EMBERS OF ANGER

ANNA ST. CLAIRE

Edited by
JESSICA CALE

Copyright © 2018 by Anna St. Claire

Cover design by Dar Albert, Wicked Smart Designs

Edited by Jessica Cale, Safeword Author Services

All rights reserved.

No part of this book may be reproduced in any form or by any electronic or mechanical means, including information storage and retrieval systems, without written permission from the author, except for the use of brief quotations in a book review.

This book is dedicated to my mother.

My mother, a retired English teacher, encouraged my writing as far back as I can remember. As a child, my mother would lead us into story starts on car trips –something that I remember as great fun and a wonderful learning opportunity. She has always been a wonderful advocate for my stories.

CHAPTER 1

New Bern, North Carolina
May 1862

The narrow road widened as the lone young woman and her horse and buggy entered the town of New Bern. Pollock Street was quiet; the old oaks and sycamores lining it didn't even whisper with their leaves, and with the glaring sun overhead, they provided little respite from the dry heat.

The back of her dress damp from sweat, Ella Grace Whitford glanced up at the cloudless sky. "Rain would sure be welcome 'bout now," she murmured to herself.

New white flags hung from the storefronts of a few businesses. "Blazes! Look who's gone and took the oath," she muttered through gritted teeth as they passed The Mercantile, its white banner hanging lifelessly over its door.

They had taken this route so often that Bess needed little guidance. Her horse slowly pulled the buggy left onto Craven Street and headed for their familiar stop.

Damn Yankee invaders have no respect. They steal anything they want from us—even our dignity.

Two months ago, the Yankees invaded the town. The battle ripped the heart out of the small city, and with it, the life Ella knew. They took over the town. *They call it an occupation, but it is more like humiliation.* The Yankees fancied themselves in charge of everything and held that over the heads of those that had remained behind.

Ella's own losses had mounted up with this war. Her father abandoned them at nineteen, leaving Ella to raise her younger brother with only the help of a few trusted house servants. They were her family.

As if on cue, four Union soldiers on horseback came at full gallop, careening around the corner, and overtook the buggy, kicking up a giant red dust cloud behind them that spread in all directions.

Her mare reared. The wagon pitched violently onto its two right side wheels, then slammed down on all four. The impact sent baskets flying from behind the seat, their contents spraying into the air and falling everywhere.

Ella tried to stand but couldn't. She fought to hold on, trying to regain control. "Whoa, girl, whoa! Bess, steady! Whoa! Calm down, old girl. Whoa!" She tried to calm her frightened mare with a white-knuckled grip. Her efforts were fruitless. "Oh my God! Bess, please stop!"

A Union soldier ran towards her from the provost headquarters just across the street.

Bess neighed and snorted trying to escape, her front legs flailing violently in the air. The soldier arrived at her side and tried to stop the horse's panicking. Repeatedly, he reached until he grabbed her halter. Gripping it tightly, he coaxed and pulled her back. She responded to his strong, steady grip and dropped, still snorting. Grasping her halter with one hand, he calmed her further with the other. "Whoa, old girl. Steady as she goes." He pulled on her harness as she reared up once again, tugging her back down.

The buggy stopped rocking and rested on all four wheels. The cloud of red dust settled down, coating everything in its path. Two baskets lay outside the buggy—one shredded from the pounding of Bess' hooves, the other empty and covered with dirt. Eggs and vegetables from the baskets coated the ground, with yellow yolks spewing everywhere.

Noticing her shaking hands, she released the reigns and took a deep breath, needing to relax. It was hard while covered in dust and runny yolks. The buggy was also spattered, but somehow Bess had escaped a covering and looked as if that violent kick-up had not just happened.

The soldier guided the mare to a spot near The Griddle.

"Ma'am, are you all right?"

A male voice penetrated her thoughts. She focused on the soldier holding onto Bess's halter. Vibrant sky-blue eyes locked with hers, and the corners of his mouth lifted into a slow, easy smile, stressing a strong jawline and white teeth. A strange tingling hit the pit of her stomach.

He motioned towards Bess. "The old girl seems to have calmed down now." He reached up and patted Ella's hands, leaving a curious new sensation of awareness spreading through her arms. She studied where he had touched her, marveling at the new feeling pulsing through her.

Ella opened her mouth to answer him, but nothing came out. She could only nod her head at the man standing in front of her. She willed her breathing to slow and her heart to stop pounding certain he could see its beat through her chest. *He had saved her life—a Yankee! A very handsome Yankee—one with arresting eyes and a warm, gentle touch, but a Yankee all the same.*

"I think your horse is fine now." He patted Bess's rump and rubbed the horse's back, smoothing down her mane. Once the mare had calmed down, he released her halter and picked up the reins Ella had dropped. He looped and tied them to a carriage post on the wooden sidewalk.

"Ma'am, let me help you." He extended his arm to help her down from the buggy.

Ella shook her head. She could only manage a frozen half-smile in response. "Thank you, suh. I believe I'm fine." She glanced at the chaos that surrounded her. "But I suppose I should get this mess cleaned up, first." *Was that her voice?* It sounded strained and squeaked as she addressed him. *Nerves?*

A wetness oozed down her arms, making her aware of the streams of dripping yolk. The cloying substance draped her arms, clothing, the seat, and even her shoes. Two eggs rolled towards the edge of the seat, and she grabbed them, saving them. Others didn't fare so well. Sickened by the wet mess, Ella snatched a towel from the basket, intent on blotting up stickiness.

The street was silent, and to her distress, she noticed that she had drawn the notice of several people walking along the boardwalk. As the yolks dripped from the sides of her buggy, mortification heated her face and she dropped the towel.

"No good Yankees!" She blurted out the words and then regretted it. She turned to face him. "I apologize, suh." Keeping her voice above a whisper, she explained, "It's just that this was all we had to sell this week, and now there's this mess... it's just so upsetting." *Well, that hardly describes my mood.*

"Ma'am, please..." He gave a cautious smile. "I understand your fright and your displeasure. Why, if this happened to my little sister, I expect she might never ride in a buggy again."

Warily, she glanced up at him and recognized the officer's insignia on his uniform. She simpered but inwardly recoiled. *Yankees are bad enough, but I am rescued by an officer!* She was unimpressed by any Yankee's rank. She had no regard for the officers running her town—or rather, running roughshod over her town.

"Suh... this mess... it was all the fault of those riders. Those men just plowed around the corner and nearly killed both Bess and me. They didn't slow down, even. There is no way they didn't see us." She tried to be civil, but her voice betrayed her. The more she spoke, the more strident her voice became. She knew he was only trying to help her... but she felt justified because he was a Yankee.

And Yankees take away anything and anyone near and dear. They rip up lives.

A year into this horrible war, and she had already seen too much ripped away.

"They will kill us all!" Taken back by the shrill sound of her own voice, she looked down, embarrassed, and fumbled with the buggy's brake stick.

He stepped back, increasing the room between them. However, his expression was one of complete understanding. "Ma'am…"

She cut him off, not wanting to hear what he might say about her outburst. Tension riveted her body. "I apologize again, suh. My nerves seem to have taken control. I think I am still unsettled from nearly being killed." *Ha!* She knew it was more than the buggy accident that had unnerved her but couldn't say that. *There should be a law against being a good-looking Yankee.*

Discomfited, she lost her composure. "Tarnation! I'm a mess now. My dress and my good shoes are all covered with yellow muck." She clapped her hand over her mouth. Tasting yolk on her palm, she gagged.

She grabbed up the towel again and wiped her hands and mouth, spitting out bits of eggshells that had stuck to the towel. Nervous and angry, she flicked the loose strands of hair from her eyes and dabbed at her dress with the towel. It was hopeless, she thought, bending over to wipe the drippy substance off her shoes.

"Oh, please, allow me to help." Without waiting for a reply, he pulled out his handkerchief and leaned in to help wipe her shoes.

Startled by his help, Ella jerked her head back, banging her head into his chin. The jolt knocked his hat off his head, revealing brown, wavy hair hanging down the back of his neck. It didn't look dirty and greasy like many other men. It looked… nice.

"Ouch." She pulled back, biting her lower lip to keep back a smile, her anger forgotten. "Oh dear!" She touched her lip with the towel to make sure she had not caused it to bleed.

"My apologies, ma'am." He rubbed his chin. "I thought to help you clean up some of this mess that my men caused you. I didn't mean to add to your misery." He drew back, grinning. "I can see I have not helped your distress."

Is that a dimple on his chin? I've always heard a dimple on a man's chin means good-natured. That wouldn't hold true for a Yankee, or could it?

"Thank you. I appreciate your help, but... I am fine." Ella squirmed a little under his gaze.

She gathered what remained of the produce she'd brought with her, then reached behind her seat and shoved it back into the baskets. Cook always wrapped her pies and packed them in their basket. They were still intact. Remarkable.

She counted what remained. "Half a basket of eggs and one basket of sticky, wet vegetables! Sara has to clean those off. Cripes!" Realizing she'd said it out loud, she clamped her mouth shut, not sure of what to say. She had already apologized for her bad humor—twice. Her temper always gave her trouble because she said what she thought when she thought it.

With no other dry option, she wiped her hands on her dress and climbed down from the buggy, planning to push past him before he could offer any further help. She wanted him to leave.

She stopped short when he again held his arm out to help her, his face showing no reaction to her harsh words. Ella drew in a slow, deep breath to quell her frustration and accepted his hand.

"Ma'am, I plan to discuss this incident with the captain who led those men. That is not how we conduct ourselves."

She reached up and touched the base of her throat. "Thank you. My heart is still pounding so fast, suh."

"That they had to have seen you and didn't even come back to check tells me they need a lesson in civility. And it's obvious they didn't see the beauty of the driver."

The officer still held her hand. It felt warm, but not the warmth bothersome in the summer heat. As soon as she got down from the buggy, she pulled it free and placed it on his arm. That at least looked proper.

He covered her fingers with his free hand. Tingles of awareness again shot through her body. *This is a wildly pleasant sensation.*

"In the meantime, please accept my sincerest apologies and some recompense for the goods you lost." He walked with her to the door of the restaurant, stopped and doffed his hat. With all of this excitement, I forgot my manners. My name is Colonel Jackson Ross. I was coming out of the provost's office across the street when I saw your horse and buggy in distress." He paused as if waiting for a response. "May I buy you a cup of coffee? I was just planning to have breakfast myself. Sara's restaurant has the best breakfasts. And I must mention those Southern grits. I enjoy that a lot." His dimpled grin almost had her nodding in response.

"I appreciate your kind offer. I do. But I have to decline." Ella released his arm and pasted the widest smile she could muster on her face. She realized it looked forced, but no matter. She didn't trust Yankees. He would find out about her and take away something more from her life. She hoped her refusal would send him packing.

"This does not make up for the fright and losing your eggs and vegetables, but please accept this." Colonel Ross pulled out three silver dollars from his jacket pocket and placed them in her hand, closing her fingers over the coins.

Startled by his generosity, Ella stared at the hand with the three coins tucked within it. It had been a while since she had held three silver dollars. She wanted to refuse them, but she had her younger brother, Aiden, and the others to consider. This was much more than she had hoped to get from Sara. They needed this money, and pride would not put food on her table.

She unfolded her fingers and stared at the coins. "Thank you, suh. This is very generous." She looked up, straining to keep from blinking, which she saw as a sign of weakness. His eyes drew her in, and she found she could not look away from him. "I hate to turn down your offer of coffee, but I have business to conduct and then I am expected at home. Thank you for helping me with my horse. I think I'm fine now." She saw disappointment and another emotion she couldn't identify flash across his face.

"Well then, would you allow me to escort you back to your home? I would hate for any further incidents to occur."

"That is a kind offer, suh, and I am tempted. But I have a short distance to go and Bess knows the way. We will be fine. But thank you." She'd lied, but she would not show up with a Yankee in tow. Ella hoped, after today, she'd never see him again. He threw her emotions into such chaos.

"Yes, ma'am. I see. Well, if you insist you are all right, I need to go back to my office for a few minutes. I think I recognized those men, and I plan to get my assistant to locate them. If you will please excuse me?"

He nodded and started across the street to the provost's headquarters.

Ella wouldn't say she believed him. She looked at the three silver dollars and reflected on his generosity. But then, it was his men who had caused her trouble. Yankees were all alike in her book.

With that thought, she felt a niggling uncertainty and... guilt.

Pshaw! She would not allow either to bother her. She was embarrassed, and yes, she was angry. She lifted her chin and pursed her lips, determined to ignore everything around her that threatened to fire her temper.

Two Union soldiers walked past as she watched Colonel Ross cross the street. She obliged them with a smile. "No accounts," she muttered for her own satisfaction between her teeth, grinning. Then, making sure the handsome colonel was out of earshot, she added, "And no manners, either." She lifted the edges of her dress and turned towards the front door of The Griddle.

Before walking in, she turned and glanced to where Colonel Ross had gone. Just thinking of him sent that strange fluttering to her stomach again. It was pleasant, yet foreign and frustrating. Until meeting Colonel Ross, she had never experienced this gentle tickling in her stomach.

Three fresh cavalry horses tied up in front of The Mercantile caught her attention. The store sat next to the provost's headquarters. A large black one stood several hands higher than the others. *I wonder if that horse belongs to him.*

She didn't plan to change her opinion of Yankees because one had saved her life and showed her kindness. Besides, she wanted to make this a quick trip to town. Her trips were getting easier, but she still dreaded it.

Runaways were everywhere. Her brother, Nolan, would get angry with her if he knew she was doing this. Well, he would get angry if he were home and not off fighting this dratted war somewhere.

She sighed. *Where are you, Nolan? You would be right. I shouldn't have come alone.*

She could have brought her overseer, Jason, but with most of the slaves gone, she needed his eyes on Silver Moon, her family home. Besides, he was acting strange—too attentive. It made her uncomfortable.

She reached into her pocket, touching the small derringer strapped to her leg—pleased that she had remembered to bring it. Nolan taught her to shoot her gun and made her promise to have it with her at all times. He trusted her to take care of things while he away. She always hit her target with it, but she was not so good with Papa's shotgun. There was just too much to remember—*pull this, slide that, cock this.* Or was it, *cock this, pull that, and slide this?* No matter. She avoided the shotgun. This little pistol was much better.

"Pshaw and diddles!" She lowered her voice. "I'm dawdling. This day is making me crazy. I need to head back home soon. One thing I don't have time for is more attention from Yankee invaders!"

With that, she opened The Griddle's door, its bells jangling, announcing her visit.

CHAPTER 2

Ella caught the door behind her, easing it closed so it wouldn't slam. Sara, her best friend, looked her way and smiled in acknowledgment. Sara was waiting on a table near the front window, so Ella took her remaining eggs, vegetables, and pies to the counter and waited for her to finish with her order. While she stood there, she glanced out the window. Both The Mercantile and provost headquarters were visible from where she was standing.

"Thank you, Mr. Williamson. You come back anytime. And please say hello to the missus." Sara shoved her pad in her pocket and came running up to the counter.

"Hello." Sara pulled Ella into a big hug. "My dear, you must be parched after—oh my goodness!" She gave her friend a long look. "What in the world happened to you?" She stepped back, staring.

"Yankee invaders, that's what." Ella hurled out the response. It felt good not to have to apologize for her temper this time.

"Well, this should be interesting. Give me a moment. I'll be right back." Sara darted into the kitchen. When she came through the two swinging doors, she held a stack of small hand towels and a bowl of soapy water. "Here you go." She placed them on the counter.

Ella reached for a towel thankful she could clean up her arms and wipe the dust off her face while Sara stooped to get the yolk off the bottom of her dress and shoes.

"You are quite a mess, but oh, you are still a sight for sore eyes! I'm so glad to see you. Let me bring you some tea from the back. It will do you a world of good." She shook her head in dismay. "I may have a dress you can change into. I keep a spare dress here in case I spill food on the one I'm wearing. The lady down the street does a great job of getting out stains. I'll take your gown to her. She owes me a favor."

"Thank you, Sara. I feel rather sticky and dirty. A clean gown would help. I don't have many gowns as you know. I cannot afford to lose one."

Sara scooted together all the dirty towels and flew into the kitchen. She came out with a pitcher of tea and a brown bundle. "I got the dress and tea. I've had so much on my mind these past weeks. Mostly Nolan. I haven't heard from him. But I'm sure he's all right." Her voice caught.

Ella looked up at the mention of Nolan. Her brother and Sara had become engaged just before he left to join his regiment over a year and a half before. "I hate to ask, but did he mention anything 'sides fighting or the weather? I haven't heard a thing from him, either."

"No, just the usual about missing me and you and Aiden." Sara bit her lip. "He said nothing that would tell us anything. I'm worried. I guess we have to keep checking the lists." Her voice almost choked to a whisper.

"He doesn't mention where he is, does he?" Ella knew the answer before she asked it, but still felt compelled to ask. She worried about him a lot; it would be nice to know where he was, so she could read the posted reports and make sure he was okay.

Sara laid the bundle down trying to change her own mood. "No, he never mentions where he is. And the letters are weeks old before I get them." Her mouth worked. "We must have faith. Your brother never told us anything he didn't want us to know. He is more protective than most and wouldn't want either of us to worry."

"Well, that's just it. I thought one of us would have heard… something. There have been so many killed." Seeing Sara's anxious look,

Ella moved them away from the subject. "You've talked me into borrowing your dress, but I insist on doing something for you." She would discuss it with Lizzy, her housekeeper, and surprise her.

"You need not do anything for me. Friends help each other." Sara nodded towards the door. "How long can you stay? Can I take Jason a cup of lemonade while he waits?"

"I should get back soon. Truth is, Jason didn't come—just me and Bess."

"Ella, are you crazy? Your brother would be furious. There is so much crime now. If something happened to you, what would become of Aiden?"

"Pish! Nothing will happen. I brought my gun." Ella tapped her leg. She kept it near although the vexing invaders weren't what frightened her. It was Jason, her overseer. "I am not worried about driving to town, but can I share something with you? I confess I don't know if it's just my imagination, but I need to talk to someone."

"Sure, can you talk out here?"

"Yes. It's Jason. I don't bring him with me to town because he makes me feel strange. I catch him staring at me. Last week when I was milking a cow, I felt like someone was watching me. I turned around, and he was staring at me from the doorway of the barn. He acted like he had just walked up. He apologized for scaring me and left. Each interaction is unsettling. It's frightening." She shuddered. "And it's happened more than once. He comes around and asks if I'd like him to take me to town, but I refuse—I tell him that Carter and I are going, or I don't know when I'll be going. And only yesterday, I saw him standing by the barn, watching me beat a rug. I pretended I didn't see him, but he had this strange grin on his face. His attention unnerves me."

"Staring? That's odd. Does he say anything?"

"No, he doesn't. But when he drives the buggy, he tries to sit closer than is necessary." She shivered.

"Ella, have you mentioned this to anyone—Lizzy or Carter? And no, I don't believe you imagine people staring at you. That behavior is disturbing."

"Thank you for believing me. I thought I was being ridiculous, but it unsettles me when he comes near. You raise a good point. I've told only you. I will mention it to Carter and Lizzy this evening."

"That's smart of you. I couldn't bear for anything to happen to you." Sara gave Ella a quick hug. "Please ask Carter to ride with you, if you will."

"I'll consider that. I promise." She smiled at her friend, her relief obvious.

Sara picked up the basket of pies, bringing them up to her nose. "Let's both enjoy this heavenly bouquet." She inhaled. "Cook's fresh-baked apple pies! This is a wonderful surprise you've brought me this morning, and I forgot to ask for any. Thank you." Beaming, she pulled one out of the basket and sniffed. "We sure need these. Everyone loves Cook's pies." She put the pie down and picked up the basket, turning it and seeing remnants of a yoke. Some had already dried. Some were still wet.

Ella's attention moved to the window and what was beyond.

"What are you looking at? Ladybug, if you stare any harder, you might burn a hole in whatever or whoever has your notice!"

"Burning holes in the backs of Union soldiers might be a good thing." She smirked. "I am watching the doors of The Mercantile. I saw a high-ranking soldier go inside. This could be interesting. With the flag already flying, I wonder what other business he could be about."

The door across the street opened and Colonel Jackson Ross walked towards the restaurant. "Oh no! He's coming here now!" Red-faced, she groaned and turned towards Sara, determined to ignore him.

"He, who? *Who* is coming here?" Sara stood on the balls of her feet and tried to look over her friend's bonnet. "Oh, that's the colonel. Nice fella. Quit your worrying. He comes every day for breakfast. It's either an order of flapjacks and grits, or grits and eggs with bacon, but always grits. Says he cannot get enough of our Southern tradition. He asks me to melt cheese on them. Have you ever heard of such of thing? But I've tasted it, and it's superb. I might put it on the menu and call it cheesy grits!" She chuckled.

Ella slapped the top of the counter in defiance. "Isn't there any place off limits to them?" At her friend's irritated look, she apologized. "I'm sorry. It's just that they are everywhere. And to be honest, it worries me. No, that's not true. I am angry. In fact, I'm livid!" She squeezed up her face in an exaggerated huff.

"Well, just you don't go saying something to set him off. He is very nice, and I better not have to remind you about manners, Ella Grace—we need nice here! This is a business I depend on and I don't want to have trouble because of that temper of yours."

"I will be nice," Ella murmured, just loud enough for Sara to hear her. She hoped she could make it out the door before her voice betrayed the simmering ire she felt and the recognition she didn't want to acknowledge.

She had never introduced herself to Colonel Ross. Seeing him could embarrass her after the deserved set-down Sara had just given her. Guilt shamed her. She had been rude to a man who had saved her life. Sara would never understand. She was the one person who didn't let her get away with anything, but their friendship always survived their squabbles. They were more like sisters.

"Let me take that dress out to the back of the restaurant and change. This sticky, gritty mess is very uncomfortable." She picked up the brown package, ready to scoot through the kitchen doors.

"I will clean off a table while you change," Sara said, her voice soft. "Hurry, I want to see how it looks!"

"Okay, I'll be back in a minute." Ella turned back to her friend, "Thank you for this." Hugging the brown package to her chest, Ella glanced back towards the door. *Maybe he won't recognize me in this dress.*

"Ella, wait! I was so thrilled about the pies, I forgot to look into these other baskets." Excited, she pulled back the covers "Ah, I see the origin of the egg yolks. What happened?"

Ella frowned. She would not get to change, and she risked Colonel Ross seeing her again still looking a mess. "Well, it's not quite a dozen today, courtesy of the Yankee invaders. This morning, I started off with a full basket—must have been three dozen. Now, I don't think I have even twelve eggs left. Those Yankees stirred up my horse. Sweet Bess nearly bucked me clear off the seat!" Her voice rose as she continued, "Anyway, those I'm not wearing, I'm looking to sell."

She managed a small smile for her friend. Her loud rant had drawn the attention of Mr. Burns and everyone else in the restaurant. That only added to her misery; she was already self-conscious about her bedraggled appearance.

Sara lowered her voice to almost a whisper. "Please be careful with what you say. And, I beg you, please, please watch that temper of yours. I can't afford any trouble, Ella Grace Whitford." She wiped her hands on her skirt and looked towards the door. "As you can see, the colonel is heading this way. Hurry and go change, and when you come back, please act natural... well, no. Just be polite to him, at least for me," she pleaded in a rushed voice.

"Fine. Please don't get so out of sorts." Ella pulled a face. She would do as Sara asked and not let her temper get the better of her. Sara took her temper in stride, but she didn't need trouble. "I promise to be polite. You should go. You have a customer. I can't stay long, anyway." She turned to go change her dress.

"Please don't leave so soon. We haven't gotten to visit yet. I have something to tell you. Stay a few minutes longer. It won't be dark for a long time and I won't keep you."

"All right. I will, but not long." Ella gave her a quick hug and went to the pantry in the back of the restaurant. It had a door and offered a semblance of privacy. A few minutes later, she returned, her stained dress folded in the brown paper. "Can I lay this here?" She motioned towards the counter.

"Yes. I'll handle it. There, now! That looks better. Don't you think so?" Sara stepped back and appreciated her, a satisfied look on her face.

"I love this color, and the material is so soft. Is it cotton?"

"Yes. And blue is your color. It highlights your beautiful auburn hair."

Before Ella could answer, Sara leaned in and whispered, "Have you heard the latest? It's about Mr. and Mrs. Smyth at The Mercantile."

"No. What happened?" Ella whispered back, half-listening as she craned her neck. She spotted the colonel. He had stopped and was talking to another officer.

Looking around before she spoke, Sara replied in a hushed, disapproving voice, "The Smyths took the oath yesterday." She nodded for emphasis.

Ella was silent for a moment before she spoke. She schooled her face to contain her temper. "I don't like it. I am shocked at the change in their sympathies. They take the oath and hang that dreadful white flag out there. I noticed there were more flags today. It may help them, but it hurts the rest of us." She shuddered. "I guess the Christian thing is to forgive, but it's hard when you have good men fighting and dying for the cause."

"I still can't believe the Yankees have been here so long—it's been two months, Ella. A lot of their men come in here. They aren't all that bad. But some are abrupt and… not clean. Sara wrinkled her nose in obvious distaste.

Alarmed, Ella looked her friend in the eye. "What if they forced you to do it?"

"I don't know. I think I would refuse. No, I know I would refuse. Nolan has put his life on the line, and he has my heart and my loyalty, as does the cause." Sara's tremulous voice betrayed her apparent confidence. She paused before continuing, "Though, I had not considered that they would ask. I should, I reckon… consider that they *will* ask."

"Well, what about your father and mother? Surely these Yankee devils won't pressure a minister of a church to swear the oath." Sara's parents had become like surrogates to Ella since the departure of her father.

"Shh! Lower your voice," Sara returned. "Mamma said they already asked." Keeping her eyes on the door, she grinned and whispered, "Papa said 'no,' that his oath was to God Almighty."

Ella snorted.

"What was that?" Sara held her hand over her mouth and laughed.

"I was just thinking about your daddy telling them no, and I got carried away."

"Yes, his stern tone would have made them sorry for even asking!"

Both laughed, until one and then the other snorted once more, which only elicited more peals of laughter.

Sara looked past Ella, out of the screened door. She nodded, signaling that Colonel Ross was almost there. "Tell me now, how is that adorable little brother of yours?" she prompted, her voice jovial and a little louder than in their earlier conversation.

Ella took the hint. Forcing a smile on her face despite her mood, she jumped into the conversation. "Aiden's great. Growing like a weed. Oh! We found a puppy a week ago. Or maybe he found us. He was scratching at our front door. I think he must have gotten separated from his mother although I know no one around who has either a female or male lab. He isn't black—rather, he's more of a golden blond color. And he has two different colored eyes. One eye is brown, and the other is blue. He was wet and hungry when we found him, but he's just what Aiden needed. He's named him Bo, and they're inseparable now. They are always playing. Aiden's favorite game is something he calls 'Pirates'".

"Gracious, what's that?" Sara laughed and shook her head.

"I'm not sure of the rules, but the two of them stay absorbed in it—"

The door to the restaurant jingled and Colonel Jackson Ross entered. The black and silver braided brocade on each shoulder of his uniform stood out, giving him an air of importance.

Ella's eyes locked onto his for a moment taking in the measure of his broad shoulders, square jaw and the vivacity in his gaze. There was much to appreciate. She caught her breath and wondered whether he would stay silent about having already met. Heat flooded her face. She hadn't even introduced herself when he had been everything kind.

The colonel smiled in her direction. He looked as if he might say something, but after a moment, he walked to the table in the far corner. The sound of his spurs moving across the wooden floor stressed his long and easy gait. He lifted the chair off the floor instead of pushing it back, so it would not create noise.

His mamma must have taught him to do that.

When he walked past her, she caught the smell of horses, leather, and spice wafting in the air behind him. She started to speak but decided against it. What could she say? 'Goodness, suh, you smell heavenly'? Or maybe I can remind him he saved my life a little earlier and thank him. No. I've already thanked him once, and I don't want to encourage any further interaction with him.

"Dearest Sara, I must leave. I need to get back to Aiden. Lizzy and Cook are watching him, but they have other chores, as we all do. Cook will have more pies for you later this week. The strawberries are almost ready to pick. I'll bring 'em soon as I can. And thank you for this loan." She smoothed her hands down the front of the clean blue dress.

"Oh, I had forgotten about strawberry season. How wonderful!" Sara clasped her hands together. "You tell Cook, we would love some of her delicious cobblers." She gave her friend a hug and a kiss on the cheek, and then whispered in her ear, "Take extra care getting home now. See you later this week."

Ella looked over one more time to the table with the colonel. He saw her and gave her a wink followed by a wide smile.

Winked! He winked at me. Her face burned with color.

"I promise." She hurried to the door, knowing her behavior was only adding to her embarrassment. Still, it felt justified. She sprinted down the steps to her buggy.

Once installed, she thought about the handsome face inside The Griddle. *No! What is going on with me? One handsome face and I am making a cake of myself. He was the enemy, the invader. He was a Yankee. Though that was one handsome face that also saved your life.* "Ugggghhh-hh!" she screamed out in a frustrated burst, as much to stop her thoughts as to protest them.

The Elders had thought the war wouldn't touch New Bern, or at least that was what they'd told everyone. When they'd found out the Yankees were coming, they'd said, "Our boys will win."

They had been wrong. Not only had some of her family and friends died or gone missing but her own life as she'd known it had changed. When her father disappeared, she had become more of a mother to Aiden than his sister. It had all happened so quickly.

Urging Bess to pick up speed, Ella cringed at the town's destruction. Boarded up homes, buildings, and broken windows, damaged from looting dominated the landscape. The colorful rose bushes and fragrant gardens from before the war had vanished, replaced by a few hardier flowers that had pushed themselves towards the sun from beneath overgrown, unkempt grass and bushes, spurred by the spring weather.

Seems like all the nicer homes are now, occupied by the Yankees. She felt her chest tighten. She had heard there were close to twenty thousand in the area, a number she still couldn't comprehend. Well, at least they were doing something useful by repairing some of their chaos. Flicking the reins, she urged the mare to pick up her speed. She couldn't get home soon enough.

CHAPTER 3

Colonel Jackson Ross watched the beauty in royal blue talking to Sara. It didn't escape his notice she never offered her name—nor that the woman was wearing something different. Recalling her state of panic and disrepair when he last saw her, he understood. Unnerved by the incident, she glanced back at him, and he winked. She blushed, and while he realized the rudeness of his behavior, he couldn't help himself. The lady intrigued him. When she rushed out the door, he broke out into a grin.

What a woman. But my God, what a temper! Funny, though, it suits her.

Despite her temper and the manner in which she had ignored him, he thought about how that gorgeous red hair would look spread across a pillow, curls surrounding her face, the first light of morning just breaking through the window, her arm across his naked chest... Heat spread up his neck as he grasped where his thoughts had just traveled. No surprise, he found his pants felt more than a little snug.

Jackson tried to focus his thoughts on what he needed to get done, but the soft scent of jasmine brought his thoughts back to her. Diverting his thoughts wasn't effective. *I might have to sit here all day.*

A calendar on the wall caught his attention. May 1862. It had been at least six months since he had been in the company of a woman, and this one was taking over, in what... minutes? She paid him no attention—tried to pretend they had not met—and here he was, suffering on her behalf.

Just who was the redheaded beauty? I'll make it my business to find out. After several long and boring months, this town was showing real merit.

Jackson Ross couldn't focus except on the memory of the woman that had just walked out the door. A green-eyed spitfire. A man could lose himself in her eyes. They were the largest, greenest eyes he had ever seen. She was a complete vision.

Yes, and I am becoming a complete fool. She was a real spirited one. What is her story?

He laughed when he thought about her face when she left. Unable to resist, he winked at her. She looked stricken and nearly ran out the door. The minx. It was clear from her silence she intended to keep their earlier meeting to herself.

Perhaps it was her scent of jasmine, a pleasant smell he had always appreciated. She smelled delightful and for the time when he was helping her, he didn't smell the stale stench of smoke that had permeated the town since the battle in March.

Christ! I am in the middle of a war and I am in charge of thousands of men.

Jackson's responsibilities with the war effort were tenfold. He was charged with protecting the town, both from within and from the outside. He was also responsible for training the men that would go on more offensive maneuvers. And then there were civic responsibilities.

It was a big responsibility with this town. There were people who sided with the Union, and then, there were the Rebs. It was a thankless job, but his military career had always been important to him.

This was a town in turmoil, and it was his town for the time being. It was his job to keep the peace. Many of the men had joined up with the Graybacks and were off fighting. But there were also many Unionists that had joined the northern army, some within the same families as those who were fighting for the South. Heated emotions and distrust dominated.

Many women in town were without the protection of husbands. The city attracted runaways because of the Union Army's presence, and households were losing slaves and servants. The climate here was a dangerous one. He hoped for wisdom and a swift end to the conflict.

The thought of danger brought him back to the young woman who had just left. Jackson recalled she had traveled here alone. He didn't know how far she lived from town. That concerned him. He needed to check into her situation a little further.

He had noticed the exchange between Sara and the redheaded beauty. No doubt about it. The owner of this restaurant knew her, and he wanted to know all about her. He needed to know who she was.

As was his habit, flirt that he was, Jackson flashed his brightest smile. Sara smiled right back.

"Morning, Sara," he said, relaxing into a lazy grin.

"What'll it be today, Colonel?"

"Let's start with some coffee—cream and sugar—and then biscuits and gravy, and grits, please."

"Oh! We got in fresh eggs. Are you sure you wouldn't like a couple of eggs sunny-side up?"

"I seem to have a bigger appetite today, and that sounds great. Yes, let's add a couple of those eggs, please." He pulled another napkin in place from the table and placed it on his lap. "And would you share the name of that pretty redhead that just left, Sara?"

～

Sara took a deep breath and considered the man in front of her. Nothing escaped her notice. She'd seen the way he was looking at Ella and felt he was more than a little affected. She might be an unmarried woman, but she knew *some* things about the opposite sex. All kinds of talk went on in there, and she listened. Might learn a thing or two, she always thought. Sara gave her biggest smile to the colonel.

"Colonel Ross, suh! You are referring to my best friend, Ella Whitford." Shifting her gaze down, Sara poured his coffee. She bit her lip and tried very hard not to smile when she noticed he had thrown a couple of napkins over his lap.

Still biting her lip and forbidding herself to grin, she thought about how much information she should give. She might be a pastor's daughter, but she grew up with boy cousins around her, and until this war, had been around Nolan.

Her heart seized a little at the thought of Nolan. It had been a long time since she had seen him. Even more concerning, she hadn't heard from him in two months, since before the battle. She wondered how he was doing… what he was doing. She had hoped Ella would stay a few more minutes, but Ella had been out of sorts and left before they could sit and talk. Sara kept her face schooled despite her thoughts.

"Care for two sugars with your coffee? And would you like some patties of sausage with your biscuits and gravy?"

She shuddered and wondered what the colonel wanted with Ella. Sara knew what Ella's reaction to his inquiry would be. Like her best friend, she hoped the colonel and his men would leave town soon.

"Your friend, she seemed to be in town alone today." He pointed towards the door that Ella had exited through only minutes earlier. "Did she have far to go? I hope I need not tell you these roads are dangerous."

"She lives on a plantation out of town apiece." Looking down at the colonel, Sara put on her most convincing smile. "Don't you worry 'bout Miss Ella. She is a smart one. The usual number of sausage patties, suh?" She prompted him again.

"No, just two for today since I'm adding the eggs." Colonel Ross smiled and nodded. "Does Miss Ella come to town often? This is the first time I have seen her in here."

Sara fought back the feelings of disloyalty. The colonel came here often. His behavior convinced her of his sincerity. There was no denying that this handsome man could be an interesting challenge for Ella, she mused, taking in the colonel's very practiced innocent smile. "Pretty regularly. She brings in fresh eggs, produce, and baked goods—whatever she can spare to sell—and today she brought apple pies."

Sara offered no other information and placed his coffee in front of him.

Colonel Ross picked up the coffee cup and took a sip. "Good coffee. And thank you for the information. I apologize for putting you on the spot with my questions, but I assure you, I am only interested in her safety."

~

Ella was in a hurry to get back. As she worried her lower lip, she thought about the handsome colonel and her stomach felt like butterflies fluttering. She had caught him staring at her when he thought she wasn't looking. How distressing that was!

Those Yankees were nothing but trouble. *Now a body can't even go to The Griddle without having to deal with their ilk.*

Guilt shot through her. He had saved her life, and he behaved the perfect gentleman in Sara's restaurant even in the face of her guile. She had felt the air leave when he walked in The Griddle.

She needed to remember that man was trouble. Not only did he look at her with those piercing blue eyes, but he touched her. Even if it was to help her, it was just too familiar. And for him to think she would allow him to buy her coffee—or anything—without an escort. It was embarrassing.

And that rascal had winked at me, by God!

Handsome as he was, he had no business winking at her in such a way. What if someone had seen? She gasped.

No, definitely not. She wanted nothing to do with him. Besides, she needed to get home to Aiden. A five-year-old could get into a lot of things. He would look for her. He and his precious little puppy would be waiting.

As much as she willed it otherwise, her mind kept coming back to the colonel. She recalled his smile when she looked back before leaving. On that, her stomach did a flip.

Bess knew the way home and moved at her usual plodding pace. Ella felt drained, and her attention kept drifting back to the near accident and the colonel.

Just before they turned away from town, they passed the train station. A train was pulling in, its whistleblowing, heralding its arrival with great gusts of smoke.

The air around her became stifling, and she gripped the buggy seat with both hands. Goosebumps ran up her arms. Ella closed her eyes, fighting against the memories that were flying back.

It was just after a spring rain when she and Bess had ridden into town. The train had just pulled into the station on schedule. It was restocking its tender with coal. Its engine sat still on the tracks, hissing while passengers were loading.

She could smell the smoke swirling around her, filling her lungs. It had come from behind the station where the fighting had been going on that day. Everyone had known the Union Army was on its way, planning to attack New Bern. They had taken it in stride, thinking it would be a quick win for their boys. They were horribly wrong.

One minute there was calm and normalcy, and then chaos. The poor Southern boys came running and screaming down Front Street, wounded and bleeding, trying to make it into town for help. The Union soldiers were fast on their heels, firing into the running bedlam.

Fear filled the air as thick as the smoke. The station was complete mayhem. Friends fought for space on the train, desperate to leave town before the Yankees could stop them.

Carriages and wagons, loaded down to excess, had pushed the horses too hard. She had never seen horses whipped. Some dropped from exhaustion. Others hit bumps in the road, catapulting trunks and packages out of the wagons. Cases overstuffed with beautiful clothing and precious heirlooms fell off wagons in every direction, their contents littering the road.

She shoved her hand into her mouth to stifle a scream. The image of her elderly neighbor, Mr. Medlum, being pulled under his carriage was still fresh and horrified her. His broken body was dragged behind his horses. No one stopped.

Oh no! It's happening again. She closed her eyes and clenched the reins as the familiar feeling took over. Her heart slammed in her chest, heaving; blood pounded with the ferocity of a thundering rain. Her lungs struggled for air, once again overcome from that foul smoke, the smell of fresh gunpowder from the battle invading her senses. She gasped repeatedly for air; her mouth was bone dry. The cloying heat enveloped her body. Beads of sweat crowded her forehead, and a loud roaring took over in her ears.

Try to calm down. Ella clenched her hands around Bess's reins. She heard her own voice screaming. "Breathe. Take slow, deep breaths. Slow."

And then it was over. Slowly, she could hear the sounds of the town again as the roar of air left her ears. Ella kept breathing. In, and then, out.

She blinked and realized she was mouthing soothing, calming instructions to herself over and over. Her horse tossed her head and swished her tail, fidgeting, reacting to Ella's own panicked behavior. This was the second time this had happened, and it frightened her. She looked down at her white knuckles, trying to relax her hands. She thought about what calmed her... Aiden's cheerful face came to mind. Her body relaxed just thinking about Aiden.

Ella smiled and made a clicking noise inside of her cheek, urging her horse on. "Come on, Bess. We're all right now. I'm sorry I got you nervous." The old horse responded with a soft neigh and a nod of her head, and she trotted away from town.

A breeze pushed her bonnet back and the wispy tresses that had escaped blew in front of her face. The sensation of the feathery fingers of her hair and the wind in her face calmed her further. As she continued to build the distance between herself and the town, both horse and driver relaxed. The fear she felt moments before disappeared.

Except for her, Aiden, and a couple of servants, the house was empty. It was anyone's guess where Papa had run off, drunk and in his usual wretched state. He had cleaned out the jar in the larder, taking with him every cent they owned.

Papa simply left, leaving no word of his direction other than informing Lizzy that he planned to find Nolan. Her brother wrote, but his letters never told where he was. As she always did, Ella prayed for her brother and she prayed for her papa.

Nolan left when the first shots were fired at Fort Sumter. Since he had graduated from The Citadel, the Confederacy called him to be an officer. They needed every trained officer they could get, he had said. Southern boys knew how to fight.

The war would be quick—a few months at most. That's what everyone said. But it had been over a year now, and several New Bern boys that she had known had come home in boxes.

Then there were also those with their names noted in the newspaper. That was a notoriety no one wanted for a son. North Carolina had only just seceded from the Union, but so many of its young men had already joined to fight for the cause.

Slaves, sensing freedom, fled in the night. Many sought and found refuge with the Yankees. Property or not, the Yankees refused to return them.

New Bern was an occupied town now. A tremor overtook her. Her home's survival was up to her. There was no one else. She promised herself Silver Moon would be there when this war was over, and Nolan came back to them. The loneliness and desolation were overwhelming. Tears brimmed and spilled over her lashes.

Ella couldn't fail Aiden. He might not have Mamma or Papa, but he had her. They had each other. They would make do.

"I don't think this was our best trip to town, ol' gal." Ella thought of the three dollars, the colonel, and her stained white muslin dress. "And I think my dress is ruined. It looks more yellow with all that yolk and dust." She felt hot and sweaty—not a good combination with all the dust. She couldn't get comfortable.

"There's no one out here to impress," Ella muttered aloud to her mare. She slapped the reins against Bess's hindquarters to encourage her to pick up the pace, hoping to stir more air as much as to increase her speed.

A loud rustle on the side of the road startled Bess and caused the mare to buck. Fear seized her. *Not again!* Grasping the reins and almost standing, she regained control again of Bess.

Twice in one day! Maybe she should not make this trip alone.

Perhaps she should not make it at all.

~

*H*e crawled out of the brush at the same moment a buggy flew past him. The horse tried to rear, and a redheaded woman struggled to hold the reins, keeping the wagon at its full pace. Was that Ella? He moved to the road but lost his balance and fell backward. Getting up once more, he reached down and brushed the beggar lice from his pants.

He wished he could have seen more of who was in the buggy, still puzzled over the lone woman driving it. He might have gotten a ride if he had gotten onto the road faster. But what a sorry sight he had become; he would have frightened her.

Nolan pulled himself up and leaned on the thick wooden post he now called his crutch. No longer was he recognizable, even to himself. His once shaven face was now gaunt and covered with hair. His shredded uniform was dirty.

If anyone spotted him, it would cause problems.

He had to stay vigilant of every person on the road. It would be difficult to explain his Union uniform in these parts if he were recognized.

After a long moment of silence, he stretched out his arm and planted his crutch ahead of him. He leaned on his stick and headed in the same direction the buggy had traveled.

CHAPTER 4

*N*olan Whitford moaned, but his words were difficult to understand. Sweat soaked his forehead. No matter where he turned, he couldn't get comfortable. Cool hands placed a wet cloth on his forehead. Nolan wanted to ask about the cloth. He wanted to see whose hands those were, but darkness pulled him back into a smoky black world.

He was there again… wet, cold, in a murky hell. Where were his men? He had expected to see them. Confusion caused him to moan again, answered by the hands, but Nolan slipped back to that day as the darkness claimed him.

New Bern March 14, 1862

*S*moke rose from all directions. With all the rain of the past days, the air was wet, and the smoke hung like a curtain. The initial advance was easier than they had expected. The Rebs had dug trenches and *fortified the area with fallen logs to protect their men, but the Yankees' initial advance must have surprised them because this battle area was empty.*

He pushed forward with his column, watching. His gun was pointed and primed. He could hear the column ahead of them already engaged in battle. Bullets ricocheted off trees and bayonets clashed. Narrow knolls of land extended like fingers into the swamp. It was hard to see them in the smoky fog.

He couldn't see their faces yet, but he knew the enemy surrounded them on three sides. Bullets whizzed by his face. Terrified, he stepped over men in gray uniforms and blue uniforms in front of him, and he kept moving.

He was with Reno's column. They broke through at the brick kiln after Foster's column had softened up the Confederate defenses. He recognized some dead bodies. They were men, friends he camped with just the night before. The situation made him weak in his knees; he used his rifle to support him.

Keep moving.

Acrid smoke swirled around him. Straightening, he picked himself up and moved forward once more. His stomach clenched with tension.

The recent snow and the constant rain made it harder to tell where the swamp ended, and the ground started. His boots sunk into the deep sand and clay, softened by the water. The knolls of ground disappeared without warning. Frigid swamp water seeped through his uniform and caused him to shiver, and he muffled a cry. It came up to his waist. He raised the gun he was holding over his head.

He inched his way forward in the freezing water towards the Confederate stronghold line. Reno pushed his men onward. The Union commanding officer's orders reverberated throughout the marsh, along with the sounds of musket balls.

Men screamed in pain as their bodies hit the freezing water. He saw faces of some dead in front of him, and he recognized friends he had grown up with here in New Bern. His heart twisted as he tried to think.

Spying could get him killed if they caught on, but it was worth the risk. He needed to see Ella and Aiden.

And there was Sara. His lovely, kind Sara... she was there, in his mind's eye. He could almost smell her molasses cookies. Was she still waiting for him to return home—if he got home?

Nolan knew he was risking his life. People living in New Bern would recognize him.

A Confederate officer and a spy! That would make a great catch for someone's career. Even though he grew up here, Nolan knew better than to test loyalties of the locals with the strain of this war. There is no telling what anyone would say if they saw him. He didn't know how the locals would react if they saw him wearing a Union infantry uniform, knowing he was part of the Confederate army.

A cannon exploded from behind him, stopping his thoughts. The ball shattered the hill some thirty feet in front of him. Scattered body parts of the enemy littered the area around him. He closed his eyes. Dire screams of agony pierced the already frantic atmosphere. Pungent, black smoke filled his lungs—the time was now.

Nolan ducked down behind the fallen log and pretended to be dead. His heart pounded so hard and loud in his ears he was sure that anyone passing by would hear it, too.

Slow breaths. Must… look dead.

He wasn't sure how long he would need to lie there, but he knew this would be his death if he didn't run, and this was the only way he saw out. Hot, sticky, wet, cold.

I don't want to die in this hell hole. I don't want them to find me here in Bullen's Branch. He squeezed his eyes shut. *Dammit, think!*

Less than two years ago, he had been working the plantation, in charge since his father had become unhinged following his mother's death. He'd had plans. He wanted to help his father, but doctors gave him no hope. Still, he planned to marry and raise a family of his own.

God, please help me get out of this disaster.

If he died like this, his family would think he was a traitor.

His heart was so loud. Someone would hear it.

The sounds of human suffering and bullets pounded his ears. He moved his arms over his head, to cover them, hoping he wouldn't draw attention.

I need to get out of here, he thought, panic sending bile up into his throat.

Loud voices penetrated his thoughts.

"Retreat! Men pull back. Now!" The man bellowed orders in a tone that brokered no tolerance for debate.

Nolan looked up, hoping he could do so without drawing attention. He had to see what was going on around him. The authoritative voice came from an officer in a gray uniform wearing a slouch hat. The officer moved from behind the cover of trees and spoke to his men. Nolan recognized him.

General Branch was counting on him to lead his own men to victory. He had to get to his men and his camp first. The Thirty-Fifth was expecting him.

But wait... Was his regiment retreating? They weren't putting up a fight. What was going on here? Why wasn't the commander telling his men to fight? The Union forces were winning.

Nolan felt the bite on his thigh before he saw it. A few seconds later, a long, dark viper slid past his head and a hot wave of nausea overtook him. Snakebite. He would die if he didn't get out of there. But how to escape?

Panic threatened to overtake his body. Taking ragged breaths, he tried to slow his heart down. He knew of little but the noise of his pulse.

He tasted the metallic taste of his blood. His lip was bleeding. He had been biting it shut to stay quiet. He could no longer hear the cannon or the wails of the dying. All he could hear was his heart hammering in his ears, faster and faster.

If I go to sleep, I will die. Got to... get... to... help... be... fore...

Nolan felt his body shutting down. Almost through sheer determination, he counted to himself.

1... 2... 3... 4... 5... focus on the numbers... 6... 7... 8... 9... must... not... sleep.

Above him, orders in a familiar voice sounded, and the firing seemed to end. He recognized Colonel Ross. "Line them up, single file men. Take weapons, Smith." Prisoners were being taken.

Then he heard footsteps nearby and voices he didn't recognize. Someone lifted his head and rubbed the hair from the front of his brow. A female voice said his name. Who?

Arms lifted his body. Carried. The darkness was overwhelming, frightening.

Where was he?

*L*ight intruded and heated his face. Sheer pain washed the reality of war back over Nolan. He opened his eyes and looked around. He was no longer on the wet, cold battlefield. He had been dreaming.

He was in some sort of lean-to, a hut. A small-framed old black woman stooped over a kettle with her back to him. She wore the clothing of a slave and had her hair up in a turban with gray wisps peeking out from the bottom. A vague familiarity struck him, but he couldn't reason why.

Without turning, she said, "'Bout time you wake up. Lucky you be alive." She twisted around and regarded him a long moment. "Massa Nole, you safe now."

"Where am I?" He struggled to place this woman in his mind.

"Yuz been asleep fer two weeks. I doctored your leg, chile, I did. Right smart bite you got, Massa Nole. I sucked de poison out and put snakeweed poultice on it. Drink des here tea," she said, shoving a cup of yellow fluid at him. "You member Ol' Indie, doesn't you?"

He blinked hard, then stared a moment, trying to focus. "Ol' Indie… I remember… but where… how did I get here?"

A gentle pair of gnarled hands held a chipped cup of tea to his nose. The tea smelled anything but good, and the yellowed cup was dirty. He wanted to turn up his nose and refuse it, but Ol' Indie was giving him this, and he trusted her.

Nolan told himself that the dirt couldn't hurt as much as the poison from the snake as he accepted the cup with shaking hands.

He lifted it to his mouth, but barely any of the liquid passed his lips. A good amount of the tea trickled down his face. The small amount he had swallowed smelled foul and created a strange sensation going down his throat.

He tried to remember. The last thing he recalled was being bitten. He needed to check on his sister since getting word that Ella and Aiden were by themselves, except for a few slaves, down from fifty. How would she get through this war on her own? Her last letter told him that Pa had abandoned them and taken all the money. A groan escaped him. *Where was he?*

He needed to get home and then back to his men. All he knew was his head hurt. He reached up and felt his face—a beard. How long did she say he had been here?

"You is in the swamp with me, Massa Nole. At my place. And you know where dat is. No one will find you until you ready to be found."

"How did I get here?"

"You been here a while now, Massa Nole. Right poorly you were. When I found you, you were laying wit' de dead men, but I checked and knew you was still alive. I seen you move. Ol' Indie was watching de big man with the Union Army pick up the dead men. Dey almost got you 'fore ah sees you move and check on you." She took the cup from Nolan. "Drink more of this. You been in and out of sleep for goin' on two weeks. This will help you can get better." Grinning, she filled up the cup and handed it to Nolan.

Nolan grimaced but accepted the cup, his hands still showing a slight tremor. He set the cup down but held on to it. "I need to find out what happened to my men. I saw them retreating. Were they defeated?"

Not getting an answer, he continued, his voice rocky. "And I need to check on my house, my family. I have to warn my sister and little brother." His voice wavered from exhaustion and weakness was taking over.

"Well, here now, you need to take things slow, Massa Nole. You look like a Union boy and I know dat your sista gonna near faint when she sees you in dat uniform." Ol' Indie sat back down in a heap in her old cane rocker and picked up her pipe. Placing it in her mouth, she stared at Nolan. "What you got to warn Miss Ella 'bout?" Nolan could tell that Ol' Indie worried about Ella. Her hands shook when she mentioned their safety. "What you figger'n to do when you feel better, boy? And drink up that potion for Ol' Indie. It'll make you strong."

Nolan drew the drink to his lips. He knew he needed it. He took a swig, trying to swallow. The foul taste was still hard to swallow, and he sprayed it from his mouth.

"What is this?" Spitting out the residue, he looked up at the woman.

"Drink up. Dis is my marshmallow root tea. It is good to keep de fever and de infection in your blood down."

He tried to clear his throat. "My sister needs to know there are dangers. There are runaways and deserters who could threaten her."

Nolan was grateful for her rescue, but Ol' Indie's presence and lack of information added to his confusion and frustration. He needed to get to his men.

What a fine kettle of fish he was in now. His orders were to move to the other side, not get bitten by a damn snake! He could hang for desertion from the Union Army. If captured and found to be a Confederate officer, he faced prison.

He needed to stay hidden until he could make it back to his men once he could figure out where they had gone. He had expected to see them when he first got to the battlefield. It shocked him to see so much battlefield unmanned. The Yanks advanced easily.

Something had gone wrong, and he wanted to know why they abandoned his carefully-laid plans and the battle lost.

CHAPTER 5

Colonel Jackson Ross had rounded up as many of the Confederates as his men could find. The prisoners who weren't injured were moved to a prison camp. The battle had been costly despite the Rebel surrender and early retreat.

The outcome pleased General Burnsides. Federal forces had taken control of the major port city of New Bern and the train that ran from Wilmington to Goldsboro. His job would be to serve as a provost marshall and restore order to the area. It would not be easy.

In the past six weeks, his men had gone to great lengths to account for all of the Union soldiers. So far, they could only find one person unaccounted for, dead or alive. Private White was the only man missing.

A small posse of men was scouring the area looking for him. Jackson didn't want to think of the man wandering around in need of medical help.

Oddly, Jackson recalled White. He had struck him as alert bright, and not the type to bolt. He was nowhere to be found. It seemed the lad was a runner. They would find him.

The military established several hospitals because there had been so many wounded on both sides of the battle. The thought occurred that he should check them, in case the young man had been improperly identified. He realized it wouldn't be easy. General Burnsides was already talking about making New Bern a regional hospital site for the wounded, and he was bringing in more doctors.

Jackson recalled previous medical facilities his unit had assembled. The government wanted more money and attention going into this area— and it made a big difference. These hospitals used the latest methods and medicines. They had buildings to work with, including the two-story New Bern Academy, and the Dixon House. Still, with so many sick men he needed more nurses. But how could he accomplish that?

Perhaps Sara Larson at The Griddle could have some helpful thoughts on the matter.

~

Heavy rain soaked the town for days. The morning the skies cleared, Jackson did something he'd been thinking about doing since meeting Ella Whitford. He headed across the street to The Mercantile. A niggling feeling tugged at him and hoped he could solve it with this visit.

Opening the door to the store, he stepped in and the bell chimed behind him. "Morning, Mrs. Smyth."

Startled by the slam of the door, the short, plump woman stopped talking to her husband. "Oh, good morning, Colonel Ross. What can we do for you today?"

Mr. Smyth scurried to the backroom, leaving his wife at the front counter, not waiting to hear a response.

Mrs. Smyth smiled at Jackson. Her hands twisted a rolled-up dust cloth tightly.

She was nervous. But why?

He grinned and moved in her direction, trying to put her at ease. "I wonder if you could help me." He lowered his voice, watching her face as he continued. "This is important. What can you tell me about a family living on a plantation called Silver Moon?"

"You are referring to the Whitfords?" she asked haltingly.

"Actually, yes." He drew up to the counter, leaning against it in a conspiratorial manner. "I met one of the members of the family. I believe she may be the lady of the house, a Miss Ella Whitford."

"Colonel, yes, yes. We know Ella very well. A loyal and hard-working young woman." Visibly relaxed, Mrs. Smyth leaned forward, keeping her voice low in case someone walked into the store. "Very nice family—well, what is left of the family. She has been running things since her father up and left her and her little brother a while back. Took all of their money, I heard. Had a strange notion about finding his son—who isn't lost. He's a soldier fighting... ah... fighting for the South." Mrs. Smyth flashed an apologetic look as she rushed on. "She depends on a handful of house slaves."

He stood there for a moment, silent, knowing that the woman he met this week was living in isolation and with no protection. He felt a strange sense of concern. She relied on the money from the eggs and vegetables. Jackson was glad he insisted she take money.

"Is her husband serving in the war?"

"Oh, no. No husband."

He tried to quell the strange feeling of pleasure sweeping over him. He hadn't noticed a ring, but he also knew many Southern women gave up their jewelry to help fund the Confederacy's strapped coffers. He wanted to smile, but paused for a long moment, thinking.

Mrs. Smyth gave him a look. "She was mighty popular growing up and would have been the belle of the ball here." She sniffed and blew into a handkerchief. "What with the war, well, things have changed. She is now a mother to her brother. She teaches him how to read and cipher and keeps food on the table. She is very devoted to little Aiden."

"Yes, and from what you've told me, she seems to have taken on quite a few things to keep her home intact."

Mrs. Smyth fidgeted with the pad and pencil she had laid on her counter. "Her mother was a close friend of mine, God rest her soul. Eleanor died giving birth to that little boy." Looking away, she wiped a tear from the corner of her eye. She was quiet for a long moment.

"Mr. Whitford loved his wife and his family very much. But when Eleanor died…he never was himself again. He up and left a year ago. Ella takes care of everything herself, and she's doing a real fine job."

The thought of Miss Whitford's vulnerability kept turning over in his mind as he listened.

She hesitated, suddenly nervous. "Is there something wrong out at Silver Moon?"

Jackson lifted his hat and stepped back from the counter. "No, no. No trouble out there that I know of. I, well, I ran into her a little earlier this week. I was unaware that there was a young woman heading up the family occupying the plantation. It's my responsibility to know this area and protect the citizens. It's one I take seriously. These are dangerous times with runaways and deserters. I appreciate the information. I do. Thank you, ma'am."

Mrs. Smyth beamed. "I'm pleased I could be of help, Colonel."

He started to leave, but recalling the cigars on display, he returned to the counter. "Mrs. Smyth, I'll take two packs of those nice cherry-blend cheroots." He pointed to the cigars on the shelf behind her. "And how about another bar of that soap you sold me last week? Sandalwood, I believe it was."

"Yes, suh. Give me one moment. I'll wrap that up for you. That'll be… erm… forty-two cents, please."

Jackson reached into his chest pocket and pulled out a small purse. He pulled out a silver dollar, laying it on the counter. "Thank you. Please keep the change. You have been very helpful."

He stepped out on the porch and pulled one cheroot out, lit it, and tucked the rest of the package inside his coat pocket. Lingering a moment, he looked towards Silver Moon and smiled. A simple plan formed in his mind as he puffed on his cheroot.

Jackson muttered, his voice too low to hear. "I think we will need a perimeter headquarters that will allow my men to spread out and practice drills. And the bigger the property, the better it serves. This will please the general." He smiled, his mind made up. He would scout out his new headquarters soon.

He headed home. Once he was relaxing in his bunk, he watched the swaying tree limbs in the window. Ella Whitford lingered on his mind, and thoughts of her were almost maddening in their intensity. Had it been too long since a woman had been part of his life?

Had it been two years since he had been engaged?

Maria had taught him a valuable lesson. Love would never be part of the equation again. He didn't want to be made a fool of twice, not over love. She had cheated on him with Nate, his close friend. Love had been placed on the chopping block for him. There was no need for it anymore. Marrying Maria had been his dream, never hers. Nate was her aspiration, it seemed.

He had his career to focus his attention on.

He had plenty of work. It was important to find a better spot for his men to camp and he suspected that perfect spot lay on the outskirts of town.

Burnsides and the Mass 21st claimed many of the vacated homes in New Bern when the wealthier residents fled just before the battle. In most circumstances, the homes were still furnished. Many were stocked with food. Hungry soldiers enjoyed the cured hams and preserves they found. As enticing as many of the homes in town were, Jackson felt a perimeter location could better serve his needs and the needs of the military encampment here.

Ella's face and green eyes flashed in his mind. A smug smile lit his face. Yes, he needed to get that perimeter location for law and order.

With that justification in mind, Jackson got up from his cot and grabbed his jacket. He pulled on his boots and grabbed his hat.

"Marshall, we will check out a new site for our men. Saddle my horse and yours. I'll meet you out front in five minutes. I'm running back to The Griddle across the street and should be back."

"Sounds good, Colonel!" Lieutenant Colonel Marshall Jameson. Jackson's best friend and sidekick gave a sly smile.

"What? Why are you giving me that look?"

"Jackson, we've been together for the last fifteen years through everything—school, women, and now war. I know where we are going. In the last couple of days, you have mentioned a plantation being run outside New Bern by one Miss Ella Whitmore. And you mention her frequently."

"You wound me. This is a sound idea." Jackson felt his collar heating. That damn Marshall knew him too well.

"Can't deny that. It is a sound idea to have perimeter security. Goes along with our need to have small militia units on some outposts."

"Thank you." He wanted to be on his way, unwilling to give this one to Marshall.

"I'm just happy to see you so excited about your job. That's all." His grin widened, and he grabbed up his hat.

Jackson bit back his retort. He would not dignify Marshall's goading. The perimeter was a sound military decision. Miss Whitford's plantation just provided the perfect location.

He strode across the street to Sara's place. The bell hanging from the door jangled as the screened door slammed closed, announcing him. Embarrassed, Jackson turned too late to catch the door.

"Sorry, ma'am," he said to Sara. "If you have just a moment, I would want to take a minute of your time."

"Well hello there, Colonel! I'm so happy to see you this morning! Let me see to this order and I will be right with you." Sara pushed the kitchen door open and disappeared.

Jackson wondered how much information Sara would give him. He wouldn't mind seeing Miss Ella Whitford again, but there was the issue of her safety. He had not realized there was an occupied plantation on the outskirts of New Bern, or at least not one occupied by a young woman, a small child, and a handful of loyal slaves. That setting would be a target for deserters and runaways and others.

The thought made him angry and stirred up his protective instinct. Uncomfortable, he shifted and looked out the screened door, waiting for Sara to finish in the kitchen.

The door to the kitchen swung open. Sara pushed through carrying a fresh pot of coffee and a basket of rolls. Nodding at the table next to her, she signaled for Jackson to come and sit.

"Would you mind if we sat while we talked? I haven't had a

moment to take a breath all morning! The breakfast crowd finally left, so I thought you might enjoy a couple of my leftover biscuits and another cup of coffee."

"Thank you. Don't mind if I do." Jackson slid a chair out for Sara. When she got comfortable, he helped himself to the chair across from her. Clearing his throat, he tried to think how to best begin. "I am headed out to Silver Moon. I need a perimeter location for my men. And until a couple of days ago, I didn't know there was an occupied plantation in this area. And I didn't realize there was one occupied by a young woman and a small child."

"Suh, are you suggesting that you will take my best friend's home away from her?" She drew back.

He lowered his voice. "You realize she could be in harm's way. Please tell me what you know about the number of servants she has on the property."

There. It was up to her. He knew Sara cared about her friend, but he was not sure he had established a level of trust with her.

While she had not taken the pledge of allegiance to the Union yet, he had detected no outward feelings of mistrust. He knew her sympathies were with the Confederacy, but he liked her. All the men felt comfortable coming to The Griddle.

Anything she could tell him would be important. Jackson stayed quiet and watched Sara struggle to respond.

Sara was quiet for a moment. "Ella is a private person. We have been friends since we were small girls. I know that she will not take kindly to your intrusion. In fact, she will see it as hostile."

"I imagine you could be right, but I feel that while it serves the Union, it's in her best interest. She will need a little coaxing."

At that, Sara smiled. "Ella has her cook, a few house servants, her overseer and a few land workers. They respect her, and she returns the sentiment." Sara's voice lowered almost into a whisper as she looked at the customers in the restaurant. "The Whitfords were always good to their slaves, treating them like they were family. Nowadays, she works right alongside her people."

Sara stopped talking as if she might have revealed too much. She was worried about Ella's reaction, too.

After a moment of silence, Jackson cleared his throat. "Thank you, Sara. I will not betray your confidence. I wanted to know what I could run into. It's dangerous around here for all of us. And I agree. Miss Whitford is taking a big chance living on her own. I plan to move out there with my men. I expect she will *not* welcome me." With that, he rose from the table.

Smiling, Sara responded, "Count on it, suh. But I have worried about her living out there by herself with the soldiers and the escaped slaves all around us. I have heard awful things!" She shuddered. "Why, just last week Mrs. Smyth told us they discovered a broken window in the back of their store. They boarded it up. But still, it just made me shudder to think of how vulnerable we could be."

"I had not heard of that. That concerns me. I will check into it. I'd appreciate it if you would let me know if you hear anything about her plantation—anything you think I should know, Miss Sara."

"I will, suh. And… good luck." Sara stood up and picked up the basket of biscuits and the coffee pot while Jackson slid the chairs back under the table. She stood very quietly. "Please be good to her."

Shielding his eyes from the sun as he left The Griddle, Jackson reached into his pocket and pulled out his watch. He winced. Ten minutes. Marshall will be waiting. He quickened his pace down the steps and crossed the street to the Taylor House.

The townhouse was the central command post and home for Burnsides' commanding officers. Burnsides had commandeered a roomy mansion a few blocks over for his headquarters.

Approaching the Taylor House, Jackson slowed down and took in the look of the town. It appeared quiet today. He puzzled over the break-in at The Mercantile and wondered why Mrs. Smyth hadn't mentioned it.

He recalled that both she and Mr. Smyth were acting strangely. They were nervous. That would have to wait. Today he had a perimeter fortification he needed to remedy. Jackson crossed the street, headed to the stables behind his headquarters.

As he predicted, Marshall was waiting. Looking up at the sound of crunching boots on the gravel, Marshall tipped up his hat and shot Jackson a lopsided grin. Jackson noticed and fought back his irritation towards his friend.

Marshall could be like a dog with a bone. Jackson could tell when Marshall thought he was onto something. Jackson didn't feel in the mood for sparring, not caring what Marshall thought he knew. Seeing Marshall with his horse, he squared his shoulders and took a deep breath.

"Ready? Let's head out of town."

"Sure. Did you get what you needed from The Griddle?"

Ignoring the barb, Jackson checked his saddle and secured his rifle. It always felt good to ride Mason. Silver Moon would be at least thirty minutes out, so he would give Mason some good exercise.

The big black stallion was a pet as much as an animal could be. Mason was special to Jackson. He was a gift from Mrs. Thomason, a lady he had the good fortune to meet in Virginia a year before.

Her husband had died trying to fight off some Rebel renegades that had invaded their farm and were trying to steal from them.

Mason was one of three horses that were in the Thomason's barn when the Rebs set it on fire. Jackson and his men showed up just in time to engage the renegades. They killed them all and put out the fire before it swallowed up the barn and killed the horses.

The horses were in bad shape, but they made it; her other livestock didn't. The Thomason family had been targeted because of their Union allegiance. It was just one of the harsh realities of this brutal war.

Afterward, they helped Mrs. Thomason bury her husband. Mason had been her son's horse. She noticed Jackson had a way with horses and asked Jackson to take Mason. With her husband dead and her barn burned, she could not keep him. Jackson couldn't refuse her request. They needed good horseflesh.

He and his men had hitched up her wagon with her two remaining horses and loaded her belongings. They provided Mrs. Thomason a safe escort to Richmond, twenty miles away, so she could live with her sister and her sister's husband.

Before he left, Mrs. Thomason got Jackson to promise he would try to find her son, Henry, a young Union recruit. She had not gotten a letter or any word on him in almost a year and feared he had been killed.

So far, Jackson's search had turned up nothing. He wished he had asked if Henry was his only given name. Why had that only occurred to him now? Whether he found Henry Thomason, Jackson knew he would never give up Mason, who had become so important to him. Reaching down, he patted Mason on his neck.

His mind was trying to test his resolve to stay free, at least since breakfast the other day. Thoughts of a young woman with deep green eyes and a blue dress invaded his thoughts.

He couldn't understand the effect she had on him and smiled almost every time he thought about her. *Just who was she?*

They had barely spoken to each other, yet her face was in his dreams, his thoughts, and now, leading his plans for his men. But he had seen the horrors of what desperate men would do when they only wanted food and silver candlesticks.

She was in danger. He could feel it. He tried not to worry but a picture of a burning barn made its way into his mind.

Marshall glanced at Jackson and leaned down to make sure his rifle was secure in its scaffold. He cleared his throat. "No rain today, Jackson. Should be a good day to explore the land."

Jackson looked at his friend and nodded. He didn't miss the concerned look on Marshall's face. "Something feels wrong, Marshall."

He urged Mason faster, and Marshall followed suit. The two men kicked up their speed, leaving a wall of dust behind them.

Nolan felt vibrations on the ground and heard the sounds of hooves racing towards him. He looked around. The only cover was a dead tree that was lying prone along the edge of the road, tucked up close to some dead brush. He rolled down over the log and pushed his body up against it, hiding under the dry foliage.

He knew he would pay for this later. No more than two minutes went by before two Union officers rode by, kicking up a furious trail of dirt. They didn't slow down, so he hoped that meant they had not seen him. Nolan let out an anxious breath and wished he hadn't.

The dust made it impossible to catch another. Where were they headed? He knew this area and there weren't many places out this way. The most notable place was where he was headed—his home. *Was Ella expecting them?*

He recognized those men. A protective feeling yanked Nolan up from the ditch and moved him towards the road. *Just where are the colonel twins going?*

His commanding officer and his sidekick were headed towards Silver Moon. That meant only one thing to him—trouble. He tried his best to dust himself off. Nolan looked at his pants and his jacket. It was useless.

His blue uniform was almost shredded beyond recognition. He wasn't sure what he should do. This was not going according to any plan he could have expected. The colonel twins would arrest him for desertion if they saw him. *Better he gets discovered there, then at his home. He might be able to explain away the desertion with the concussion and the bite.*

But if they found him at the house, he would be a suspected spy. Everyone there knew he was a Confederate officer. He was unarmed except for the stick he had sharpened into a spear. *What did Ol' Indie do with my weapons?*

He touched his face and pulled at his rough beard. That is if they recognize him. He had seen his reflection and didn't even recognize himself. He would frighten Ella if she saw him.

Reaching inside his shirt, he pulled out the locket that hung from his neck and opened it. His beloved smiled up at him, her face framed by layered curls. A lock of her hair was tucked in the locket. "Sara," he groaned aloud, his throat seizing on him.

He hadn't seen her since the conflict began. He closed the locket and pushed it against his chest protectively. Grabbing his large stick, he continued making his way home.

CHAPTER 6

A soft wind whispered through the trees as the men rode up to the gates of Silver Moon. Silver maples and stately magnolia trees lined the road leading to the plantation house gently swayed back and forth. Behind them sat a wooded area edged by a wide field of snowbells.

The effect was beautiful. It was hard to imagine this plantation could run without its full contingent of help. As they moved on, the driveway took Jackson and Marshall from the wooded and naturalized garden area, to a region where tall overgrown grass and weeds dominated.

The tall grasses and weeds wildly grabbed all the land available, drastically minimizing the loveliness of the stately maples and magnolias. This area needed to be cleaned. Dangers could easily hide here. Finally, a small curve in the drive led them to a brick-paved drive, and the big house came in view.

The driveway ended in a nicely formed wrap-around in front of a Georgian-styled columned home. Large sections of white paint peeled on parts of the house, and black shutters hung askew. Still, Jackson could easily imagine the massive drive having led carriages to the house, host to lavish parties of the past.

Horse posts and a dry trough stood off to the side. It must have been a welcoming site for the dusty travelers before this war.

"So, here we are." His spoken words served almost an affirmation of his own plans and were met with silence. He climbed off his horse and led Mason to the post. He couldn't help the feelings of anticipation. "Let's see who is at home."

Another feeling gripped him that he couldn't identify.

It was dread.

~

The jangle of boots disturbed Ella from her chores. She parted the curtain and looked out to see *him*. He raised his hand, and she opened the door before he could knock. She attempted to hide her shotgun in her skirts. She didn't want to shoot him. Yet.

Ella opened the door. "Gentlemen. Colonel Ross, Lieutenant Colonel, suhs. Can I help you?"

She was at odds with herself. Normally, she would have answered the door with the shotgun cocked and ready. She hated Yankees, but for reasons she couldn't understand, had ignored her instinct and answered the door without cocking her gun. Her face warmed as she realized she was staring.

He cleared his throat. "May we come in? I feel like what we have to say would be best discussed in the parlor." Colonel Ross pulled his hat down in front of him.

"Suh, you have come to my house for reasons unknown to me. I only just met you, so I don't think so. Anything you need to say to me, you say it here." Ella adjusted her shotgun alongside her skirt, making sure it was no longer hidden.

"Miss Whitford," Colonel Ross began, "I think formal introductions are in order."

"How do you know who I am?" Ella reflexively raised the gun.

In a swift movement, the colonel stepped in her direction and placed his hand on the gun, pushing it away from them and holding it firmly.

"You are correct, we were never properly introduced. A failure on my part, I assure you. I am Colonel Jackson Ross of the United States Army. This is Lieutenant Colonel Marshall Jameson. We are here on behalf of the Union."

Ella narrowed her eyes, trying to pull her gun away. "Suh, you have your hands on my property." She jerked the gun back, forcing it up sharply. Her hip hit the stock and her finger accidentally pulled the trigger.

An ear-splitting explosion sounded as the gun went off, blasting a hole in the ceiling. Chunks of plaster rained down from the doorway on top of all three of them. Colonel Ross threw himself over Ella as the three of them fell to the ground.

For a few moments, all Ella could hear was ringing, but she could feel vibrations of footsteps that were getting heavier.

~

"Miss Ella, Miss Ella, you be all right?" Male and female voices spoke simultaneously, both pulling up shocked.

"Oh, my dear Lord." Lizzy looked first at the ceiling and the front door, and then at the large chunks of plaster and wood lying on top of a powdered white stack of bodies and let out a scream. "Miss Ella! Oh Lordy! Miss Ella, is you in there? Help me, Carter! Goodness! Miss Ella!"

Lizzy slung plaster away from the bodies in a panic. The mound of bodies began moving, and she screamed again, falling onto her backside.

She threw herself at the bodies and began pawing the plaster away, looking for her mistress. "Miss Ella. Where you be? Mercy! What done happened here?" Lizzy pawed furiously at the pile of rubble, as a man began to rise, dressed in blue and covered in white powder. "Who is you men? And what has you done with Miss Ella?"

"I'm... umph... uggh... here, Lizzy." A muffled female voice came from under the mound. The top body rose up slowly to his knees. Almost at once, three white powdered faces looked up from the pile of white plaster and boards into the worried faces of Lizzy and Carter, Ella's house servants.

"Oh my! Here now, let me help you up, Miss Ella." Carter bent down to help Miss Ella up from the floor. The two men pushed themselves up from the floor and began to dust the plaster off their uniforms.

Lieutenant Colonel Jameson kicked the pieces of plaster to the side of the room and took in the damage. "I believe the lady made her point," he smirked.

Lizzy rushed over and began fussing over her, checking her from head to toe. She glanced back over her shoulder, casting a cold expression towards the two men still dusting themselves off.

~

Ella waited a minute, trying to get her temper under control before she responded. When she stood up, she realized Colonel Ross had flung himself over her when the plaster fell. Again, with the brave man stuff! She was annoyed that the closeness of his body didn't feel so bad. She wished Lizzy had waited just a moment or two more before rescuing her. His arms were corded with muscles; they were so strong. That tingling feeling emerged from her nether region—something she had felt once before. Warmth shot up her neck. She shook her head, trying to clear it.

"You are hurt." Before anything could be said to stop her, Lizzy lifted the edge of her skirt and ripped a piece of her slip. She held it to Ella's head to stop the bleeding on a forehead cut.

"Oh...I'm bleeding!" Ella glared at the men. Livid, she walked up to the colonel and poked him chest. "Now see what you caused? We were fine until you came to...*save* us."

Of course, she knew it was her loaded gun that went off, but it was still his fault.

"What business do you have with us, Colonel?" She angrily turned to the other man. "And you can wipe that smirk off your face. This isn't funny in the least."

Colonel Ross dusted off his hat. "Miss Whitford, we need to set up a perimeter post for the town and your plantation is the perfect site for our camp. We will primarily use the grounds and will take as good a care of it as we can, but we fully intend to set up camp here with at least four hundred men. Of course, we will also be conducting drills."

He looked around and nodded toward the fencing that was down. "We've noticed the overgrown trees and grasses, and the shrubbery is creeping over the tops of the lawn and completely covering parts of the fencing. I mention this because I want you to know that we will do our best to maintain your property."

"Suh, you are insulting. You are talking about my home."

Clearing his throat, he continued. "I will have my men help with house repairs, as well as repairs to the land, in an effort to ease some pain of our imposition, as part of our keep. We don't intend to ruin your home."

"Suh, you just being here will ruin my house."

"Miss Whitford, these are perilous times. I share in the responsibility for the people here in New Bern. And I have a responsibility to the military. This is more than fair.

"Fair?" She stomped her booted foot, hugging her arms folded tightly across her chest.

"In addition, I am authorized to pay you a fair price for supplies and lodging. That is something I will insist on.

Flabbergasted, Ella just stared. He was taking over her home, and at the same time offering her rent. She hadn't heard of that happening in town. Of course, the homes that had been taken over had been abandoned. She opened her mouth to say something, and closed it, momentarily at a loss for words.

This was stunning. She could certainly use the income. There would be little to no cash crops this year; she had limited help in the fields—there was only herself, her house workers, a few of the laborers, and an overseer that had stayed on when the Yankees came.

This thought renewed her anger. She was being taken over, just like the town. It hadn't worked to keep her head down. They discovered Silver Moon, anyway. "And what if I refuse?"

"You can refuse, but we will be here, anyway." Colonel Ross readjusted his hat, knocking off more of the dust. "We don't mean to cause you any trouble, but there's one more thing. We will need quarters and an office inside. We will periodically have meetings. May we look around?" He nodded towards the library behind her.

Heat rose up to her neck and bile burned her throat. She wanted to speak but knew she would embarrass herself. Still, she needed to say something even though she realized that she didn't have any recourse. She had to relent. "I won't pledge." She bit out her words and stared at him, waiting.

Lieutenant Colonel Jameson stepped forward. "Miss Whitford, I know this is most inconvenient, but if you will allow this willingly, it will save us a trip out here tomorrow with more men."

Colonel Ross continued, "Your plantation is where we need to place our perimeter security post. And ma'am, it's simply not safe for a... beautiful woman and a young boy to be unprotected in times such as these. You have no idea of the perils—"

Ella shot him a look. "I assure you I can take care of myself and my brother." She grabbed her shotgun. Her left hand comfortably cradled the barrel and her right covered the trigger and stock.

Colonel Ross arched his brow. "Miss Whitford, just because you can handle a shotgun, that does not mean you can shoot one. Please hand over your gun, for your own protection." He looked over at the damaged door and then up at the ceiling. His hands reached for the gun, grazing her arm.

Warmth passed through his glove where it touched her skin and moved up her arm. Ella felt her body react to the intrusion of his touch and recoiled.

"I will not! And you will not come here and demand my personal property, and squatter's rights, too." She raised her gun, determined. "My gun is for protection, and I will not turn it over to you or anyone. What happened... here." Ella looked down at the mess on the floor and then glanced at the ceiling. "This is your fault. You, suh, overstepped yourself and grabbed my gun!"

"Miss Whitford, you can either make this easy or hard. I propose we make a very equitable situation. To show you the earnestness of my offer, I will pay you for anything we use, including your supplies." Jackson reached into his jacket and pulled out his wallet. He held out some crisp bills towards her. "Please accept this."

Ella made no move for the money.

"This is for the damage. Of course, I plan to see this fixed. I will have men out here tomorrow to mend this—with me. We will be good tenants."

Ella felt the weight of his glare, instinctively knowing he wasn't going to relent.

"Now, Miss Whitford, I would ask you again to see the lower floor. We won't require your upper floors. They will be left alone for you to use as living quarters for yourself and your family. My men that enter will be respectful that this is also your home. I will post a guard here at all times."

Tempted, Ella looked at the bills. It was more than she would make with six months of deliveries to The Griddle, but it was about pride. Just who did he think he was?

"Suh, you can just keep your dollar bills. You won't be staying." She pointed the gun towards the door. "You men can see yourselves out."

~

Heat rose past his collar; Jackson was infuriated. He had never met a woman who did not respond favorably to him.

Jackson studied Miss Whitford. Her reaction was one of anger. He was offering mollifications that were rarely given yet she just glared. He had smiled, cajoled, and even offered her payment for *use* of her property. The other homeowners weren't getting that. He was determined to make this a peaceful coexistence but was running out of options. What was he missing?

He could barely hide his irritation. "Miss Whitmore, I plan to take your home as my command post with or without your permission." Jackson didn't need her permission, but he wanted it. Moving closer, he lowered his voice. "Now, are we going to work together on this? Or will this be a *hostile* takeover?"

"Suh, you have invaded my home, sought to steal my gun, and scared me and my family near to death. I would judge it a hostile takeover *as if* there was any doubt."

He fought to maintain his temper. Why was she so stubborn that she couldn't see he was trying to help her? Her unwillingness to accept an opportunity to be protected irritated him. He was also angry that he was being told 'no' by a woman. This was new territory for him.

∼

He was too close. Ella could smell his sandalwood cologne. Her body shuddered involuntarily. She hated these men... *didn't she*? Clenching her hands tighter around the shotgun, she took a deep breath.

They aren't leaving because I want them to leave. Perhaps there is some level of compromise I can create. Or at least, if she could have more time, she could find a way to get rid of them.

Ella stepped aside. "Lizzy, please show the colonel... the *colonels* around the lower floor. And Carter, would you mind finding Aiden and bringing refreshments to the library?"

"Thank you, Miss Ella." Colonel Ross took off his hat and paused at the door, scraping his boots before entering the hallway.

"Follow me, Colonel, suh." Lizzy walked slowly through the hall with the two men in tow. As Colonel Ross passed her, his arm brushed Ella's bare skin on her arm. A multitude of butterflies passed through her and her gaze followed him down the hall.

She took full notice of him. How could she not? Those broad shoulders almost pushed out of his corded uniform. There were so many men in New Bern now, but no one that looked like him. He took her breath away.

Now there would be over four hundred Yankees on her property, alone, but she had no interest in any of them. What was it about this one? Her traitorous body sent an answer tingling straight up her neck.

Ella glared at the backs of the colonel and his friend, their voices and footfalls echoing through the rooms as Lizzy showed them around the first floor. They were in the dining room.

Her arm still tingled from his touch when he brushed past her. If she *had* to have the Union Army here... no! What was she thinking?

Ella took the few minutes the colonels were distracted to place her shotgun behind her desk in the library, hiding it before they returned. No way was anyone confiscating her gun. She stood next to the door, waiting.

Footsteps with the jangle of spurs got louder as the two men approached the front entry hall where Ella stood waiting.

"Miss Ella, I'd be happy to get some tea for everyone." Lizzy's eyes grew large, and she nodded her head subtly in the direction of the library.

Caught off guard by Lizzy's actions, Ella stumbled. "Uh... yes. Well, some tea would be nice. Let's go to the library." Ella wasn't sure what Lizzy was about, but they had grown up together. She trusted her as she would a sister and followed her lead.

"Well thank you, Miss Whitford. That would be nice." Jackson looked at Marshall and shrugged. "Lead the way."

"This was my papa's library." She paused. "Now, I guess it is Nolan's, or will be whenever he finally gets back home." She opened the doors and led them inside. A heavy oak desk sat in the middle of the room, facing the doors, its back to books. Intricate carvings laced the panels of the heavy wood. Two armchairs sat at angles in front of the desk as if waiting for visitors.

Bookshelves lined three walls, from the floor to the ceiling, with a moveable ladder on runners hooked to the wall. To his eye, the books appeared to be dusted and well maintained for the number of staff that existed here.

The windows alongside the fireplace were covered with thick burgundy velvet curtains although the velvet was rather worn. The ceiling was made of dark wood and matched the floorboards. A thick burgundy Wilton carpet covered the floor. A small gaming table sat in the corner of the room. Clearly, this was a man's room of escape.

"Yes, this room will serve my needs." His tone turned solicitous. "I haven't seen this many books in a while. Your father must have loved to read." Jackson absently pulled a leather volume from the bookcase behind the desk. He examined it, turning the pages gently.

~

"He did. And he encouraged us to read as well. We all have books in here and were always welcomed to come in and use his library." Ella watched Colonel Ross put one book back and select another, and then another.

"I can see that the books are well maintained. We will make sure that we are careful with the room. I like it. It will be a wonderful room to entertain the general and some other officials in though." Clearly pleased, Colonel Ross was busy looking at the room and didn't notice the look that Ella had on her face.

Ella closed her eyes. Her lawn wasn't perfect, but now she saw it full of tents and invaders everywhere. Her barns and the stables would no longer be hers. Their horses would be tied and corralled everywhere. Men would be coming in and out of her home at all hours. How had this happened?

One minute this was home, and she was making do. And the next, *he* was here to save her? How was that, again? Oh yes! He planned to make this his *perimeter camp*. The words almost soured her mind just thinking them. She would become a prisoner upstairs in her own home.

Aiden would be confined. Her little brother would no longer be able to play on the front lawn with his puppy. *No, this wasn't going to happen.* Her outrage started building again.

"You are quite serious. You think to take over my home?" She bit her tongue in an attempt to quell her rage. "This won't be proper, suh. I am an unmarried woman. I am sure you can find another property that will better serve your purposes." She bit the words out deliberately.

Standing off to the side, Lieutenant Colonel Jameson was quiet. Tipping his hat, he gave Ella a slight smile and edged towards the library door. "Hey, maybe three is a crowd here. I think I will let the two of you finish discussing this. I'll wait in the foyer, Jackson."

Leaving the doors open, he walked into the foyer but muttered just loud enough for Colonel Ross to hear. "This is your battle, buddy. I think I'll let you handle it."

He smiled at her. "No, I am sure this will be perfect. And Miss Whitford, I assure you that your virtue will be secure."

He looked again at the large desk and the books behind it, seeming to Ella that he was lost in thought. He failed to notice her step towards the bookcase.

A blue and white vase hurled past his head, crashing into the fireplace wall.

Startled, Colonel Ross spun around to face the furious face of one Ella Whitford and the smirking face of his best friend.

CHAPTER 7

Jackson felt lucky to get out of the house with his head intact. She had excellent throwing ability and a horrible temper, but he couldn't help the smile that came over him.

Mentally, he ticked off his list. The perimeter coverage had become paramount in his mind. He was pleased with his own timing. It had only taken him a day or two to get things pulled together.

Jackson thought about the hospitals and realized they still needed more help and more space. That was another problem. Slaves were turning up in epic numbers, many sick and hungry. They had no home, no way to earn an income, and no education. This new freedom of theirs was not without a cost. Providing them hospital care was going to be a tougher problem to fix.

No one seemed on the same page in this damnable war. Jackson didn't want to waste any more energy being irritated by this problem. He needed to do something, now.

"Marshall, come here!" he bellowed. He never spoke to his best friend that way. He would be apologizing. This day was not going well, already.

~

Marshall slid back his chair slowly and walked into the backroom that served as the colonel's office, a slight grin pulling his lips.

The vision of Jackson Ross ducking the vase played over in his head. "So, when do we leave? The men are packing their bedrolls, and Cook has stocked the wagon. They can be ready in a quarter to a half hour."

"Yes, that is excellent. Yes. We will leave shortly." Turning in his chair, Jackson faced Marshall, still rolling a nub of a pencil back and forth. "But we need to get some things set up quickly. Schools. I'd like to leave those under your guidance. Your sister is a teacher, and I am thinking that you can consult her for direction. I've been told we've got slaves and their children swarming into the area with no place to live. They need some help. Let's organize shelter and schools for these slave children and their parents, too. Can you handle these items for me?"

"Sure. Jackson, I was thinking… you reckon there is anyone that can tutor them? I don't recall meeting anyone wanting to teach, so far. Seems that anyone that had anything to do with educating kids abandoned this town when they heard we were coming." Marshall paused.

"Send word and see if any schoolmasters are out there that want to try their luck here in the southern parts. General Burnsides had mentioned the school concept earlier. It's needed. I don't want it to get lost in this transition. Let's check with his office and see if he has heard of anyone interested, and we'll go from there."

Marshall scrawled a few words on a piece of paper and stuffed it into his pocket. "I'll follow up with this, Jackson."

"There's a lot that needs to be done before we can get our men settled. Sanders is loading supplies. The fences need mending. Glass panes, wood and paint will also be needed. I'm certain this perimeter camp will not be without its problems." Jackson stood and pushed the chair under his desk, the legs scraping the unvarnished wood. "It's almost eight hundred hours."

"Yes, sir." Marshall grabbed his hat and stood next to the door, waiting to leave. He could not wait to see what Miss Ella Whitford had in mind this time. Chuckling to himself, he pulled the door closed behind him.

∽

"Time to get out to Silver Moon." He checked his pockets but couldn't find his notes. "I'm sorry. I left something inside I need." Quickly, he walked back into his office. Jackson spotted his list on his desk and stuffed it into his chest pocket, then hurried back out the door.

Marshall chuckled when the door closed.

"Marshall, you have something to say?" Jackson looked up at his friend, his brows arched.

"No, sorry. Well, yes. I do have a little something. I've never seen a woman get under your skin in what… seems like just a few days?" He quickly added on his fingers and looked up with a grin. "Yes, in less than a week's time, as a matter-of-fact."

Jackson shot him an angry glare.

Marshall cleared his throat and quickly changed the subject. "Ahem. Yes. Colonel, I was just thinking about how fast Sanders and his supply wagons got loaded. I don't think I've seen our men move so fast. I think we're all ready for this assignment."

"Good. There's much to get done when we arrive." Jackson's tone was terse. He mentally chastised himself for a display of temper he couldn't seem to stop.

"I'm thinking we should get some coffee before we leave. It will be a long day. What do you think?" Marshall nodded in the direction of The Griddle, across the street.

Jackson was already on Mason. He glanced over at The Griddle, thinking of Sara's great eggs, toast, and warm coffee. His stomach started rumbling. "That is a stellar idea." *Of course—hunger! He had forgotten breakfast.* "Let's tie up and get some grub, then we head out. I've got Sanders meeting us out there at ten hundred hours and if we're not there first, we may be attending his funeral." Visions of a fiery redhead and a shotgun caused him to choke back a laugh.

"Sergeant Sanders is one of those by-the-book people who will probably get right in her face. Before he knows it, she could have his grill on the end of her shotgun." Marshall hooted.

"My thoughts exactly." Jackson dismounted. "More likely, he would try to arrest her." That thought upset him. "We'd better hurry so we can beat him there."

He tied up Mason, and the two men walked into The Griddle.

The door to the restaurant jingled loudly as it closed behind them. Smiling, Sara picked up her pot of coffee and two cups and led the two men to their favorite table.

~

Ella woke up and grabbed her dress off the back of the chair. Quickly putting on her stays and her dress, she pulled her hair back into a tight chignon and splashed water on her face.

She realized she was taking shortcuts getting dressed, but she didn't have the luxury of having her own maid to help her dress these days.

She grabbed a towel and dried her face, hands, and arms. Picking up her small looking glass from the corner of her dresser, she stared at her reflection. *My hair never looks shiny anymore,* she thought wistfully. *He is coming here today.*

Admittedly, he was very pleasant to look at, and if that was all there was to it—looking at him—that would be one thing, but he was taking over her home. *Her home.*

She needed to get that man off her mind. What about a diversion? Yes, that was just what she wanted so she could think about other things she needed to do, like… well, like gather eggs.

"Lizzy, are you up here?" She walked out of her room onto the landing and looked around.

"Yes, ma'am. Here ah am." Lizzy came out of Aiden's room carrying a pile of clothing.

"Those men are coming today. They expect to stay here. I feel like I am in a bad dream." Ella wrapped her arms around herself, her fingers tapping fiercely on her upper arms. "What do they expect to do for food? We just have a few animals and they are not going to be given over to the Union Army. And those are *my* horses!" Ella tamped down her rage. She needed to stop. Her chest was heaving, and she hadn't even brushed her teeth. How had she forgotten to brush her teeth?

"I know this ain't what you want to hear, but I suggest that we try to get on as normal as we can. Truth is, you been trying as hard as a body can, but you could use the help they gonna give us. And besides, there ain't much we gonna be able to do 'bout them coming."

"Oh, Lizzy!" Tears of frustration brimmed in her eyes, and she brushed them away. "I know you are right about us needing help, but they are Yankees. I don't want to have them here."

"Miss Ella, best you get yourself together. They will be here this morning."

"I'll try. You are right, of course. I don't know what I'd do without you." She took a deep, calming breath. "I'm taking Aiden with me this morning to gather eggs. It's time he learned to help milk the cow. What do you think? Bo may enjoy that, too. That is if he doesn't tear up the poor cow's nerves." She shook her head and smiled.

"Yes, ma'am. It's a good idea." Lizzy smiled. "We are doing the laundry this morning. If I can have your dress, Miss Ella, I will see if I can get some of that dust from it."

"Oh drat! I left it folded across the end of my bed. Lizzie, I hate to ask you, but you mind grabbing it as you go past my room?"

Lizzy nodded and left, and Ella turned her attention back to Aiden. He made her smile—he and Bo. This child with his soft brown eyes and blond hair had stolen her heart the day he was born. It was up to her to make sure that his life was safe, that he had plenty to eat, and that he got a good education. Sometimes it felt overwhelming, but she couldn't imagine her life without him. She would do what she had to in order to keep their home. Lizzy was right. She needed to try to keep her life as normal as she could.

Aiden is almost six, she realized with a start. *Has that much time gone by since Mamma died?* Her eyes misted. She sure missed her mamma.

She wished Nolan had stayed home. Aiden needed a man around here. If Nolan were here, she wouldn't have this situation with the dang Union Army.

Well, *maybe* she wouldn't.

She scowled. It *could* actually be worse.

Nolan was a colonel in the Confederate States Army. She might not see him until this awful occupation was over and he could come home. A colonel in the Confederate army couldn't just show up in occupied territory. She shook her head in frustration. There was just so much here to do to keep things running. *I really miss my brother.*

"Aiden, time to get up, my little one! Let's go. We have chores to do," she said gently, as she shook his shoulders. She walked over to the windows and pulled open the curtains, letting the morning sunshine stream into the room. Aiden slowly rose as golden floppy ears emerged from under his covers.

"Aiden, we talked about Bo sleeping in the bed. We agreed that he could sleep in your room if you make him sleep in his *own* bed. That one." Ella nodded towards the empty pallet on the floor next to the bed.

"But Ella... he was cold!" Aiden gave his puppy a hug and scooted out of the bed. He leaned over and began changing into the clean clothing that Lizzy had laid out for him. When his sister didn't respond favorably, he sat back down and pulled on his black boots. "Come on, Bo. Time to work." The little blond puppy pushed himself out from under the covers. He leaped off the bed, shook himself off and trotted over to where Aiden stood. The two of them looked up at Ella plaintively.

She grinned. These two made her laugh in the face of everything. Ella knew she couldn't even fake being upset with her little brother. "Come on, Aiden—you and Bo. Let's grab some grits and eggs, and head outside, hmmm?" She leaned over and gave them both a kiss on their heads. The puppy licked her hand, and she reached behind his ears and scratched them. The three made their way downstairs to the dining room.

"Who were those men yesterday?" Aiden peered up at his sister expectantly.

"I don't remember seeing you when those gentlemen were here." She put down the dishes she had lifted from the cabinet and looked down at her brother. "Where exactly have you and Bo been playing?"

"Well, first, you gotta promise you won't get mad."

"Where you have been playing on this plantation? You and I have talked about this, and you have boundaries, young man."

"We were in the barn. Miss Kitty done had her babies. I was showing them to Bo."

"Aiden! Dang it! Leave Miss Kitty alone. She doesn't want Bo nosing around her babies, and I don't want you in that barn by yourself." Ella shuddered involuntarily. "I've done told you. Our Negroes are not all here with us, and it's hard to be sure it's safe everywhere. You must promise to stay by the house when you go outside. If you can't find me, make sure you let Lizzy or Carter know where you are. I want to keep you safe." She glared at him, biting her lip to maintain her stern look. "One more time—do *not* go anywhere but around the porches or just around the house unless you go with someone. These are unsafe times."

"Yes, ma'am. I'm very sorry." Aiden got up and hugged his sister around her waist, burying his head in her skirts.

Noise on the lawn got their attention, and they both ran to the window to look out. A soldier was hammering a board on their fence, fixing the broken posts.

"Tarnation! Wait here." Abruptly, Ella pushed back from Aiden and rushed from the room. Her baby brother and Bo followed in her wake.

As she approached the front door, knocking sounded from the other side. She was moving at a rapid speed, intending to grab the handle, but the knocking brought her to an abrupt halt.

Ella peered out the window. Taking a deep, steadying breath, she smoothed her skirts and her hair and opened the door.

"Why hello, Colonel Ross, Lieutenant Colonel Jameson. I see that you have started making yourself at home already."

"How are you, Miss Whitford? And whom do we have here? Young man, what is your name?"

"My name is Aiden, suh." Her little brother held his hand out to shake it. Bo lunged and barked, making it clear that the visitors weren't welcome.

Colonel Ross shook the little hand and winked. He was such a cute little boy. "And what is the name of your puppy? He is a cute little fella, too!"

Bo wasn't having any of it as long as Aiden was close to the stranger. He stood back, barking,

"His name's Bo." Aiden looked meaningfully at his pet. "It's all right, Bo. I can tell. He's not gonna hurt us." Turning to the colonel, he asked, "You *ain't* gonna hurt us, are you?"

He chuckled. "You do get right to the point. No, Aiden, Lieutenant Colonel Jameson and I are bringing our men here to begin setting up camp today. We plan to protect your property. There could be bad men out in the area that would hurt your family and we want to see that it doesn't happen."

Nodding towards the sounds of hammering, he added, "And we intend to fix up a few things, too, to make sure that we pay our keep." He looked up at Ella and smiled.

Ella's arms remained crossed. As if fighting any softening of her heart towards his charming manner, she pulled her arms closer. "Well, we should get this over with. Hopefully, we can come to a better agreement." She looked pointedly towards the colonel. "I still don't agree with your squatting here, but I'm determined to make this meeting go better than yesterday. After all, your men are already fixing our fence. I should be, well, I *am* grateful for that." She punctuated her words and looked away from both men, giving her practiced response.

"Ma'am, we are not squatting." Jackson's expression was rigid.

She smiled tightly. "Let's head on to the library. I believe that is the room you are most interested in, anyway."

"But why they got interest in our library, Ella?" persisted Aiden, holding her hand. Bo followed Aiden and Ella into the library.

Ella squeezed his hand. "Manners, Aiden," she admonished quietly. "Colonel Ross is here *temporarily* and *temporarily* will be using our library as his office. He feels we need *protection*. The rest of his men will be bivouacking. That *is* the right word, isn't it, Colonel? It means camping on *our* land outside of *our* house while they watch over *our* property." Not giving him a chance to respond, she continued, "It is my hope you mean to use the land area towards the back, Colonel. Would that be right?"

"Well, yes and no. A few men will have responsibilities on the front side, here, in order to properly cover the property. But men will be posted on all flanks... err... sides of your property. We'd like to take a look at the rest of the property, with your permission. Do you ride?" He tilted his head and nodded slightly, pointing their attention in the direction of their horses, which were visible from the window.

"Why, yes, I do. I suppose I could show you the land. But it's been a while since I've ridden properly, I mean, well..." She hesitated. "I no longer have a riding habit. I have been using my brother's old pants and shirt. They fit me, and that will have to serve."

~

Jackson hadn't fully decided where they would post their tents, past getting her acceptance and starting to fix the property as a goodwill gesture. He needed to see all the land. And he hated to sound tentative.

The animation in her face at the mention of riding gave him hope. She was doing her best to hide her enthusiasm. The thought of riding alongside excited him though. He didn't plan to miss that opportunity.

"Let's adjourn outside, Colonel, Lieutenant Colonel." She cut into his thoughts. "That is if you have seen enough of the library. Aiden, you and Bo need to come with us, please. Stay where I can see you, love."

The four of them had almost made it to the front door when Bo gave a piercing bark. Aiden stopped and looked at his pup. His face lit up with excitement. "Bo and me will play pirates outside, sista. We promise to stay close." Before she could stop him, Aiden ran outside, and then hurried back to the doorway. "Don't worry. I will shut the door." He pushed the door shut, too hard. The vibration of the slamming door sent another large chunk of the unsecured plaster to the porch floor.

~

Watching the scene on the porch from the safety of overgrown shrubs and briar bushes about two hundred feet from the front door, Nolan grimaced.

What was going on here? He made it to the plantation the night before. Afraid that his appearance would frighten his sister and brother, he had waited for the light of the day. Now, there was this to contend with.

"Dang Yankees!" He recognized the Union officers. Why were they here? What was with the repairs going on? Who was paying for this? This was *his* land, and that was his sister.

Ella didn't look pleased although it was hard to see much from this distance. He certainly could not hear a thing above the noise of hammering.

Aiden had shaken the colonel's hand as if they were old friends. Stress mounted when the group went inside the house.

He felt strange. It was hot outside, being the beginning of the summer, so why was he feeling so cold? He knew he was hungry, but seeing his family was his priority.

He recalled the remnants of beef jerky stuffed in his pocket. It would do for now. As if objecting to his thoughts, his stomach rumbled so loudly he almost shushed it.

Nolan eyed the scattering of Yankee soldiers working in different areas on his property. It frustrated him. What the hell was going on? This didn't look like it was going to end too soon. He needed to figure on another plan for the time being.

Two men were working on the porch, fixing the ceiling. They made their displeasure in repairing it a second time known.

"What happened there?" he muttered aloud to himself. Hammering from the side of the house redirected his attention. The shutters were being repaired. These men weren't going anywhere for a while.

There would be no answers and no food right now. He would have to remain hidden until nightfall, or until the area cleared.

Nolan ducked back into the bush, not feeling well at all. Sitting quietly, he spotted the root cellar off to the side of the house. At least it would offer shelter and he could get better rested before he saw his siblings. There could be food in there, too. He just needed the right opportunity to make it there.

Confident that he was well hidden, he leaned back and drifted to sleep. A small ray of sun pushed through the brush, heating his face. More heat was something he didn't really need at the moment. He had been cold, but now he was warm, very warm. Slowly, his eyes succumbed to the pressure to close.

"Bo, I seen something over here. Shhhh. It could be the pirates." Moving his finger from his mouth, Aiden drew his sword, stepping forward with exaggerated moves. He clutched the small stick that was his sword tightly. The boy and his dog slowly approached the tall stand of grass and brush.

"Bo! This here is Captain Hook, his self! Looky here! He is a real pirate. Boots and all." Using his sword Aiden nudged the grass open to get a closer look.

Nolan's movement agitated a dog into a barking frenzy. Not sure of where he was, Nolan jerked awake and stared into the face of a wide-eyed and scared child with a barking dog. *Of course, Aiden!*

He might not remember him, Nolan realized with a start. Nolan sought first to quiet the dog and tried to grab him. Missing, he fell forward into the dirt. "Aiden, it's me, Nolan... shhhh! Shhhh!" He spit dirt from his mouth. "Dang it, Aiden, can you hush up your dog?"

"Nol'n? My br-brudder Nol'n? No, my brudder is fighting the damn

Yankees." Aiden pulled his shoulders back and pushed out his chest. Stepping forward, he reached for his puppy, trying to grab Bo and hold the sword up for protection at the same time. Bo was relentless. He continued his furious bark at the now moving mound of brush.

"Please, Aiden, please get your dog to be quiet. If I wasn't your brother, how would I know your name?"

Aiden peered closer at him. "Uhhh... well, you don't look like Nol'n." He tugged hard on his beard. "B... but you *do* know my name. But my brudder is away at his army job." He reached up and scratched the back of his ear.

Deciding to chance it, Aiden stepped up to retrieve Bo. "Bo. Shhh! Bo. It's all right. Come on, boy." The puppy at first resisted, but Aiden's soft words of encouragement finally pulled his attention away from Nolan. He knocked Aiden down, licking his face.

"It's good, boy. This here's my brudder Nol'n. 'Cept I don't member him looking like this." Suddenly, Aiden grinned. "If you are my brudder, then, who is my sister?"

Nolan barely had the energy to pull his face from the dirt and look at his little brother. "Ella is our sister, and you have been a fine young master while I have been gone. I can only be home for a little while, but this has to be our secret. Aiden, can we have a secret between brothers?"

"I'm a pirate. Bo here is a pirate, too. Pirates keep secrets good, Nol'n. But why can't Ella know, too?"

"I will tell Ella, but not today. I'm not feeling too good. Can you help me hide until tomorrow—in the cellar, over there? I can't let those men see me, or they will take me away for good. I will explain everything to you and Ella. But can you trust me?"

Aiden put his chubby little hands on his hips, pushed out his chest, and looked into his brother's face. "I will help you, Nol'n. But how we gonna do it?"

"Well, first... keep a look out. I need help to get to the root cellar. Are those men gone?"

"Yea, well, Colonel Ross, he and the lieutenant colonel, they left a little while ago. But the other men, they are staying in the tents out back." Aiden stepped close to Nolan, peering closer into his face, almost nose to nose. He lifted up his brother's beard and looked underneath. "You smell bad, Nol'n. And why you got a beard?" He wrinkled his nose and covered it with the palm of his hand to keep from smelling him.

Nolan gently touched his brother's cheek. The little dog, Bo, sat still watching both of them. Remarkably, no one had reacted to the barking dog. The continuous hammering must have camouflaged the noise.

It worried him a little that his brother could be outside and not be noticed. He would talk to Ella about that when he finally saw her. But right now, he needed to find a place to sleep. His body was failing him. "Aiden, can you help me get to the root cellar? I am going to stay there for a while, just to rest."

"Sure, Nol'n, but we have your bed upstairs. That might be better."

"No. Remember, Aiden, I cannot let these men see me. Trust me for now. Please. Just help me get to the root cellar. There is a bed in there."

Satisfied that no one could see them, the three of them quickly made their way through the tall weeds and brush. When they got close enough, they bolted to the root cellar on the side of the house.

Opening the door, Nolan climbed down the steps. He paused at the top step and gave Aiden a small hug, conscious now of how bad he smelled.

"Remember, this is our secret. I will sleep here tonight. We'll figure out something else tomorrow. You need to stay away from the cellar, so no one will see you. All right?"

Slowly nodding his head, the little boy straightened his shoulders.

Nolan could see he was trying to look like the pirate he wanted to be. It was clear that Aiden didn't understand why Ella couldn't be told he was home. Causing his little brother pain hurt him.

"Come on, Bo. Let's go." The two of them ran together to the front porch, leaving Nolan staring after them. He closed the cellar door, latching it from inside.

Reaching along the wall, Nolan felt for the lamp they kept on a small shelf near the top of the steps. Grasping it, he turned up the wick and lifted off the top. Nolan took a match from his pocket and struck it on the underside of his boot. He lit the wick and replaced the globe. The light helped. He looked around and noticed that there wasn't much food. His sister and brother didn't appear to be starving, but the plantation looked as sparse as this cellar.

He wasn't going to get a full stomach here. He noticed a barrel of apples that were being stored and grabbed up a couple. This would have to do. He had hoped for something different—more.

He lifted the lid off of a crate and pulled out some old blankets for the bare cot in the corner. Sleep would be welcome. He didn't feel too well.

CHAPTER 8

The wind whistled as it blew with force. Parts of the house groaned in response. It had been raining for over a day and the fields looked like marshes and small ponds. Ella peered out her front door and surveyed her property.

In the week since Colonel Ross and Lieutenant Colonel Jameson had first shown up and invaded her home, things had changed. She had to admit it was for the better.

Crossing her arms, she examined the results. The fences were mended and painted. The shutters were back, secured, and painted just in time. The house itself needed painting, but she certainly didn't expect *that* to be done. That was her responsibility. All of it was, really. It was an amazing amount of work, and not one penny had she put forth.

How did all of this happen?

It had to be due to Colonel Ross.

She hugged herself to restrain the tingling feeling that took control of her spine.

He came into her life—well, *stormed* into her life—and while he was intrusive, she found it strangely comforting having him around, something she would never admit to another soul.

She looked at the almost fifty tents that had been set up on the grounds, and the parked wagons. Her home felt under siege. She knew more men and their tents were coming once this storm finally let up.

Colonel Ross had several hundred men under his command. He planned for all of them to camp here. Where in the world would so many men stay?

The thought that her home would be providing a place for them to stay ready for battle was distressing. However, when she just focused on her vision of the colonel, or even his voice, butterflies swarmed her stomach.

What did that mean? Surely, she wasn't really becoming soft. She would not be a traitor to her brother or her people. They were the invaders, and she should remember that.

She tried to keep her mind on the anger she should feel about his intrusion, but at the same time, the thought of him nearby gave a sense of comfort she hadn't felt since Nolan and her daddy were there.

She couldn't reconcile this feeling. She was glad things were going better than she had thought, but then, life never stayed good. It would mess up. It was going well before Nolan had left home.

Then her daddy stole what little money they had, the money she thought she had hidden. He found it and took it, leaving her and her little brother penniless. They had nothing but debt, a dwindling plantation to keep going, and fifty mouths to feed.

Now things seemed better once again. Her brother was still out there. While that wasn't the best circumstance, at least he was still among the living, and when this war ended, she felt hopeful that he would be home.

The colonel really had made things better for all of them. She felt safer. She tried to reason that Colonel Ross was just a cog in the larger Yankee wheel, and he *was* trying to help her.

No. She needed to get past these ridiculous feelings. She shouldn't expect this time of contentment to lull her into a feeling of false security.

She watched the small current that had formed in her yard, noticing small limbs and other things fighting for position as they floated past. Ella had never seen this much water on her property. She wondered how the men managed to live in those tents. Absently, she leaned her head against the pane of the window.

"This dratted rain doesn't show any sign of stopping. I'm tired of being cooped up inside. Lands sakes! Now the wind is picking up. This storm is just getting worse and worse," she railed out loud to herself, easing her conscience about the possibility she was losing some of her animosity and distrust towards the troublesome duo.

As if to reinforce her thoughts, a very large, very dead magnolia branch crashed to the ground in front of the porch. She jumped back, and her foot caught on the corner of the doormat.

Ella flailed her arms in an effort to remain standing, but she fell anyway. She knocked the sconce off the wall on her way to the floor, sending the glass globe and its base crashing into pieces when it hit the wooden flooring. Luckily the candles were not lit.

When she opened her eyes, the broken glass was all around her, but she managed not to sit on any. *Geez! That could have been painful.*

The crash echoed throughout the first floor of the house. Almost immediately, footsteps raced down the hall and slowed at the door where she lay.

"Miss Ella? Miss Ella! Is you alright?"

"My pride. Just my pride. I think we will need a new entry light though." She pointed to the wall where a sconce used to sit. She looked at where her foot had caught and still didn't understand how it happened. "I tripped on the carpet," she lamented.

Lizzy helped Ella up. "There you go, Miss Ella. Now what had you so p'occupied that you didn't look where your feet was step'n?"

"I was thinking about how I didn't feel..." She swallowed. "I don't hate them as much." She nodded toward the library. "And it bothered me. I don't completely understand how that happened."

"Miss Ella, you just reacting to how they treat'n us. The colonel gave his word. When you can let go of some of that anger, you can see other things." Seeing the door propped open, Lizzy stepped outside on the porch. "My goodness, there sho gonna be a powerful storm here, soon. See those dark clouds over yonder? I hadn't seen one of them in a while," she said with a note of astonishment. "It may be what they call a hurricane. Wonder what Ol' Indie would say about it?"

"I don't recall ever seeing clouds like these." Crossing her arms protectively, she stared at the broken glass. "This persistent storm...I'm tired of being cooped up. I feel like a chicken in a pen. Why, I feel like I should lay an egg. That's how long I've been holed up in here. This storm won't let up. It's so dark."

"It looks bad, sho' nuff."

A feeling of alarm swept through her. "That's what I was afraid you'd say. I have never seen one, but my mamma used to talk about a fierce storm that happened when she was a young girl. She said the wind was horrible, and the rain kept going on forever until it flooded fields and houses. The river swelled really big with waves and washed over the land. Many people died." She thought about her mamma's story. "I think we need to get the windows boarded. Those with shutters should be locked down. Let's hurry!"

Lizzy and Ella rushed upstairs and started opening window sashes and securing the storm shutters. The ones in the front of the house were larger. She would need Carter to help with those. "Where can we put the livestock to keep them safe? We don't have much, and we can't afford to lose what we have." She talked as she worked, glancing at Lizzy. "I hope Colonel Ross does something about his men. They cannot stay in tents in this storm. I may not like Yankees, but I cannot wish them harm. They may be cruelly hurt or die."

She was beginning to care and could not account for this sudden feeling. It made her uncomfortable, and she felt disloyal. Still, Ella's focus was on saving the lives of the men.

"We need to close these shutters. Lizzy, find any servants you can to help you. Maybe Carter can give us a hand. Wait, no. We can handle the shutters. Send Carter to find Jason and have him warn the rest of the people and the men in the tents." She stopped for a moment to gather her thoughts. "If Carter can't locate Jason, there has to be someone in charge who can warn those men to take cover. Have you seen the colonel?"

Lizzy was still staring up at the clouds. "I hear Carter now. He is looking for Aiden."

"Aiden? What do you mean looking for Aiden? *Aiden's missing?*" Panic hit her. Ella realized that she had not seen Aiden or Bo in the last hour. "We have to find him!"

Terror pulsed through her. She sprinted downstairs with Lizzy behind her. The pitch of her voice elevated in panic. Without looking back, she flung open the screen door and pushed her body against the onslaught of wind and rain. "Aiden, Bo, where are you? Can you hear me? Aiden, Bo? Are you out here?" The wind blew harder and almost completely muffled her voice. The rain pelted her face, and it was difficult to see anything.

"In this storm? Miss Ella, surely the boy is in the house somewhere. We will find them."

No longer listening, Ella was already making her way down the front steps. Cupping both hands together above her eyes in an attempt to shield them from the pelting rain, Ella ran around the house. "Aiden, Bo…answer me! Aiden, can you hear me?" She screamed as loud as she could but could barely hear herself over the sound of the wind and rain. The wind was strong and pushed her against the trees. She struggled free and moved back towards the house.

Ella fought against the panic making its way through her body. *Where has Aiden gone?*

As she turned the corner of the house and started towards the back, the cellar door to the house opened. Ella jumped back with a cry of alarm. Out poked two arms holding one casserole dish. The arms placed the casserole dish on the ground. A black skillet and a kitchen towel followed.

Stunned, she stopped and watched the small arms move the dishes out of the way. Now she was curious. A little blond head of a five-year-old boy emerged with a golden yellow puppy. He turned around and tried to push the door closed but was blown almost back into the opening by the wind.

Stunned beyond words, Ella moved to help him just as he managed to push the door closed.

"Aiden Terrance, there you are! What in the world are you doing coming out of the root cellar?" More relieved than angry, Ella forgot the storm for a moment and grabbed him. She sniffed and screwed up her nose at an odor. "You stink. What in tarnation have you been into? Oh, my goodness! You smell awful, like you been rolling in… in… refuse."

She gently moved Aiden aside. Bo yipped at her and tried to block the door. She pushed the puppy aside and pulled hard to open the entrance to the cellar. The wind took it from her hand slammed it back against the frame, leaving it open. Holding the edge of the door as securely as she could, she peered down. A waning lantern cast light from the bottom of the steps, illuminating a man lying on a pallet of blankets.

She started to scream but stopped when he looked up. He looked vaguely familiar, but she couldn't remember anyone with that much hair. Blond hair. She turned and looked at Aiden, who was firmly looking down.

"Aiden? Who is that? Do you know? You do! What are you…" she admonished him. She wasn't going to get any answers from him. "Wait right here. Do you understand me? I have never taken a switch to you, Aiden, but if you move from that spot, I will. Do not move."

Instantly, she regretted the threat, knowing she would never be able to carry it out. Aiden looked up at her, his eyes brimming with tears. She looked back at the blond-haired man and her heart seized. Ella recognized who it was.

Tears ran down her face unchecked. She dropped down and pulled her brother close to her, holding him against her body to protect him from the pelting rain and wind. They both cried.

"Nol'n is real sick, Ella. Bo and I, we tried to feed him and make him betta. But he didn't get betta and now he can't talk to us. I think he might die, like my frog, Twigs."

Squeezing Aiden tightly, Ella understood that her brother was very sick and quickly needed help. She looked around and knew one thing had to happen now. She needed to get her brother out of this root cellar.

Ella studied Nolan for a few moments. She could see his body slightly rising and falling. It was obvious that he hadn't had a bath, clean clothes, or real food. She noticed remnants of cake and smuggled dinner lying on the floor. Aiden had indeed been trying to take care of his brother. A gnawed-down corncob thrown in the corner told her that this had been going on for the past few days. They had corn two days before.

Tears spilled from her eyes as she saw the lengths Aiden had gone to help Nolan. How had they kept this a secret? When had Nolan come home? Nothing made sense.

"Aiden, you and Bo come with me. We have a bad storm coming, so come and hold my hand tight." She gripped his small hand.

"But Ella, we can't leave our brudder." He tried to tug his hand away.

"We have to leave him right now. But I'm going to help him, I promise."

Once they made it inside, Ella stooped down and looked into Aiden's eyes, wiping both the wet hair away from her face and the tears from his. "You and Bo are to stay in the parlor. If anyone comes looking for me, do not tell what I am doing. Anyone, understood?"

Aiden peered up at his sister. "You mean like Colonel Ross? Nol'n don't like him being here."

Startled by her brother's revelation, she took a moment to think before responding. "Yes, most definitely the colonel. Tell him... tell him that I'm getting dressed. If he comes. Which he shouldn't. At least I don't think he is supposed to come. Will you do as I ask?"

He nodded. "Me and Bo will sit in the parlor."

Her anxiety level was climbing. Her brother was home, but he was very sick, and she had the Union Army camping on her lawn. *Dang it!* How much more complicated could this get?

If Nolan didn't want her to know he was home, there had to be a reason. She fought back a scream of frustration. Aiden said Nolan knew about the colonel and was hiding down there. How long had he been here?

Well, there were many questions she needed to get answers to, but they would have to wait. Right now, she wanted to get Nolan out of there before Colonel Ross arrived.

Ella felt slightly frantic. She stepped outside to go to Nolan, but she realized she needed assistance.

"Lizzy, Carter, come quickly." She hollered into the hall; she knew one would be nearby, but would they hear her? The wind was so loud. Deciding not to take the chance, she pulled on the old house bell.

That cord had not been pulled since both her parents lived here. She shivered at the thought. Surely hearing the bell, they would realize this was urgent.

Footsteps running through the hall calmed her worries. Carter and Lizzy both arrived before the bell stopped ringing, concern written across both faces.

"Miss Ella, you is all wet and gonna catch a chill." Carter's voice cracked with concern.

"Come, please come with me." Running to the root cellar, she pulled on the door, finally pushing it open against the wind. The lamp-lit cellar clearly surprised Carter and Lizzy.

She latched it open and carefully lowered herself inside and moved down the steps. Carter and Lizzy followed.

Nolan was lying on a pile of dirty quilts in the corner. As they approached, he moaned. His body trembled violently.

Ella started to put her hand on his head, but Lizzy jerked her back. "Stop."

"What?" she asked, indignant. "We have to get Nolan out of here. Colonel Ross is coming, and so is the storm. This root cellar will collect water and it's too cold for him down here." She pointed at Nolan's shivering form on the cot.

"Miss Ella, he may have the fever. I've seen this before. We need to move him, but we need to have someone that has survived the fever already move him." They both turned to Carter.

Ella suddenly felt queasy. "Oh no! Aiden and Bo, they have been down here with Nolan for days I think. I didn't know he was here. Oh, dear Lord!"

"Now you just relax Miss Ella. The young Massa isn't showing any sign of it yet. We got time to get him help."

"Lizzy, *please* call him Aiden." Ella retorted, barely covering the irritation in her voice. "You are family. You *know* how I feel about you and Carter." She gripped the wall for support, fighting the bile that was rising in her throat. Nolan was home, but had he brought something so horrible that it would take both him and her little brother away from her? "Lizzy, what can we do?"

"We need to get Ol' Indie."

Carter stepped around his wife and picked up Nolan. "Miss Ella, my mamma, you know dat she can fix dis up, but I got to go get her." He reached over and hoisted Nolan over his shoulder. "I sorry, Massa Nol'n, but dis is de only way I can carry you. My! I figured you to be heavier den dis."

Nolan only emitted a groan.

"Where do we put Massa Nolan, Miss Ella?" Carter mounted the steps, pulling himself up carefully so his precious cargo didn't slip off. "Lord-y, if I can say so, I ain't never been 'round anyone needs a bath more!"

Ella stopped and sniffed the air. "Oh, my Lord! Truly, it is horrible." She pinched the end of her nose closed. Her brother smelled vile. The ludicrousness of the situation hit her, and she began to laugh. "Oh, he stinks… the worst I think I've ever smelled."

Lizzy and Carter looked at each other, not wanting to insult their mistress, but they couldn't help it. It stunk. The three of them laughed. No one could hear them because of the storm. It was so freeing to be unafraid of being overheard.

"Glad you find my sit-u-a-tion so amusing, d…dear sister," Nolan managed to squeeze out with quiet emphasis.

The laughter stopped, and they looked at Nolan, who had woken up from the noise of their mirth.

"Nolan, you are awake!"

"Stating the ob-obvious, Sis."

"Always the jokester. We are sorry, it's just that you uh… well, you need a bath. But you are a sight for sore eyes. I've missed you so! I'd hug you, but you could be very sick. We've got to get you to a different shelter. When you are better, we are gonna talk about how many years you just took from my life!"

Her brother tried to pull the cover to his chin, his efforts exposing his feet.

"Scaring me to death like this." Ella pulled the cover back over his feet. "Aiden thinks you are dying like his frog. He is quite upset. Nolan Whitford, how *could* you try to keep your visit from me?" Her voice got louder with repressed anger. "Let's get going, Carter. Where will we put him if he has the fever?"

"The fever?" Nolan's voice was weak.

"Hush. Don't you worry none. We're gonna get you better."

Carter shifted his load and Nolan groaned louder this time. He seemed to be in pain. "I think we need to put him in the tunnel room and I will bring Ol' Indie here. She can get in from the kitchen if I just distract Cook, and you can get in from behind the cloak closet." Hearing no objection, Carter took a breath and continued. "Lizzy and I keep the passageway clean of spiders and other critters. We were preparing in case the Yankees come and we got to hide you and little Massa Aiden in there. There's a stash of food in there, too."

Unprepared for this revelation, Ella felt a little humbled at the two servants that were more friend than anything to her. They had been with her family for most of their lives. They met and married here. This was their home as much as hers. "Yes, thank you. That is… so good of you two to have taken care of us like that." Her throat felt suddenly full. "Let's move him quickly."

CHAPTER 9

Ella blew out the lamp and closed the cellar door behind them. They trekked against the rain and wind and entered from the side of the front porch, moving slowly, hoping not to draw any attention. The Union troops were just on the other side of the house.

Once inside, they quietly opened the door and entered the secret tunnel that led to the safe room. Wall sconces provided light to the room that her ancestor had built a hundred years before when the first house was built on this site.

Her ancestor had been a privateer, and the room served as a hidden storeroom for gold, brandy, and other treasure he'd bring back. Of course, that bootee had long since been removed. During the revolutionary years, the room served as a place to hide on more than one occasion. The family safeguarded the room and, outside of the few slaves that were close to them, no one was aware of its existence.

The warmth of the room was the first thing she noticed. Insulated by earth on all sides, it maintained a constant temperature. The doors to the tunnel were well hidden.

No one had ever found them as far as she had been told. Had the knowledge not been passed to her, she would have never known it existed.

A small corner pantry was full of food. A cedar chest nearby was kept relatively clean and stocked with candles, blankets, and other items that would not spoil easily.

It was furnished with things that had been gradually replaced over time in the house, lightweight furniture that could be easily transported through the tunnel so that some comfort was available.

A table and chairs, two beds, and a chest of drawers dominated the space. The walls were stone and covered with heavy woolen tapestries to help insulate and maintain a comfortable feel. Area rugs that could be easily removed and cleaned from dust and other things covered the bricked floor.

A small stove with a chimney sat towards the back corner. The chimney was expertly vented through the wall, channeling the heat and fumes out through a side flume of the chimney. It was fashioned to allow heat and provide some level of light cooking. A second ventilation system diverted smoke through the rock and outside to the cookhouse.

The cookhouse had been relocated many years before to conceal the room. This was primarily used in the summer when smoke from a chimney would be suspect. There was an outside entrance to the tunnel, and that was hidden within the cookhouse itself.

Cook didn't even know of the existence of this room. It was for the family. Lizzy and Carter were family; they knew all about the secret room.

"Nolan, we are going to get you through this. Ol' Indie will soon be here. And you need to listen to her, *please.* I will be back when I can go check on you." Pausing, she looked back at her brother lying down on the small bunk and smiled. "I love you, big brother. I wish I could hug you. We've missed you so very much!" Quickly, she turned and left through the tunnel, heading back before she was missed. She left Carter behind to settle Nolan before he left to get his mamma.

Ella and Lizzy got back in the foyer just in time to hear the jangle of boots coming up the front steps of the house.

"Lordy, Lizzy. I'm a mess. My face, my hair. I am *drenched—and so are you!* Do you think he might stay occupied in the library? Come on before he asks why we are all wet." Lizzy followed her up the steps. Ella wondered about her little brother, hoping she could count on his discretion. But then, she might not need to worry. He had kept Nolan's secret, had he not?

Ella ran up the stairs to her room. On the top of the stairs, she realized she was trembling. The shock of seeing Nolan, finding him sick, and then having to move him so rapidly had been hard enough. Now with a storm bearing down, the stress consumed her. *This day—was it still day, even? —surely couldn't get worse, could it?*

CHAPTER 10

Jackson shook the rain off his hat and stomped his boots hard as he approached the door, hoping to shake the water and mud from them. Once inside, he opened his trench coat and breathed a sigh of relief. His clothing had managed to stay dry underneath.

The wind was blowing hard gusts of rain, making it difficult to tell if that had been the case. It blew sideways half the time, and with such force that he barely managed to see. It wasn't supposed to be night yet, but it was already so dark, it was as if dusk had fallen over this area early.

Marshall should be right behind him with the cook wagon, but he wondered if they would make it. Now he wasn't sure that it was the best idea to have the cook wagon come in this tempest.

This storm was worse than anyone thought it would be, and it had rained for a day and a half, with little break. The wind was picking up. He noticed the huge limb that had fallen right by Miss Whitford's front porch. That could have been dangerous.

Almost fifty tents had assembled out there already. He needed to do something with the men that were here now. The storm was getting worse. He wasn't quite sure what he would do at the moment, but he couldn't leave them out in this mess.

It was just the luck of timing that the rest of the troops hadn't mustered here yet. He expected them here by the end of the week since they were moving in groups. Thunder and lightning joined in with the storm, the combination spurring on the wind and rain.

He raised his arm to knock, but the door opened up before he could. Now, that seemed a little strange—were they expecting him? Lizzy stood before him, her right hand holding open the door and her left hand nervously opening and closing by her side. Her hair was damp and glistened from the rain.

"Hello, Colonel Ross, suh. If you are looking for Miss Ella, she will be down directly. You can wait for her in the parlor."

"Lieutenant Colonel Jameson is coming up behind me with a contingent of men and a cook wagon, but this storm is bad and is getting worse." His smile helped hide his surveillance of her wet appearance.

The housekeeper turned to leave, but Jackson stopped her.

"Lizzy, I don't want to put you ladies out, but I must do something for the men that are already here. Could there be any place besides the barn that you can think of that could shelter about seventy-five men?"

Lizzy looked at him for a long moment before answering. "Well, Colonel, we have some homesteads from the folk that left. They are just simple cabins, but they are built good and betta than the tents, I expect. There are right many that are empty now. And the barn, well, it's full of what little livestock we got. Miss Ella, she had Mista Jason, de overseer, bring the cattle and horses in there. We hoping they be all right. It's sturdy."

"Thank you for that information. I'll wait in the parlor for her. I'd like to speak to her before I move the men."

"Yassuh, Colonel." Lizzy left him in the entry hall at the door to the parlor. As he entered the room, he heard a sudden energetic rustle.

"Colonel Ross!" The boy bounded off the sofa dragging a pillow, with his puppy coming up behind him.

"Well, young man. What you doing down here? I thought you

would be… well, I'm not sure where you would be." He laughed. "It's been a while since I was a boy and had to suffer through a bad summer storm such as this." He roughed Aiden's hair affectionately.

"Your dog is one handsome fellow. I just noticed he has two different colored eyes! That's very unusual."

"Yes suh, he does. The blue one shines when he's happy. The brown one shines when he is upset. I just figured that out." Pleased, he petted Bo.

"That's quite an observation, young man. I noticed your sister's shine when she's angry!" They both chuckled. "So, what are you and Bo doing down here?"

"My sista told me to stay put while she changed clothes. She was mighty wet." As if he had been told to, he quieted very quickly.

"Oh? Wet?"

Soft footsteps sounded behind him as Ella walked into the room. "Yes, Colonel. I was quite…wet." She smiled sweetly at them then gave a level look to Aiden. "I had to go out in this…weather…and find this little rapscallion."

"You were outside in this storm, Aiden?" He regarded the little boy, whose expression changed from excitement to embarrassment and something more. He wasn't quite able to discern what it was. A look passed between the brother and sister that he couldn't help but notice. Something was up here, but Jackson couldn't fathom what it was. He glanced from one to the other. Nothing.

"Yes," Ella continued, seemingly unaware of Jackson's scrutiny. "Aiden and Bo were soaked clear to the skin. They were playing, um, pirates, I think, but they didn't notice the storm until it was upon them. It frightens me to think how they could have been hurt or worse in those high weeds out there."

Ella walked over to Aiden and kneeled. "Come here. Let me check your head. You too, Bo." She moved her hands carefully through his hair.

"Are you checking him for lice?" Jackson was curious. The child seemed clean.

"Ha! Well, you see, we live in an area that is known for these bugs that latch onto the head. I don't like to have them on my brother. I usually check him after he comes inside."

"Bugs that latch on your head? I've not really heard of that too much. Are they dangerous?"

"I don't know, really, but you surely have seen them with your men out in the fields so much. They attach themselves with a bite. Their poison gets into the blood. Yes, it's quite disgusting." She shuddered. "I don't even want to think about lice." She shook her head and then erupted in laughter.

"What's funny?"

"I'm sorry. Here we are, suh, discussing the unseemly topic of bugs in the hair." She turned away, grinning.

"Yes, well, it seemed that the conversation just took us there." Jackson couldn't help it. Her smile was contagious. He almost forgot what he needed, something that seemed to happen a lot lately when she was around him. "Oh. There *is* something I want to discuss. How could I forget? The men. They need shelter. Miss Lizzy mentioned that there might be empty cabins that we could take up—the ones that the Negro folks have abandoned. I have to get these men out of the wind."

"Yes, that is a great idea. You need to help your men. Don't let me hold you up. Please. I'm just sorry I had not thought to offer that. I noticed their situation earlier and was concerned."

"Marshall should be here about now. I'll get him and the sergeant to help me move the men." He started to leave but turned. "Aiden, you must listen to your sister. These tall weeds are not the best place for you to play. We will cut them down shortly but stay close to your house."

"Yes, suh. I will!" Cheerful once more, Aiden bounced up from where he was sitting on the sofa. He offered to walk Jackson to the door, and the colonel readily agreed.

Once outside, Jackson looked around. The storm had calmed down. The wind was barely noticeable, but the clouds were getting even blacker if that was possible.

There was a feeling of eeriness in the atmosphere. He needed to get the men in the shelters as quickly as possible. Grabbing the reins to Mason, he pulled himself up on his horse and cantered into the camp area. Marshall and the cook were already there. They were just standing, waiting. Irritation at the veiled jab rushed through him.

Marshall flashed a wide grin as he rode towards them,

"Hello, Marshall."

~

"How is the lovely Miss Whitford?" Marshall couldn't help stirring Jackson up, but just seeing him smitten did something to him.

"She is fine. Stop the innuendos."

Jackson could deny it, but Marshall sensed the attraction. His game was to always protect his heart, but this time, well, this time it looked like his friend's effort to keep his heart out of the way wasn't going to work. He saw the sparks passing between them, even if the two of them didn't see it yet. He wanted his friend to find someone—especially after what had happened with Maria. No man should suffer that humiliation. She lost out in that exchange. Nate would never be the man Jackson was.

Jackson jumped down from Mason. "Look, Marshall, this storm has just given us a breather. Let's get these bedrolls and tents pulled up and moved to better shelters. Miss Whitford says there are a number of cabins on the backside of the house. They are empty except for a few of the Negroes that decided to stay. We can use the rest of them. The men will have to double up, but let's do it. Move them out. This break won't last, I fear."

"Yes, sir." Marshall turned and passed the orders to the sergeants that were there. The command went out to roll up the camp and move to the cabins.

Tents started coming down en masse as men ran back and forth, depositing their tents into stalled wagons, and running to the cabins with their bedrolls in hand. The ominous look of the storm overhead was all the prompting they needed.

"Jackson, what about the horses?"

"I didn't ask, but we need to move them, too. Let's pull the wagons closer to the barn and give them more security. We'll un-harness the horses and move them to the corral near the structure. Several horses and cows are already in the barn. The barn is small, but twenty or so horses should not take up too much more room."

Within an hour, the men had moved their bedrolls, tents, and all the rest of the camp equipment. Soon the area that had been covered with tents and wagons was a vacant field, once again. There were paths worn into the ground and any grass left had been worn down, but other than that, there wasn't a sign of the camp.

The back of the house was abuzz with activity as the cabin community became alive once more. Doors from the cabins where a few of the field help still resided opened up and heads popped out to see what was going on.

Seeing what was needed, the cabin occupants all came out to help the soldiers get sheltered. They passed out candles and lanterns from the supply house. Some women brought pieces of wood to help cover broken window glass. The last few horses were led to the barn.

As the barn door was latched shut, the wind began to kick up, and the rain started once more. This time, rain came down with a fury. Lightning crashed, and thunder boomed. Jackson and Marshall lost no time as both took off for the front door of the house.

~

Ella looked out the library window and watched the men picking up the camp. She didn't have long to get Ol' Indie to Nolan. How was this going to work? If Nolan were discovered, he would be arrested.

But then, there was the matter of the deep blue uniform he was wearing. That was confusing. She had not had a chance to ask him about that. It was barely noticeable, but Union issue, all the same. What in the world had her brother been doing wearing that?

She was sure that Aiden had not noticed that or there would have been questions. Had he killed somebody? *Well, silly*, she thought to herself morosely, *of course, he has. This is war. Nolan is an officer.*

Yet here he was, at home, sick.

She wondered about that. She was afraid it might be yellow fever, but Lizzy called it ague. What if Aiden caught it? How long had he been exposed to Nolan?

Her hands fisted in her skirts. Ol' Indie would know what to do. She was the closest thing to a mamma that Ella had. The dear woman always took care of Aiden, just as she had when she and Nolan were children. She nursed them. When her mamma had died, Ol' Indie kept Aiden alive. She found a nursemaid. She had wanted to be free, so they gave her papers. But after she had them, she had stayed. Her family, she said, was here.

Well, you cannot get too much done staring out the window, now can you?

There was a lot to do. Ol' Indie needed blankets and water for Nolan. Grabbing up the stack of quilts by her side, she walked to the closet in the entrance hall. She opened the door and quietly pulled it closed behind her.

Stepping to the back of the cloaks, she pressed on the back panel in its secret spot, allowing it to silently slide open revealing the tunnel opening.

Ella turned up the oil on the sconce on the wall and the light brightened the path. The door shut behind her, its sound soft on its hinges. Satisfied she could see well enough, she slowly descended the steep stairs to bring the quilts down to Nolan.

He was still resting there, but now he was shivering violently. "Ol' Indie should be here soon," Ella spoke softly, assuring her brother that she was here.

"No, don't get close to me," Nolan muttered, his teeth chattering loudly.

"You are awake. Here, I've got blankets." Her nose wrinkled a little from the smell even though she tried not to let that happen. "You don't smell as bad as before."

He opened his mouth to talk and then shut it. He tried again. "C...

Carter cleaned me up. S... s... said I s... s... stunk. He l... left a l... little while a... g... go" Frowning, he pulled up the covers, trying to get what little warmth he could.

"Shhh. Don't talk. We will catch up soon. But right now, save your strength. We have problems. I need to tell you that the Yankees have decided to camp here."

She felt a little guilty when she said it that way. *But why?* Ignoring that niggling feeling of remorse, she went on. "They intend to set up what they are calling a per-i-meter. They say that they need to be here to defend me, humph! And they are looking for renegades and others, determined to keep them from harming the citizens."

She huffed and continued her rant. "And of course, that isn't all of it. They intend to set up stuff. A hospital. Oh, and schools for the Negroes. But not on our property. At least, I don't think so. It wouldn't be a bad thing, though, if they did." She hesitated. "And Nolan, they are planning, no insisting, on staying in the house—our house. The library has become their office."

She was out of breath when she finally got it all out of her system. Curiously, she wasn't as angry as she had been before. Maybe she was slowly getting used to the idea.

Maybe she was attracted to the colonel.

Shaking her head, she persisted, "The colonel and lieutenant colonel seem nice enough, but I cannot let them know about you." She looked around the room. "You cannot stay here, Nolan. Not now. It just isn't safe."

A tear escaped and rolled down her cheek. She was turning away her own brother, but it was for his own good. He would be captured if he stayed. Maybe killed. Another tear followed the first. This was his home, too. *Damn those Yankees. They caused this.*

"I s... saw." Nolan rasped.

"You saw the colonel? Then you know how dangerous..."

A door opened on the other side of the room and Carter and Ol' Indie entered. The tension was so strong that Elle leaped up from where she was and hugged Ol' Indie.

"Now, girl." Ol' Indie gently wiped the tears from Ella's face. "Carter says our boy's sick again."

"Again?" Ella sniffed and looked over at Nolan.

"Yes'm. He was bit purty fierce by a cott'nmouth on the battlefield. I was looking over deem men that wuz hurt, seein' if I could help. But I seen him lying there. I know'd Massa Nole soon as I seen him lying yonder on dat field. He was wet and 'peered to be 'bout dead. Mo than cott'nmouth got him down. He had da fever."

"Nolan, you had the fever?" Her voice strained. "Could he have it again?"

"It be like that with some people. When Massa Nole's fever broke, he left. I figured he be okay, but then, in my bones, I started feeling that sump'um was wrong. Next thing, Carter came and brunt me here." She looked down at the young man she had always nursed back to health.

"Oh heavens! Aiden was with him. Ol' Indie, my little brother… will he get sick from Nolan?"

"Calm yourself, Miss Ella. We best get Massa Nole okay again. I'll see to Massa Aiden, directly. Does he show signs of being sick?"

"Not yet… but he was with him…" Her face turned red. "I'm sorry, Ol' Indie. I'm not going to borrow trouble."

"It's natural for you to worry. But let's get Massa Nole well. You is a good little mamma, Miss Ella." She smiled at her former charge, then, cleared her throat and placed her hand on Nolan's face. Ol' Indie looked up at Ella, concern etched on her face. "He got a bad fever. Has he been throwing up the black?"

Ella shook her head. "Not that we know. He smelled really bad. Carter cleaned him up. He had been hidden in the root cellar. It stinks, and we still have to clean it, but there was no black stuff that I saw." She took a deep breath and exhaled slowly. "I'm worried about Aiden. I can't help it."

Ol' Indie looked down at Nolan. "De fevers kin come back right smart. If young Massa gets sick, you send for me. It's hard to say if he will catch it. I think Massa Nole here might be with the ague. He has de fever and the waters. I may have sump'um for it." She dug into her pockets, bringing out a small vial. "Tonic from the cinchona bark. Let me tend to Massa Nole. And now you should get upstairs and leave me to my bidness." She gave a quick, pointed nod towards the door.

Ella left through the hidden access in the pantry. She stayed as quiet as she could to make sure the coast was clear in the kitchen. Silently, she left out of the kitchen into the yard and walked back in through the front door. She briefly opened the front closet to make sure it looked the way it should look. Satisfied, she pushed the cloaks back in place and secured the closet, before heading into the parlor.

Her little brother and his puppy were both curled up on the floor in front of the fireplace. It was unusual to have the fire going on a day like today. As wet as it was, it seemed to help cut a chill out of the air. Aiden snored softly, with Bo curled up next to him. Picking up a small shawl from the back of a nearby chair, Ella used it to cover the two sleeping adventurers.

What a long night this was going to be. She listened as the storm raged on outside. Branches banged against the library windows. The loud noise reminded her that they still needed securing.

She couldn't sleep with that going on. She would have to see to them. Carter tried hard, but with so much to do, he couldn't get everything done.

Lizzy came down the stairs just as she was heading to the front door. "Miss Ella, I seen that the colonel is finished getting his men in the shelters."

"Good, *I think*. But that means he will be back here to do whatever they plan to do with the library." Ella smirked. The colonel could secure all the remaining windows. If he was going to live here, then he could make himself useful.

Returning to the parlor, Ella picked up her book and sat in the large wingback chair next to the fireplace and Aiden and Bo. She realized she had not relaxed all day.

Ella tried to focus but found it nearly impossible. Her mind kept drifting back to the safe room. How was this to work out? Her brother lay sick, likely to be arrested if he is found, and she was hiding him under the nose of the enemy. And she felt confused over the way she was reacting to the colonel. If he accidentally touched her, her body tingled in places that had never had such a feeling. And her thoughts... her thoughts continually drifted to him. She constantly wondered where he was... what he was doing... was he smiling? She loved his grin. He was so strong and a natural at taking charge. Yet he was kind. Even Aiden and Bo were becoming attached to him. She found herself becoming more and more attracted to the enemy.

That varmint was taking over her property, commandeering her privacy—all this and a horrible storm, too. She felt frustrated and powerless to do anything. There seemed to be nothing for it. At that moment, Ella decided to do that, exactly—nothing. She leaned back and closed her eyes.

~

The loud knocking on the front door should have roused the whole household, except it competed with the furious storm raging outside. Lizzy opened the door, showing the colonel and the lieutenant colonel to the parlor. Soft snoring drew their attention to the sleeping boy and his dog.

Bo raised his head, looked, then lay back down. He seemed satisfied that these men were okay.

"Miss Whitford, we have secured the men and the horses. I wonder if you would mind if we bunked in the library. That has never been my intent, but the dry space was limited, and we ran out of room out there."

Ella shushed him with her finger to her lips. "Gentlemen, they just went to sleep. We anticipated your need. Lizzy created pallets hours ago. You both can sleep here." Ella stood and walked towards the library. It was worth it to see the looks of surprise on their faces. Ella bit her bottom lip to keep from smiling. "We are staying in the parlor tonight together. I think it's best for us all to stay on the ground floor. You'll be much more comfortable down here with the rest of us. This will not be a habit, I trust?"

"We will be fine in the library. We appreciate your hospitality. I will make better arrangements tomorrow. I don't want to head back to town in this."

Ella put on her biggest smile, hoping it conveyed she was accommodating. "Should you need anything, just holla. Oh, the windows. Colonel, if you don't mind, I would ask a favor of you. Could you secure the hurricane shutters for the parlor *and* the library? With so much to do, we didn't get a chance to do latch them, and Carter is helping to ready other areas of the house. He will be finished any minute, but I've got another item or two I need him to take care of for me." She locked her eyes on Colonel Ross's. "Would you mind, terribly?"

"No, no we wouldn't. Marshall, come with me." The two men left to secure the windows.

Lizzy glanced at Ella and both exhaled slowly. This was not what she had imagined, but for now, she would stay in charge of her home, and her wits—at least until things were resolved with Nolan, whatever that meant.

CHAPTER 11

Strange dreams plagued her. She was running from someone. His face was unclear, hidden by shadows, but she could hear his voice. She tried to identify it. Who was he?

Still shaking from the dream, Ella lifted her head from the sofa and looked up at the window. She wanted to see if there was any damage. A large crash sounded from outside. *What was that?* Shuttered windows kept her from seeing a thing. Thunder and lightning had raged all night, and now only an eerie stillness, a quiet stillness, filled the room.

The fire was out and the room was cold. She shivered. *How did we let the fire go out?* Wiping her eyes, she glanced over at Aiden and Bo, still cuddled together under the heavy quilts near the fire. Aiden's innocent face ignited her emotional side.

She caught herself brushing back a small tear. He could not play outside since the invaders had arrived, and now water soaked the ground.

Loud drops fell on the ashes in the cold fireplace, drawing her attention. She gave her head a slight shake. *Guess that answers that!* No doubt the fire had been out for hours. At least the two small beings tucked under the quilts stayed warm. Nolan was in the safe room with

Ol' Indie. She worried about him but had absolute faith in the care that their cherished healer could offer.

The warnings that renegades and deserters could be out there must have caused her dreams to be so frightening. The large goosebumps on her arm were not part of her dream, though. That was from the cold room, but the dream had been scary.

She remembered the dream. The man chasing her was trying to kill her. Dark shadows hid his face. Arms came up and grabbed her. She couldn't see anything but darkness. Ella shuddered as she opened the front door. Dreams like this foretold.

She pushed back a branch that had fallen against the front door and stepped outside on the porch. A faint breeze stirred. It was a far cry from the roaring winds of the last night. She ventured out to survey the front of the land.

The sun was up over Silver Moon, and the birds were trumpeting their survival. It was almost as if the birds were trying to tell everyone it was over and safe to come out now.

Water stood in the areas beside the house where a small creek once ran. There was no way to identify where the creek meandered. Today it looked like a glistening lake. Had the tents and bedrolls not been removed, they would have been floating. Those men were lucky to have gotten a better shelter. She hoped the cabins held. It would be a few days before the men pitched the tents again, judging from the standing water.

Large boughs from the graceful magnolias hung heavy with water. Once the water finished running off of them, perhaps their shape would resume. Some of the heavier boughs had split from the tree and sliced through the fencing.

In one area, six sections of smashed and broken fencing lay scattered on the ground. Luckily, the pasture being used by the horses and cattle was a little hillier and attached to the barn area on the other side. They still had access.

Leaves and branches littered the driveway into the plantation. The closer to the road, the worse the conditions became.

A small branch of water behind the plantation house ran into the

Neuse River. The river ran to Kinston, some forty-five miles west of New Bern, and dumped into the inlet. The fingers ran into the main streams and ended in the main river.

Normally, the stream on the plantation was an innocuous little threadlike creek. It barely had movement of water. The depth wasn't more than a foot or two. That was before the storm. The overflow from the storm would take time to recede, maybe weeks. The increase in wetland only magnified the dangers of the mosquitos and snakes that were already hazardous in the area.

Ella grabbed her arm to quell the shiver that ran up, thinking of those creatures. She looked up at the sky. While the rain had stopped, for the time being, clouds still filled the sky. There would be more rain soon. Shivering from the cool breeze, she wrapped her arms around herself.

Colonel Ross and Lieutenant Colonel Jameson had spent the night in the library. Ella wondered how they slept. She imagined them bunking on the floor, huddled under their blankets—not together. A giggle escaped.

Their fireplace was likely cold. She had offered more blankets, but they had insisted they needed none. The weather was unusually cool for the eve of a summer's start, a product of the storm.

She thought about Colonel Jackson Ross cleaning up and washing, and a warm feeling took root and moved up to her face, heating her cheeks. Was he awake yet?

As if in answer to her question, the door to the library opened and the colonel walked her way. She turned her attention to the nearest window and pretended to look outside.

"Morning, Colonel, suh. I trust you slept well. Looks like the storm passed, but we have a mess." Her bottom lip quivered a little, possibly from the spring chill in the air.

He came up behind her. He wasn't touching, but his presence was so close she could almost feel the heat from him. Her body reacted, pushing warmth to her core. She didn't understand this. He was an irritant, trouble, and she liked him.

She grinned, but a quiver stole through her. This man complicated life with her brother. Nolan was in danger while he was there, but still, she felt safer somehow with the colonel. It was confusing. Why? She had not felt unsafe before he arrived.

"Miss Whitford, we will be in close quarters. I would like it very much if you would feel comfortable calling me Jackson."

His first name? Would that be proper? "Suh, I'm not sure we should be so familiar. You are the...conqueror." She paused for emphasis. *Why did she still needle him?*

"Ouch! Must we still be enemies? I am trying very hard to be your friend, Miss Whitford. I would like to be friends."

"Well, your men cannot go back on the land for the time being, but the cabins can remain theirs if they are comfortable there." A ripple of a shiver shot down her neck, straight down to her belly. He was here with his men, and they weren't leaving soon. "There is so much damage out here. I do not understand what else has happened."

"I'm waiting to hear from Marshall—er, Lieutenant Colonel Jameson—on how the men fared. The winds beat the barn and the buildings, but only some shingles and a roof or two ripped off. Men in the cabins affected moved to another one. We tried not to overcrowd those. We can fix the damage. Thank you so much for the generosity you extended towards my men." He hesitated. "If you don't mind, the cabins provide sound shelters for the men. We might use some of them for a sickbay."

"I think would make an excellent use of the empty ones. I had not thought of that."

"Thank you."

"And the horses? They are good?"

"Yes. As far as we can tell."

"I haven't seen my overseer, Jason, yet today. Have you met him? We tried to catch up with him yesterday before the storm, but Carter said he was gone. I'm not sure where he was, but hopefully, he was back just before the storm hit."

"Can we go back to our earlier conversation... I asked that we be friends, and for you to call me Jackson." He waited for her answer.

Her eyes shuttered. "Yes, I suppose we could be friends. Thank you... Jackson."

He leaned forward and touched her shoulder. "Thank you very much, Ella. You've made us feel welcome, despite your... protestations."

She looked at him and saw that cute dimple of his. A slight smile formed on her lips. "Suh, the only thing I could ever object to with you and your men is that you are all on the wrong side." *That and my dear brother was sick and in the safe room and you could do him harm.* "Let's see what we can rustle up for breakfast." She wanted to move him away from the front of the house.

Stopping at the parlor, she leaned in and didn't see Lizzy. Good. She had hoped she and Aiden could sleep a little longer. The past day had been very challenging for all, and Lizzy seemed beyond exhausted last evening.

"Miss Ella, breakfast is on the table." Lizzy walked up and let them know that the grits and eggs were cooked. "Lieutenant Colonel Jameson is already at the table. Shall I get our little man up, Miss Ella?"

"Yes." She sighed. "I had hoped you would have gotten a little more rest. But since you are up, yes if you don't mind. We should rouse the little bugger." She turned to the colonel. "Let's get breakfast." They walked side by side towards the dining room.

∽

*H*ad he really asked her to be friends earlier? The word was out before he could pull it in. *He wanted more than to be friends.* He wanted to see her hair fanning across his pillow. That gorgeous red hair drew him like bugs to a light. Would she never stop the antagonistic tone?

"Ella," He stopped her with a touch. "I wonder if we could talk later. This storm gave me some ideas and I would like to get your opinion." His voice held just a touch of raspiness to it. He could see goose bumps had broken out on her neck, despite her unwillingness. Perhaps he had an effect on her.

"Certainly," she inhaled. "I'd like that very much."

Small feet sounded behind them. Turning, Ella caught Aiden as he leaped up into her arms. "Ummph! Aiden! Control yourself, my little man! You know it's rude to act so in front of other people. You are almost as big as I am!"

Aiden winked. "Don't frown, sista. I ain't ever gonna leave you like Nol'n."

"Oh! You little ragamuffin! I'm just sad thinking you will grow up and one day won't need me as much," she rejoined, grinning.

Jackson glanced over at Aiden. Did he wink? He didn't think he had seen too many children his age wink. Well, no matter, the little tyke's good mood was contagious. Ella was smiling and no longer snide. Aiden liked him and he liked Aiden.

Bo, however, wasn't as trusting and friendly. His sharp barking sounded at the heels of the colonel and continued down the hall.

"Quiet, Bo! Colonel Ross is nice." Aiden shushed his little companion, holding his tiny finger up in front of his lips. Bo seemed to understand because he quieted down. After looking up, he sniffed the colonel and followed. "Ella, where did Colonel Ross live last night?" Aiden looked up at him with his little hand on his hip.

～

*E*lla swallowed her smile. Just when did Aiden try to become the man of the house? How did that happen? How should she handle this? Knowing he also held Nolan's life in his hands, she didn't want him to blurt anything out about that, either.

Nibbling on her lower lip, she pondered how to answer his question.

Lizzy trailed behind Ella and heard Aiden ask his question. "Mista Aiden! You know not to ask things like that! You are fixin' to get yourself in trouble." She tapped Aiden on the shoulder. "Well, little man, have you washed up yet for breakfast?"

Relief moved across Ella's face, but it was only a brief break. She would have to address Aiden's concerns and make him understand what is going on with the Yankees. How could she have felt so comfortable a few minutes ago? Jackson was making her life a mess.

His presence had complicated everything. Thoughts flashed to Nolan and Ol' Indie in the room downstairs, then she remembered the fixin' up he had had his men do for her. And he had just asked her to discuss ideas with him. She felt guilty and heaved a sigh.

As they approached the dining room, they heard Cook moving around. Breakfast was ready. She could smell it. They walked in to find cornbread, ham, eggs, and grits set out family style for them.

Jackson hurried over and pulled out the chair for Ella. He picked Aiden up and helped him into a chair nearby. Bo retreated to the corner of the room.

Lizzy withdrew to the kitchen with Cook. Ella called to her, but when she came back in the room, she met Ella's expression with a strange one of her own.

Not wanting to question her in front of the men, Ella waited until later, but there was plenty of room at this table for everyone today.

"Thank you for this, Miss Whitford… Ella. This looks wonderful." He nodded towards his friend and took his first bite, but Aiden cut into his action.

"Can I say de prayer?" He cocked his head towards his sister, a serious look on his face.

"Yes, Aiden. Please."

"Thank ye, dear Lord, for this food. Bless my sister and our people, like Cook, Lizzy and Carter. And please watch over," he glanced up at Ella before continuing. "Please look over my brudder Nolan and make sure, Lord," Aiden regarded the colonel, and then he winked as big as he could at his sister, "that he is okay. Keep him warm and safe and please don't let him have no sickness. Amen."

With that, he picked up his fork and ate.

"That was very nice, Aiden. We appreciate this meal." Jackson picked up his fork and knife and nodded to Ella.

"Thank you, Aiden." Aiden's wink stunned Ella. She wasn't sure she understood it, but when she scanned the table, both of the colonels were staring her way, a perplexed mien on both of their faces. *Uh oh.* Eager to change the subject, she moved it to one everyone would show interest in. "Let's eat. Then we can check out the damage to the house." She nodded towards Jackson and continued, "You wanted to get my thoughts on some things. That could be a good time."

Silence descended upon the table as everyone ate. The sound of plates, glassware and the occasional clank of a utensil hitting a plate was all the noise heard. No one talked for several minutes.

"Pass the bis-gits, please," asked Aiden, breaking the silence. He reached for the bowl of white fluffy rolls. Lieutenant Colonel Jameson passed them down the table, wearing a grin on his own face. When the bowl of biscuits came his way, he reached for it. He pulled out two, putting one on his plate and lowering his hand under the table with the other one.

Bo, seeing the signal, walked over to the table, ducking under the corner furthest away. He moved to the biscuit and removed it from Aiden's hand, and laid back down to eat his own breakfast. Bo held one paw over the biscuit and licked the top, savoring what was to come.

Once breakfast ended Cook came in with Carter and, with Lizzy, cleared the dishes. Ella kept watching the three as they carried on as if the war had never taken place.

Before Colonel Ross and Lieutenant Colonel Jameson had come, her life was one of helping with everything. She planned to speak with her friends and find out what was amiss. They were in this together, and no one needed to eat in the kitchen. So, what was this pretense about? She would ask Lizzy later.

"Miss Whitford, can you accompany me on a walk around the back of the property? I think there is damage, but I'd like to have you with me as we assess it."

Startled, she looked up at the colonel. "Yes, I'd like that very much.

The damage could be bad. I fear for all of those men and the poor animals."

Ella pushed back in her chair and she stood. The colonel cleared more room for her. She rested her hand on the arm he extended to her. At their touch, a familiar current shot up her arm.

CHAPTER 12

*E*lla wanted to pull her arm back from his, but he had clamped his hand over her arm. It was such an unfamiliar feeling... but it felt delicious. His hands were warm and comforting. She looked up at his face, searching. A smile warmed his face. He seemed guileless. She couldn't object to that.

They walked down the steps behind the house. What awaited them, surprised them, both. The slave cabins were largely untouched. Only the roof from one hut lay in the common area. The shelter was all but decimated, but the men inside had escaped.

The barn held, but there was damage—the wooden shutters and the barn door were gone, and hay was everywhere. The horses and cattle were still in their stalls, but the chickens were running around the yard.

An officer walked up to Colonel Ross and saluted.

"Yes, Smith. What do you report?"

"Sir, there were no casualties, although six men need to go to sickbay because they were hit with flying debris. The roof from a cabin blew off and barely cleared two of their heads when they ran for shelter. No livestock was injured, as near as we can tell. There was minor damage to the barn and six cabins sustained damage."

"Where did you establish the sickbay?" Jackson spoke up before Ella could say anything.

"Sir, we have cleared out a cabin and have designated that area for the sick."

"Thank you, Smith." He nudged her around the fallen debris of the cabins and directed her towards the barn.

Ella looked his way. He treated everyone with kindness and fairness, and it was obvious the Lieutenant Colonel thought so much of him. She didn't want to pay him attention. What was it about this man that made her body betray her so? Every time there was an opportunity, she stared his way. He had a commanding presence that exuded confidence.

If only he wasn't on the wrong side.

Wait, what was she *thinking?*

He looked down at her and her eyes opened as big as saucers. Did he hear her thoughts?

"Miss Whitford… Ella? I do like that name." Not waiting for her response, he kept talking. His voice emitted almost a velvety feel to her ears. "I have something for you. You have been very gracious. We agreed to pay you something for the use of the land, food and materials we are using and expect to use. I hope this is enough." He placed a small brown envelope in her grasp, clasping her hands in his for an extra moment.

Ella quavered inside from the contact as she opened the envelope to find US currency. There were twenty-five dollars in that envelope. Real money. Federal currency. That was more money than she had seen in what now seemed like forever even though it was going on a year-and-a-half. That was a fortune for her. She had not expected it from him, especially when they had already been fixing up the plantation. "Err…yes." It was all she could mutter. She was trying to process all of what he said to her.

"Yes?"

"Yes…um…I." She stopped and smiled up at him. "I like it very much when you call me Ella." She looked down again at the envelope before she placed it in her pocket. "This is totally unexpected. I mean, I recall you told me you would pay me something. We never discussed it further. I never considered it and certainly I didn't expect it. But it will help me very much." Her throat clogged with emotion.

She gazed up at him, locking his eyes with hers, and said, "Thank you, Colonel." A tear moved from the corner of her eye, creating a lone stream down her cheek. She wanted to brush it away but fought against calling attention to it.

∽

"Please, call me Jackson." His tongue suddenly thickened, causing him to stammer. "Well… I uh, I like it when you call me Jackson." He stumbled over the words. This wasn't going like he had rehearsed. It was embarrassing.

She was the first woman in years that he had any interest in and his damn tongue had to tie itself up in a knot. It made for a difficult speech. Without realizing it, Jackson placed his hand over her hand. Shock waves shot through him. He had never felt this way around a woman before; the only feeling he recognized was the sudden tightness growing in his trousers. He would very soon face humiliation.

"Yes, well, it is the least we can do for your generous support." He cleared his throat and tried to move forward, bringing her attention to what was around them. "The horses and cattle seemed to have fared well."

Except for the animals, they were alone in the barn. His hand was still touching her hand—holding it—as they walked into the barn. How many people had seen that?

Where is Marshall? I will probably hear of this. What is it about this small mite of a woman that has me so befuddled?

Jackson pondered for a moment as his eyes continued to search for his friend. He stopped when he noticed she was watching him.

"Jackson," she said tentatively, as if testing the strangeness of saying his name aloud, "I should head back into the house. I want to grab my egg basket and come back out. I'm thinking the chickens may have put out a bumper crop over the last night. Unless fear makes them react the complete opposite." She nibbled her lip wearing a look of hesitation.

"Wait. Let me escort you back." He fought the urge to kiss her, wanting his moment to become theirs, but knowing that would not happen. Jackson released her hand and pressed the small of her back, directing her back to the house. "After you, Ella."

They took their time heading back. Both were quiet.

~

Ella gathered the eggs and the extra milk she could sell. She was surprised she had so many eggs left over with the addition of these new tenants. *Twenty-six eggs!* Maybe she could make it to The Griddle without breaking them. It was a source of income she could count on, and she needed the money, even with the money from the colonel. She wouldn't allow herself to count on money from Jackson—Colonel Ross.

It was still hard to call him Jackson, but it felt nice.

Sara counted on Ella's contribution—not that she was the only one bringing eggs. Goodness, Sara could never run the restaurant on her small offerings. She laughed out loud at the thought. It had been almost a week since the hurricane, and that was a few days too long since her last visit. She needed to see her friend.

So much had happened. Should she tell Sara about Nolan? Her brother and Sara needed to see each other, but how could that happen? Just thinking about this made her head hurt. Nolan was feeling better, and he needed to leave—soon.

Ol' Indie and Carter planned to get him out, and she would rather not know how that happened. They knew the swamps and the river better than anyone she knew.

The soldiers reassembled their cook wagons and tents on the lawns. As if the storm had never happened, they continued their daily maneuvers. It was truly something to watch. She didn't understand much of what they were doing unless they were shooting. But she noticed there were fewer and fewer birds on the plantation. The guns probably scared them.

CHAPTER 13

Two weeks had passed since the hurricane. She had checked every day on Nolan. He was getting better. Soon he would need to leave. She knew that. Nolan was well enough to express his anger over Jackson's presence, and he was doing just that every time she saw him. It was tiring.

Ella had a difficult time explaining their presence to her brother. She didn't fully understand it herself. It was as if they appeared one day and said they were staying. Well, *that is* what they did. Ella almost defended their stay, and even to her thinking, that was too far. However, there were benefits. She caught herself smiling at the thought.

She could not argue that she felt safer. Stories she heard in town about desperate men seen on the fringes of the countryside frightened her. Jackson immediately sent a squad out to find them. His job was to keep the town calm and safe.

She constantly worried about Nolan being found. Truthfully, as much as she loved her brother, her gut was in a constant churn over the possibility of Nolan being found here. She knew that would be bad for him. He could be shot or hanged.

Nolan made no secret that he was bored and wanted to get back to his unit. His unit was in Kinston, about forty-five miles west. As hard as it was for her to see him go, knowing he would at least be nearby felt a little better. She had not even known where he was since he left for the war until he showed up the day of the storm. She hated him being sick and knowing this could come back on him if he wasn't careful concerned her. Hopefully, Ol' Indie could give him something to help him if he got it again.

Jackson and Marshall were off doing maneuvers with the men, or something. An officer named Foster had asked them to work with them. She eavesdropped as much as she could on their conversation in the library. Unsure what she was listening for, she told herself she would know it when she heard it. Ella stayed as vigilant as possible, so she wouldn't get caught, but if she did, what could they say? It was her library. Well, Nolan's.

When the men left the library, she was only aware that they were leaving. She very much wanted to speak to her brother. This was the perfect opportunity.

Lizzy had Aiden occupied upstairs doing lessons on his math and other studies. Ella could not find a better time not to be disturbed. Lizzy was a blessing, and a big help. Teaching her math and reading years ago had been one of the best things she had ever done, for so many reasons. Now she could be gladder for it because Aiden listened to Lizzy cipher better than her.

Curiously, Lizzy refused to let any man see her cipher. She did her ciphering when the men left the house. But she helped with the books, and that was a great help to Ella.

She pulled the entry hall closet door closed and tapped on the wall in front of her as she had been taught and a panel opened, gaining her entrance to a hidden underground room.

The room smelled better. His sickness had cleared, and he was getting his strength back. *It's strange how sickness can dominate the smell of a room.* It reminded her of her mother's room. Momma lingered for a short time once Aiden was born but never recovered. Her room always had that certain sweet smell.

"Nolan? You awake? I brought you refreshments." Ella moved carefully down the steps, balancing the cool pitcher of tea and the basket of biscuits and marmalade.

"Sis! You remembered. Thank you. Marmalade. I love it." Nolan had the biscuits and jelly out of her hands before she could clear the final step. The fact he was up and about made her happy and sad at the same time.

"Hi, Ol' Indie. I didn't realize you were still here. Let me fetch another glass, and we can all share the tea and biscuits."

"Chile, I'm fine. You don't need to run back up those stairs. You and your brother just sit a spell and enjoy each other's company. The older woman walked over to a chair by the stove and sat down. "Now yu'uns can talk, Ol' Indie will just close her eyes and nap a spell. Massa Nole, you mos well now, but need to take it easy. We still got to keep you quiet or de fever might come back. We need a few mo days here. I sho don't want you to fall sick and Ol' Indie can't be dare."

"Thank you for all that you have done." Ella looked over at her brother lying casually on the cot with one arm propped behind his pillow. "Nolan, now that you are feeling better, I want to ask you a few things before Carter and his mamma take you to your men. I am curious." Pulling out one of the only chairs around the table, Ella smoothed her skirt and got comfortable.

"I promise. I will just sit here and talk to you. I know you want to know what I can't tell you, but I will tell what I can." Pausing, he looked at Ella, who sat quietly and stared at him, her hands folded in her lap and a curious smile on her face.

"You know the rules. You get to ask a question and then it's my turn to ask." A smile lit up Nolan's face as he returned his sister's attention.

Ella looked him in the eye. "I'm first. Okay. Why were you wearing a Union uniform when we found you? You must know we're curious. What have you been up to, dear *brother*?" She dragged the last word out.

"Whoa. That's two questions." He laughed. "I cannot answer either of them. So, you get another question. That's the rules."

"Confounded army!" Ella muttered and glared at Nolan.

Ol' Indie opened one eye and looked over at the two. "Now, Massa Nole, if you don't tell her that you were shooting on the other side, I'm gonna do it."

Ol' Indie's remarks took him by surprise.

"What? You're a traitor?" Ella covered her mouth with her hand, shocked.

Ella's shocked response brought his focus back to her. "'Course not!"

"Well, what am I to think? You were in a tattered Union uniform when you arrived. Now I hear that you were firing on your friends? Nolan! How could you?" Ella pushed back from the table and stood, covering her stomach with her hands. She felt sick. "It was no wonder Papa never found you, you were in the wrong army!"

"No, Ella, you have it wrong." He walked to her and grabbed her shoulders. "No way would I be a traitor. I was…" He looked down. "Okay. Look. Look, I was spying. There! I told you both. You should know that knowing this puts you in danger. You cannot tell *anyone*."

Ella stood there, shocked. She wanted to understand, but all she could feel was anger. Her brother was spying? "They will hang you if you are caught. And what about Aiden, Lizzy and Carter—and everyone else? I can take care of myself, but they rely on us, on *me*. We must get you out of here as soon as we can."

"Ella. Calm down. I don't intend to be found. No one knows of this room, do they? I plan to leave in a couple of days."

"Don't tell me to calm down." She lowered her voice to an angry whisper. "You promised me you would take care of yourself. You think spying is a good thing?"

"Yes, I did promise. And no, spying is not good, but it is necessary in these difficult times."

"Well, you say you have plans. Can you share them?" Her eyes narrowed, she sat back in the chair and crossed her arms.

"I know you may not understand, but I am an officer and I have to do my duty. Share none of this with Aiden. He will ask questions. If he asks, tell him I had my uniform taken and they left me with that one." He looked away for a moment. "I was on a mission. It failed. *I failed*.

But I have to get back to Kinston, to my men, so I can report what I saw. I must get back there soon."

"Well, what did you see?" She knew he would get irritated, but she wanted to know.

"Ella, you go too far. I cannot discuss that, and I will not discuss that." Seeing she would not be satisfied, he continued, "I was more concerned about what I saw happening on *our* side."

"*Our* side? But we lost the battle..." She was afraid to hear what he had to say. Boys she had grown up with had lost their lives. If she heard something she didn't want to, it would diminish them somehow. If she knew that they did something wrong, it would make her feel awful, but not knowing was killing her. She had to know. How could she get him to tell her?

"I see that look on your face. We will not discuss my mission further, beyond how it affected me. I have to get to my men and report. What happened wasn't what I expected, but since I saw what took place, I have to report it."

"How were you supposed to get to your men?"

"I cannot discuss that." A crooked smile lit his face. "Now, it's my turn to ask questions." He pointed at the ceiling. "First, what is the Union army doing here?"

"They are here because this land offers them a good place to set up what they call a *per-i-meter* camp." She sounded the one word out slowly. "I still don't understand why they came out here, but they have been very helpful, and they are paying me for the use of the land."

"Right. They are building their skills to kill more of our Confederate brothers and using our land to do it."

"No. Well, I guess they are training, but they are more about keeping the peace. I'm alone, Nolan. Except for the few hands we still have, Carter and Jason are the only men I can rely on for help, and... Nolan, I don't know if I'm just imagining this, but Jason acts very strange. I find him watching me. He leers. He insists on driving me to town if he finds out I'm going. I've tried to go without him because I am afraid of him."

"You made trips by yourself to town?" he interrupted, disbelief and anger evident. "I remember seeing a woman fighting to control her wagon on the road here. I wasn't sure at the time, but now I realize it was you."

"What? You saw me? Where were you?"

"Ella, what did I tell you about the dangers? You promised me."

"Nolan, lower your voice, please!" He saw her that day. *His presence was what spooked Bess.* "I just explained—"

"And you worry about a little harmless attention. Compared with being set upon by some deserter or a runaway slave intent on harm, you single out flirting?"

He wasn't listening. She was tired of men thinking they knew it all. "You are right about the deserters but please... about Jason—"

Nolan interrupted her. "I don't believe you need to worry about Jason. He's harmless."

"And you are so sure of that? I too, remember the day Bess got spooked. *You* spooked her." She shook her head in disbelief. "You cut me off and won't even take my concerns seriously. I am not comfortable with him. He leers, and is always watching me..."

"Ella, I didn't know I spooked Bess. I was sick and stumbled out of the brush, but you were already beyond me. But it could have been someone else coming out of the brush. That is a reason you should not be driving alone. And Jason—has he said anything inappropriate to you?"

"No. I said it's the way he watches me and it's what he does. He wears a weird smile when he looks at me, and he moves entirely too close to me on the buggy." She heaved a sigh. "I know you worry about me, but you aren't listening. You won't even try to see things from my point of view. I can see this exchange is going nowhere, so we might as well stop now." As long as she had the colonel at the house, she would feel safe. No way could she say that to Nolan.

"Going back to an earlier question, sister—how long are they staying?"

"I don't know." She wanted to change the topic. "Do you plan to see Sara?" Ella narrowed her eyes.

At the mention of Sara, Nolan looked away. "Yes, I would love to see her, but I don't know how to make that happen." He glanced up at Ella.

"Well, maybe you should leave that to me. You focus on getting better." Ella got up and gave her older brother a big kiss on his forehead. "I'm glad you are home. I wish it wasn't under these circumstances. I've got to get back upstairs before I'm missed. A man named Foster came to see Colonel Ross and they are outside doing the maneuvers. He must be very important because everyone saluted." She squeezed his hand. "Nolan, I don't want anyone looking for me."

A soft snore rent the air and she looked over where Ol' Indie was spread out on the chair. Softly, she reached over and touched her arm.

The older woman woke with a jerk. "What? Oh, Miss Ella. I must have dozed off. Please, 'scuse me."

"I hate to wake you, but I need to head upstairs. Please let me know if you need anything else for Nolan. You have done such a good job doctoring him." She kissed the old woman on the forehead. "We love you and appreciate it."

Nolan touched her arm. "Wait! You said Foster? What did he look like?"

"Oh, I don't know. He wore an officer's uniform. Dark hair. Broad hat. Mustache. Nothing much to look at, if you asked me." She covered her mouth, embarrassed, her face heated behind her hand.

"If you hear anything, please let me know. I understand he is over all of the troops here. He is smart, likes order, and has placed two of his most trusted men here. He is likely to share something that could be useful to me. You may hear things." Nolan thought for a moment. "I wish he was on our side."

"And what if I hear something? What could you do with that information? You are stuck here."

"Just let me know if you hear anything. I wouldn't ask you, but this could be a matter of real importance."

She shook her head in exasperation and hugged him. She whispered in his ear, "I will. I love you."

Ella left weighted with worry. Somehow, her brother needed to get to his unit. How could she pull that off with the colonel here? And he wanted to see Sara. She sighed. *Another impossible task.*

~

*C*olonel Jackson Ross.

Shivers ran down her arms and her back at the thought of him. What was happening to her? He was the enemy and now he had someone here that might be planning to hurt her brother and his men very soon.

Her brother was of similar rank, she reminded herself. He was very smart and would be okay. She decided to tell him anything she heard or saw.

Jackson was nothing but kind to her. That made little sense based on what she knew of the Yankees. He had not demanded she take the pledge. Lately, she couldn't even get angry at him.

Ella had thought he might kiss her the other day in the barn. Goodness knows she wanted that kiss, but when he didn't make the move, she had said she needed to gather eggs. *Eggs!*

Botheration! She was falling for him. She never allowed herself to fall for any of the town boys because of the talk of war, and here she was falling for the enemy.

That could not happen, could it?

"Bess, I have to do this trip for my brother. He will leave soon." Ella muttered as she hitched her horse to the wagon. Ensuring the eggs and milk were placed under the front seat, she climbed aboard. "Hold still, Bess. This'll just take a minute. Here. I've got it." She secured her horse onto the wagon, then she climbed aboard. Touching her hip, she felt for her gun. It was there. Small comfort. It would still be a long, hard ride.

Ella wanted to talk to Nolan before he disappeared back to his men. Getting time with him now that Jackson and Marshall and their men were on the grounds made things difficult. At least he was better.

She picked up the reins to go. "Come on, girl," she urged. Opening her mouth in an exaggerated grin, she made a clicking noise. "Giddy-up, Bess."

"Whoa! Wait for me, Ella!"

Ella stopped the buggy almost as quick as she started. He stood in front of her, his hands out in front of him to stop her.

"Hey!" He grinned. His spurs clanged as he covered the short distance to the buggy seat. "I was looking for you. I also need to go to town. Would you mind if we go together? I can ride Mason alongside you. Or we can ride the wagon together... if you'd like the company."

"Why, I suppose we could ride together. I mean, why put two horses through the travel?" *Why did I say that? I have to talk to Sara, and his going would make it difficult.* He was smiling at her and those adorable dimples were making her forget how difficult.

"That's really nice, Miss Whitford. I would enjoy that very much."

He was back to calling her *Miss Whitford*, now. She wasn't sure she liked that.

"Give me a couple of minutes to let Marshall know we are going."

"Marshall?"

"Yes, I will put him in charge. He can carry on without me here. There is still much to do. There are repairs out back that he will take care of, and we also found your cellar door unhinged. Marshall will make sure it gets done properly." He looked at her for a moment, then, hurried back up to his office—*her library.*

Marshall was in the library—so close to the secret room's entrance. Her insides twisted at the thought of Nolan leaving, but it was getting hard with him chafing at the bit to get out of the hiding place, and Jackson and Marshall often in the house. Plus, Jackson had insisted on posting a guard on the porch. The whole situation made her nervous, especially with her brother's restlessness.

She felt relieved he would be leaving soon but scared she might never see him again. What a mess this war had made of her life. Jackson Ross and his men had sent her life into a tailspin.

She was beginning to have feelings for the man. She enjoyed being around him, and that just made things worse. It flew in the face of her beliefs, making her now doubt her judgment. Ella needed to talk to Sara. Alone.

Suddenly she recalled him saying something about the cellar. What had he said about the cellar door?

Oh, no! If they go down there, they might find out that Nolan had been here. But if she said anything, it would raise suspicions.

Keeping Nolan hidden was getting harder. Having Jackson and his friend Marshall here, and all of those men—there was no choice about that.

Ella needed to help Nolan get out of here. He had mentioned that he needed to get back to his men in Kinston, and Carter was ready to get him there. He knew the river.

Tomorrow night.

~

As Jackson ran up the steps to the house, his spurs announced his arrival. When he had seen her hooking up the buggy, he had wondered if she intended to go alone. It was dangerous out there, and he didn't want her to drive by herself.

He asked Ella to let him know when she needed to go to town, intending to protect her. Jackson barely caught up with her today. Stubborn woman. She acted indifferent when he advised her about the dangers, as if she would not be vulnerable.

There had been reports of vicious attacks on the outskirts of town involving deserters—beatings and robberies. It appeared they were Rebs. His men tracked and shot them, but with the last attack, they couldn't get there before the farm was burned and pillaged. The animals were slaughtered, and the husband was shot in the head and left for dead. These men must have wanted guns. Still, the attack was more vicious than he could have imagined. They could have taken the guns and not done the killing. It was disturbing.

The evidence they found at a camp showed there were two, maybe three more of them that were out there. His blood chilled to think of Ella driving alone.

"Jackson, good to see you!" Marshall looked up from the ledger he was working on as Jackson walked into the library.

"Thank you, Marshall. I'm riding into town with Miss Whitford. The obstinate woman planned on driving herself." He looked down at the stack of papers on the side of his desk. "I haven't read through these. Is there any further word on the absconders spotted in the area?"

"Nothing more yet." Marshall gave a concerned look as he put down the ledger. "And we have gotten no closer to finding our own deserter. Wherever Private White has gone, he's eluded all of our tracking efforts. He is either good… or damned lucky. We have all others accounted for either in sickbay, dead, or working."

"Well, that is concerning." Absently, the colonel rolled a pen in his hand and looked out the window. "He cannot have just disappeared into thin air."

Jackson felt like he was missing something. The hair on his neck prickled, but he attributed it to the worry he had over Ella. "Perhaps these defectors met up with him. They could have done something to him. Might be a question to ask if we can capture any of them *alive*, this time. They weren't supposed to kill those two men."

"Okay, I will look after things here, but could you do me one favor?"

"Sure. Well, on second thought, I will try." Laughter crinkled his brow. "What would you like? No, I am not bringing any women out here." He had no idea what to expect from Marshall. This should be good.

"I only want some of Miss Sara's homemade cinnamon rolls. Just thinking about them makes my mouth water. Just thinking about *her* makes my mouth water!" Marshall broke out in easy laughter. "Sure, you cannot tuck her in the back of the wagon and bring her back?"

His shoulders relaxed. "No, yes… I mean, I will bring you the cinnamon rolls. Just keep things hopping here." Jackson pulled his hat off the hook, a smile on his face and a new pep in his step as he took off to join Ella.

Ella stirred feelings in him. He had almost kissed her in the barn. It wouldn't do to mix business and pleasure. He needed to get his baser instincts under control.

Although General Burnsides had no care about it, he felt it wasn't the greatest of ideas to get involved with these townsfolk. And, with tracks already on his heart, he wasn't eager to repeat that.

~

*E*lla felt for her small derringer tucked in its hiding place on the side of her leg. It was habit. She felt safer already just knowing Jackson would ride with her.

She had heard about the women that were accosted and the one that was attacked. Too many details of that had gone all over town. *Don't these Yankees know that some things just are not discussed?*

"Okay, Bess, let's keep it steady, old girl." She smiled shyly at Jackson, thinking about the first time she saw him. "Sara likes getting our eggs, but I doubt she wants them scrambled." Flicking the reins, she guided the wagon down the road. His nearness was comforting. It was much nicer already with company on this trip.

Any noise or movement on the side of the road caused Bess to jolt. She became edgy in the same spot on each visit lately, so Ella anticipated it and held on tight. Probably a nest of animals. Expecting it before Bess helped.

Perhaps she should mention it to the colonel to see if he, too, believed it was animals.

No, it would just bring up his need to protect her. She could handle herself fine.

"Great job, Bess! Easy does it." Her white-knuckled hands held the reins tight, but her voice denied any sense of panic. Cotton filled her throat—or was that fear? She was glad he was with her.

*J*ackson wasn't fooled. "Would you allow me to help? I can take the reins. Perhaps a little break would refresh you before we arrive."

"Well, I *thought* I was doing fine."

Jackson heard the ire in her voice. She was reacting to his offer to take the reins. He reminded himself not to be so heavy-handed. He wanted her grateful for his help, not angry or thinking he diminished her abilities.

Biting her bottom lip and looking straight ahead, she passed the reins to Jackson.

Bess didn't seem to notice the difference in drivers.

His skin tingled where their legs touched. He wondered how it would feel to touch her thigh. He itched to move his hand closer but decided against it. She was gripping her seat tightly, and they weren't going fast. Best keep his hands to himself.

He cleared his throat. "I noticed the disturbance in the bush area, too. Probably wild animals, maybe a deer."

His mind remained on those bushes back there—certainly something he needed to check out. That was *not* a deer; it made way too much noise. If she had not been with him, he would have stopped and checked, but her safety was more important.

As she got closer to town, Ella shared a startling thought. "Colonel, are the people in town aware that you are staying at Silver Moon—you and your men?"

"I didn't pass information around town, but we both know that once The Mercantile hears that I have been setting up the perimeter on your plantation... well, I'm sure it will make its way around."

If it hasn't already gotten around. That is one gossipy old woman at The Mercantile. With sudden clarity, he realized that in trying to both protect Ella and do his duty, he might have created gossip that could injure her.

Jackson cleared his throat. "But your reputation will not be affected. My word."

No, I don't want to ruin your reputation, but I would like to kiss you, hold you. I cannot get you off of my mind. I am unbelievably attracted to you. Heaven help me.

Why had he promised to guard her reputation?

~

"Jackson, I was wondering what you think of the South. The land and people, I mean."

"Well, until we came to New Bern, this war held nothing for me but pain and suffering—seeing men die and killing." He looked at her. "Then I met someone that made things very interesting for me."

"Oh." Unsure of his intent, she ventured further. "Could you describe *interesting*?" She looked down and clasped her hands in her lap, still a little miffed at his heavy-handedness and unwilling to look his way.

"Well, yes. I could." He looked over at Ella and shifted the reins to one hand. With the other, he touched her chin, shifting her attention to him. "I find you interesting, Ella."

Her eyes widened. A fluttery feeling stirred in her stomach, actually lower than her stomach. She fought to subdue her feelings. "Well, I find *you* overbearing, Colonel Ross," she huffed in response and pushed his hand away. "Suh, you overstep…you insisted on driving without a care to how it made me feel. And what if Bess doesn't like your driving? I cannot afford any more disasters like broken baskets of eggs or damaged vegetables." She wagged her finger at his face. "And there's another thing. You don't need to chauffeur me. I can drive my buggy. I've been doing it since I was twelve." Ella stopped talking when she saw the look on his face. *What?*

He was staring at her with a curious look. It was not the look of someone who had just received a tongue-lashing. She felt conflicted and accused him of things she *wanted* to feel. Truth was, she liked the way he made her feel. He slowed then stopped the rig and she didn't object.

They were alone. She looked at him, her breath coming in short, rapid bursts.

Jackson leaned in, his lips softly brushing hers. A delicious shiver moved down her spine, and she offered no resistance. His hands moved inside her cloak, then down the sides of her arms. Fighting the feelings, she was experiencing, she tried to push back, but he was holding her arms, gently pulling her towards him. They inched her closer and closer to him. She could smell leather and sandalwood. *Oh my, it's almost overpowering.* No longer trying to restrain herself, Ella relaxed, and time seemed to stop.

His mouth moved to her hair and he nibbled on her ear. It sent delicious feelings down her body, down to her toes. He moved to the other ear, his kisses burning a trail as he moved to her neck. His soft caresses elicited gentle moans as his mouth covered hers, this time with more intensity. His teeth gently nipped at her bottom lip, enticing her, and she opened her mouth, gaining his slick, warm tongue entry. As it swirled around hers, she boldly met it with her own, the kiss becoming more intense, their breaths intermingled and frenzied.

She knew she should stop this, pull back, but she wanted his kiss, his touch. Ella felt the warmth of his hands caressing her breasts, rubbing, sending shivers down her neck and awakening her to a warm moistness between her legs. Her body was responding in ways unfamiliar to her.

Jackson stopped kissing and touched his forehead to hers, then gently unbuttoned the top buttons of her gown. She could not react. With a few more scalding kisses to the base of her neck, he moved to her breasts, his breath heating her skin. Her hands reached for his hair, twining her fingers within it, toppling his hat off. Still kissing her breasts, he leaned her down on the seat, his upper body covering hers. They stopped for a breath, and this time, she moved in and kissed him.

Realization of what was happening slapped her senses aware. *Not this, and not here. What if someone saw them?* Her palms against his chest, she pushed back forcing Jackson to lift his head and meet her gaze, chests heaving. Scrambling, they righted themselves.

"I apologize. I should have never taken such liberties. But I find myself attracted to you, *fiercely* attracted to you, Ella."

Whap!

Ella gave him everything she could muster in that slap across his face.

"What the hell?" He pulled back, his hand covering the side of his face.

"What? You want to know what? You…took advantage of me, suh. I am shamed!" Her breath came in bursts as she scrambled to explain the slap for a kiss that she wanted. "You have laid claim to my property, and now you are trying to take over my person. And you are a Yankee! No! I cannot allow it." She turned away, her chest rising and falling, as red heat moved up her neck.

"I said I apologize. You didn't object during that kiss. Why did you have to slap me? You were enjoying it as much as I was."

"That isn't true. You…" She couldn't finish. Truth was she *had* enjoyed it. Her face flushed red as she tried desperately to hold back angry tears. "I've just never been kissed…well…like that. And, I'm not a woman of loose morals." She added that quickly, unwilling to let him know this was her first kiss.

"A beautiful woman like you, never kissed… properly?" He shook his head and looked hard at her. "You should be kissed. And I would never think you to have loose morals. Now, please don't be angry with me. I don't want eggs sailing my way." A smile lit up his face.

"Well, I am…no, I'm really not upset. My emotions are a little… confused." *They are new. I want to be furious with you, Jackson Ross, but no, I'm definitely not angry.*

She licked her lips and looked over at him.

"Ella, I have feelings for you. I am not saying that what I did was right. But I will say that what we did felt right. Maybe this was not the place, but it's the first good opportunity I have had to kiss you, and I've needed to kiss you for a long time."

She sat still, taking in what he had just said. Her feelings were in disarray. She had enjoyed his caresses and his kisses. This war had not given her an opportunity to properly court any boys.

Jackson had stormed into her life. Now he was stealing her heart.

~

Seeing her lick her lips nearly undid him. His body reacted. The discomfort of his tight britches reminded him of her influence over him. He had not planned on any of this, but she ruled his brain. *I want to kiss you again. I want more with you.*

"I apologize, Miss Whitford, but not for finding you attractive. Nor for wanting to kiss you…"

Bess snorted and jerked the wagon. That gained their attention, and they both looked at the horse. Did she see something? He looked around. Nothing. *Well, we needed to come to our senses.*

"She must have grown bored," Ella's smiling eyes searched his face, a grin lighting up her own face.

Jackson chortled. He reached up and touched the spot on his face, his cheek still fresh and stinging from her slap. Well, if the cost was that slap, he felt he had gotten a deal. He wanted to know her, know her passion.

For now, it would have to wait.

Jackson picked up the reins and looked around. No one was about, so they had not been seen. Good. The last thing he wanted was to compromise her. He should have never gotten so carried away. *What was he thinking?*

"Perhaps the middle of the road to New Bern is not the best place to have expressed my interest. I ask for your forgiveness, Ella, sincerely. I can only plead that I was swept away by your beauty."

Looking up, he noticed the sun high in the sky. It was noon. "We need to get going if we want to get back by nightfall. I don't believe this is the best place to be at night." Clicking the inside of his cheek, he urged Bess onwards. He thought he saw a small smile before Ella turned her head and looked ahead.

He tipped his hat to the ladies that passed by them as they came into town and caught the side looks of a couple of his buddies. It was important to address that later. Sometimes good-natured teasing was misunderstood. Jackson would make sure that no one made comments about Miss Whitfield. He dropped her at The Griddle and promised to return soon, before moving Bess across the street to his quarters.

Alone, he could think. He had not expected her fury. Damn, he had given no thought to how she might feel, and that made him feel like a cad. He glanced over. She didn't seem angry now. His feelings towards her were becoming a force, and he needed more control. Still, that kiss had been very satisfying. He smiled. No question there was smoke between them. He looked forward to the ride home. He missed her, and that was a feeling he hadn't had in a very long time.

It scared the hell out of him.

CHAPTER 14

*E*lla almost ran into The Griddle. Sara was finishing up an order in the back, so Ella signaled to come up to the front. "Hurry," she mouthed, looking behind her out the window.

It took what seemed like an inordinate amount of time, but Sara finally finished and came up to give her hugs. "It's been over a week. How are you holding up?" Sara winked at her as she made for the kitchen. "I'll be right back. Let me put these few dishes in the sink." Sara pushed through the half-doors and they swished back and forth in her wake.

Not sure what to make of the wink, Ella was taken back. What in the world was Sara communicating? Oh, never mind. She was worried Jackson would come back before she got to talk. "Just hurry!"

Ella saw him come down the steps to his headquarters on his way to The Griddle. "Damn!"

When Sara looked up sharply from the kitchen doors, Ella realized she had cursed out loud. She always tried to keep those words to her thoughts—ladies didn't curse, her mother would have said. Heat flamed up her neck.

"Sorry, Sara, but hurry."

"What is so important that you have to defame yourself with such words?"

"Come on, Sara. It's me. We both think those words. Stop trying to make me feel bad. It's not like I cursed in your daddy's church."

She looked back out the window. Relief was evident when she saw Colonel Ross stopped by some young officers to talk about something. "Sara, look! They're back." She waved her friend over to her side.

Sara walked over, and Ella immediately turned back to watch out the window. "He's home!" she whispered loudly, the excitement nearly ripped the words from her mouth.

"He...*who?*"

"Sara...don't...oh!" With her mouth open in an O, Ella's voice lowered her whisper, "Nolan."

"Nolan? *My* Nolan?" Sara's voice was barely audible. She scrambled to get a better view.

"Yes, but he is leaving in two days. If you want to see him, you will need to—" she paused and checked to see if Jackson was still detained. "Come out to the house. I've thought of your excuse." Ella leaned in, her heart beating fast. She was nervous.

"But what can my reason be to go there? You bring *me* supplies. And I have my restaurant."

"Tomorrow is Sunday. You're closed. It's been a long time, and you are coming out to help me get started on canning. Besides, you need to leave this building now and then. You work downstairs all day and you live upstairs." Proud that she had thought of what she felt was the perfect reason, Ella beamed.

"But what will we can? You bring me all of your extra food to sell."

"Oh!" Ella felt deflated. Sara was correct. There was nothing they could can. A conversation outside the restaurant drew her attention. "Tarnation! He's already back."

The door jangled open and in walked Colonel Jackson Ross. He looked at Ella and then at Sara. "Did I interrupt something?"

"Why no, Colonel, suh." Sara chortled. "We were having a little girl talk is all. Ella, I'll be back in a moment." Hesitating, she turned and gestured to her friend. "Would you mind helping me, dear?"

Ella nodded. She pushed her baskets away from the edge of the counter and started after her.

Sara stopped and turned around. "Oh, bring the eggs, Ella. We can put those away and I can pay you from my office."

"Sure, glad to." Ella tittered, "We should be right back."

The doors swished behind her. Ella looked around at the very pristine kitchen. Even the dirty dishes Sara had brought back only minutes earlier already soaked in a sudsy sink. *How does she manage this? It's incredible.*

An arm reached out and pulled her towards the pantry. Without a word, Ella complied. "Shhhh!" Sara reminded. She held her finger in front of her lips, and then, pointed back towards the dining room.

"So," began Ella, "I need to let you know. Nolan was very sick when he came home. Ol' Indie has been at the house trying to get him well. I've been afraid to leave the house. Today, when I tried to leave, *he* came with me!" She nodded towards the swinging doors. "I cannot get rid of him."

"It must be very stressful. Help me think of an excuse to my being out there, and so soon after this visit. I know! I will bring a birthday cake out there for Aiden. His birthday is this week, right?" She winked and smiled triumphantly, slapping her hands against the pleats of her skirt.

"That is a marvelous idea! I like it. And Aiden doesn't keep up with what month this is. He won't know we are celebrating early."

"It's settled, then. I'll be out there with a—"

Before she finished her sentence, the doorbell jangled and Jackson pushed his head through the swinging doors. "You have a customer, Sara." Seeing no one, and hearing no reply, he stepped into the kitchen area. "Ella?"

"Ella, please take this for Aiden." Sara spoke loudly, nodding towards the footsteps. "I will bake his cake and bring it to you. I may stop by tomorrow while I deliver a couple of meals to some of the shut-ins."

"He will love that. Your cakes are the best. Thank you, Auntie Sara. Remember…six candles." Ella smiled. Picking up a cake pan, she gave Sara a quick kiss. "Perfect!"

"Ladies?" Jackson smiled at both. "Sorry to intrude, but you have a customer, Sara. I didn't think you heard me, and I thought you might want to know." He smiled and tipped his hat.

"See you tomorrow, if it works out." Sara winked at Ella. "And I may help you with that dress a little." She turned and gave her biggest smile to the Colonel.

"Oh yes…you know I am terrible with the needle…but I'm trying." Ella felt her head, making sure she tied her bonnet. They were ready to go.

"Colonel, perhaps I will see you again soon. Aiden's birthday is in a few days, but I may bring his cake to him tomorrow."

"Oh…I almost forgot." Jackson grinned. "Marshall asked me to bring back some of your delicious cinnamon rolls, Miss Sara. Would you have any baked today?"

"Oh my! Yes! Please bring the lieutenant colonel these." She picked up a small tin of cinnamon rolls, wrapped them in a towel, and handed them to Jackson.

∽

"Miss Sara, I would prefer that you had an escort to Silver Moon. There are quite a few miles to cover, and the roads are isolated and lonely. Not to alarm you, but we believe we have men—we suspect former slaves from a nearby plantation—that have attacked people. They are still running loose, and that could pose a danger to you. We are trying to track them now."

Jackson watched her, familiar with Ella's adverse reaction to anyone helping her.

"Of course. Would there be someone who could leave about noon? We close tomorrow, and I have some shut-ins to visit in the morning."

"Yes. Let me head back to my headquarters and plan. I will return in ten minutes."

~

*E*lla and Sara looked at each other as the door shut behind him. Sara's face showed alarm. "Now what? How will I see Nolan if I'm surrounded by his men?"

"Ah! You now understand my dilemma," Ella smirked. "Well, just leave that to me. I will take care of the colonel's man."

The next few minutes passed quickly. The bell to the restaurant rang, announcing that their time for plotting was over.

~

*J*ackson entered and approached the two conspirators at the counter.

"All set. Sergeant Johnson will drive you. He will be here with a wagon at eleven-fifty tomorrow morning."

"Thank you, Colonel. You are most thoughtful, suh."

They are guarded, he thought. About what, he hadn't a clue, but he was sure it wasn't about their kiss. He knew Ella well enough to know that she kept things to herself until she was ready to share. He hoped when she shared anything about their kisses, it would be with him. Maybe there could be another…moment.

Jackson smiled and tipped his head. "I think we should get back on the road, don't you, Miss Whitford? It's getting a little late, and I think it would be a good idea to travel the road in the daylight."

"That's probably a good idea. I hadn't noticed the time." She gave Sara a quick hug. "Everyone will be so happy to see you."

"You be careful around Jason," Sara said, speaking low into her ear.

Ella nodded and clutched her basket.

Leaving the restaurant, Jackson looked up at the sky. "We should hurry. It'll be dark soon. It's one thing to drive back myself at dusk, but I don't want to have you on the road."

~

*E*lla felt irritation at his remarks, but she noted it was much less than she usually felt. Perhaps he was getting to her. She looked up at him and couldn't help the smile.

Taking her hand, Jackson helped her into her buggy, and then hoisted himself up beside her. As he touched her hand, a familiar but nagging surge of heat coiled in her stomach. She studied Jackson, the warmth of their touch still on her mind. He was concentrating on the drive, but she was concentrating on him.

Ella tried to hide her smile, but when she couldn't, she looked down at her lap, still thinking. *It's hard to dislike him—he's such a gentleman, and so kind and thoughtful. And his gorgeous eyes don't hurt.* She had to concede that he looked better than what she was used to around here. There had been little to look at since the war started.

"So, did you have a good visit?" Jackson smiled in her direction.

"Yes, I did. Thank you kindly for escorting me."

"Do you mind if I ask you a question?"

Guarded, she nodded. Ella noticed his face had turned serious.

"I overheard Miss Sara's comment about your overseer, Jason, and I can't help but wonder why she was cautioning you.

Ella was peaked. *How dare he listen in on her private conversation? He goes too far!* Her face heated with anger. Balling her fist into her skirt, she started to convey her anger, but stopped. What was wrong with her? He was in the room and Sara had not whispered. Of course, he could hear it. Maybe she *should* tell him.

"He frightens me." She responded and went silent, trying to decide how much she should say.

He slowed the wagon down and faced her. "It's important. I have reason for asking."

"He follows me with his eyes whenever we are close. And when we are on the wagon or go to town, he gets too close and…well, he slides real close on the seat. And there is this smirk he always wears lately. Our interactions are…disturbing." She felt relieved sharing this fear of Jason with Jackson.

"Has he ever touched you?"

Ella thought about that. "Yes. I find it very inappropriate he tries to sit so close that his leg touches mine. He slowly slides towards me, thinking I won't notice. May I ask why you ask?"

"Well, I noticed him staring at you this week, so I approached him and pretended I needed information about some of your folks still working your land. Instead of answering me, he told me I was paying too much attention to you and said your brother asked him to protect you."

She shuddered. "I don't know what to say, except that cannot be true. Nolan would have told me." The concern etched on Jackson's face was palpable. She trusted him. "I try to avoid him."

"Thank you for sharing this with me. The behavior I witnessed seemed odd—almost possessive, but I did not think it dangerous. However, it bears watching. Would you let me know if you notice anything else?"

"Thank you, I will." She smiled, feeling a sense of relief for having shared her fears with him. He didn't dismiss her anxiety but listened and offered support. This just added to the feelings that Jackson stirred in her.

Colonel Jackson Ross muddled her thoughts when he was around, yet she was most comfortable when he was near. That sudden realization alarmed her. His presence was making her life very interesting, but maybe not all in a bad way.

CHAPTER 15

Ella woke the next day amid a hubbub of activity. Jackson had started his project. She looked briefly at the bell pull that hung in the corner near her bed. It had been years since she had pulled it. No, she insisted on making her servants—her friends—feel they were part of her family. Before that, her mother had done the same. She was always working alongside her help.

A cup of hot chocolate would suit her right now. She always associated hot chocolate with her mother. These thoughts brought melancholy, a feeling she was experiencing more of late. She needed to shake off the errant thoughts. She didn't want to feel sad. Resolute, she moved her feet over the side of her bed and pushed them into her slippers.

The sun broke through the curtains. Daylight. The day promised plenty of stress. *Maybe there will be some happiness, too.* She smiled.

Sara was coming today to see Nolan. She would also bring Aiden a cake.

Ella realized she still needed to tell Aiden that it would be his birthday. Today or next month, Aiden wouldn't know the difference, and she'd fill Lizzy and Carter in on the plan. Her little brother liked surprises and would most likely enjoy a little celebration, something she hadn't thought she could do this year. Nolan could share in the party somehow. She couldn't think too much about that; she needed to get things ready.

Jackson was smothering her with his concerns, and this Yankee stuff going on was taking over her entire life. She didn't want to give up her life to a man, especially to a man that could harm her brother.

It was time to get up. She needed to let Nolan know Sara would be here soon.

"Lizzy! Could you help me with a few things?" She leaned over the balustrade, hoping Lizzy was nearby.

She finished her toilet and once again checked the hall for her friend.

Lizzy came up the stairs, arms full of linens. "Miss Ella, I heard you call. I hope you didn't mind the extra minute. I grabbed the clean linen."

"Goodness no! I would have helped with that." She reached over and took the top of the stack. "Let's put these up together. I want to fill you in on my plans—but we must hurry." She lowered her voice to a whisper. "Sara is coming today."

"But, Miss Ella…"

"Shhh. We must be quiet, or he will hear us." Smiling, and then placing her finger over her lips, she whispered, "Nolan plans to leave soon—maybe tomorrow. I wanted to give Sara a chance to see him. I need to work this out without the colonel or his sidekick seeing or suspecting."

"You are so right. They always be showing up exactly when you don't want them." Lizzy grinned. Fishing around in her pocket, she absently jingled her house keys and then smiled. "My! I thought I had misplaced these. I was hoping they'd turn up." Lizzy started down the stairs but lowered her voice into a collaborative tone. "Come, I have clean linen for Master Nolan. I started to take them to him, but the colonel showed up. He's in the library." She shook her head, "I think this might have to be a two-person job. Do you want to distract the colonel, or would you rather I do it? And when do you want to share the birthday news?" She turned and grinned at Ella.

"Lizzy, what would I do without you?" A smile lit up her face. She felt good about her plan. "Well, there's not a moment to lose. We should do this."

~

*J*ackson waited in the library. He needed to speak with Ella about yesterday. His impetuousness could have injured her reputation, but he couldn't bring himself to regret those moments. The thoughts of their intimacy—even though she had gotten angry—stirred him.

She was on his mind constantly. The night before, he had looked over at his pillow and wanted to see her next to him. He wanted to caress her, taste her lips, and know her in his bed. The thought made his pants tighten.

That was just what he needed.

He heard light footfalls coming down the hallway. They were coming towards the library. Yes, timing was everything. He quickly sat down behind his desk. Marshall was observing some of the field training and would be away for a while.

Three quick knocks on the open library door drew his attention. "Come in." He looked up expecting to see her.

It was Lizzy who entered. Almost instantly, his mood changed. "Is Ella not well this morning?" he ventured. He could feel his body cooling.

"No, she is well." Lizzy arched an eyebrow at him.

Noticing her expression, Jackson realized he was still sitting, an unusual greeting from him. Lizzy had noted it.

He slid out from behind the desk. He never sat when a guest entered the library unless he could not move. His mother had drummed manners into him from the time he was in leading strings.

"Suh, we could use your help. We want to get a small party together for Massa Aiden. It's his sixth birthday this week. Could we bother you to help move furniture? Carter pulled out his back, and I was hoping not to let him hurt it again."

That was odd. He had just seen Carter carrying a large pack of woodchips to the barn. He hadn't appeared to be injured.

Well, he didn't want to pry in their relationship, but it seemed Carter was putting something over on Lizzy.

Or was someone putting something over on him?

Nah. It would be obvious. With my military preparation, I would be hard to fool.

Still, something didn't feel just right. Jackson followed Lizzy to the ballroom to see what was needed.

"Miss Ella thought a small party in this room would be fine. With Bo in the mix, we need to have plenty of room. The young Massa mentions often how much he admires you." She looked up at Jackson. "We want to give him a pirate party. It would be just the thing for a six-year-old. If you feel like it, maybe we could borrow one of your tents, or make one? With the storm and now all of the men, Aiden isn't allowed to play outside unsupervised. Since he seen your tent, suh, it's been all he talks about."

"Well, I'd be honored to help." Flattered that they would think to include him in the planning, he decided a cleaner tent would be the thing. "Have you any spare linens?"

"Yassuh. What would they be used for, if I can ask? Would tablecloths work?"

"No, no, I think we should design Aiden a tent. Ours are all in use, but they are dirty anyway. I will work with Marshall to make him a fine tent. He will be able to use it anywhere in the house." Jackson headed towards the door.

"Suh, where are you going?" Lizzy's voice stopped him.

"Sorry, I got carried away. I'm going out back to get the wood cut for the frame. This will be fun." Jackson's smile ignited his face. He felt like family, being able to do something for young Aiden. He still wanted to talk to Ella, but that would have to wait. This was important, too.

*E*lla heard Lizzy and Jackson talking in the back of the house. She felt bad about the deception, but things being what they were, she had no choice. She grabbed up the stack of clean linens and scooted into the entry closet, heading to her brother.

Nolan was sitting in the chair, sipping a hot cup of, well she wasn't sure what he was drinking. He had a terrible look on his face. It must have been one of Ol' Indie's potions. "Hello, brother dear!"

Making a weird face, he gulped down the rest and put his cup on the table, almost with a slam. Good thing the noise down here was covered up with the ground and the walls between. No one heard anything that happened in this safe room.

"Well, how are you feeling?" She placed her hand on his forehead. It felt cool, normal.

"Ol' Indie says I'm betta. I need to get back to my regiment. I hate to leave you, but I've already been gone too long."

She gulped, agonizing over the thought of him leaving again, and placing himself in harm's way, but if he didn't leave, he would be a deserter, and her brother would never allow that. She hadn't told him, but Ella was proud of him. The least she could do was get him and Sara together for a visit. They needed to see each other.

"Let's not talk about you leaving. I know it's coming." She gazed around the room at the starkness. Her brother had stayed here, undetected, stealing out in the night for fresh air. He had a lot of determination. This war had dealt him circumstances she would have found objectionable.

Maybe it was as Mamma had told her—men were built differently from women. They could do things women could not tolerate. Exactly all of what that meant, Ella wasn't sure, but she thought this could be part, even while a small measure of her had questioned the veracity of this adage.

"I'm so sorry that you have been stuck down here." She noticed that he was staring off. "What are you worried about?"

"You." He grimaced. "Had I known Father would abandon you and Aiden, I would have found a way to stay. I feel negligent. I've left you to fend in a desperate situation. We all thought the war would end quickly, but I fear that will not be the case."

"Don't fret so, Nolan. You have not been negligent. Anyway, I have plenty of help right now." She rolled her eyes and looked behind her up the steps. "I have too much, I think."

"Yes, him. I sense you want to tell me something about him, but I'm afraid to ask."

"No, there is nothing there." Ella blushed and she could feel the warmth travel up her neck.

"Ahh. Yes, I can see that." His brows drew together. "I am familiar with the reputation of the colonel. Even though his men revered him, it was because of his fairness towards his men, not because of fear. He was a good leader. I admit, the man is being good to my family. I cannot hate him. He *pays* you, you say? That's incredible."

She nodded. "I do declare I was surprised. He *insisted* on payment."

"They may pay, but it rarely happens. Tell me, sister, what else is keeping you busy. It pains me I cannot be more involved."

"Oh! I have a surprise. I need to get upstairs soon, so I must tell you." She watched his face. "I visited Sara yesterday. I told her you are here."

"What? Why? Do you realize that you are placing both of you in danger, sharing information like that? It's bad enough you have had to risk your life putting me up while I healed. But—"

"Shush! Sara and I have this worked out. Now, please don't be mad, just listen." She took a deep, calming breath before continuing. "Sara is coming here to see you. We are calling this Aiden's birthday. Before you object, it won't make that much difference to Aiden. And, it'll really be only a little early. Aiden won't know the difference. She plans to bring a cake."

"Still, you two are putting your lives at risk. Do you know what they do to spies? It would be hard to explain my presence if we were found out." He studied her.

"I know. I hate…well, I hate these people being here. They have taken our home over, and I feel like I have become a boarder."

Seeing how upset he made her, Nolan backed off, changing his tone. "Well, I am still upset you have done this; however, I confess I cannot wait to see Sara." He grinned. "When will she be here?"

"There! That is the brother I recognize—smiling, handsome and confident. And healthy-looking again, instead of looking like a back-woodsman in rags." She crossed her arms and regarded him. "Hmmm, you've gained weight. It looks good."

"You are stalling. When? When will Sara get here?" He walked around the table. "I need to clean up." He grabbed up a straightedge and looked into a small mirror, allowing it to move around his chin as if looking for a whisker.

"Where is Ol' Indie?" Ella noticed her absence.

"She left an hour ago. That old woman is great at getting in and out. She leaves through there." He pointed behind him towards the kitchen entrance. "She and Carter are getting supplies ready and they are trying to be seen around so she seems familiar to the army folks. They don't know everyone who lives here, or that she isn't one of our slaves."

"Workers," Ella corrected.

"I know that you don't like to call them slaves, but they are slaves, sister."

"Nolan, we will always disagree about this. Outside of you and Aiden, they are all the family I have here, and Lizzy is helping get Aiden's party ready, so Sara can slip down here." She folded her arms across her chest and tapped her foot.

"Okay, okay. You win this round. I just want you to be safe. Now, when will she be here?"

"Anxious?" Ella smiled at her brother. "I'm not sure. Sara plans to visit some shut-ins, first. Jack...err, *Colonel Ross* made her wait and ride with one of the men from his headquarters." Her face flamed. "He worries that there are renegades out there. Doesn't want us out alone. He has gotten so darn bossy." She huffed.

"He has gotten protective. You may not need me to come home." He quirked a brow at her and smiled.

"Nonsense. Anyway, we plan to have a small party in the dining room. I'm gonna try and fool them into thinking that Sara is helping with some clothing that I have been trying to sew. So that he won't question her absence while she visits you, she will be in my room, until the coast is clear. Now, I have to go."

Ella leaned over and kissed her brother on his forehead and hugged him. She left the way she had arrived, listening to make sure there was no one near. The colonel was pretty noisy, and so was the lieutenant colonel.

Hearing no one, she stepped out. The coast was clear. Fighting the impulse to run up the stairs to her room, she walked quick. Sara would be here soon. She needed to have the rest of the props. She also needed to see what Lizzy had accomplished.

CHAPTER 16

*E*lla had not seen Aiden all morning. Where was he? She had heard nothing out of Bo, either. The two were inseparable.

Walking to the back of the house, she checked the closets, just in case. No Aiden or Bo. She would stay calm. He was in the house somewhere.

She was in the dining room when she heard Jackson and Lizzy approaching, and picked up the pinned dresses that she brought down from her room, earlier.

"Miss Ella, there you are. Your nice colonel has been good enough to help me this morning."

Lizzy's choice of words gave her pause, but she recovered and smiled at both. "Pshaw, Lizzy! You know he isn't *my* colonel, but he is a most accommodating and obliging man. Jackson, thank you for helping her. I'm afraid that Carter overdid it and has reinjured his back."

She held up her pinned dresses. "Lizzy, when Sara comes, please don't let me forget to have her look at my dresses. I never took too well to the needle, and I am forever begging her help. Sara is a genius with the needle and thread."

"We were fixing the ballroom for Aiden's party. I thought of what I plan to give him."

"Yes, Miss Ella, the colonel is *making* him a present. He's gonna fix the young Massa a tent…a real tent for him."

Lizzy was pleased with Jackson's contribution.

Ella nodded and smiled in acknowledgment. "Thank you, Jackson. He will surely enjoy that." She clasped her hands, wringing them together. "Speaking of Aiden, have either of you seen him and Bo? I am looking for them. I realized that he has been especially quiet. Is he in the house somewhere that you have seen? I've asked him to play in the nursery or in his room unless he goes outside with one of us."

Before anyone could answer, a loud knocking sounded at the front door. Ella hurried towards the front of the house in time to see Marshall hang Sara's cloak in the front closet.

"I just got here. Let me see where everyone is," Marshall looked up and saw Ella, Lizzy, and Jackson approaching. "There they are. Miss Sara, can I help you with the cake?"

Tittering, Sara glanced at her friend and then up at Marshall. "Oh, yes. Thank you. This is Aiden's birthday cake. His party will give me the opportunity to spend time with Ella." Sara handed Marshall the cake and untied her bonnet. "I'll just hang up my bonnet." She opened the entry closet door and laid the bonnet on the top shelf above her cloak.

"Hello Ella!" She walked to her friend and hugged her.

"What flavor did you decide to make the cake?" she asked, pretending that she didn't already know. Ella grinned. Marshall, and then Sara, had each gone into the closet. She wondered if Nolan was standing near the top of the safe room stairs but dismissed the concern.

"Chocolate, his favorite." Sara nodded, smiling. "The lieutenant colonel kindly took it for me. I believe he took it to the kitchen."

"Excellent. Welcome. We are arranging the ballroom. I plan to join everyone, but Aiden is missing, again. I want to look for him. He's probably outside playing 'pirates' somewhere I've asked him not to go out alone. I will be back soon. I hate to ask, but I wonder if you could look at a couple of things for me?"

Lizzy understood her signal. "Colonel, would you be able to help me with the chairs? I think one is broken, but I believe we'll need about ten. We should have enough."

"Marshall and I will both help you. If you have a couple of broken chairs, we should get them seen to. We are happy to be of help."

The two men followed Lizzy down the hall to retrieve chairs from the dining room. As soon as they were out of sight, Ella relaxed.

"Whew!" She nudged Sara. "I didn't realize that espionage in my home could be so complicated."

"Ha! You are a sly one. I need to keep an eye on you, my friend." Sara hugged her again. "I cannot wait to see him."

"I will take you to him. Wait for me to come back for you. Or Lizzy. I'm taking you to a special safe room. Swear secrecy to me." She smiled at Sara. "You are my friend and almost my sister. I know you would never share this information. Quick. Come." She led Sara back to the entry closet. Pulling her in, she put her finger to her lips, signaling that they needed to be quiet, and closed the door.

Sara's eyes widened in surprise as Ella pushed on the secret panel and opened the door leading to the safe room. Wall sconces and candles lit up the passage down the stairs, but Sara was gazing at the illuminated body at the bottom of the steps. It was Nolan.

Ella noticed he was wearing clean clothes and his hair was slicked back, still wet. *Thank goodness he bathed.* She wanted to pinch herself to make sure that this was happening. It made her happy to see her brother and Sara together.

"Sara, I'm gonna leave you two down here. Will that be okay with you? Ol' Indie and Carter may come in from the back entrance. Nolan knows their schedule. Will you be comfortable being alone with your betrothed down here? I cannot stay. I need to be upstairs."

"Yes... oh yes! Ella, thank you." Without another word, Sara dashed down the steps as quickly as she could.

As she started out, Ella turned once more to see her brother holding Sara. She felt really good about this. She just hoped that everything would work out as she planned.

Once up the steps and back in the closet, Ella listened before opening the door a crack. She made sure that no one was around when she stepped out of the closet. *I should think about using the back entrance occasionally. Using the pantry would make it a little easier to get past the men. I have to find Aiden and Bo.*

Ella walked back to the ballroom where Lizzy had the colonels working. The three of them were cleaning and arranging the tables and chairs. Her heart warmed at the sight. How she got the men to help clean, she couldn't fathom. She took a deep breath, pleased that her plans were going as she wanted. Lizzy had opened the drapes to clean the windows, allowing more light than usual into the room. Peeling paper and cracks in the plaster drew her attention. Things had not been repaired outside of the main rooms since Nolan left. Perhaps she would be able to get this repaired before the chandelier fell. There were some dangerous looking cracks near that.

"Hi, you three! Thank you all so much for helping, Colonel. You too, Lieutenant Colonel." Ella gave them both a smile. "I left Sara up in my room with my dresses. I need to go out and look for Aiden. I shouldn't be gone too long. I'm gonna peek in his favorite spots. He doesn't appear to be in the house, and that bothers me greatly."

Ella left them and hurried to the front door. The hair on the back of her neck was standing up, and she couldn't account for why she had that awful feeling. She had a nagging concern that it might have something to do with Aiden. Scurrying around the back of the house, she found the shortened stick that he usually used as his pirate's knife. It had the ribbon tied in a semicircle on the end, where he hung it from his belt.

Ella grabbed up her brother's stick and ran to the barn, calling for both Aiden and Bo. The only response she got came from Mason, Jackson's horse. He snorted and stomped his feet. If she knew horses better, she might believe him uptight and rather unhappy about being in a stall. She grabbed a handful of oats from the bag Jackson had hanging in the stall and fed him. "Here's a quick treat, Mason. "She gave his velvet nose a quick rub and a small kiss. The horse seemed calmer, so maybe getting some oats and the nose rub was just what he needed.

Bess snorted from the stall next to her, demanding equal time. She took oats to Bess and rubbed her between the ears, her favorite place. Chuckling, she realized the source of Mason's ill temper. He wanted to get over to Bess.

"Okay, I need to keep looking for Aiden." She said it almost to herself.

She took another quick look in on the two horses and went scurrying outside to the wooded area where the tall grass grew. *Aiden better hope I do not find him in here.*

"Aid-en, Bo!" Ella came out of the barn calling their names, as loudly as she could. No answer. The eerie silence fueled her panic.

Walking around to the back of the barn, she heard rustling in the brush. "Bo, Aiden. Come out of there, right now." Ella noticed the ground in front of her had large drops of blood. Terror took over and she ran mindlessly into the brush, slapping it out of her way. "Aiden, Bo! Are you back here?"

A muffled cry sounded out and Bo barked. "Aiden! Is that you?" Ella fought her way through the snarled briars and brush until she finally saw them. Aiden stood behind Bo, who was barking fiercely in her direction, guarding his buddy. *Is he barking at me?* She started, unsure of what was going on around her. *No, he is barking at something behind me.* Before she could look behind, a heavy object slammed into her head. She tried to scream for Aiden, but her voice was gone. Blackness took over as she felt herself falling.

∽

"Ella! Ella!" Aiden screamed. "Leave my sista alone! Stop hurting my sista! What'd you do to my sista?" Wiping his eyes, he ran towards her, with Bo in tow. A man hit his sister with a large stick and flung it hard at his barking dog. Aiden pulled Bo close before the stick landed. Two large black hands grabbed Ella and slung her over his shoulder, then disappeared into the brush.

A third man, the one that tried to grab Aiden, left him alone and ran after the others. His red shirt was flapping in the wind behind him and snagged on some brush, tearing it. Bo broke loose and sprinted after him, barking at his heels.

Aiden followed screaming Ella's name over and over. He tried to keep up with Bo, but broken limbs, briars, and rutted ground caused him to trip and fall repeatedly.

"Ella! Bo!" Crying and nearly hysterical, he stopped running and stood there, hiccupping sobs and shaking. Terrified for his sister, Aiden knew he needed to get help. He turned and ran back towards the house, screaming for Colonel Ross.

Rustling in the brush behind him startled him. He slowed down, hoping it was Ella. Bo came running through the scrub carrying a man's leather shoe.

"Bo!" The sobs got louder. The little boy and his dog ran to the porch. "Help! Colonel Ross, help us. They took my sista!"

~

Jackson heard the crying and commotion and ran out onto the porch. "Aiden! Bo!" Waves of panic coursed through him at the sight of Aiden's torn clothing and bloodied face and arms.

Aiden was nodding, crying, and running. Loud hiccups and sniffles made it hard for the little boy to talk.

The child ran up the steps and grabbed Jackson's shirtsleeves, pulling hard and crying. "My sista, they have my sista!" Aiden tugged his arm to get him to follow.

"Aiden, talk to me. What happened? What do you mean they took your sister?" Jackson felt the hairs on the back of his neck stiffen. The small boy tried to hiccup a response, only frustrating Jackson more. "Where is your sister?"

Bo dropped something at his feet. The dog backed up and barked furiously until he turned and ran into the brush at the edge of the yard.

"Bo! Come here, boy!" Jackson struggled over whether to run after the dog. But a moment later the puppy re-emerged, this time carrying a piece of red fabric. The dog dropped the cloth and barked frantically.

Not willing to believe Ella was gone, he called out over his shoulder, hoping this—whatever it was—was a mistake, and she would 'round the corner of the house and come from the barn or anywhere, as long as she was okay. "Ella…Aiden's here," he shouted. Nothing. He scanned the front yard and then saw the leather shoe and the red fabric in front of Bo for the first time.

"The pirates took her." The small boy stood, sobbing and choking on his tears, and struggling to breathe. "They hit her on the head and kilt her." Aiden hiccupped his words through bursts of tears.

Bo wouldn't stop barking. Again, and again, the little dog ran to Jackson and backed away, as if trying to get him to follow. The puppy nudged the old shoe and the piece of red cloth towards Jackson and backed up, still barking.

Jackson reached down and picked up Bo's offering. The puppy leaped in the air, barking. Bo was giving him a clue. Whoever had taken Ella had lost this shoe. Examining the footwear, he noticed that it was the same type given to field slaves, and it was very worn down. He clenched it, his stomach heaving.

I need Aiden to tell me what he saw.

"What happened, Aiden? I must know what you saw. Calm down and talk to me." Jackson felt a chill fill his body. *Ella.*

Marshall and Lizzy ran out onto the front steps. "We heard screaming. What's going on?" Marshall looked from Aiden to Bo to Jackson.

"Where is Miss Whitford?"

Jackson suddenly realized with sickening clarity that Ella Grace had been kidnapped—she may be dead. He was silent for a long moment.

"Whose shoe is that, Jackson?" Marshall persisted.

"Aiden said the pirates hurt her and took her." Jackson was not sure who the pirates were, but he would find Ella if he had to move Heaven and Hell to do it.

"Miss Ella? Oh Aiden, you are hurt." Lizzy brushed past Marshall and picked up Aiden, hugging him.

Jackson summoned his reserve of emotional strength. "Lizzy, please take Aiden and Bo into the house and clean him up. Keep an eye on him. Don't let him outside. Marshall and I need to look for Miss Whitford." Acting calmer than he felt, Jackson checked his gun, making sure it was loaded.

He looked down at Aiden and Bo. "Lieutenant Colonel Jameson and I will find your sister, but I want to make sure you are okay. She would be very mad at all of us if anything happened to you and Bo here. Promise to stay put."

"We promise, Colonel." Tears continued to stream down his small face.

Jackson's heart tugged. "Please go with Lizzy and stay in the house. Lock the doors and windows until I get back. We will alert the men to watch the house until we return."

What had happened to the guard he had posted there? Jackson just realized the man was gone. "Wait." He reached for Aiden, taking him from Lizzy, and wiped away his tears as he hugged the little boy tightly to his chest. He put him down and patted his rear, urging him back to Lizzy.

Marshall disappeared inside then stepped back outside, the screened door slamming behind him. "I've got my sidearm. Let's go. You can fill me in."

The two men retrieved their horses from the barn and took off in the direction Jackson had seen Aiden running from. They circled the barn. It was obvious an animal or something had been in the tall weeds. Blood and scrub marks created a path to follow, and soon they could identify where it appeared someone had been dragged. They followed the tracks as far as they lasted. There were two sets of tracks for much of the way; one track was obviously a man's foot. The third set of tracks joined them.

"I see three sets of prints. One set gets heavier here." Marshall pointed at the more substantial tracks.

Jackson stopped his horse. He slid out of the saddle and pulled the shoe Bo brought him from his leather saddlebag. "One set of the footprints got heavier back there when the dragging stopped." He kneeled and fit the shoe over the bare footprint. "This matches the size of the print next to it. These tracks are heavy. They are carrying her. They can't have gotten far. Let's keep going."

The two men kicked their horses into a canter, still following the tracks. Aiden wasn't able to give him much information, but these tracks gave them plenty. He felt certain they would find Ella.

It took only a few minutes to dash his hopes, as the tracks ended abruptly at the creek. Jackson looked up and scanned the creek up and down. "Reckon they had transportation, or do you think they are following the creek? If they followed the creek, it would be a guess as to the direction. They may have had a boat or something here. Maybe somebody was waiting."

"If they have hurt one hair on her head, I will tear them limb from limb." Jackson bit out the words, his pent-up emotion spilling out.

Marshall touched his friend's shoulder. "We need more help. I'm going back to get some more men."

His shoulders dropped. He worried that waiting more time could mean Ella might be hurt badly, but Marshall was right. If these were the same men that had been hitting the area, they were dangerous. There appeared to be three; they would be outnumbered. He wanted better odds with Ella's life hanging in the balance.

Marshall looked over at his friend. "We will find her, Jackson. I promise. You let Lizzy and Carter know what is going on. I'll pull together a tracking party and meet you in ten minutes." Marshall rode toward the tents. Jackson rode to the house, his heart full of dread.

It was wartime and Jackson had fought many battles. But the fear he felt now was different—worse. He dismounted and ran up the front steps. "Lizzy! Where are you? Come quick." The screened door slammed behind him.

"Suh, what is it? You got Miss Ella?" Lizzy looked behind him and then locked onto his face. "You don't have her," she intoned. Tears welled up in her eyes. "What's happened to Miss Ella?"

"I don't know, Lizzy, but we will find her. Marshall is getting a tracking party. We found blood. I need to speak to Aiden again. I have questions to ask him about the men he saw. Their tracks led to more tracks."

Aiden heard his name and came running into the room. "Did you find my sista? Ella!" Seeing only Jackson, he stopped. All hope disappeared from his face.

"No, Aiden. But I promise I'm going to find her. Try not to worry, son. I need to ask some questions, and what you say will be very important. It could help find Ella." He blew out a large breath, trying to calm himself down so that he could focus and ask without getting Aiden any more upset. The child was still crying. She was his mamma, even if she was his sister. The thought slammed into him. "Tell me. Tell me everything you can remember."

Aiden nodded. "Bo and me were playing Pirates. Then, they snuck up on us. There were three of them." He held up three fingers, struggling to hold his thumb and pinky down. "They were the pirates. And Colonel Ross, they hurt my sista." Red-rimmed eyes looked up at Jackson.

Jackson's heart twisted. "Can you describe them to me?"

"They were dark people, like Lizzy and Carter and Cook. But one man wasn't black. He was white." Aiden clasped his little hands together. "I remember. Bo and I, we knew that white man." A cry tore from his lips as he told who it was. "It was Jason, the man that lives yonder." He pointed towards the fields. "He lives out there with our people." Aiden sniffed, trying to catch his breath. "They hurt my sista, and Jason, he tried to kill Bo. But I saved Bo."

"Tell me what you remember."

"They tried to grab me. Jason grabbed me and slapped me when I screamed, but Bo bit him and we got away." He stopped crying and continued to tell Jackson everything he could remember.

"Did Jason say anything?" Jason was the overseer. Ella had mentioned not being comfortable with him. A chill went down his spine when he recalled what she had said, and how the man was none too friendly with him. "Did any of them say anything?" Jackson talked slowly and emphasized his words.

"Before I got away, the man said that they gonna kill my sista if I didn't calm down and stop crying." He hiccupped. "But then she was looking for me, and one of the men came up behind her and hit her on her head with a rock or something. Ella fell down. She was dead!" Aiden started crying uncontrollably.

Jackson picked him up and hugged the little boy to his chest, trying to calm him. Rage blinded him. She couldn't be dead. He needed to find Ella quickly. Her life could be in danger, and if these were the men that had been raiding the area this past month, she may only have a short time before they did kill her. Several innocent people in the area, families, had been attacked and some had been brutalized.

No, he couldn't let his mind think on that.

Aiden was a little calmer, so he set him down and nudged him slightly in Lizzy's direction. "Lizzy, Carter. I need you to tell me all you know about this Jason character," he implored.

The two looked up at Jackson, worry evident on their faces. Lizzy pulled the little boy to her skirt, gripping her small charge by his shoulders.

Carter spoke first. "Yassuh. Jason, he was hired before Massa Nole left. He tol' us he come up from Naw'leans. His folks back there, he always said. The folks in de fields, they talk about him. Say he has a mean streak. But they clam up when I asks about it. Jason talks about find'n a wife and leave'n. But he don't say who. Miss Ella, she stop riding with him. He right mad 'bout that." Tears streamed down the man's face. Carter wiped his face with his sleeve. "You find our Ella, now, hear me? She be like a little sister to me. I know I not her brother but we, Lizzy and me, we been here to see her grow up into a fine, fine young woman. And Miss Ella, she got a good heart." Carter's voice cracked with emotion. "Please find her, Colonel Ross, suh."

Carter knew about her fear of Jason by observing, *and I didn't do enough when she told me. I should have taken it all more seriously and acted on my own concerns and observations.* "I will do my best. I promise."

This seemed bigger than renegades ransacking properties and wreaking havoc in the area. This was kidnapping. "Carter, have you seen or heard anything else about Jason's activities that might be important to know?"

"No suh, he just a mean man. Don't look you in the eye—that kind of man. He beat a young boy here, near to death."

Could Jason be the ringleader? "He was with two or possibly three men—they were probably slaves that he was working with, but from where? And why take Ella?" A cold shiver ran down his back. Had Jason planned to take her away with him?

"They be so many slaves done runaway from all parts, Colonel. I got no idea who dey could be."

Confound it! What am I missing? The two men his posse tried to capture earlier in the week weren't slaves. They were white. The posse shot them before the men could be questioned.

He hoped the death of those two men would end the plundering and violence. The two appeared to be alone...but could they have been part of a bigger band? A farm was hit a couple of days ago.

"Aiden, Marshall will be here any moment." He picked up and hugged the little boy once more, giving him an extra squeeze before putting him down. "Your sister will be home soon." His chest seized. *She has to.*

"Massa Aiden, you come with me. We need to clean you up." Wadding up a corner of her skirt, Lizzy wiped the smudges from his face. "Let's stop by the kitchen and get something from Cook." She lifted her nose and sniffed. "Mmm. Can you just smell that? That's Cook's fine fried chicken and mashed potatoes—and I know you love fried chicken! What you think 'bout that, Aiden? Hmmm?" She smiled at him and squeezed his hand. "Come on now, boy. We'll find something good for your doggie, too." Nodding to Jackson and Carter, she pulled Aiden with her. The two of them headed for the kitchen. Bo trotted behind.

Marshall should be back here with the men any moment. Jackson grabbed his rifle and hat. They would need horses, plus an extra one or two to bring back the men. Maybe a wagon would be better.

He met Marshall at the barn. His gut was churning. They needed to find these men before they got too far—before they hurt Ella.

I care for her, perhaps more than anyone before her. He didn't deny it. His heart was affected.

CHAPTER 17

Her head throbbed, and her throat was parched. She wanted to reach up and feel her temple, but her instincts told her to stay quiet.

She could hear voices of several men around her. Her name was mentioned. How did they know who she was? Where was she? Who were these men? Where was Aiden…was he safe?

She felt her eyes well up and struggled to hold back the tears. Her head hurt. She tried to look through her lashes without opening her eyes but a crack, hoping she could figure out where she was. If she were lucky, no one would look her way. She saw men's backs, and things were blurry. She eased her eyes closed and tried to keep her breathing low and even.

Ella stayed that way until the men's voices sounded muffled. Her spine stiffened with fear at one voice. She'd know it anywhere. Opening her eyes slightly, she confirmed her fear. *Jason!*

He was here with two male slaves she didn't recognize. All three had bloodstained clothing. And they smelled—*blech*! The stench wafted across the room. She tried not to gag at the gamey odor. Ella hated foul smells.

Jason was barking orders. He was furious and the other two looked nervous . Cold fear ran through her, and she trembled. He terrified her and now she was at his mercy. She wished Nolan and Jackson—if even just *one* of them, had taken her fear of the man seriously. Nolan had dismissed him as harmless. Jackson had expressed concern about him, but hadn't felt he posed a real danger to her.

A clutch of panic hit the pit of her stomach. *Get it together, Ella Grace. Calm down and think.* She slowed her breathing down and focused on stopping the trembling. She had to let him keep thinking she was unconscious.

While her hands were bound, she noticed she still had some freedom within the bonds. Did she still have her gun? She always strapped it on her thigh. Had she lost it, or was it still on her? If they turned, she could move a little and find out. She couldn't tell if it was in the holster.

Suddenly Jason drove his fist into one of the men's faces. She heard the crunch and then swearing from the two runaways. Smothering her gasp, she remained still and acted asleep.

"I should kill you." She knew him. He had a look that could terrify a person when he yelled. No one else she knew made her feel uncomfortable like he did. It was a menacing look and she could imagine he wore that look on his face now. "Why did you hurt her? I told you not to harm her in any way!" Jason unleashed his temper on his accomplices.

"Massa Jason, she walked up on us and had a weapon. We had no choice. Don't hit me, Massa."

Jason reached over and snatched up Aiden's stick. He laughed. "You call this stick a weapon?" Jason slung the stick, not caring where it went. His voice mocked them.

Something landed next to her feet. *The stick...that's Aiden's pirate sword.* He and Bo...she tried to remember...Bo barked at her, and then everything went dark. She prayed they were safe. They had to be. I have to get away. Her hands were going numb from the position they were in; they felt cold. She needed to shift her body, somehow.

Slowly, she moved her hand to feel her thigh. Good! The gun was still there. They had not found it. She grimaced against the pain. Jason had no idea she could shoot, but he was fixin' to find out.

The men's voices were getting closer. Ella closed her eyes and relaxed, determined to appear still out of it.

"Massa Jason, we best get moving. Dis here cabin, well, it's too close to da middle of da swamp. The big witch woman lives out here and she watches the family. And it's still on her property, you know," he said, nodding at Ella. "If we get caught, we won't be able to run. We be stuck right here, and I don't want to meet my Maker in this here cabin. That army man we seen there will be looking for her. He'll have dem army men hot on our trail. Dey so many of dem." The shorter man's voice exposed his fear.

"Shut up, damn it! I need to figure out what to do. I'm thinking." She hated Jason's voice. His thick Creole accent repulsed and terrified her.

Ella didn't have to work hard to keep her eyes closed. Her head throbbed. She focused on staying alert.

Her head hurt, and she wanted to sleep, so she focused on the voices, listening. Did they mean *her property*?

"Damn! She has blood on the back of her head. I certainly cannot go into town after Doc." Jason's fist slammed the table near the fireplace. "I should kill you! Find someone who can help her."

The arguing got louder, and Jason swore words she didn't understand. No doubt it was more Creole.

Would anyone know what had happened to her? She didn't know how much information Aiden could give…and to whom? Who would come for her? Her head hurt so much. It was hard to focus on anything. So tired. Her fists relaxed as darkness claimed her once again.

*J*ackson and his men were barely out of view when Lizzy called for Carter. He came running. "Carter, we got to help Miss Ella. We both know what our little man told the colonel. He says they was two stranger slaves and Jason. That doesn't make sense. Do it?"

Carter sat down at the news.

"Carter. What you know? You betta tell me."

Miss Ella had always been his favorite in this house. Now, she was hurt and gone.

"Lizzy, I does know sump'um but I cannot think what it is. It's something that I heard from Jason. 'Bout a month back, I brung some food to the field hands. Jason showed up and yelled. He took a whip and beat a young boy near to death. But it was what he said that I can't remember. And I think it is important." Carter's head was down, and he tried to focus.

"Carter, she our family. You should have tol' her. You never even said nothing to me. Miss Ella needed to know this."

"I not say anything 'bout the beating because he told me it be his word 'against mine, but I see him beat dat young boy. He near killed him over a scrap of food. I know how Miss Ella feels 'bout her people. She wants to give her people a home, but he be the Devil. The ones dat left, dey run because of him."

Carter put his head in his hands, "I been notice'n him round Miss Ella. I don't like the way he looks at her. He mentioned something 'bout a place…he called it *his place*," Despairing and wringing his hands tightly—Carter tried to recall more details about that afternoon. Jason hitting the boy was a scary thing, too. "I can't recall what more he said, 'bout his place."

"I know what we need to do, Carter. Massa Nolan, he got to be 'tol. Keep an eye on the little massa while I go tell him."

Lizzy was out of the door before he could respond. Carter checked Aiden's room. The littlest Whitford and his dog were curled up on the bed in front of the fireplace. It was still cold, even though it was spring. Carter rubbed his chin as he watched them. He wouldn't let anything happen to Aiden and his puppy, not on his life.

It was good that Aiden was able to sleep. He looked so much like his older brother when he was asleep. He could remember Nolan at that age clearly and couldn't help taking a moment to think about those happy memories.

"I hope you be dreaming sump'um good, boy." Carter gently closed the door and went downstairs to find Cook.

※

Lizzy took her time. Making sure no one saw her, she opened the pantry door and stepped in. Closing it behind her, she moved to the back of the closet and pressed the wallboard in the upper corner. The wall opened slowly and she moved into the stairwell, closing the door behind her. The kitchen entry had been used a lot. There was no dust. Probably Carter and Ol' Indie.

Knocking lightly on the inside wall to alert Massa Nolan she was coming, she made her way into the safe room. "Hello…Massa Nolan…Miss Sara…I'm coming down. I need to talk to you, Massa Nolan. It's very important." Lizzy hoped that she was doing the right thing, though she wondered what he could do to help.

Two whispering voices sounded rushed. There was rustling. She waited a minute then made her presence known. "Massa Nolan, yo sister is gone, and the colonel and his men have gone to find her."

"Gone? What?" Nolan and Sara rushed to the back stairwell at her words. "What do you mean, my sister is gone?" Nolan thundered.

"She been afraid of that man, and now he—that no-count Jason—he took her. Carter, he witnessed bad stuff from that man. He and two slaves hurt your sister in front of Massa Aiden. They tried to grab Aiden, but he got away, he and Bo. You don't worry 'bout them. But Miss Ella, she was taken."

※

Terror filled him and he looked around for his weapons. "I have to help find her."

"Now how you s'posed to do that—you being wanted yo-self? I just needed to tell you. You needed to know. The colonel and his men, they gone after the men that took her. They will bring her back."

"I cannot just sit here. That no good Jason!" Anguished, he recalled an earlier conversation with Ella. "She was trying to tell me something about Jason, and I cut her off. If I had only given what she was trying to tell me a chance. I should have listened to her."

"Nolan, you can't go." Sara pleaded with him. "You could be caught. The colonel is a smart man. He will find our Ella. He will bring her back to us."

"Sara. This is Ella we are talking about here. I have to find her. I promise I will come back to you. But I have to find her." Images of his sister wiping his brow and nursing him through the fever flashed through his mind. "She risked her own life to care for me. I will find Jason and if he hurt my sister, he will be a dead man." He meant that. He needed to know as much as he could. No way did he want to get caught, but he would give his own life for his sister. He wasn't staying here while she was in danger.

Nolan took a deep breath, trying to calm himself. "Lizzy, thank you for telling me. Aiden is okay?"

She nodded.

"Is Carter here? I need to see him."

"Yassuh. He is. I'll send him to you, but you will want to know the rest." Distress was evident in her voice as Lizzy continued to relate all that she knew. "Oh, Massa Nolan, there is one thing you need to know. The colonel added another guard to the house, here. They are now watching the front and the back of the house. He is very protective of Miss Ella and Aiden." With that, Lizzy left to find Carter.

He looked for Sara and saw her sitting on the cot, her arms wrapped around her legs, drawn up under her neck. There was so much he wanted to say to her. What if he was captured and never got to tell her? He went over to her and dropped to his knees. "Sara, look at me."

With the tip of his finger, he nudged her chin up and kissed her. "You understand, don't you? I have to help. I could never live with myself if I didn't try to find my sister."

"We are both lucky to have you, Nolan Whitford." Wiping tears, she smiled up at him. "I'm gonna be here when you get back."

"I love you, Sara." He started to say more just in case he got captured. But he wiped that thought away. He would be back, and he would see his sister home. He needed to get to his daddy's guns, and he hoped they were still where he left them.

It wasn't long before she heard Carter coming back to the kitchen. Lizzy was sitting at the table, waiting for him. His face looked grim. Cook had taken some scraps to the pigs and was out of the room when Carter returned. Lizzy needed to talk to him about being careful when he came in that pantry door. She also wanted to hear what he and Nolan had discussed.

"I remembered something—Jason said he had a place. He called it *'de cabin.'* Do that make any sense to you?" He looked towards Lizzy. His hands clenched into fists by his side. "I let Massa Nolan know about it."

The pantry door slammed open and Sara appeared, breathless from taking the steps so quickly. "Nolan took off to look for Ella. I couldn't stop him. Took one of his daddy's guns. The posted guard walked around the corner of the house, and he left in the other direction." Fear colored her voice as she wrapped her arms around her middle.

Carter jumped up and helped Sara to a chair.

"Miss Sara, you know he had to find his sister. Those two are closer than most." Lizzy thought of Nolan and his antics when they were all growing up, and it made her smile. She and Carter were slightly older than Ella and Nolan, and the four had known each other most of their lives. "Massa Nolan will be back. Can I get something for you to do to take your mind off things? I know how you feel about this family. My mamma always 'tol me that when you can't do nothing more to change a bad thing that's happening, find something to occupy your mind. Would you like to work on a sampler? You know Miss Ella has never been able to finish one." Lizzy tried to laugh.

"Yes, she was always more interested in riding and doing things with her daddy." Sara laughed and wiped at her tears.

"You are right there! She'd come in from the fields with her daddy and her dress be torn. The missus tried to change that, but she quit when she seen how happy Miss Ella was running around with her daddy and then, Nolan. She told me she figured Ella would find her a special husband one day—one that could do his own stitching." Her voice weakened with a slight tremor, as she continued. "But her mamma also knew Miss Ella could do anything she set her mind to do. The missus adored her beautiful girl. They adored each other."

"Well, I guess I could pick up one of Ella's samplers. Yes, that would help. Your mother was a wise woman, Lizzy. I will do it. Wait. Ella said she has a dress she has already cut out. I'll work on that. You are right. I need something to stop putting this wrinkle of worry on my forehead. Ella will wear her old dresses until they disintegrate on her before she will start another one." She gently touched Lizzy's hand.

"I'll go get it. She cut one or two dresses out, but Miss Ella never worked any more on them. Shoved them in her closet. She doesn't know, but I've been working on one in my spare time." Lizzy reached into the closet and after rustling around pulled out a large brown package.

"Well, then. It'll give us both something to do to keep our minds off this mess we are in here. We can't do anything until we know more. I'll meet you in the parlor." Sara accepted the package from Lizzy and picked up her basket.

Nodding at Sara and Carter, Lizzy left to retrieve the stack of mending that needed attention.

Carter and Sara walked past the library, and Sara stopped and looked inside. The gun cabinet was still ajar. "Carter, can you help me fix this so no one notices the gun missing?" The two moved the remaining items around, and Carter took the key and put it back in the desk drawer.

"Reckon we should get on to the parlor, Miss Sara."

Sara glanced back at the gun cabinet. "Oh Nolan, do be careful," she said, softly, before the library door clicked shut behind her.

CHAPTER 18

Ella awoke slowly and found she was lying in the middle of the same bed where she had been earlier. She tried moving her arms a little, just to get the blood moving. The covers underneath her felt gritty.

Oh! Was that something crawling? A spider?

A cold chill went through her and her body jerked. She was deathly afraid of spiders. She wanted to look, needed to look, but how? Her arms were going numb from their bindings. They had not been tied so securely earlier, but they felt much tighter now. At least they were in front of her. Small consolation, but she'd take it.

The sun had long since gone down, leaving the room chilled. She heard no sound in the room so she chanced to open her eyes and look around. It was dark, but after a minute, her eyes adjusted to the darkness. She could see the door and an old fireplace on the far wall. The fire had burned out long ago.

The bed smelled bad. No, it *stunk*. There was no telling what prizes it was bestowing on her hostage body. The thought of bedbugs—or any bug, sent a shudder through her. Something moved across her forehead--it had to be a spider. She rubbed her bound hands over her forehead as panic gripped her. Sweat soaked the back of her dress, and she fought to stay in control, aware her life might depend on being alert. Ella closed her eyes and took slow, even breaths.

Stay calm. Inhale. Exhale.

Turning her head, Ella noticed a window with a broken pane. *Glass, or even the pane, might cut the ropes off. I have to get to the window.*

How much time did she have? They mentioned finding someone to tend her wounds. How long could that take? And who would that be?

Ella listened to the footsteps and sounds outside the room. She recognized Jason. He sounded angry and loud. Another man sounded nervous. The door opened, slamming against the wall.

"Gunner, I will kill you if she doesn't wake up." Still raging, Jason stood over her. Ella willed her breathing as shallow as possible, feigning sleep. Angry she had not awakened, he huffed and stormed out the door, banging it shut behind him.

The door opened again, and another man entered. She dare not open her eyes, even a hair. She tried not to react to noises, but that last slam frightened her and she almost gave herself away.

Ella heard his heavy breathing. *Was this Gunner?* He stood over her. She smelled him--his foul breath on her face and his dirty body assaulted her senses. He touched her face, smoothing her hair back, behind her ears.

"I didn't mean to hurt you bad." He harrumphed. "I know you isn't dead, but dat crazy man might make you wish it." He said nothing else and left the room. She recognized him as the nervous one.

She took a deep breath when the door crashed opened again. Jason. "You are a beauty." His Creole voice sickened her. Ella struggled to breathe out slowly. She wanted to kick, yell, fight…anything but lie still. But she knew better.

Her captor touched her lips. His clumsy and heavy hand moved down the front of her dress. Shame threatened to burn her up. She tried to forget what he was doing to her.

He thinks I'm still passed out. Stay calm. She could feel her heart pulse in her throat. *My gun is strapped to the other leg. Please God, don't let me have one of my attacks right now.*

Ella paid close attention to her breathing, keeping it slow and even. Trying not to cry or let him know she was awake was so hard. He stood over her prone form, lifting her dress enough to touch her inner thigh.

"Damn dark room. I want to see your body. All those days wanting to touch you. You can't move away now."

His sweaty smell was pungent. She knew that odor from riding into town close to him. It was hard to remain still when her nose needed immediate attention. She normally turned her head and covered her nose to avoid the stench, but he had her at a disadvantage this time.

God, please give me the strength to stay still and help me get away. Don't let him see my gun...

His hands were all over her. He was touching her breasts. What was he going to do?

Oh, God. What do I do?

She lay perfectly still. *Think of Jackson...his smile, his smell...so clean and wonderful.* Would he know she was missing? Rage replaced fear. She wanted to slap Jason. How dare he abduct her! How dare he touch her!

If my brother finds out...if...I can just reach...

Ella strained but still couldn't reach her gun. It was impossible without a free hand.

The bottom of her dress moved up again; he was looking at her. His hand inched up her inner leg. Her skin reacted to her fright, breaking out in goosebumps to what he planned.

If he doesn't stop he will discover—</p>

The front door to the cabin opened and slammed shut.

"What are you two stupid men doing?" Jason shouted profanity in his native Creole at his partners and jerked her dress went down. She opened her eyes to see him leave, slamming the door closed behind him.

Bound or not, she had to escape. Jason would not leave her alone. She got up and went to the windowpane she had seen earlier. Jason's shouts rose above the ruckus in the front room. She hurried back to the bed and tried to lie down, closing her eyes just enough to still see beneath her lashes.

"You bring her out of the sleep. You hear me, old woman? Make her well. Your life depends on it." Jason pushed the door open and shoved Ol' Indie inside and followed her.

Ol' Indie watched Ella for a moment. Them reaching into her bag, she pulled out a small white jar of salve. "You men, you get outta here while I min'ster to de lady. Or you find someone else."

"Don't threaten me, *sorcière*. Wake her up. Now!" Jason pulled out a knife and jabbed the tip to the woman's ribs. A trickle of blood stained the front of Ol' Indie's dress.

"You can threaten Ol' Indie, but I need to be afeard you to be skeered. And, I ain't skeered of you. I ain't doing nothing 'til you leave the room. Kill me now or get out." Ol' Indie held her ground, her eyes never leaving him.

"You think you need privacy? She's out cold. She ain't going anywhere." Jason jeered at her.

"I am not afraid of you, Mista Overseer." Ol' Indie starred at Jason, saying her words slowly. "I know you been sniffing after des here girl. I seen you. But she be out and be injured bad. If 'n you want me to care for her, you will leave da room." Ol' Indie's fingers were behind her, fumbling in her skirts for something.

"Fine. Five minutes. Do what you need to do. We will be right here. Try anything funny, and I will kill you both." Jason looked at his pocket watch. Satisfied that he knew the time, he nodded to the short black man, and the two of them left Ella and Ol' Indie alone.

The door closed.

"I know you be awake, Miss Ella." She lowered her voice to a soft whisper. "I see your eyes move. Girl, they gonna hurt both us if I can't get dat cut on your head fixed right. That man, he a Devil man." Ol' Indie shook her head sympathetically as she looked at Ella.

"Where are we?" She tried to sit up and rub her head. "I hurt so bad, and my hands…" Ella wanted to cry, but choked out the words to Ol' Indie's sympathetic ears.

Ol' Indie soothed as she talked, rubbing circles on her arms. "Mista

Jason done stirred up a hornet with da colonel. Why your colonel is on his way with lots of men. They gonna find us. We just need to stay alive, you hear?" She rubbed Ella's cold hands.

"Does Nolan know I'm gone?"

"You been missing a whole day, Miss Ella. De men—dey *all* looking for you."

"Not…not Nolan. He can't show himself. He will be arrested."

Ol' Indie gently pushed Ella's head forward and examined the back. "He is okay. Don't you worry about Massa Nole." She harrumphed and moved her hands gently around Ella's scalp. "Miss Ella, you got a powerful knot back here. Chile, you gonna have a bad headache. We need to keep you awake. Been practicing my cures long enough to know if you hit yo head like this, you betta not lie down to sleep. I know you just woke up." She took a deep breath. "My heart 'bout broke in two when I see my baby lying here." She soothed Ella on the arm. "But then, I sees your eyes flutter a little…just a little…and I knows you was awake."

Reaching into her pocket, Ol' Indie withdrew a jar of something. She opened it up and dabbed her hand inside, withdrawing some of the foulest smelling stuff. "I'm gonna put this on the big cut on the back of your head, Miss Ella. Be still. It could sting a little, but it will help. Your head been bleeding, and I want to make sure this cut don't get any worse. Heads bleed bad with a little cut. You are lucky it ain't no bigger. I know it hurts."

"Ol' Indie, did you see where they have us? I recognize none of this. Pew! Why is it that everything I come into contact with in this room stinks? My nose wants to cry." Ella started at Ol' Indie's blood-stained dress. "You are hurt!"

Ol' Indie sniggered. "It's gonna take more than a little cut to hurt Indie. And I got them thinking I do Black magic. Maybe that could help us."

"But you never do magic anymore. And besides, it was always good magic. I will admit though; a little disappearing spell would be good about now." Ella smiled at her old nurse.

"The tall black'un they call Hokum, he tried to blindfold me.

Grabbed me when I was heading back to de house to see your brother. He wasn't good at putting on an old blindfold. Reckon I'm too scary for him." Indie tittered. "I 'tol him I'd set a spell on him if he touched me. He grabbed me and then hurried and tied me up and let me go." She cackled. "Den, he told me it wasn't his idea to snatch me. I thought your disappearance and him getting me might be connected, so I came to be here with you."

The old woman paused and motioned towards the door. "Des here cabin is on the property just outside your Papa's land. It's near de marsh at the back of de properties."

Ella could not recall a cabin at the back of the adjoining property. Her head pounded in pain, making it hard to think. She knew the land. She and Nolan used to ride horses and had been everywhere, but she struggled to remember a cabin.

Ella was eager for more information. "Who lived in this old cabin, Ol' Indie?" Ella shivered. "I declare, this bed is full of bugs. I hope you got something to get those bugs off us. It's just awful. I had something crawling on me. And Jason, he put his hands under my clothes—all over me." She flushed.

"Oh, Colonel Ross, he not gonna take kindly to anyone touching you." She shushed her charge and tried to soothe her. "Dis here property, I think it's the overseer's hut off the next-door property. The Brices, your neighbors, dey didn't do right by people. Dey had slaves, but Mista Brice, he was mean and nasty to them. He even kilt some, but tortured them, first. These two -- I recognize them. They are from de Brice plantation."

She paused a moment. "Massa Brice must have been real bad to dem for they to be working for de likes of Mista Jason." She drawled the last words out slowly as if lost in thought.

"Anyways, I dropped some stuff on the way here—until we meet up with an old wagon. Hokum didn't see me. I'm hoping dat Mista Jackson sees what I dropped. He surely will find us."

~

The two women sat alone in the room for what seemed like a long time when Ella remembered the broken window. The panes were gone. It was their chance. " Ol' Indie, help me to the window."

"Miss Ella, he said five minutes. He'll be back."

"We must be quick then."

Ella placed her binding over a jagged edge of glass and sawed. She felt the rope give way. One loop and then the other fell off.

Suddenly free, she reached under her dress and grabbed her gun, placing it in her pocket. Taking a log from the fireplace, she cleared the rest of the broken glass, while there was noise out front. "Come on. Let's go before they come back."

Ol' Indie stepped behind Ella, but her focus was on the door. She mumbled a prayer as the two worked to escape.

The window was a little high, but Ella grabbed a chair. She stepped up and hoisted herself onto the broken pane's ledge and looked down. A large prickly bush stood between them and freedom. Looking around, she spotted a man standing off to the side.

Damn!

It was Nolan.

Oh my God! My brother came to help me.

As joyful as she was to see Nolan, she wished it was Jackson. She immediately felt guilty. Nolan made a huge sacrifice coming for her.

"Come on, Ol' Indie."

"Lordy, I don't know if I can…"

"I'll help you. She helped Indie put her legs over the outside ledge and then pulled herself up next to her. They were almost out the window when the door opened, and Jason thundered back into the room.

"Five minutes is up! You are awake, I see."

Desperate, Ella tried to nudge Ol' Indie into a jump from the window.

Jason jerked the old woman from the window and slammed her on the floor, out of the way. He grabbed Ella before she could jump, pulling her back towards him. She saw Nolan move towards her, but Jason's arms were too strong. He tore her dress dragging her across broken glass. Pain shot through her as jagged glass raked her back.

Ella saw Ol' Indie's still form and blood coming from her head. *She wasn't moving.*

"You killed her!" Rage won. She reached into her pocket and grabbed her gun. She had one chance. With her pocket still covering it, she pulled the trigger and a shot went off, hitting Jason's foot. "Damn it. Why didn't I aim higher?"

Startled, Jason stared at her and down at his foot, the blood oozing all over.

Jason's look of fury registered too late. "You bitch!" He slammed his fist into her face, and she fell backward to the floor.

Two shots rang out in the front of the cabin. Ella struggled to hold on. She heard something heavy fall.

Footsteps thundered towards them.

Jason grabbed her up and placed a knife at her throat. Slowly, he backed towards the window, keeping her nearly limp form in front of him. "Stupid woman. You better not move. I'll kill you." His voice was low in her ear and his breath was hot.

The door burst open. "Jackson," she whispered, her eyes wide with fright.

"Drop it, Jason, and lower her…slowly."

He *had* come for her! But where was her brother?

Jason pressed his knife into her throat. A small stream of blood oozed down her neck. *He cut me!*

The overseer yelled back and forth in English and in his native Creole. "Mister Colonel…you can just back out or this knife will slice her throat and there will be no soft, lovely Miss Ella." He kept screaming orders, but quickly his words lapsed into rapid Creole.

Ella fought to stay awake, but the room had turned into a swirling picture of which she no longer felt part. Her body felt heavy and her vision narrowed.

Jackson pushed forward. "Let her loose and move away or I will shoot you where you stand." Jackson aimed his gun at Jason's head. His forefinger covered the trigger.

"No! I assure you that your bullet will go into her first, should you be foolish enough to shoot. And I will finish the job with my knife." He sneered. "I have the upper hand, as you see."

"Let her go. Your two accomplices can no longer help you. One is dead. The other is tied up. My men have surrounded this cabin. You will not make it out alive. Should you hurt her, I will delight in ripping you apart, limb from limb, and cutting out your organs for the buzzards—all before I free you to go to your maker."

Jackson never stopped advancing. He moved slowly and seemed to be looking behind her.

Her heart pounded in her throat. She could not think with a knife to her neck. *My gun...*

Moving her free hand into her pocket, she grasped the handle of her weapon. *He forgot to take it. There might be one shot left.*

"She will never be yours, Colonel Yankee. She is mine. I intend to keep her." Jason reverted to Creole again, his voice raising and lowering, as if in a conversation with himself.

Ella couldn't understand a word, but she recognized he was losing control. That, and her arms were going numb. How could this work? She wasn't sure she could fire her gun again and live. He would kill her, even knowing he would die as a result.

Trembling, she worked her gun into her hand. Ella thought hard. She had to do something. Squeezing her eyes, she found the trigger and—

BANG!

A shot rang out from behind her. Jason crumpled, pulling her to the ground with him. She never fired her gun.

Nolan.

"What the hell?" Jackson raced towards her, kicking Jason's knife away. "My men were waiting for my order, so they didn't..." He rolled Jason over with his boot. Blood poured from his head. "He's dead."

Ella succumbed to her panic and fainted.

She heard Jackson talking to her in the tunnel. "I know you are in there, Ella. Can you hear me, my darling? Open your eyes. Yell at me… anything. Just please look at me."

She tried to get to him. Slowly, her eyes fluttered open. Blood ran down her neck and over her shoulder. Ella tried to feel pain from where the bullet must have struck her. Her body was playing tricks. She could feel only the pain from the glass in her back. Were those cuts responsible for all of this blood? Was she…no, she couldn't be dead. She could smell the fresh air that must have come in with Jackson and his men.

Jason's face stared up at her, sneering. Even in death, he frightened her.

She recalled the soft voice that pleaded her name only moments ago. "Did…did you call me darling?" Ella whispered. She reached up and her trembling hand touched Jackson's face.

A smile edged his mouth in answer. Lifting her chin, he drew her close and kissed her sending a tiny tremor running through her. She laid her head on his shoulder and took full advantage of his warm breath whispering soft words of endearment on her neck. She felt safe, finally.

Heavy footsteps announced Marshall's arrival. He pushed Nolan into the room, one hand gripping his collar, the other pointing a gun into his back.

"Found this one lurking outside, Jackson. He fired the gun. We were waiting for your order."

Jackson glanced up. "Private White," he uttered in a whisper.

Ella pushed away with remarkable force. "Nolan! Oh my God, it's Nolan. Let go of my brother! Can't you see he isn't a threat to you?"

She strode to Nolan, slapping Marshall's gun away. "Get that gun out of my brother's back. He is my *brother*." Anguished, she turned to Jackson, her face streaming tears.

"Marshall, we don't need that. He's not going anywhere. Put your gun down."

"Colonel…" Marshall nodded at Jackson and holstered his gun.

Undeterred by Marshall's grip on her brother, Ella clung to Nolan and buried her face in his chest, crying. "Nolan, it was awful. Jason killed Ol' Indie. We tried to escape but he caught us and slammed her into the wall." Her chest heaved with sobs.

"Shhhh. My brave little sister, look! He didn't kill her, Ella."

Ella lifted her head. "But I saw her hit the wall, her head had blood…"

The old woman stirred. She rustled around and pushed herself up into a sitting position. "Now there. You both know it takes more than a wisp of a man to kill Ol' Indie." Using her hand, she winced at the pain as she wiped the blood from her face.

"Marshall, it's true. This one—" Jackson nodded at Jason's lifeless body "—held a knife ready to slit Ella's throat."

He pushed Jason's body with his booted foot. "Just checking. Habit. He's gone." He moved over to Ol' Indie and helped her up.

CHAPTER 19

*J*ackson watched the sister and brother. He didn't miss the lack of surprise he thought should have been there for two people who haven't seen each other for over a year. He debated whether to mention his recognition of Private White. Sweat collected over his brow.

Not an easy decision. To give this information could cause a lot of trouble. If he arrested Nolan, the arrest would be in front of his sister. That would be the first bad move. He struggled to read Ella's face. She seemed in shock— understandable. This had been traumatic. Jackson exhaled, releasing a calming breath. He rotated his shoulders, releasing the buildup of his own tension. *Any longer and Ella could have been...*

He forced the thought from his mind.

Where had this man been hiding? He noticed the clean clothes and the absence of facial hair that should have been there by now. Something else was going on here, something he could not quite figure out yet. He stayed quiet about the identity right now. She would hate him if he carried out his orders in front of her. Did Marshall recognize him?

Nolan's reckless nature won out, and he pushed himself out of Marshall's grip. Marshall pulled his gun.

"Allow me to calm my sister without a gun in my back." Turning slowly, Nolan looked Jackson in the eye, defiant, and then glared at Marshall. "As you can see, I'm not the enemy."

"You may." Jackson returned in an even tone. He stepped aside, ignoring Nolan's unrestrained challenge, and allowed the two to have time together.

Disregarding the other two men, Nolan gently pulled his sister nearer, holding her shoulders. "Your neck is cut."

She put a hand to her throat. "His knife nicked my neck."

"I saw him pull you both away from the window. I was so worried, Ella." He squeezed her shoulders affectionately. "You may not believe this…Bo led me here." He nodded his head towards the window. "He's a good dog. Our little brother has a smart companion." He snickered. "The pup is a natural tracker, but I hold little hope you will allow him to hunt, considering what happened to Rover when we were younger."

Nolan whistled, and a yellow flash of fur bounded into the room.

"Bo!" Ella bent down and held out her arms. The puppy jumped on Ella, nuzzling her and giving her kisses.

Self-conscious, she grabbed the torn shoulder of her dress and pulled it up, covering her exposed skin. The movement caused her to wince. "My back, it hurts. I think I may have a bad cut from the window."

"I have sump'um for that." Ol' Indie reached into her pocket and pulled out a small brown jar of salve. "I always have some ointments with me." She handed it to Nolan.

"Let's get you home, Ella. We can sort all of this out." Jackson moved out from behind Nolan, retaking charge.

Nolan pocketed the salve for later.

"Marshall, please help Ol' Indie stand. Have the men come and pick up this body and put it with the other. Bring the one still alive and lock him up tight. We need to find out if there are others." Jackson acknowledged Nolan with a curt nod.

Nolan stepped aside as Jackson moved to comfort Ella. He took his jacket off and draped it around her shoulders.

~

A tinge of elation hit her body when Jackson put his jacket over her shoulders. She realized that the animosity she once felt had faded. However, this was not a happy circumstance. Not with Nolan. Somehow, she would make sure her brother didn't get punished. She wasn't certain how or knew all his sins, but she had to try.

Ella nibbled her bottom lip. She hadn't wanted to hurt Nolan, but she couldn't help her reaction to Jackson. It made her happy to be around him, this same man that had once made her beyond furious. She still hated the damn Yankees, but…well…not this one.

Good grief! How did that happen?

Her thoughts struggled only a moment before Jackson gently directed her arms through the sleeves of his uniform jacket. It felt warm from him. She snugged the jacket around her front, covering up her torn dress, and put her arms around his neck to hold on as he lifted her.

"Wait, Ella, that would not be proper." Her brother pushed past Jackson, who stepped aside. "I will carry my sister." Nolan picked her up and carried her outside. Ella gave no objection. She needed to maintain proper decorum to anyone that could see them. She didn't want her brother to get the wrong impression.

"Nolan, take the spare mount. You ride back with your sister. We will carry Bo."

The dog barked and pulled closer to Nolan, who looked from his sister to Bo.

Ella recognized the conflict emerging with her brother's dog. "Nolan, Bo will follow, but he gets too close to the legs of the horses. Aiden would be heartbroken if something happened to him." She could not allow the pup to be hurt.

Nolan considered what she said. "Would you feel comfortable

riding back with Colonel Ross? I feel sure he will treat you with high regard."

Something passed between her brother and Jackson that she didn't understand. Their nods to each other were subtle.

Jackson turned to his men. "Marshall, see to Ol' Indie's in the wagon. And please help Mr. Whitford secure the pup in the saddle." He mounted Mason and reached out to help Nolan as he handed his sister up.

"Yes, sir." Marshall nodded curtly at Nolan and indicated he and Bo should follow him.

Ella would have pinched herself from pure joy if she thought she could tolerate more pain. She sat in front of Jackson. With one arm around her waist, he held onto Mason with the other.

"Nolan, please take the mare tied to the back of the wagon for you and Bo.

Jackson smiled and clicked his steed. Ella was tucked tightly in his arms.

~

The door burst open when the posse pulled up out front, and Aiden ran out. Sara, Lizzy, and Carter followed him. The slamming door woke up a drowsy Ella.

"My sista is back!" The little boy ran down the steps and latched onto his Ella's leg, still sitting on Mason.

Unchecked tears ran down Ella's face. She knew Aiden could have been hurt. As it was, her head and back were the only casualties.

Well, there *was also* one dead overseer and one of his accomplices. She, however, couldn't summon any remorse for either death. Jason would have killed her and Ol' Indie—or Aiden and Bo.

Marshall dismounted and hurried over to help Ella down from the horse. Jackson alighted behind him.

Nolan handed the puppy down to Jackson. But Bo leaped out of Jackson's arms and ran heedlessly to Aiden, jumping up and licking his face, glad to see him.

"Bo, where have you been? I woke up from my nap and you were gone. I looked everywhere." He grabbed Bo's neck and returned the kisses.

Nolan spoke up. "Bo led us to the bad guys. He helped save our sister, Aiden—your puppy is a hero!"

Before Nolan could dismount, Jackson walked over to him. Gripping the back edge of Nolan's saddle, he spoke. "Nolan Whitford, we have things to discuss, you and me. Go nowhere." He looked hard at him.

Marshall moved to Nolan's side. His voice was low, but Ella still heard. "Let's go to the library, Mr. Whitford. We will meet Colonel Ross there."

Nolan nodded and forced his mouth into a terse smile.

Ella held her stomach, uneasiness stirring at the exchange. She looked up at Jackson with tear-rimmed eyes. "Surely you can allow my brother to catch his breath. He saved our lives."

A noise sounded behind them and Ella turned in time to see Ol' Indie stumble. Jackson and Ella reacted, each grabbing one of the older woman's arms and steadying her.

"Come, Ol' Indie. We'll get you to bed."

~

*J*ackson regarded Ella as she followed Carter carrying her old nursemaid up the stairs. This would be tough. He needed to meet with Nolan Whitford, or *Private White*. Whoever he was, he wanted answers.

Marshall had seen Whitford, as had the three other men in the posse. He had to remember his duties, even if it risked his heart. He stopped Ella as she returned downstairs, hoping his voice sounded stronger than his resolve felt. This was his responsibility.

"Ella, I have to talk to Nolan, and find out more about this. It's my duty. You and I have things to talk about. Sara is here, and Aiden thought he lost you. You go with them. I will catch up with you soon." He tried to offer a smile of assurance, but it came out tense and of no help. He reached down and squeezed her hand, almost as if he could signal to her that he would do all he could allow himself to do.

Damn! His heart was already involved.

Ella burst into tears and fled upstairs to her room.

Jackson looked over where the posse had been sitting quietly. The men had already taken the bodies and secured the remaining rogue slave for the time being. He dismissed them back to their duties.

Jackson wanted to say more. Instead, he tied up Mason and walked into the library, joining Nolan and Marshall.

CHAPTER 20

Jackson closed the library door and took his time getting comfortable in his chair, all the while taking in the mood of the room. Nolan sat across from his desk, a cynical smirk on his face. Marshall leaned against the fireplace with a look of expectation.

"Marshall, thank you for your help this afternoon. We may have captured the men responsible for some rapes and other violence around the outskirts of town. I had hoped that they were already dead, but that could be a false assumption."

He looked at Nolan, his look hardening. "I suppose you are to be thanked for your help." He extended a hand to Nolan. "Thank you," he said, shaking Nolan's hand. He noticed that the grip was steady, not clammy or tentative.

"So...Whitford. Tell me about Rover." Jackson smiled affably, his eyes watching Nolan's reaction.

"Well, I would be glad to tell you about Rover. But I find it strange that you call me into my library to ask me about my dog that died years ago. How is that relevant?" Nolan unflinchingly responded and focused on Jackson.

"Humor me." Jackson wanted to know more about this man. He

suspected what Nolan had been doing as Private White, and it created a sense of dread in his stomach. He nodded tersely at Nolan, a reminder he was waiting.

After what seemed like too much silence, Nolan shrugged and started. "Rover was my dog. I was about twelve and Ella was about eight when we got him. Had him for several years. I think my father traded cotton for him. But that is not important. Fact is Rover was my Christmas gift." He smiled in remembrance.

"He was a Tennessee tree-hound. Ever heard of them? They are made for the land. Smart dog. He was supposed to be my hunting dog. But Ella domesticated him—made him sweet." He laughed.

"I know that breed," Marshall interjected. "Jackson, remember they had two dogs like that back at the fort? The handler kept them in the cages. They were handsome dogs. But you let this animal in the house?" He laughed. "Why did I ask that? Bo is in the house and he will be a big dog."

All three men laughed at that. It helped ease the tension.

"Well yes, we did. To go on, Rover did whatever Ella asked, followed her everywhere. The only thing he loved to do with me was fish. When I'd bring out my fishing pole, he would quit whatever he was doing and come with me."

Fidgeting slightly, Nolan reached into his pocket and pulled out the jar of salve from Ol' Indie.

He placed the salve on the desk. "We should get this up to Ella," he said, and pushed the salve forward, towards Jackson. His head nodded towards the library door.

Marshall moved forward and took the jar. "Okay. I'll take it. Be right back. I will give this to Miss Lizzy." He touched his hat and closed the door behind him.

"Ahem. Private White?"

Nolan looked unabashedly at Jackson. "Who?"

"Don't toy with me, Whitford. I know that you are White. What I don't know is if Marshall recognizes you as White." He shook his head. "Honestly, I don't know what I am to do with you. I know that when I arrest you, your sister will be heartbroken."

Jackson stared up at the ceiling as if it held some answer, then, glared at Nolan. "I know you realize I care for her. A lot. I don't want to see her hurt, but I'm a soldier. I have a job to do. And you and I, sir, have a lot to discuss." He kicked his spur against the foot of the desk and moved behind to take his seat.

"But I want to know about you. Continue. Tell me more about your dog, Rover." He studied Nolan.

Heavy footsteps sounded toward the library. "Please continue with Rover's story. You mentioned him earlier with Ella."

Marshall opened the door. "Did I miss anything?"

Nolan looked at Jackson and grinned. "No, suh. We were just passing time for a couple of minutes while you delivered the salve."

Jackson puzzled. *Why the deference to Marshall while the caginess with me? He knows I know what he was doing. Why provoke me?* Jackson couldn't read Nolan Whitford and needed to know the man, so he could know his own mind. This wasn't the time for rash reactions. He wanted to think about his options before acting. Absent divine intervention, he needed to figure out what those options were. He didn't like this feeling of being compromised, but there was nothing for it.

This smirking man in front of him was not Private Angus White. *Was there ever an Angus White?* he wondered. "Mr. Whitford, please continue."

"Well, there's nothing much more to tell here." His lips moved in a momentary smile as he talked. "Rover didn't like dead things, and he wouldn't kill anything, even a fish."

"If I'd hook a fish, he barked relentlessly, and then he would gently pull the fish out of the water to the shore. After I'd unhook him, Rover would play with him. He'd toss the fish around and bark. He seemed to know he couldn't do it long—that the fish would die without water.

"After a few minutes of that, he'd bring me the fish, and I'd pop it in the fish barrel. He'd do the same thing every time we pulled in a fish. That was our routine. Crazy dog." Emotion flickered in his eyes.

"Papa decided we would take Rover hunting and teach him he wasn't a 'prissy dog,' as he called it. Ella cried and tried to hide Rover. I thought he would be fine. But he wouldn't pick up the dead birds because they couldn't play with him. Then Papa shot his gun off too close to Rover and the noise caused him to bolt. It was the next day before we found him. He was wet, sick, and cold. For a while, it was touch and go, but he came 'round."

Nolan picked at his collar. "Look, I'm not sure what talking about a dog is all about. I...*we* loved our dog. End of story."

Marshall was the first to break the silence. "You Whitfords sure have a knack for finding good dogs." He smiled and nonchalantly slapped his leg. "That Bo is smart—and one heck of a tracker!"

Nolan grinned, more relaxed. "Yes, it seems my little brother Aiden also has a way with dogs. Bo wouldn't let me near the house because he didn't know me."

"Which brings me to ask," Marshall continued. "Where did you come from today, and where have you been?" A flicker of irritation and impatience shone in his eyes as he glanced first to Nolan, and then Jackson.

Silence descended on the room.

Nolan watched Jackson. The atmosphere was tense as they tried to read each other.

"I had just gotten home. I ran a high fever and was hospitalized for a long while. A small leave gave me time to get to my next post. But after word came that my sister was here alone with my little brother, I wanted to check on my family. Got word that my Papa up and left. No one knows where he is, but he left almost a year ago." Nolan emitted a growling sigh of displeasure. "I returned home to find out Ella had been abducted and Aiden near got kidnapped himself. I took off after her. Aiden helped me with Bo. Lizzy filled me in on you and your men being here. But I had to choose... Anyway, I love my sister." He heaved another sigh but maintained eye contact with Marshall.

"Well, that was great timing." Without missing a beat, Marshall stood. "I suppose you are a Johnny Reb?" He stared at Nolan, expecting an answer.

The question took Jackson by surprise, but he noticed Nolan's calm composure was unchanged. He thought he saw a fleeting look of sadness in his eyes.

"Suhs, I am a Confederate soldier." He turned his focus to Jackson. "I have a question of my own."

Jackson nodded. "Go on."

"What makes you think you will ever be good enough for my sister?"

~

He knew this could happen—arrest, prison, maybe death. It was a risk he took to save his sister.

I had hoped to rescue Ella and bring her home, or...damn! Maybe I should have listened to Sara and didn't give that enough thought. All I knew was Ella was being harmed.

Nolan was determined not to show any emotion. Especially fear. He focused on his throat, hoping to maintain his cool exterior. They thought to throw him off by asking him to talk about Rover. Jackson was smart, but he had also learned those tricks. *I enjoyed thinking about old Rover.*

This meeting could mean the difference between freedom and imprisonment for his family. What the hell? He came home to find his family forced to host the enemy. He knew little about Jackson—only what he had observed in his brief time as Private White. His men had respected him. But that didn't recommend the man being here with his sister. Nolan grasped that his was not a good position, but he vowed he would protect his family, somehow. To do that, he needed to survive this ridiculous interview.

Nolan bit the inside of his cheek to maintain a look of deference, something that was necessary if he was to get past this mess. There had been jams before in this war. He regulated his breathing, to control his outward appearance of emotion, thoroughly trained in the body language. He knew what indicated lying. While he couldn't control his pupils, he sent commands to his body, hoping to maintain a calm exterior.

The cards were in the Yankee's hands, *except one*. He didn't want to go there, but Nolan realized it may come to that.

Marshall interrupted his thoughts. "Well, soldier…Mr. Whitford, what are you doing this far from your unit, and what unit would that be?" Marshall said, a meaningful look in his eyes.

This was a problem. If he gave the right unit and escaped to it, they would know it was nearby. In fact, these two probably knew where all the Confederate units were at this moment… at least the major concerns. He had to be careful.

Nolan was sure his regiment, the 35th North Carolina, was still in Kinston, but they may still believe he was dead unless Captain Wilson got the message he'd sent days back. He knew other regiments likely to be around. They would want to take New Bern back and would watch or creating the chance.

"The 26th Regiment, North Carolina, suh." Nolan prepared to embellish this story.

Marshall remained focused on Nolan. "Where was your unit when you were…given leave?"

Marshall was fishing. He'd give him something to think about. "Suh, my unit left me behind because of illness—I mentioned the high fever, but I also had a nasty rash. I believe they thought I had smallpox and feared a spread." He maintained eye contact with Marshall.

Marshall backed up.

Nolan fought to hold back a grin. Pleased Marshall had bought his story, Nolan pressed on, hoping to give enough information that other questions weren't asked. "I wanted to see my sister, and when I got here, she had been kidnapped." Nolan glanced over at Jackson. The man was scrutinizing him. "I don't think there is anything I could add to that."

"You appear *well*, Mr. Whitford," observed Jackson. "The 26th North Carolina, you say? Hmmm… an interesting development came out of that regiment. It spread like wildfire after the New Bern battle. Something about a woman and her husband both fighting in that unit? Do I have this right, Marshall?"

"Yes. I believe you do. What were their names?" He glanced at Jackson with a machinating look, and then back to Nolan, a silent demand he answer.

Jackson pulled a cigar and match from his inside pocket. "Care for a cigar?" Jackson lifted two more cigars from his pocket and passed them to Nolan and Marshall.

"Light?" Jackson struck a match on his boot and held the flame out first to Nolan, then Marshall. He struck another match and lit his own cigar, then tossed the matches in the spittoon near his desk.

How quaint. Next, he'll offer me my own brandy. Nolan slowly puffed his cigar and took his time answering. He gave Jackson time to puff on his cigar, while he pretended to ponder the question. He wanted—no, needed—his answer to satisfy the needs of these two men.

An offense is always the best defense.

Uncrossing his legs and taking a deep breath, he sat up.

"I feel I'm being tested here," Nolan drawled. Holding back a smile, he nodded towards the men. "You could be talking about Private Black, Sam, and her husband. Well, now *they* refer to them as the Blacks—husband and wife soldiers." He shook his head and continued. "Sam is a woman. It's outrageous, women joining ranks of soldiers, but it's not unheard of with this war. This surprised the lot of us. She got wounded in the battle and her husband found her. He was in a different unit, same regiment. Colonel Vance was angry at the deception. He discharged them both two months ago."

"No one in your unit was aware he was a *she*?" Jackson raised a brow and looked over at Marshall. Both men smirked.

"No, suh. That isn't the thing you'd expect. She kept to herself. Bound her chest, and from what I understand she cut her hair short. She also wore male clothing. She didn't look, or act, like a woman with her deceptions. I got my leave not long after their discharge." He thought a little longer before he continued. He walked a tight line trying to give enough detail but also keep his story consistent.

"I don't know where she and her husband went, but in my opinion, there was something off with them. I was not in agreement with turning them out as angry with the Confederacy as they were. I think their sympathies…" He looked first at Marshall, then at Jackson and continued, "Their sympathies are now with you and the Union. Word is they were bushwhacking innocent Southerners and raiding land in the name of the Union." He scowled as he spoke the last words.

"They are brutal," he added, "almost as if they are working off their grudge on innocents."

Marshall looked over at Jackson, concern etched on his face.

"*What?*" Nolan looked at both men.

"Well, several local people have been murdered. Families bushwhacked, their homes ransacked, and livestock stolen or just slaughtered and left for the buzzards." Jackson's voice was steady and low.

"We had not considered a woman could be part of this. It provides a possible reason we haven't been able to locate them. The unrest since the battle is significant outside of the town. Our patrols found two men we suspected of the killings, but they weren't able to capture them alive to question them. The arresting posse killed the two men. We felt that they were traveling with more, but now, we have to go on what we had determined. Your information helps. Doesn't sound like the Blacks would work with others."

In a swift change of subject, Marshall looked up at Nolan. "So, just who are *you* to the Confederacy, Whitford? What is *your* rank?"

Silence hung in the room for several moments.

"Major, suh." Nolan blew a ring of smoke to his left. He resisted telling them his real rank— lieutenant colonel—afraid it could be more trouble for him. Union command often treated higher ranking captured officers brutally.

He had risen quickly in his ranks and was supposed to resume command of his own regiment—the 35th, North Carolina. Hopefully, they were still in Kinston, waiting. They could be called away. He needed to get back to them. Caution kept him from revealing his real regiment.

The Blacks gave him an opportunity here. He only knew about them because he ran into a Confederate picket when he left to rescue Ella from Jason. The picket was looking for weakness in the Union lines around New Bern. He *knew* what that meant.

Thank goodness for small favors. A reason to appreciate Jackson flared in his mind. The Union forces were here with Ella and Aiden.

An unprotected woman and a small boy—his family—would be prime targets for renegades and soldiers looking for physical pleasures or revenge, like the Blacks. His home would not be an easy place to attack because of the Union numbers and their readiness.

Fortunately, the picket had recognized him. He updated Nolan with the comings and goings of the various Confederate units in the area, including information about his own regiment. Nolan updated him and told him to expect him back shortly. By now, he hoped his message made it to his command, so they would know he had survived. He needed to get back.

Jackson glanced at Marshall and subtly nodded towards the door.

Marshall understood the unspoken command. "Well, I will leave you to Colonel Ross here. I think it's time I check on the household and the men and see how things are going." He nodded at Jackson. Taking one more look at Nolan, Marshall exited, sauntering out of the library. His heavy footfalls grew fainter as he moved further from the room.

The hair on his neck prickled at that remark. It struck Nolan as personal, the tone too knowing. He felt unsettled, more than he had during any of this questioning. No way would Marshall have referenced his sister like that in front of Jackson. He wanted to get back to Sara. But *how* was he going to be able to accomplish *that*, with the attention of these two?

"So now it's you and me, Whitford." Keeping his eyes on Nolan, Jackson took one more puff and put his cigar out in the ashtray next to him.

CHAPTER 21

Jackson wasn't sure what to make of Marshall's questions. Did he recognize Nolan? He had given him free reign with the questions. Nolan's appearance seemed too coincidental. He had just shown up, as he said, but there had been and still were posse combing the surrounding area looking for any renegades, and they were looking for him as Private White.

There had been no leads on Private White. The whole thing frustrated him leading him to wonder if White even existed—though he had met him.

How had one man slipped through the lines? Even more perplexing was the question of how he had gotten to the house after the kidnapping. There was more to this, he knew it. *Patience*, he reminded himself.

It was Jackson's job to take Whitford prisoner, but if he did that—no, *when* he did that—it would be the end of anything he might have with Ella.

His body warmed at the thought of her. She was no longer sharp and dismissive with him. Her tone had softened, and after the rescue, he was certain there was a spark of interest—or at least she had relaxed considerably towards him. Hope took root.

Whenever Ella smiled in his direction, his heart felt hopeful, not weighted down by the dismalness and death of this war. Aiden's tearful description of her kidnapping brought him to his knees. The guards that missed those men were still working off his anger. The thought of her hurt had all but sucked the life out of him. He'd had to find her. The moment he had seen her, *he* felt rescued. Would she be able to feel for him what he felt for her...ever?

Who was he kidding? This was wartime. Her brother was on the other side, and he was Jackson's prisoner. Hadn't he said as much? *Definitely, a non-starter.*

Her brother wants what is best for her, his heart kept whispering in his head. *I can handle this. I just need a strategy—one that keeps Marshall from knowing Whitford's other identity.*

Jackson fought to sort out his conflicted feelings. He was not a man of inaction. He needed to decide on his approach. If they both suspected Nolan was a spy and didn't arrest him, not only would it mean his career, but Marshall's as well.

He would not risk Marshall's career. Truth be told, he wasn't sure *what* he was willing to risk.

Jackson reached into his pocket and found the familiar pencil nub. He pressed on it and rolled it around for comfort. *Why sacrifice anything? I can work this out. Her brother loves her.*

Schooling his features, Jackson moved to the front of his desk and perched on the corner, leaning forward and looking at Nolan.

"Whitford, I like you. I think if this war wasn't a factor, we might be good friends. I asked you earlier about your dog, Rover. The reason was to find out—" Jackson spoke slowly and paused for effect.

"More about me," Nolan finished the sentence. "I understood what you were doing. I don't mind, actually. Rover meant a lot to my family. I rather enjoyed reminiscing about him. I admit it took me a while to understand why we were discussing my deceased pet."

Jackson had not expected such candor.

"We are sworn, enemies. You are also in *my* home, suh." Nolan recounted, his ire rising. "I felt my sister was in danger and I love my sister. I..." His comment trailed off.

"Let's be candid, Whitford. It's just you and me right now. Obviously, there is more to your story. Depending on what I find out and what I'm comfortable with, I may have to arrest you. It's no secret that I am rather fond of your sister. I know she is an honest person. She also loves her family." Jackson stopped and pushed his hand through his hair. "I'm not sure why I'm taking this chance."

"*Chance?*" Nolan looked up, his attention riveted to Jackson's eyes.

"Don't pretend you don't know what I'm dealing with here. I know you are a smart fella. You handle yourself with more aplomb than the average soldier." He blew out a long exhale. "Look, I confess I find myself in a bit of a pickle. I can divest myself of the problem. But for the first time in a long time, I would like to see if my relationship with Ella has a future."

"Whoa! I knew of the attraction. Hell, everyone can see that. But what *relationship?*" Nolan pushed up from his chair, all but shouting.

"There is a connection between your sister and me." Jackson stood nose to nose with him, locked in a glare with Nolan. "You will sit down, sir," he ordered, his words coming out deliberately, his eyes never moving from his opponent's face. "She has not only my support but my respect."

Nolan gave the barest nod, and returned to his seat, his face unflinching.

Resolved, Jackson sat on the corner of his desk, still facing Nolan. "My choices are few. If you are arrested, she will see my involvement, obviously, and I will never have that chance." This was his heart speaking, obviously, set on mucking things up. Jackson persisted. "If you take the pledge, word will get out you are a Confederate soldier. In other towns, we have had questionable—no, bad activity towards Confederate soldiers that have come forward. I can account for most of my men, but I am one of three placed in provost positions." He lowered his voice. "This war won't last much longer, and God willing, I would like to think I will outlast it."

Nolan was silent.

"You aren't making this easy, Whitford. I thought I was in charge here. Maybe I'm slipping." He grinned. "What I'm asking you is for permission to court your sister."

Nolan sat silent for a moment, his eyes impenetrable to Jackson. "Do you love her?"

Jackson shifted uncomfortably. "I think so, yes. What I mean is that it's been a long time since anyone affected me the way Ella does. I am…" His voice trailed off. "Yes. I am in love with her." He looked Nolan in the eye.

"And your intentions? What are they?"

"I have not spoken of anything with Ella. She's hated my very existence until recently." He smiled, half to himself. "But I think she is mellowing towards me. Surely you noticed the repair to the ceiling in the foyer? Her gun went off the first day I came here."

Nolan cleared his throat. "Yet she missed. Suh, my sister, and my brother mean everything. They are the reason my life is in the position it is in at this moment… sitting here with you, my very existence on the line." He shifted in his seat and leaned towards Jackson. "How you *know* you feel about my sister means a great deal. Can you allow me the insight on your intentions?" He paused. "I warn you, suh. If it is other than marriage, let me tell you now, I will not agree."

Jackson pulled the pencil nub he had been turning from his pocket and placed it on the desk beside him. Crossing his arms, he considered the man in front of him. "Whitford… er… Nolan, you seem to be the protective brother Ella has spoken of, and I can attest that your sister displays similar bravery to yours. She would die for her family, I believe." A moment of silence passed.

The question loomed over him. Jackson swallowed, and he realized that his heart had been completely taken over by one Confederate belle. "Yes, I would like to pursue Ella with the hope of marriage. However, we are still getting to know each other. I had not planned to get married too soon."

"So, you would string her along? While I cannot fathom liking my sister and my property in the hands of the enemy, I will not see her heart broken." Nolan glared, his eyes shooting daggers.

Jackson fought the urge to be sarcastic, considering Nolan was *his* prisoner. But this was also Ella's brother. He felt challenged, just as he was when he had faced Maria's father years ago. He shook off any appearance of nonchalance. "No, of course not! I am a gentleman and an officer. I would do nothing to hurt Ella. My intentions are honorable. I want to court her, with your permission, as difficult as it seems in this environment."

Nolan narrowed his eyes, and his voice was tight. "Ella is a grown woman, I won't tell her what to do. But I can't like her aligning with the Union." He rested his hands on his thighs, leaned forward, and locked eyes with Jackson. "Make *sure* she doesn't get hurt."

"Well, that brings me back to my initial point. I am proposing that you disappear."

Nolan raised his eyebrows, looking alarmed.

"That didn't come out right. Look Whitford, there is something I have not conferred. There have been problems with young Confederate soldiers coming home and *disappearing*. I can't believe I'm discussing this." He shook his head. "I suspect it is an officer within our ranks, but I cannot prove it yet. Marshall and I are suspicious of one or two people. And I don't want to take a chance with your life." He let out a long sigh and ran his hand through his hair.

"I will let you go. I want you to leave. Tell me what I can do to make that happen. I know this is probably a mistake, and I could lose my career, but I'm willing to take a chance on you. Don't ask me why. Don't make me regret this decision."

Jackson got up and walked to the corner of the room and opened the top flap to the glass book cabinet. He pushed the false books out of the front and pulled out a bottle of brandy and two glasses, setting them down on the desk between them. Nolan had heart and loyalty, evidenced by his willingness to risk his own life to save his sister. There was no doubt in Jackson's mind that Whitford would trade his life for Ella's.

He noted Nolan's amused smile. Waving at the brandy, he smiled back. "Would you have one with me? I discovered this hiding place a week ago, and it seems a great place for concealing libations."

Nolan's eyebrows rose slightly. Jackson nodded towards the

cabinet to his left, "I noticed the cabinet stock has not been touched in a while, and I felt no need to use your house liquor."

This will be the toughest thing I think I've had to do in this war, seeing this through, but it's what I have to do.

He needed this drink if this would continue, and hoped that wherever Marshall was working, he stayed there.

Jackson passed a glass with a couple fingers of brandy to Nolan. He raised his glass and was met with a stare. Leaning forward, Jackson took a swig. "Ah well, we are at least making progress. And this helps clear things up."

Nolan studied Jackson from across the desk. This was surely not what he thought would be discussed. He had suspected his sister was interested in this man, and he was right. The man had control of his home, his library, and his booze, but he was taking good care of it, and he didn't appear to be abusing his position or his sister. The alcohol still sat in the cabinet in the same spot where he had left it after he and his dad toasted, just before he had left the previous April.

If not for the war, he agreed with Jackson, they would be great friends. Maybe they still could be, if he could trust him... at least with his home and his family. He suspected—call him crazy—that Marshall had an interest in Sara, but he planned to handle that. He wanted more time with Sara before he left, not knowing how long it might be before he saw her again.

"You must have some thoughts on what we've discussed. If you don't mind, I'd like to hear them."

Jackson's remark jolted him from his musings. "Yes, I do, as a matter-of-fact. I believe we have points to... discuss." His sentence waned as a noise outside the door to the library caught his attention. Nolan put his finger to his lips and jumped up.

He stepped quickly and opened the door. Aiden lost his balance and stumbled into the room, landing in a heap with Bo right behind him. Nolan helped his brother up from the floor. Aiden dusted off his pants and seemed unconcerned at having been caught eavesdropping. He casually walked over to Nolan. It was almost as if he understood the elephant in the room.

"Nolan, when you gonna get back to work?" His absence from home had been explained to Aiden as a job—his military job to serve his country. His little brother didn't think past the concept of working and not working. Nolan hadn't understood the impact of what had taken place on the land around him until the simplicity of his brother's question caught him off guard.

"Not sure, little man. But you know I will take you fishing before I have to go, so you don't worry too much." He ruffled his brother's hair.

"But I want to know. I asked Lieutenant... uh," he looked up at Jackson, "I asked Mr. Marshall, but he won't answer my questions. He sits there with Miss Sara and they talk in the parlor." Aiden folded his arms and looked at his brother, waiting for an answer to his question.

Nolan stiffened. Tousling his brother's hair, he smiled. "I will be going back to work soon, and I want to take you fishing before I do, but maybe not today."

"But why? There ain't no clouds today. Miss Sara is working on a dress for Ella and Ella is taking a nap. If I go near there, Lizzy will make Bo and me take a nap, too. I'd rather go fishing." He wrinkled his nose.

"Well, it's almost somebody's birthday, and it could be *we*"—he nodded at Jackson— "were having a private conversation." Nolan narrowed his eyes at Aiden, making his point. It was hard to get upset with him.

"Oh brudder, Bo." Aiden's voice was somber. "It looks like everyone has better things to do than spend time with us." Eyeing the two men, he continued. "Don't forget your promise. You said you would take me fishing."

"Yes. Now you head upstairs and catch that nap. You have been through a lot these past few days. I will be up to talk to you later."

The little boy and his puppy reluctantly left the room.

The door closed softly behind them. Nolan was still fixated on what was going on in the parlor. *What was Marshall up to with his girl?* He understood that she probably had said nothing about them, so he would have to just solve this problem a different way.

He was unsettled about what to say to Jackson but decided to trust him—a little. "I need a Confederate uniform. My uniform has been lost." Nolan didn't miss the look that passed over Jackson's face. He didn't want to say or do anything that could change the way things were going for him. "I appreciate you aren't in the habit of outfitting our side. I can probably get one issued once I get back."

"*Where* exactly is it you will get back to, Nolan?"

Nolan eyed him before trusting him. "I need to head upriver to the Lenoir County area and catch up with my men. They are waiting."

"Your men?"

"Yes. I have not been exactly honest where my position is concerned. I feel that for the sake of our relationship, I should let you know that my rank is that of Lieutenant Colonel. I am a graduate of the Citadel." His eyes followed Jackson's every move and reaction as he spoke to him. He thought about how he could end this conversation without spilling the beans about the runner who had been keeping him flush with current information on his men. "I'm sure you understand my hesitation in sharing this with you and the lieutenant colonel earlier."

Jackson sat in silence for a long minute. "Okay, I will accept that. Is there anything else you might want to tell me? I warn you, I am already struggling with what I have discovered you have done. I don't suppose you would care to enlighten me as to why you were in my unit posing as a private?"

"Not really, suh. Is it okay if I call you Jackson since you are calling me Nolan? I do realize you have the upper hand here, but it would make it more comfortable." Nolan reached for his brandy and studied the glass for a moment. "I will say that the mission was unsuccessful, and it won't be repeated. I cannot say more. I'm sure you understand."

"Yes." Jackson swirled his brandy, slowly, thoughtfully. He didn't doubt that what Nolan told him was true. "I trust you, Nolan. I hope someday we will be friends and not just brothers by marriage." His mouth turned up at the corner. "But for now, you will leave the day after tomorrow, so say your goodbyes with no one being the wiser. You will slip off without the formal opportunity to say much of a goodbye. I am risking my neck here, and I've rather formed an attachment to it. Don't make me sorry."

"Agreed. I will be ready. I would like to take Aiden fishing. That will be my goodbye to him until this conflict ends." Resignation etched on his face, Nolan took a swig of his brandy. He swallowed, but the large knot that had suddenly risen in his throat made it difficult. He would miss his family. It had been hard enough to leave the first time.

He had hoped this war would be over quickly, but now he felt differently. He didn't see a resolution that would work for both sides. Would he live to see the end of it? The pain was raw and as sharp as a knife to the gut.

He wanted to give Ella some brotherly advice about this relationship with Jackson. He winced. She wouldn't like it. She'd probably reject it, but he was her brother and it was his duty to protect his sister's heart.

He had watched them together and knew her heart to be already engaged even if she didn't realize it yet. He thought about his approach. It would be fruitless to be negative about the relationship. He wasn't, and that felt odd.

It was important that he speak to Sara soon. Nolan downed the rest of his brandy. Jackson had gone to catch up with Marshall. He was sure that he would not share their conversation, knowing that Jackson's honor would not allow him to jeopardize his friend's life and career. Nolan knew he was lucky Jackson was an honorable man.

Setting down his glass, he left the room to find Sara. Marshall's pursuit of *his* girl angered him, but he trusted Sara. He could not give her any details, but he would share his hope that they would be together soon.

It was time for goodbyes.

Two days.

CHAPTER 22

*E*lla lay awake in her bed and stared at the ceiling. She could hear voices downstairs and was surprised they weren't raised. Nolan had risked his life to save hers, and now his own life was in jeopardy again. He was meeting with Jackson and Marshall now. What was being said in there? What if they sent him off to a horrible Yankee prison yard like those she had read about in the posts?

She would not spend another moment gazing at her ceiling and wondering. Ella acted. Swinging her legs over the side of her bed, she found her slippers but decided against putting them on her feet.

The cool floor felt good against her skin. She padded to her closet and took out her half boots and her white muslin dress. A cheerful look would be best even if she felt just the opposite. True to her word, Sara had returned the dress to her in perfect condition.

Hmmm. My hair needs attention. Ella pulled her hair up into a chignon, releasing soft curls around her face. She pinched her cheeks and checked her image once more. Satisfied, she left the room, closing the door behind her.

Everyone expected her to remain in her room. As much as she felt the need for rest, she had to know what was going on. She wandered downstairs, hoping not to draw awareness to herself. As she reached the last step, the door to the library opened and Nolan stepped out.

Thank goodness he isn't in irons. That's a good sign. She felt hopeful.

"Nolan, where are you going?" Ella kept her voice light and enthusiastic.

"I want to see Sara… have you seen her? I had hoped to see her before she went back to town."

"Well, you are in luck. She will be here for Aiden's party. Sara doesn't plan to leave until tomorrow."

"Aiden's birthday party?" He laughed and shook his head. "Oh yes, the party. Pity the man that thinks he is smarter than you two ladies. You girls have always had the ability to throw me off my game."

Ella smiled. "Sara and I sort of moved the party up a bit. And even that was delayed…" She swallowed. "Anyway, it was a reason for her to be here, to see you. I couldn't let you be here and not spend time with her. And now, you even get to come to his party… I hope." Her face turned serious. "I know I shouldn't ask," she lowered her voice to a whisper. "But Nolan, I have been so nervous. I know that they know. What will happen?"

"Sis, we will talk later, but it's gonna be fine. I think it will. Try not to worry." He held her softly by the shoulders and gave her a kiss on the cheek and whispered in her ear. "You said Sara is here, still? Do you know where I can find her?"

Ella's voice was almost a murmur. "I haven't seen her in the last little while. I've been resting upstairs. Lizzy might know where she could be. Or you could check the… front hall closet." She nodded her head towards the front door. "She needed to put a few things in order."

A smile lit his face. He squeezed Ella's arms affectionately and took off towards the front of the house. Checking to make sure the coast was clear, he moved into the closet and closed the door. He headed down to the secret room.

Ella listened for noise. It did her heart good to see him cheerful and filled with hope. She suspected Sara would be down there waiting for him. They had such little time together, and Sara was heading back to town after the party for Aiden.

Ella was not planning to intrude and would see Nolan later. She decided to find Jackson and see to things herself. The worry was not helping. Relief could only come with answers.

How had things spiraled out of her control? Her big brother had helped save her life, and for that, he might lose his. Tears welled up in her eyes. Her hands clenched into tight fists as she attempted to control the tension and fear. She was feeling so many things right now as she wandered into the kitchen to check on the cake. "It's still here." The cake was covered in a cake tin in the larder. She thought about taking a small taste but changed her mind. *I need answers.*

She headed towards the front of the house, her steps slow and her shoes barely making any noise on the steps.

Prickles of fear ran up her spine when she noticed the library door cracked open. Had someone noticed Nolan going into the closet? Ella paused at the library door, her hands in her pockets with her fingernails digging into the palms. Deciding not to knock, she pushed it and let herself in.

Jackson was leaning against the back of his desk, staring out of the window.

I hope he came in while I was in the kitchen.

He turned when she closed the door behind her.

∽

*J*ackson was apprehensive with Ella, suspecting why she was there. He sipped a brandy, swirling the amber liquid between swallows.

He had done nothing like what he was planning. And he had never felt so conflicted. If he were caught helping a Confederate to escape— much less a Confederate officer—he would be court-martialed for treason. He could even be charged with collusion with the enemy and hanged.

His career had always been the most important thing in his life. If this went bad, his family would never understand; they would have lost their son, brother, and grandson. His grandfather, his father, and now he, had all served their country—each earning high honors for their devotion and sacrifice. A family tradition of service and honor would be sullied.

Jackson shook off that thought, not wanting to focus on bad outcomes. The decision was made—it was the one his gut told him was the right one to make. He didn't want to question that decision any further. He needed to be confident he could remove Nolan from this house without creating suspicion. Ha! That false confidence was why he was drinking brandy. How did his life get so complicated?

Ella.

This high-risk, career-ending decision was being made because of one woman. He had been resolute to never let his heart get involved again after the way it had ended with Maria. But she wasn't Maria. She was genuine in her feelings, honest. He trusted her and, considering their beginning, that was quite a step. The door to the library opened and the object of his thoughts stepped inside.

"You're up. How are you feeling?" Jackson pushed his glass away and walked around the desk to where she stood.

A gentleman would back up a step and give her space.

The thought was only fleeting. He didn't feel like being a gentleman.

Jackson pulled her close to him, careful of the cuts on her back. The tension in her shoulders was palpable, but she didn't pull away. The proximity of her body heated his blood and fired his imagination, pushing away the thoughts of career and failure. A familiar vision of his dreams caught his thoughts, one with her auburn hair covering his pillow and her green eyes looking into his face, warm and inviting. He wanted to kiss her and lose himself in making love to her. His body was already responding to those thoughts.

"I suppose you have questions for me," he murmured, admiring her beautiful face, her lovely cheekbones, and her lips. He was in love with her and could no longer ignore that truth. He wanted to make love to her, right here, right now.

But Jackson was no fool. It wasn't like Ella to be so pliable. She wanted something, too. He expected directness from her. He had answers, but he also had questions.

Would she be honest with him? Did she have answers to his questions? The jasmine in her hair filled his senses. He closed his eyes, battling the effect it was having on him.

"Yes," she nodded, clearing her throat. "I want—no, I need to know what you plan to do with my brother." She pushed away. Her arms folded about her, she looked him in the eye.

Jackson watched her, studying her face. He was trying to decide how to respond. It wasn't an easy answer. He knew there was more to Nolan's story than he had let on, but right now he wasn't interested in hearing that.

He spoke, his voice steady as he kept her attention. "I will help Nolan leave." He trusted her. "I don't know when. Quietly say your goodbyes to him, Ella. It will be soon. And I am confident you will keep this to yourself. That is most important. If others hear of this, it would be bad… for both of us."

She dropped her arms, her eyes wide with astonishment. "Why are you doing this? I'm—I mean—I had not expected you to…" She let the statement dangle, as if unsure of how to finish it. "How are you planning to do this? Does—does Marshall know of your decision?" She stepped forward, touching his arm and peering into his face. "I'm still uncertain I heard you right."

"You did. I'm doing this, Ella. Can I count on your discretion? And Marshall does not know. I need to keep it that way."

She nodded, her mouth agape.

"Good." He took advantage of her silence and pulled her back to him. His finger skimmed her chin, cupping it in his hands. Her lips looked warm and lush. He wanted her.

Jackson slanted his lips and brushed hers softly. Feeling no resistance, he kissed her again, this time longer and with more force, more passion. His hands released her shoulders and moved down her arms to caress her waist. He tugged her closer, his hands covering her rear. His body was reacting—strongly—with need.

His mind battled his conscience while his lips conquered hers. Should he continue to hold her so closely? She would feel his arousal. That was only a fleeting thought. He was not letting her go.

She opened her mouth as if to say something, and he slid in his tongue. Their tongues met and caressed before he swirled his around the inside of her lips. He could feel her pulse responding, sending his own heartbeat into a faster rhythm. The kiss set his blood on fire. She tasted of honeyed tea and cinnamon. He wanted to possess her.

Scraping feet sounded from upstairs and reminded him the door was not locked. Nuzzling her, he glided his kisses along the edge of her chin and down her throat, eliciting soft moans from her as he edged the two of them towards the door and locked it. He looked down at Ella to see if she objected. Hearing none, he backed her up and pushed the paperwork off the desk.

"Jackson, someone might hear."

"Then let's keep it low." He nibbled on her ear. He felt alive when she was near, and he needed more of her. Jackson unbuttoned the front of her dress, lowering the sleeves from her shoulders. He brushed Ella's lips, then lifted her up and sat her on his desk, still kissing her. Lifting his lips only slightly, he peppered kisses down the column of her neck and onto her décolletage. Tugging, he released her breasts from their confines and suckled them, first one, and then the other. Her breathing increased its pace. He could hear her heart pounding. She was affected, and she wasn't turning him away.

His hand sought the bottom of her skirt and moved up the interior of her thigh, finding its way to her center, its outer curls moist with desire.

He inserted his index finger and moved it in and out. She gripped his shoulders, moaning. Her hands broke their grip, and she grabbed his hair, fingering the curls at the nape of his neck as she pulled his head towards hers. His ears filled with sounds of her heated panting, igniting him.

Desire consumed him. Jackson leaned her back and stood over her, his eyes lost in the forest green of hers, his member straining against the confines of his pants, throbbing against the wet heat of her core.

Her eyes shuttered as her pulse quickened and her panting became louder. He reinserted his finger and added a second, increasing his pace. She opened her eyes, and he covered her lips with his, stifling her scream as she shook with pleasure. He moved the edges of her skirt out of the way, pushing it up and laying it on her stomach He could smell her scent of sex and wanted more. He pushed her knees apart and crouched between her legs, his tongue probing and licking as she writhed above him.

He moved up and kissed her lips and then stood and moved a step away from her. They were both panting. He wanted so much to keep going, but he couldn't allow himself. "Ella. I should not have done that, but I cannot say I am sorry. I wanted this, and I want more. Ella."

Her eyes searched his face. A long moment ticked by before she responded. "I rather liked it. I know I could have stopped you... but I didn't want to stop you." She looked away, a blush stealing its way up her neck and face. "I have never... I have never been kissed by a man before you. And I have never imagined these feelings. My body feels tingly and hot. I think it must mean I want... more."

With misted eyes, she gripped his arms. "I had no idea what it could feel like. I wondered, but would have never imagined..." She trailed off into a whisper. Pushing forward, she reached her arms around his neck and brushed her lips against his.

Jackson didn't need a better invitation to kiss her. He pulled her close and coaxed her mouth open with his tongue, nibbling her lip. She opened for him and he poured himself into his kiss.

Holding her shoulders, he broke the kiss and pushed her back to see her face. "We should stop. If we get carried away, someone could find us here. I want you. I do." He brushed his lips along the edge of her chin, trying to slow his own heartbeat.

She held his hands and looked up at him. "Mmm. I think I want you, too. Is that why my body feels so strange?"

Jackson felt a shot to his heart. "Perhaps that is happening."

Ella rested her head on his chest, her voice a soft whisper. "Thank you for what you are doing for my brother. I realize what you must risk, to help him. All you've done since the first day I met you was look out for me and my family." She pulled back to look in his face.

He held her hands and gazed into her eyes while his thumbs circled her inner wrists. "I plan to help Nolan leave, but he cannot come back until this war is over. You understand that, right?" He stared up at the ceiling for a moment, thinking about what he was about to say. *I know that there is more I should know here. I need her to tell me if I'm to help.*

His fingers stilled, and he studied her face. "I know there is much that I still don't know about your brother's presence here. His story is too simple. I cannot help but wonder if… can there be anything else that you can tell me?" He waited. "You can confide in me. I want you to trust me. The more I know about how he could sneak onto the plantation, the easier it might be to make sure he gets out of here undetected." He looked into her eyes, unsure of how she would respond or if she would trust him.

"I'm not sure what else I can tell you." Ella wiped her hands on her dress and then clasped them in front of her. She looked up into Jackson's eyes. "You trusted me. I want to trust you, believe you… but this is crazy…"

She nibbled her lower lip, struggling. "Nolan showed up weeks ago burning with fever and we weren't sure he would survive." She moved away and folded her arms across her chest, hugging her sides.

Anger surged through him at the thought Nolan Whitford had been right under his nose for three weeks, and he had seen nothing. He fought his emotions, clenching and unclenching his teeth. He tried to quell his anger, rationalizing that he was doing this—helping her brother—of his own free will. He wanted a chance with Ella, and he again justified his decision.

Jackson's thoughts traveled back to an earlier conversation with Ella. She had seemed preoccupied. There had been no telltale signs, but now he realized she must have been complicit in hiding her brother.

This is going nowhere. Get over it, Jackson. You've made your decision.

He needed to get Nolan away from here. If Ella's cooperation with the enemy were known, her life would also be in danger.

He had promised her he would not hold him, but this news upset him. Jackson fought not to show his frustration.

How could he have been here all this time? Where was he?

Jackson stepped away, allowing only a slight shake of his head in disbelief, careful not to betray the depth of his disappointment.

He had already promised her, and he was a man of his word.

"Where? I want to know. Where was he all this time?"

The sound of boots coming down the hall stopped their conversation. Heavy steps halted at the door, and then there was a knock. "Jackson? Are you in there?"

Marshall. His timing is awful sometimes.

Jackson schooled his features and tried to calm his ragged breathing. Holding his finger in front of his lips, Jackson signaled for her to be quiet.

Ella answered with her eyes, then straightened her dress and quietly sat in the chair in front of Jackson's desk. She was careful not to make a sound when she sat down. She folded her hands in front of her, but she had to work to calm her breathing.

Satisfied Ella wouldn't be seen as compromised, Jackson called out from behind his desk. "Marshall. Come on in."

"The door appears locked." Marshall rattled the door handle and then shook it again. "If you are busy, I can come back," he added with a teasing tone.

"No, no, not at all. I'll be right there." Jackson smiled at Ella and allowed his chair to scrape against the floor marking his movements.

He walked to the door, unlocked it, and opened it in one swift movement.

He waved him in. "We were just catching up. Miss Whitford—Ella, was asking what happened to the men that held her at the cabin. She is feeling more herself."

Marshall strode through the door and smiled at Ella. "Hello, Miss Whitford. It's nice to see you up and about." He tossed a folded paper onto Jackson's desk. "Seen this?"

"No. What is that?"

"We might be on the right trail. Bushwhacking and murder on small farms in the area—gruesome stuff. One even happened when Jason and his men were holding Miss Whitford. Read it. It's unbelievable. It details the exploits of two former Confederates from the 26th that were discharged when Vance was made aware that they were married to each other." He paused and glanced in Ella's direction. "This is the thing we discussed with Nolan." Marshall moved his gaze back to Jackson and continued, "They are suspected of killing innocent Southerners—women and children. They kill the homesteaders and then steal horses. Nolan was right. They seem to be on the side of the Union. I think we need to send a detail after them."

"Any sign where they went?"

"No, sir. One of the latest victim's children hid and came to town after seeing her mother killed." His throat worked; he struggled to speak. When he did, his voice was full of emotion. "The child secreted herself under her bed and had to watch what they did to her mother and siblings. She was picked up on the road to New Bern by a patrol and brought to town. She described them as a man and woman dressed as soldiers. Confederate soldiers. Her description matches the couple Whitford told us about."

"Who? Who was killed so viciously?" Ella struggled to stand.

"I don't know the names, but they are in there." Marshall pointed to the paper sitting on the corner of Jackson's desk.

Ella's eyes widened as she read the paper. "This is horrible. I know he is okay, but I have this overwhelming need to check on Aiden." She gripped the chair. "What are you going to do to protect us?"

"We need to organize a large posse to protect the citizens of the town and the surrounding area. Ella, would you be willing to help us map out where there are other families in the remote lands around us?" He was anxious at this news.

"Yes. I will do the best I can." She wrapped her arms around herself.

"Right. I'm on it. Jackson, we can ride out tomorrow."

"Thank you, Marshall. I'd like you to be in charge, but let's give the others a little time to get involved in this manhunt." Jackson was trying to make it seem like he was being fair to everyone. He wanted less attention between where he was and about thirty miles west.

"Thank you. As you say, Colonel." Marshall saluted. Turning on his heels, he left the room.

Alone again, Jackson turned his attention back to Ella. His breathing still felt ragged despite his efforts to slow it down. He wondered if Marshall had noticed. Their passion had exploded earlier, and he knew if he touched her, they would be back to where they were before Marshall's abrupt arrival. He couldn't chance that again… not here in the library. He needed her near him. Her presence helped make sense of this craziness.

While he said nothing, Jackson had followed the news on the Blacks, and Marshall had just provided the opportunity he had hoped to find. Nolan needed to go west. He would send Marshall and his men east, on a circuitous route around the area to search for this rogue couple out pillaging the landscape. There would be a lot of activity.

If my hunch is right, their direction will be to head east. Nolan and I need to leave in two days.

CHAPTER 23

Nolan had said his goodbyes. He tried to focus on what was before him, but his heart kept tugging on his mind. This war was costing him more than he had realized.

When he had taken Aiden and Bo fishing, he hated to pull up stakes and go back to the house. Aiden had caught on so fast. The little fella had grown up in the space of time he'd been gone.

His little sidekick, Bo stayed by Aiden's side. After the kidnapping, it seemed the dog had also matured. He was more protective of Aiden, running alongside him, rather than ahead or behind him. He was a true friend for his brother.

His biggest concern was Sara. The thought of her made his chest hurt. He had been in love with her since her father had taken over their church near New Bern. The blonde little girl with braids was always with his sister and had become part of their family, as had her brother, Charles.

He and Charles had been best friends. Charles had followed his father's footsteps and become a pastor at a church in Virginia. What was the name of the church? Shaking his head, he tried to recall.

He hoped to see Charles again, but he knew Charles's activities were also dangerous during this war. Nolan didn't want to do anything that could compromise him. He and Charles had always been the best of friends. One was never without the other growing up.

As they had approached manhood, Charles had left for seminary. The war had begun, and it wasn't long before Nolan got the call to help his Southern brothers in gray.

When he ran into Charles, it was unexpected. Charles was performing a service for several dead Union soldiers near Richmond. Nolan had just begun his mission and was undercover as Private White. There had been a tense few minutes when Charles recognized him in the Union garb, but his friend seemed to sense there was more to it. He had nodded towards Nolan and invited him to join. They talked afterward.

Charles saw his role as more than a pastor. He felt responsible for souls. While he felt God's calling for all souls, none were dearer to him than his Southern brothers. He was doing what he could, as opportunities presented themselves, to help the cause.

He shook his head. Friends and family were all in different directions. There still had been no word of his pa. Ella said Pa had taken off one day to look for him, but he had received no notice of someone looking for him. His pa could have been pressed into service, or worse, he could be a prisoner of war in one of those horrible camps.

Nolan shuddered violently, causing his horse to whinny beneath him. These thoughts weren't helping.

"Easy, girl." He pulled her reins softly and patted her behind her ears. Nolan looked around. Seeing he was still alone once again his thoughts wandered.

He had heard awful things about the prisoner camps. If that happened to Pa, there was no telling where he could be at the moment. A lump formed in his throat. Pa could be dead and in an unmarked grave. He could be anywhere.

His heart pulled at that thought. As upset as he had gotten over his pa's leaving his sister and Aiden, this was his pa and there had been no word of him. He'd have to look for him as soon as he was able, but that would have to wait.

There had been a lot of waiting with this war. Hurry and wait—that seemed to be the way of things right now. Never knowing if they would have enough men, ammunition, or even enough surprise on their side—his men would hurry up and wait.

They waited to hear whether the war would be over soon. It seemed not.

Sara said she would wait.

He loved Sara. They would have married before the war, but that seemed unfair to her. What if he had gotten killed or badly injured? She would have to mourn for a year or possibly live with a cripple. No. This was the right thing. Sara had understood and promised to wait for him. She could change her mind if she wanted. He hoped she wouldn't.

The night before Aiden's party, he had gotten carried away. Things shouldn't have gone as far as they did. But they were pledged to each other, and he planned to wed her the minute he came home from war. Until then, their memories would have to keep them warm. Nolan hoped the precautions he had taken to keep her from becoming pregnant had worked.

Lieutenant Colonel Jameson's flirting drove him nuts. The thought of Sara in another man's arms made him crazy with jealousy.

She assured him she was not encouraging the lieutenant, saying he was just being kind, and that her heart belonged to Nolan. Damn it. Stop this. I trust her.

He wanted to see her once more, to tell her he loved her. Sara was his touchstone. She was home to him. There would never be enough time for all the kisses he wanted from her.

Unfortunately, that was not to be. Sara left the house the day after Aiden's birthday party. That damn Lieutenant Colonel Jameson escorted her back. Marshall hadn't said a word when he got back, just wore a big grin.

Nolan shook off the maddening thoughts. He had to get back to his men. There was no choice. He hoped the letter he had left on his bed would convey his love to her. Ella would find it and deliver it to

Sara. He had also left one for Ella. She was more than any person could hope for in a sister.

He was confident Ella had not shared the location or existence of the family's secret room with anyone, nor would she. He was sure the letters were safe.

Melancholia overwhelmed him. Jackson insisted on leaving that day but offered no explanation. It puzzled Nolan about how he planned to accomplish getting him out of here. Pickets were everywhere on both sides. He had seen them. Just how would Jackson explain his presence if they were caught?

Jackson had instructed him to dress in a plain pair of pants and an old shirt and to be here, behind the barn, at six in the morning. He pulled his hat down and waited.

Jackson could be trusted. While Nolan worried about his sister, he knew Jackson would care for her. At least that was one good thing. If the war ever ended, he could be a decent brother. He liked the man. The only thing he could hold against him was his bad choice of loyalty. On that, Nolan laughed quietly to himself.

The sound of another horse approaching shook him out of his reverie. Nolan backed his mare behind the building. He felt for the gun in his saddlebag. It had been his father's gun and had hidden in the library. He hated to take it but didn't know how he would defend himself if trouble came along. Ella had her small derringer.

His right hand gripped the handle of his gun. He cocked it, keeping it out of sight as he waited.

～

Jackson trotted up to the barn and pulled back on Mason's reins. He hoped Nolan was there already. He trotted towards the side of the barn, the designated meeting spot. This was the right thing for him to do. If he had turned him over, he would be hanged or go before a firing squad. Spying was a serious crime, and he didn't think he could protect him.

He wasn't about to let that happen. Others in the Union command would not support his decision if they knew, but this escape—the word was difficult to even think—was happening. It had to be successful; he wouldn't think otherwise.

Foster had taken over for Burnsides, who had left for Virginia earlier in the week to aid in another major campaign. Foster had just confirmed a rumor that had circulated. He had reason to believe young Confederate soldiers who had returned home due to injury or illness and had taken the oath were being lured to their deaths. His belief was that it was someone in the upper brass, and he wouldn't share his suspicions. Foster had asked that he and Marshall stay to discuss it after the Monday officers' meeting at the command center.

He assigned the investigation to them. There were rumors. If they were to be believed, one or more of the Union brass was doing it. Suspicions swirled around a captain in New Bern.

As they talked to men, Captain Holland's name kept coming up. He had shared how he hated the Confederates. His youngest brother had been killed at Fort Sumter and perhaps that was what had given him an ax to grind. Soldiers returning to the area were given a choice—take the pledge of allegiance or face imprisonment. That was the law, and they were sworn to uphold that law.

The captain didn't think that was good enough. It was rumored that Captain Holland had visited the men at their homes and ordered them to come with him. Sometimes he offered a flimsy excuse. Sometimes he ordered them to leave with him. These stories were just coming to light.

Some were found shot to death a half mile from their home. This had been happening for the last couple of months. Holland was reported to have been the last one to see many of the men. It was too much of a coincidence.

Now that Jackson and Marshall had realized this, they planned to look into this quietly themselves. Jackson wanted to be there in case Holland's involvement turned out to be true, but first, he needed to get Nolan away.

Clicking softly, he urged Mason towards the back of the barn. Nolan was waiting, just as they had planned.

Jackson pulled up alongside Nolan and heard the undeniable soft click of a gun. He drew his lips together as he looked over at Nolan.

"Sorry. Instinct. I un-cocked my gun." Nolan winced and brought his hand out of the saddlebag. He grabbed his saddle horn, so Jackson could see his hand.

"Where did you get a gun? I didn't know you had one." Jackson spoke deliberately as he evaluated the man in front of him. Did he read this man wrong? Was this a mistake?

"Sorry, Jackson. I took my pa's old six-shooter. Habit. I thought we might need the extra gun."

Jackson let out a small whoosh of breath. He realized how tight his body was from stress and tried to relax. He lowered his shoulders and took a deep breath, letting it out slowly.

"That's fine. You are right. We may. So, here is my plan: we will ride towards Kinston. I will get you within two miles of your camp—at least past where I know Union scouts and details to be—and then I'll head back. Meanwhile, if Union pickets stop us, let me do the talking. I will assess the situation as we get into it. Maybe we will get lucky and have clear sailing. Just don't act surprised with anything I say—play along. I want to make sure we both get away and I can get back in one piece."

"Certainly." A moment of silence passed. "Jackson, thank you for this. I know what you are risking. I hope I would do this for you if the situation was reversed."

Nodding, Jackson relaxed, a grin spreading across his face. "You know how I feel about your sister and your brother. And who knows? You could become my brother one day. I want that day to come. This is the only solution."

"Brothers. That could be good." Nolan reached out to shake Jackson's hand as their horses stood side by side. "Thank you."

"Let's ride." They trotted away from the town that held both of their hearts.

Jackson cleared his throat to get Nolan's attention. "I have a Confederate officer's uniform sewn into this blanket roll behind me." Jackson jerked his head to his right, pointing towards the back of

Mason. "Before we separate, I plan to give you a gun, ammo, and the uniform. It's one that had been confiscated from a Confederate body and found its way into my camp."

Jackson didn't comment further on that incident. He looked at Nolan to gauge his reaction.

"You've thought of everything," Nolan acknowledged. "I don't know what to say, except thank you."

Jackson chortled. "I hope you can say that you can cook. If this trip takes longer than we anticipate, we will need meals. I didn't pack anything more than hardtack and water."

"Yes. I did learn to make a couple of things. Rabbit stew and some simple things like that. We learned to live off the land as young men. You had to be able to cook what you killed."

They rode in silence for a while. Nolan cleared his throat and broke the quiet.

"I know a way. It's not obvious, and it's really just a trail, but I think it would keep us off the main road that takes so many back and forth to New Bern if you are game."

"Sure. I figured you might know a better way." He smiled at Nolan and he turned off the road behind him. They rode into the wooded area and soon found themselves on a well-worn trail that ran alongside the river.

A half-hour later, they smelled smoke. "Looks like something is burning up ahead. That's Charlie Summer's place."

"You know him?"

Nolan nodded. "The Summers are our neighbors and members of our church. I've known them all of my life. Can we take a minute and investigate?"

"Yes. We can't pass it without looking in on them. But let's agree that if it looks dangerous or if it looks like we would be in over our heads, we need to keep going." Jackson worried about the cause of the smoke.

"Agreed."

They both kicked their mounts into a run, moving along the perimeter of the property. As they neared it, they noticed the barn was already smoldering. The house was consumed in flames. There were no obvious signs of life, people or horses. Dead livestock lay scattered everywhere. They had all been shot. As the two men got closer, they spotted bodies lying face down in front of the house.

Without a word between them, they both hurried to the bodies.

A bad feeling reached the pit of Jackson's stomach.

"Oh, no!" Nolan threw his reins aside and dismounted.

Jackson looked around, studying the landscape. There was an eerie silence. Nothing stirred. He saw no signs of anyone else on the property. He couldn't shake that suspicious feeling. The barn and the house had to have been set on fire in the last hour. His bad feeling just got worse. He dismounted and walked to the bodies where Nolan was kneeling.

The couple, an older man and woman, lay face down together. Their bodies connected by clasped hands. Nolan pulled their hands apart and rolled Mr. Summers over. He had a bullet in his chest and had died instantly. Mrs. Summers had been shot in the head.

"They have powder burns. They were shot at close range," Jackson observed.

"Rinny!" Nolan gently laid Mr. Summer's body back down and moved to the Brittany Spaniel laying nearby. He touched his head, and the dog opened his eyes and whimpered. "Hey, boy." He rubbed his head slowly. The dog's eyes struggled open.

Wide-eyed, he cradled the dog's head in his lap. "He is still alive. Jackson, I've known this dog since he was a puppy. His name is Rinny. He was their companion."

Nolan noticed Jackson scrutinizing the grounds, keeping his hand covering his holstered gun. He hoped he didn't have his back to the people that had done this if they were still around.

Jackson's subtle movement reminded Nolan to cover his own gun. He pulled the gun from its holster and placed it beside him before he turned his attention back to Rinny. His voice cracked. "I used to take Rinny with Rover and me when we went fishing. The fastest dog around! Rinny must have tried to defend them."

At the sound of Nolan's voice, the dog tried to lift his head to lick his hand, but his strength failed and Rinny's head fell back onto Nolan's lap. His tongue hung out of his mouth.

"He has a gunshot wound here, left of his chest. Looks like it missed his heart." Nolan probed the wound and looked closer. He laid the dog's head down. Pulling out his pocketknife, he stood up. "I will get the bullet out, but he also needs water. He's parched and might die of thirst before the bullet kills him."

He walked to a small well that was still standing on the side of what used to be the house. Turning a crank, he pulled up a bucket of cool water and unhooked it. He took his pocketknife over and held it to the smoldering wood to sterilize it.

When he got back to Rinny, he steadied the dog and ladled water into his mouth. A few minutes later, the injured dog moved his tail. It was an attempt at a wag.

"This is gonna hurt, boy." Nolan worked on the wound a few minutes while Jackson held the dog's paws and stroked his head.

"Got it!" Nolan held up the bloodied bullet. "Okay. I need something to stem this flow of blood." He took his knife and heated it again. After cauterizing the wound, he tore off part of Mrs. Summer's petticoat and wrapped it securely around Rinny's chest. A small trickle of blood surfaced, but after a few minutes, the wound closed. Nolan gave the dog more water while he tried to lick his hand.

Jackson couldn't help but be moved by the wounded dog trying to repay a kindness. He never had a dog of his own, but always wanted one. A twinge of jealousy at the exchange of feeling between Nolan and Rinny hit him. The dog loved him. He wanted to have that someday—a home and a dog.

"I guess we have to worry about infection."

Jackson looked up at the brilliance of the sunrise, a sharp contrast to the smoky curtain floating up in front. "We can't leave these bodies for the buzzards. We need to bury them. They must be shallow graves, for now. We'll mark them with stones. I'll get a detail and come back to retrieve the bodies later and give them a proper burial."

"Sure." Nolan fought back emotion. He loved this dog. These were his people. They were part of his family. What could they possibly have done to merit such treatment? He looked over at Rinny stretched out in the heat. Feeling a little overwhelmed by this tragedy, Nolan picked the dog up and carried him to the shade of the nearby oak tree to cool him while they buried the Summers.

Jackson watched Nolan as he gently rubbed Rinny's back under the shade of the tree. They had already spent too much time, and they had miles to go. Saving the dog's life could cost them theirs.

It was useless thinking along those lines. They wouldn't be able to leave the dog, so he needed to think of something.

The two of them buried the couple in a shallow grave close to the well and marked it with large stones in the sign of a cross. Both men remained quiet, reflecting on what had happened and what they had just done.

Jackson was the first to break the silence. "Good thing you found those shovels. You seem to know this property well."

Nolan looked up. "Yes, I do. Mr. Summers was my father's cousin. We saw them every Sunday for most of my childhood. He was part of our family. They had no children. Ella and I spent a lot of time here while we were growing up."

"I understand. We need to get moving." Jackson used his hat to dust his pants, giving it a slight shake before putting it back on his head. He motioned towards the well. "It will be very warm today so let's make sure our canteens are full." He pulled his canteen from his horse and filled it from the bucket. Once full, he passed the bucket to Nolan and wiped off the water that escaped his mouth with the back of his gloved hand.

Nolan took the bucket of water and poured it over his head to cool himself, and then he filled his canteen. He took a drink and headed to his horse.

"I cannot leave Rinny here to die. I can't. But I have an idea." He waited for Jackson's reaction.

As if Rinny understood he was being discussed, the dog lifted his head and licked Nolan's hand. He was improving a little.

"It's okay, boy. We're gonna help you. I know you tried to protect them." Nolan gave Rinny some water from his canteen.

Jackson gazed at the man and the dog in front of him. This day had gotten off to a bad start. What had been a mission he thought would go smoothly was changing pace and getting out of hand.

Nolan was right. He couldn't leave the dog, either. The dog would just die. Rinny was a hero, and he didn't leave heroes to be eaten by buzzards. "Okay, what is your idea?" He watched Rinny try to thump his tail.

Pointing to the swamp, Nolan replied, "Ol' Indie. Her home is not too far from here. She knows medicine and she can help Rinny. We can leave him there. When he is better, Carter can bring him home. Ella will keep him for me."

"Ol' Indie lives where?" The information that the soft-spoken black woman lived in a swamp shocked him. "The swamp?" Jackson had heard of people who lived in such places, but it was in books. He had never seen one.

As he thought about it, it made sense. The woman had been given her independence from the family, and she would protect that. What better place to live than in the swamp? It was hidden from people she wanted to stay away from, and it was a place few would venture. He didn't want to go there.

"Okay. Wait. *What?*" His mind reeled as clarity hit him. He recalled the confidence she worked with healing Ella. That was why they could never pick up a clue as to Nolan's whereabouts. He was in the swamp.

He grimaced at the realization that this swamp was their only good solution. "What direction does she live? Do we need a boat, or is it on land so we can reach it?" He thought of the slimy creatures that inhabited the swamp, forcing a shudder through him. "Let's make this fast and get on our way. There are things I want to tell you—some things I think you may need to know."

Nolan looked up at Jackson, concern imprinted on his face.

"Marshall knows nothing about this... escape effort." Jackson continued. "He's been my best friend for most of my life and is more like a brother than my own brother was. If I'm caught, I don't want him involved. That is why I kept this from him. I told him we would meet in a couple of days to discuss several situations over which we have to gain control." Jackson pulled up the reins and pointed his horse to turn around. He surveyed the farm once more and snarled in disgust at the smoking remnants of the house, the barn, and the stench that had started because of the senseless slaughter of the animals.

I should tell Nolan that Marshall is out with a contingent looking for the Blacks.

This looked like their work. They might be closer to him and Nolan than to Marshall and his detail. He started to say something but changed his mind. They needed to get their journey underway, and he didn't want to be overheard in case the couple was still hanging around. He still had this bad feeling that all here was not as it appeared.

"Can you carry Rinny on your horse? Your blanket isn't sewn together and can cover him. It might help keep him from going into shock."

Nolan nodded and grabbed his blanket roll.

The two men carefully enveloped Rinny in the blanket and gave him a little more water. Once Nolan mounted his horse, Jackson gently hoisted the dog onto his lap and secured him.

He mounted Mason. "You lead. Let's get out of here."

The two men kicked their horses into a gallop. They needed to travel fast. Nolan kept one arm wrapped around the dog and the other on his reins. They headed towards a copse of trees ahead on the river's edge.

CHAPTER 24

The light left them as they entered the thicket of vegetation. Their pace slowed to a trot, and they picked their way over fallen trees and other low brush and debris. The much cooler air was a relief.

Ten minutes went by and Nolan recognized the familiar remnants of an old burned homestead. The fireplace was the only thing partially standing, but it was enough to serve as a good landmark. He slowed his mount even more and signaled Jackson to fall in behind him. Their path ended at a dark copse of brush. He carefully moved aside a false front of the thicket with his free arm, and gestured Jackson to follow him onto a narrow path hidden behind it.

Once they secured the thicket entrance behind them, the two men moved carefully down the path. The sound of crickets chirping got louder. A narrow crevice of light broke through the trees and shined on the water's edge, illuminating its surface. It made the black water seem almost crystal-like, but it was only a couple of feet deep and was swamp.

"There is a flatboat moored here somewhere. We can use it to get down the river after we drop Rinny off with Ol' Indie."

Jackson pulled up and dismounted. He held Rinny until Nolan could alight.

Nolan had only been here once, but he was confident he could recall all the steps to the flatboat. They would need it to move the horses once they got Rinny settled.

Luck was with them. He tied up his horse and walked over to a large hollow log. Carefully, he pulled the log back, moving the almost woven thicket and giving them entrance to a hidden dock.

"The flatboat should be here. I want to check while we have good light. Let's secure this entrance in case we are followed."

They led their horses forward and moved an identical log pulling a cover over the entrance from the other side. They walked up to a dock that was almost hidden by the brush. The flatboat was anchored alongside of the dock.

"Okay, we can tie the horses on this and move up the river. We won't go far on it, but it will help cover our trail."

"You've been thinking about this. This looks like a good plan."

"I have the advantage of knowing the land." Nolan nodded. "Thank you for doing this. I know your reasons and I realize you are still questioning your judgment, but I appreciate your kindness. I understand the chance you are taking for me."

Nolan was also glad for Jackson's vigilance. He recalled seeing Jackson watch the Summers' lands carefully, even readying his gun—something Nolan missed doing.

"Do you think the horses will be okay if we put them in the lean-to over there?" Nolan pointed to a covered area about twenty feet from them. It was partially hidden.

Jackson followed the direction Nolan pointed. A lean-to large enough for the two horses stood in front. "Well, err... yes. But I'm surprised to see these accommodations. It's a good use of this rather obscure land. What other uses does this area have?"

Nolan smiled at Jackson. "Well, I know that this is part of the underground. Slaves passed from here safely most of the time, headed north to Ohio. I'm not sure of the next stop, but this was one of the best places they left from, as I understand. This war will change all of that."

"But you still have slaves, although many ran off, according to Ella."

Nolan nodded. "Yes. You may have noticed it, but we feel differently about our workers than most. We grew up knowing we had to respect the system. We don't like slavery, but this is the South and being different isn't tolerated too well. We tried to do things different where we could. We made our money on the crops and we gave our slaves a share of the crop money, and a place to live. Profits always supported our way of doing things. We rarely had runaways—until the war, when they were freed." Nolan harrumphed.

"You don't agree they should be freed?"

Nolan thought for a minute. "Yes and no. I know that we practiced slavery here. We still have slaves although Ella doesn't think of them as slaves. They are our people, our friends and family. It's the way we were raised. Our parents always tried to help our people. We couldn't do things like teach them all to read, 'cause word would get out and it would cause trouble for everyone, including the slaves. But to free them without first making sure they can provide for their families is wrong. They need trade skills to earn a living, and they need to read, write, and cipher.

Jackson considered what Nolan told him. "It makes sense, what you say. Your people are very loyal to you and your family that much I have observed. They know they are free to go if they want, yet they stay."

"My mamma and papa were great people." Nolan stopped. He realized he used the past tense when he mentioned his father. "I guess you know my papa left shortly after I did. We haven't heard from him. I know I will need to find him, but don't know the first place to look." He looked away from Jackson, not at anything in particular. "Let's tie up our horses there. We'll use the post, hurry over there, and get back." He pointed to a small knoll of land that had a tree stump in the middle. "Not too many horses come back here, unless it's Carter. He fixed up hooks on it."

They secured their horses. Jackson took Rinny down, getting a lick for his efforts. Once Nolan got off his mount, he got Rinny and walked to the bridge.

"Okay. Let's head over to Ol' Indie's."

They got through the thicketed entrance and looked back to ensure the spot was as hidden as they found it.

"Which way?" Jackson looked at the wooded, damp area that surrounded them.

"This way." They backtracked a little along the path they initially came through, but then turned right into an area that seemed to be darker than the rest. Two old oak trees stood side by side, almost like an entrance. Once they passed the oaks, the crickets and other night noises started up.

"Careful. Let's go one in front of the other. Ol' Indie's hut isn't far ahead, but it's a little difficult to see and get to."

The two men meandered. Now and then, Rinny would raise his head a little, but Nolan patted him, calming him.

They came to a tiny muddy beach. More light seemed to break through here.

"There's her hut." Nolan pointed to a hut over the water, about thirty yards out. "The bridge is attached with ropes on all sides. It is an elaborate system that serves as both handrails and functions as a pulley to move the bridge to the hut and back." The light ended at the beach, leaving the hut in a dark, shaded area. It faced the south, catching the early sun; by noon the trees cast it into a shadowed darkness.

"You have to know this is here to notice or find it."

"Yes, I think that was the idea. Ol' Indie always wanted to have her own place. Her people used to practice medicine and when my papa freed her, giving her papers, she didn't go far. She tries to help anyone she can. Ol' Indie found me on the battlefield. I woke up here after she had doctored on me for a while."

Jackson reflected on that information for a moment before responding. "That explains a lot."

"Yes. I found my way out, and well, you know the rest." Nolan didn't want to shine a light on that again. He needed to get Rinny over to Ol' Indie and get going.

At the water's edge, he laid Rinny down, picked up a small stone, and threw it at the hut. It ricocheted off the wall and landed in the water. "It's a signal." The two men and the dog got on the flat floating bridge and pulled it towards the hut.

The door opened and Ol' Indie stepped out. "Lordy. What you brung me, Massa Nole?" She peeked closer to the dog. "That's Massa Summer's dog. What you do 'in with Massa Summers' dog, Massa Nole?"

"Someone murdered the Summers—not sure how or by whom. Rinny was left for dead. He probably tried to defend them. Can you help him?"

"Oh Lordy!" she glanced over her shoulder. "Carter. We need your help."

Her son emerged from the hut and helped bring Rinny inside.

"Carter. I wondered if you were here." Nolan shook his hand.

"Yassuh. I brung Ma some baked bread and beans from supper last evening, and I see she has herself some warm cornbread and bacon going." He grinned at his mother.

"I didn't see a horse, Carter. How'd you get here?" Jackson checked behind him, as if making sure he hadn't overlooked a horse.

"Why, I walked and rode the flat float, suh." Carter looked confused as to what this visit was about.

"I'd love to stay and have a longer visit, but we need to get going. I'm heading back to my unit. Colonel Ross is taking me part of the way."

Jackson looked at Nolan, a puzzled look on his face.

"Yassuh." Ol' Indie nodded her head several times, focusing on Rinny. "Well, you leave des here dog with me. I think I can doctor him up just like new. You want us to bring him back to de house when he feels betta?" Ol' Indie lightly scratched Rinny's head. At her soft touch, Rinny tried to raise his head.

"You think you can heal him?" Nolan's voice caught. "We couldn't leave him to be pecked to death by buzzards."

"I sure do, Massa Nole. Don't you worry about des here dog. He gonna be just fine." Ol' Indie nodded to her son, signaling him to bring the dog closer to her medicines.

Carter placed Rinny on a pallet that Ol' Indie placed near the stove and her herb cabinet. Rinny tried to raise his head as if to say goodbye but couldn't. Nolan leaned down and petted the dog almost reverently. "I'll see you again, Rinny," Nolan whispered. "Thank you, Ol' Indie." He stood and gathered himself. His eyes misted.

Without looking back again, Nolan left the hut to join Carter and Jackson, who were waiting beyond the door.

Jackson gave a polite salute. "Thank you, Ol' Indie. I'll be heading back soon. Maybe when you stop by, you can let me know how Rinny is doing?"

"Yassuh, Colonel, suh. I will do that. And Massa Nole, this pup will be home to greet you when you get back." Ol' Indie looked tenderly at her charge, and then stepped outside. Her sharp eyes took in the sky and riveted back across the swamp to where the horses had been hidden. "You must hurry, all you boys. I hear noises in de swamp. You boys go, quickly now! Carter, show dem dat shortcut, and make sure they know about the dangers."

"Yes, Mamma." Carter hugged his mother and rushed to catch up with Nolan and Jackson, who were already walking back on the water bridge. When they got to the other side, Carter unhooked the ropes and put them back on the bridge. He gave a short whistle and Ol' Indie stepped out and retracted the bridge, section by section, back to the house.

Each section tilted when the right pressure was on it, and the next layer slid under it. Finally, the three wooden and vine segments were together, and Ol' Indie secured them at the edge of the hut. She released a rope and a large tangle of branches woven together moved down from above the hut and covered the entrance. The branches were living vines that concealed a skeleton branch.

"Let's get the horses, suh. Follow me. There is a quick way out; but, we need to hurry."

The three of them quietly made their way along the edge of the swamp facing the hut. Tied up on the shore was the large flatboat they had seen earlier, hidden beneath branches. It looked wide enough for two horses and the three men. They secured the horses to a post in the center.

Carter pushed off and grabbed the steering rudder on the back. He pointed to the poles lashed down on the sides. In a quiet voice, he broke through the crickets and other noises of the swamp. "We need to pole to the entrance over there." He pointed to a stand of vines and trees in the distance ahead of them.

The three men moved the raft and the horses in silence, going deeper into the swamp towards the river. Five minutes later, they swung their craft east, poling slowly down the still waters of the river.

"It's still. At least we don't have the current to paddle against." Carter's voice was low and hopeful. Holding onto the rudder, he leaned down and picked up two large paddles for the other men.

Nolan grabbed the paddle and slowly worked it through the water. "We should be able to get close enough to Kinston once we hit shore, Colonel. Carter will take the raft back. Unless we see some of my men, you can probably ride safely back using the main roads."

Jackson nodded, digging his paddle into the water.

Nolan swallowed back the lump in his throat. "Jackson, please take care of my family for me. Ella is a very special sister. And my baby brother... well, he already looks up to you."

"I will see to your family best I can. You try to stay alive in this conflict. Your sister will count on you coming back home to her." Jackson held his paddle for a moment. "I think under different circumstances we could be friends, but this war..." he said, dropping his thought. "I do, however, wish you safe passage to your men."

Nolan smiled and reached over to pat the neck of his mount.

They had only covered a few miles of the river when they heard a man and a woman's voice coming from the shoreline behind them. The riders were still too far away to see their faces, but the men knew the raft had been spotted.

Carter picked up a paddle himself. All three of them put their shoulders into paddling as hard as they could, their distant goal in sight.

Carter spoke first. "I recognize them. Those people were camping in the swamp right much. They both got soldier uniforms, but it sounds like they is a man and a woman. Can't tell from a distance—I didn't get too close 'because they look like trouble. They stay away from Ma's hut. Ma says she heard voices of a woman over the water, talking to a man about the voodoo woman in the swamp. It's hard to sneak up on Ma's hut. The voices carry loud over water." Carter chuckled softly and passed a sly look to both men. "They may think Ma will cast some kind of spell on them."

"Does she really know voodoo?" Jackson's eyes widened.

"Oh yes, suh. She does. Our people be from the islands. They pass that knowledge to my ma as a chile. But Ma, she only uses the good healing powers. She doesn't believe in doing bad things to people. Ma says I don't have the right concentration, so she doesn't plan to waste her time teaching any of the medicines to me." Carter snickered. "Lizzy may learn, though. Ma says she at the right age to learn."

"Just curious, but about what is the right age to learn?" Jackson whispered.

"Well, a body grows up learning and knowing. But Lizzy is 'bout twenty-five years," Carter responded. "We were raised together. I'm older by a bit, maybe ten years."

"Carter and Lizzy have lived with our family as far back as I can remember," Nolan interjected. "I recall Pa discussing Lizzy as being about five years older than Ella. They have been more family than anything else."

"We both feel that way, Massa Nole."

Nolan swallowed. The clarity of Ella's argument dawned on

Nolan. They were family to her, and he was seeing her point about their people. "Carter's right. His ma only uses her medicine to help people. She has been helping people all over the plantation. She saved many with her medicines and her knowledge. Ol' Indie is a wise woman; she has always been part of our family." His voice conveyed concern. It was important that Ol' Indie wasn't thought to be a witch among these Yankees.

Shots fired along the shore grabbed their attention. The horses spooked and stamped to get away. Jackson passed his paddle to Nolan, then, turned to the horses, quieting them.

It took a few minutes, but the horses calmed down. The three men together looked around the river, at least the part they could see.

Nobody. Where had they gone? They hadn't imagined the shots.

~

Jackson couldn't decide how he felt. On one hand, he felt like he had made the right decision, considering the danger Nolan would have been in had he been turned over to take the oath—not that he thought that process would have born results. He knew better. He would have been confined to the plantation, until being moved to a prison camp, since he was an officer. If it became known that he spied as Private White, he would have been hanged.

He thought about the meeting he and Marshall had with Foster; they talked about almost ten known Confederate soldiers who had returned home and then disappeared only to be found dead later.

These soldiers had taken the oath and should have been able to live without fear of retaliation. They bore no threat. It had to be someone in charge that could order these young men out of their homes.

His gut twisted at the thought of Ella facing bad news of her brother. Helping Nolan escape was the best immediate solution.

At least that's what he was telling himself.

This day had taken a turn for the complicated. Jackson had the uncomfortable feeling that he had launched himself into the middle of a wild adventure. Backwoods, swamps, voodoo magic, hidden rafts, and the death of two prominent citizens—not to mention saving a dog. He had even taken refuge in the middle of some of the darkest marshes on the river.

A few of his questions about Whitford got answered though. He wasn't sure how he felt about all of that yet. He would need more time to ponder over the day.

At least there was a small measure of comfort in the realization that there was no way they could have found Nolan Whitford. The young man had been hidden and well cared for by none other than sweet Ol' Indie. Had it not been for her, he might have been found.

A chuckle escaped, and he looked around, hoping he hadn't laughed aloud. No one seemed to hear anything. He relaxed.

No one would have found her hut. Jackson wasn't sure how he felt about that, but now wasn't the time. She had been good to all of them and had probably saved Ella's life as much as he had. She put her life in jeopardy, walking herself right into that trap just to get to Ella.

Now they were saddled with the Blacks, cast-outs from the Southern army ranks who were probably responsible for the brutality being reaped on unsuspecting families in this area. Carter's description of the two people sounded like the Blacks.

They seemed close again. Where was Marshall? Had he picked up the Blacks' trail? As much as he hoped their trail was in the other direction, it could be hard to explain what he was doing if Marshall happened upon him and Nolan here together.

The shots made him nervous. If it wasn't the Blacks, who could these people be, and what were they after?

They were dangerous that was certain. He didn't want to be a target in the middle of the river. Had these people followed them from the farm? Were they planning to attack? There had to be a purpose as to why they were being tracked.

There were so many questions. He rubbed his forehead, trying to delay the pain he felt moving from the back of his head. Jackson adjusted his hat back a little. The shore was close. He had the unnerving feeling that trouble could be, too.

Fifteen minutes went by and Carter directed the party onto a jutting branch of land almost hidden by hanging vegetation. They pulled the raft up to the shore and disembarked. The horses neighed and stomped their feet, letting everyone know they were glad to see hard dirt.

"Suh, I think I will lie low and wait a little while before taking the raft back to the swamp." Carter dropped the rope around the steering oar and pulled it onto shore, wrapping it around the largest shrub.

"Be careful," Jackson replied, looking around.

"Well, yassuh. I will. Massa Nolan, be careful getting to Kinston."

Jackson looked at Nolan. He seemed pensive.

"Colonel Ross, you a real good man, suh. We 'appreciate what you are doing here for Massa Nolan." Carter reached out to shake Jackson's hand.

"I asked Carter to be an extra set of ears for you and make sure he keeps an eye on the areas around the home," Nolan added.

"Fine. Let's move away from the river. Carter, any advice you can give would be appreciated. Thank you very much for helping us. We wouldn't have made it this far without your help."

"You welcome, suh." Carter gave a quick nod, appreciating their words. He shifted his shoulders, standing up straighter. He motioned towards the small brush covering up the entrance to the makeshift pier. "Okay, go straight through that pass yonder and it will take you clear to a main road. Don't know what the name is, but we call it the river road, since it mostly follows the river. Head east going on six miles. You will come to a small farm just a stone's throw from Sassers' Mill. You 'member that place, don't you, Massa Nole? Your daddy would take the grain there every season." Carter looked at Jackson. "Now, Sassers' Mill is a stronghold for the Confederates. We see them all the time, their people patrolling."

"We?" Jackson had to ask. "Who do you mean, 'we'?"

"Us Negroes, of course. We move in the brush, so we aren't seen. You may not even know we are around. We learn to move quickly and quietly to stay away from the slavers. Even us free ones, we know better than to be caught, and these times, many Negroes work for the Union Army, running errands back and forth."

He hesitated. "Colonel Ross, suh, Massa Nole is like a brother and you and Miss Ella be getting on good. My Lizzy and me, we don't want you boys harmed."

"Why thank you, Carter." A smile covered Jackson's face. "And I enjoy your company."

Carter nodded. "Well, now. Best that I finish up, so you folks can get on your way. There's six hours to nightfall and the heat is still rising. I think it be best to move at night. It could take longer, but you will have cover. Try to stay to the sides of de road, keeping your eyes peeled. There be some of my folks, Colonel, that would do you harm. They'd let the Rebs know you on de road, mostly alone. No offense, Massa Nole. But, these things are important. They turn in a man such as yourself, Colonel. It brings a reward."

Carter cleared his throat. Nolan and Jackson nodded.

He continued. "Once you get there, if you head east, Lower Trent Road takes you to Kinston. Massa Nole, you 'members the way." When you get to Wyse Forks, head to Kinston. Colonel, head west. West puts you on Upper Trent and takes you back to New Bern. Remember—try to keep to de shadows if you can and be watchful. The Confederates have a line set up at Southwest Creek, 'bout five miles down Lower Trent. Best you be on the lookout for scouts. I see them often.

"There be some farmland up here, close now. They have a big well and you can water the horses, most likely without being seen. The family be done gone. Headed out of town when the Union soldiers came. Might be a good place to stop and rest. It's just beyond the first turn in the road going east."

Jackson nudged Mason closer, and he shook Carter's hand.

Nolan hugged Carter. "Take good care of Rinny for me. I'll do my best to come home. I promise. Keep everyone straight for us, Carter." He winked and mounted his mare. The two men headed quietly towards the main road.

CHAPTER 25

"Lizzy, have you seen the lieutenant colonel? Nolan and Colonel Ross left at daybreak today. I heard the horses leave. It's unusual that he hasn't come by for anything. He seemed almost too quiet when he returned from taking Sara back yesterday." Ella poured a little of the oil and apple cider vinegar mixture on her rag, rubbing it into the wood on the desk slowly. "Something's not right. I feel it."

"No, Miss Ella. I haven't. Carter is gone, too. He left last night. This house just seems empty today."

"Not only empty, but more. Since Sara left and then Nolan this morning, things seem different, sad. I pray he stays safe wherever he is right now."

Ella fumbled around with the gun cabinet, the rag wiping around the front panel. She was doing anything to push away her sudden case of melancholia. It was empty now, but her guns were close-by in the hall closet in case she needed them.

Since her horrible ordeal with Jason, she needed her shotgun nearby at all times. Jackson never said a word when she had pulled Papa's gun from the cabinet. When he had asked, she had told him she did it. He didn't seem alarmed about the gun, only about her.

So much had changed since her abduction. She felt protected—he held her, and she didn't hate him. His kiss still burned in her mind. His touch reduced her to mush within minutes. She didn't understand all of what she was feeling, having never courted. He tantalized her thoughts. What she was feeling was beyond courting. She warmed as she recalled his lips burning a trail down the side of her neck, her arms—right here in this room.

She looked around. This library had become a different room for her. Not just a room for books and bills, but one that had given her even more knowledge. It held memories of her body awakening and her heart opening.

She wasn't too sure about everything, but she knew she wanted Jackson here with her. She wanted him here now. The feelings he made her feel... she never knew a body could feel that way. It was addictive.

She was safe but feeling safe was not the problem. After all, how could she not with hundreds of soldiers right here?

There is that, but it didn't keep me from being kidnapped.

A cynical laugh escaped her. The thing she couldn't escape was the feeling of helplessness that the assault and kidnapping had given her.

Lizzy started at her laugh. "Miss Ella, you are here, but you are also somewhere else."

She walked up to Ella and picked up the discarded rag and the oil mixture for the furniture. Handing Ella another rag, the two women worked together and finished the desk and the other exposed hardwood areas. Some furniture had been in the family for over one hundred years.

"Lizzy thank you. I appreciate you showing me how to take care of the furniture. I want the house to be okay when this war is over, and Nolan is home."

"Miss Ella, I was right worried when I saw you spying on the colonel and your brother outside the library. Carter and me know you done lost your heart to that man. He a good one even if he is fighting against the South."

"Yea. I guess lying that I was worried about the state of the furnishings with the men and their cigar smoke got me a lesson on polishing and more work."

The two women giggled.

"I know you were spying. Miss Ella you betta be careful about hurting the colonel. He cares for you and you aren't a spy. You are not a person who can remember to lie."

"Lizzy, I suppose you are right." She sighed heavily and absently rubbed the oil blend into the pianoforte. "I'm so worried about Nolan. And what are we going to tell Aiden when he looks for his brother?"

"I know you are worried. The colonel gonna look out for you." She paused smiled across the piano at Ella. "Your brother will be back, you'll see. I feel it."

They finished conditioning the piano and pulled the door to the music room closed, both heading for the dining room.

"As far as what to tell Aiden, say just what Massa Nole told you. We tell him he went back to his job, but he will be back as soon as he has a chance, and they will go fishing again—and to mind you, of course. Oh, do you think we should add that he needs to be more attentive to Bo's need to go outside for his business a little more often?" Lizzy chuckled.

"Brother worship can go a long way." Ella broke into a big smile and laughed, feeling like a weight had been lifted. She wasn't sure if it was the fear of Nolan getting punished by the Yankees or the fact that she understood her feelings about Jackson. She could do worse.

He was a Yankee, but he was her Yankee.

"Jackson said he would be back in a day or two. He asked that we tell Marshall he would catch up with him if Marshall asks about him." She stopped. "That seems strange to me. I thought the two men knew each other's comings and goings. But I will do as he asked. You too. Should he ask, you know nothing of his whereabouts. But ever since Monday, Jackson and Nolan have been discussing something." Ella lowered her voice. "I cannot even hear inside the library when they are talking. They kept their voices so low. I don't know what could be so important that they can't talk in normal voices." She harrumphed and spun around to check the desk drawers. "Of course, they are locked."

"You know he locks that desk. You have your secrets, and he has his. No disrespect, but you don't plan to share information about the safe room with him, do you?"

"Certainly not. And no disrespect taken. That safe room is something only the family knows about." She smiled at Lizzy, her meaning clear. "Come on. Let's wash the linens. It's still early. Perhaps that will move my head in a better direction. I want to think about anything but this war. I already miss Nola

Ella headed for the safe room, but Lizzy stopped her.

"I got that earlier." She reached into her pocket. "I almost forgot. Here are some letters Massa Nole left."

"Thank you, Lizzy. I'd like to read these.

"You need to be out here for when young Massa Aiden wakes up. The less he sees that his brother is gone, maybe he will accept it easier."

"You are right, of course. He should wake up about now. After we finish this, I'll rouse him from bed."

"Miss Ella, I probably should not say this, but we be talking about everything but the elephant in the room. You know you need to talk about it to someone," Lizzy soothed. "The colonel is helping your brother escape. If he gets caught, he will probably be hanged as a traitor. That must make you feel something inside."

"I've never had these feelings before, Lizzy. My heart tells me what to say instead of my head. And my body feels odd when he's near. He makes me feel special and giddy at the same time. These emotions and sensations are all so new for me." She worked her throat. "But I always feel comfortable talking to you..." Her voice trailed off for a moment, smiling. A moment later, she shook her head, trying to clear it.

"What you describe, Miss Ella, is what lots of women feel when they meet their special man."

"I know," was all Ella whispered.

Ella felt almost relieved to have a reason to talk about what was going on in her head. "I... I don't know how I feel, truth be told. I think I'm at such odds with myself. Lizzy, do you think I am conflicted?" She was rambling. "And I'm so anxious. I'm real worried about Nolan and Jackson." Her voice quivered.

"You got a right to be worried, Miss Ella. He is doing something for you that could get him into bad trouble. And he is doing it because he feels something for you, I think."

"That man has come here and taken over my life. He smothers me. He insists that he has to escort me whenever I go into town, something I have been doing since I was a girl. He wants to know where I am, what I'm doing, and what I am thinking." Ella stopped. She knew this was just a rant of frustration. "I have feelings for him. And I am troubled sick about him. What if something happens to them?"

"Shush. Don't even talk like that. You know that's bad luck."

"It was easier when I hated all the Yankees, but I could never hate Jackson or Marshall." She paced the floor in front of the desk. "Not now that we know them and see they are normal like us, and nice. They don't see the whole picture. They don't see our side."

Even as she said it, she knew she was wrong. Jackson was extremely fair. The man had gotten under her skin. He was in her heart. She wasn't sure she liked the feeling. It scared her. What if he gets hurt? There was Nolan, and now there was Jackson. Both could get hurt or killed in this war.

With a jolt, she realized that she loved him. What would she do if something happened to Jackson?

This vulnerability was harder than she imagined. Maybe this was what love made a person feel. Her mamma and papa had loved each other.

Her papa.

She could understand a little better what Papa might have felt when he lost Mamma. The thought of it made her feel the loss of both of her parents all over again. Nolan mentioned he would look for Papa, wherever he was, and find him. She hoped so.

"Miss Ella? You be miles from here."

"Lizzy, I've been thinking—about everything. I feel so torn inside. This life we have, it isn't what any of us thought our lives would be like. And I would have never thought I'd hear these words from my mouth, but I think I love him. It cannot come to anything, what with both Jackson and Nolan on opposite sides in the war. How would that work? It makes me feel... vulnerable. I can't tell him. What would it mean to him? He has mentioned nothing about a future. No, I wouldn't know how to do that, and I don't know how he would react. But I think he likes me. Oh, pshaw! It's unfair for the Union Army to have men like Jackson. He's gentle, giving, fair, protective, strong, and very handsome. He understands me and likes me. How's a girl supposed to ignore that?" She almost squeaked that last sentence out. Hearing it out loud, she broke out in a rare case of giggles. She had laughed little since before Nolan had left to join the Cause.

"Miss Ella, as your friend, I see that he more than likes you."

"Why do you say that?" Ella needed to know.

"He is always looking in your direction. Always. He knows where you are, and most of the time, he seems to find a way to spend time with you. His face... he panics if you aren't close by. It's been worse since the kidnapping. I know it must be hard on you. I worry 'bout Carter, too. But we can never know when they will run into danger, doing what they are doing."

"You are right, Lizzy. I need to be more positive. I don't know what has come over me."

"Love, Miss Ella. I saw it with your mamma and papa. And I love my Carter. Love has come over you." She gathered up the rags and the oil. "Now, I'm going to the kitchen to get Cook to fix a good breakfast for Massa Aiden. You go wake him."

"Thanks so much for our talk. I know you will keep it between us."

"'Course."

Ella headed upstairs to wake Aiden and Bo while Lizzy headed to the kitchen. Her mind seemed possessed today. She missed the protective feeling she got when Jackson was here. And she couldn't get the feel of his rippled chest off her mind. She didn't see it, but she touched it, and the sensations were more vivid in her mind. Needing more, she wondered what he would look like without his uniform. Would the rest of his body look as beautiful as his face and his hands?

Small butterflies chose that moment to create complete chaos within her stomach, sending that tingling heat radiating up her neck. Her body reacted whenever she thought of him. Best get that under control or she would never survive his absence. She pulled up her collar and strode towards Aiden's room.

CHAPTER 26

The day had heated up since leaving Carter at the river. Nolan had forgotten the difference in temperature that the over brush around the river provided. August was always hot, nearly unbearable. The farm he spoke of had to be just ahead. As they rode along, they took the trail that ran along the road, canopied by the overgrowth, thinking it to be cooler. Besides, it looked like some hostile action had occurred on the road.

Charred trees lay along the edge of the road opposite them. The brush alongside the road on that side showed signs of regrowth. What concerned the men were the signs that the small path they were on now had been traveled. Most of the taller grass had been tromped down to form the pathway, and the grass was still green. It was wide enough for two horses side by side to pass through. Other than that, there was no sign of people.

Nolan broke the silence. "I recognize some of this. It's been a while since I've been this way. It amazed me how well Carter knew this area." He paused. "You can trust what he tells you, Jackson."

"Yes, both he and Lizzy are easy to be around. I'm feeling almost part of the family, despite how I came to your plantation." Jackson regarded Nolan. "If it wasn't for this war, I would feel more comfortable talking with you. There are things I want to say but can't or won't. I care for your sister, Nolan, and she is why I am doing this. You know that. I expect you to take care of yourself and come home when this war ends. Whichever side wins, there will be a need for strong leaders such as yourself, both militarily and in the community."

"Thank you, Jackson. Yes, when the war ends, I'm coming home. And I hope when I do, I can call you brother. I wish I had not left sometimes, but I was asked, and felt it my duty. The two of us have fundamental differences of opinion where this war is concerned." He scoffed. "Seems strange to be having this conversation with you. Having gotten to know you, though, it's harder to think of you as my enemy."

Jackson nodded. "Same here. You meet people that seem to share your beliefs and values. I wonder why differences couldn't have been worked out without so much bloodshed. I can see that you and Ella don't agree on everything, but you don't draw blood." He chortled.

"Yes, well not since we've grown up a bit." Nolan sniggered. "There are things I'd like to say to you, as well. Regardless of your motivation for helping me leave Silver Moon, you are a good man, Jackson. I believe you and my sister will be happy together."

He searched Jackson's face. "Tell me again, no, swear that you will be a gentleman to my sister and do right by her."

"I promise." Jackson gave an easy smile. "She is on my mind more than duty is, I confess. She has become my beacon of light."

"I know what you mean, I feel that way about Sara. I love her, you know. We are to marry when I get back. I wouldn't marry her and risk her becoming a widow." He grew quiet.

∼

*J*ackson took a moment to look at the man riding next to him. What had started as a quick decision to free him and get him to safety had turned into much more. This man would be his brother and this trip had forged an unexpected bond between them.

He meant what he said. It was hard to think of Nolan as an enemy. He was not just a man in the ranks as Private White had been. Perhaps that made this mission more right in his mind.

When he got home to Ella... Grinning, he realized that she was his home. He was comfortable and happy when she was around. The idea of marrying Ella made him smile. When had getting married stopped making him want to run?

Jackson realized the anger towards Maria had vanished. She ran off with his good friend—no, former friend—a week before their wedding. He had been crushed and angry with her and Nate and anyone he thought was in on their secret. He realized that was unfair, but for close to a year-and-a-half, she had been his. They had planned a life together. He had built a home for them. The promises they had made to each other never meant a thing. He thought he loved her and that she felt the same. When she jilted him, he swore he'd never risk his heart again.

But now, knowing Ella, he saw it was more that his pride had been wounded. His heart had never been in play until now.

Holding onto his anger was futile. Without meaning to, Maria had done him a favor. She freed him, so he could find Ella, and Ella was who he needed. She was the woman he had been looking for—a woman who, with a look, could set him on fire. He was happy all the way through. When he got back to camp, she would be there, and that was a good feeling.

"Why are you smiling, Jackson?"

He was smiling. It felt good. "Well, your question made me realize that what I once thought was a terrible blow was actually a favor. That's why. And I was thinking about what I will do when I get back to the house."

"I left letters for Sara and Ella. Ella will find them, I'm sure. I didn't want to leave, but I wanted them to know I'd be back. And if I don't make it back, I wanted them to know how I felt."

"Letters? Where?" Jackson had considered nothing about his aiding this escape would be written. That could be bad if the wrong person saw it. He thought about Marshall, who might not understand. He needed to explain.

"I know what you are thinking. You can relax. I never mentioned you in my notes." Nolan grew silent, reflective. "Ella has always been strong-willed, but this war has made her strong. She has been the backbone of our family and has been Aiden's mother for his whole life. With my father missing—" Nolan swallowed and pushed on. "Things have been extremely hard. When I left, I didn't realize my sister would be so vulnerable." Nolan's voice softened. "Papa left my sister alone, and defenseless."

"Ha!" A laugh escaped. "Have you met your sister? She nearly took us out with her roof when Marshall and I surprised her. She is anything but defenseless. She is a strong woman of conviction. I'd never underestimate her backbone. Ella said you helped her learn to shoot."

"Yes." Nolan joined him laughing. "Papa and I taught her. She was always more interested in riding and target practice than anything Mamma tried to teach her. I should tell you, she is a fair shot."

"Yeah, she almost took out the top of the house." Jackson snorted. "You keep yourself safe. We will keep an eye on Sara. Before I even knew you existed, I figured she was sweet on someone—it was obvious her heart was already taken. The men weren't immune to her beauty, but she is resistant to them. She gives none of them the time of day." As if reading his mind, Jackson added, "Including Marshall. It's the chase for Marshall. And Miss Sara exasperates him." He snickered.

Nolan's face relaxed. "We've been promised to each other since our childhood, but our parents pushed back. They told us to grow up first." He grimaced. "This war was supposed to be quick, but it's been anything but. Brutal, lonely, and everywhere. I pray it ends soon."

Both men grew quiet, focused on the road ahead. The path was ending, and they would be back in the heat again. Crows cawed from the trees around them, breaking the silence. "Sara once mentioned her brother. Does he live around here?" Jackson was curious. She never talked much about him.

"No. He moved to Virginia. I haven't seen him in a while—doubt he'd even recognize me."

"Oh! That reminds me." Jackson slowed Mason's canter and pointed behind him. "The uniform I spoke of is in here." He patted his bedroll. Don't forget to get it when we stop. Put it somewhere you can get to it as you get closer to your men. Don't want to get you this far only to get shot by your own boys."

"I appreciate this, Jackson. Thank you. Are you sure you are on the other side?" He chuckled.

"Yes, well, I have to admit some surprise myself over all of this. I trusted Ella and Lizzy with our leaving, but I needed their help. They used some of your clothing to take your measurements. They tried to alter this one to fit you as a surprise. The real surprise would have been forgetting to give it to you."

"I keep thanking you because suh, I'm speechless over this..."

"Me too." He laughed. If he were caught with that uniform by anyone there would be hell to pay. How would he explain it? Who had he become that he would take these chances?

A man in love. He was in love with Ella. It felt right.

They rode in silence once more. Jackson thought about his life. He felt good about Ella. He couldn't wait to start a family with her. And Aiden. He wouldn't forget Aiden. That child melted his heart when he met him. Pirates, indeed. He would help to raise Aiden. Ella had already proven she was a great mother. He looked forward to having her meet his family. She would get on well with his sister. Both were feisty, confident women.

A tree limb fell in front of the horses and shook him from his ruminations.

A lifeless farm loomed just ahead of them.

Ten minutes later, Nolan and Jackson could see a large track of cleared land ahead. Spurring their horses, they pulled up to the outskirts of a homestead that connected to the main road.

Just as Carter had described, the farm had a big well out back. It also appeared abandoned. A shudder ran down Jackson's spine. He looked over at Nolan to see if he sensed something. Nolan was looking west of the house in the direction of the barn. They did need to water their horses and fill their canteens.

Both men slowly headed to the well, loosely tying their horses to a tree limb nearby. They were thirsty and tired. Rest was what they needed. They decided to rest until dusk, and then get back in the saddle.

~

Nolan worried they would oversleep. If they did, it might push them to travel in the heat and light of the day. That could be dangerous.

He itched to get to his men. The mission hadn't gone the way anyone had anticipated. Not at all.

New Bern was lost, at least for now. He had almost faced a prison camp, or worse, except Jackson, chose to risk his career—his life, really—to save him and get him out of New Bern. They planned to part soon, once they got past the Union forces, and as close to the Southern forces in Kinston as they dared.

It was hard to figure this man. As much as Nolan wanted to dislike Jackson, he couldn't. He believed him and didn't think he had read the man wrong.

"Toss your canteen to me and I'll fill it up."

Jackson's voice jarred him from his thoughts. "Here." He tossed the canteen, smiling.

~

Jackson slowly reeled up the bucket from the well, bringing up a pail of water. He sniffed it and smiled. "Yes, just what we need. It's good and cold." He caught Nolan's canteen and filled it, then handed it back. "Here, you can have the first drink. I'll look around and see if I can find another bucket to use for the horses. We may need to use this one." He walked into the barn to look around.

The barn looked deserted, but the straw appeared fresh. It was still a healthy yellow color. Spotting two buckets in the back corner, Jackson grabbed them up and started to walk back to the well. A saddlebag half-hidden under some loose straw caught his attention.

Who could be using this as a shelter? It's military issue –Confederate.

He opened it. The name Sam Black was written on the inside flap.

Soundlessly, he eased his sidearm out of its holster and cocked it. He scanned the room, taking in all the stalls, looking for anything out of place. Peering in each of the stalls, he saw nothing.

One stall appeared to have been slept in, but nothing was left there. He looked up and scanned the loft.

They appear to be alone. Weird. This belongs to one. How could they have been so careless and left it? Are they still here? Are we being watched?

"Here, let's fill the horses up with these." Nolan walked in. The buckets were in his left hand and the saddlebag was over his shoulder.

Jackson silently tapped his gun when he saw Nolan, who immediately put his hand over his own, easing it out. Both men stepped back out and looked around.

Nothing moved. There were wooded areas to the rear and west of the house. Jackson squinted in that direction, but nothing appeared to move.

He nodded towards the barn and then down at the saddlebag hanging over his left shoulder. In case they were being watched, he tried to act nonchalant. He kept his voice low. "The straw is fresh enough inside and there is a loft. We will need to check it out. I think we can use the back stalls. It appears empty. There is a back escape we can use if need be. The barn can be secured from the inside. Found this." Jackson pulled the saddlebag open, the coarse name standing out.

Nolan studied the saddlebag. "If this belonged to one of the people that hit the Summers' farm, the people on this one were lucky to have left when they did. We'll use the back stall behind the ladder. That will give us some protection."

They checked both entrances to the barn, making sure they secured the doors from the inside. Within minutes, the two men finished watering the horses and took a bucket of water inside the stall for themselves to quench their thirsts. They tied both horses in the next stall, putting a bucket of water down for them.

"I thought about taking their saddles off, but I think we should leave them ready to ride."

Nolan nodded. "It's been strange. I don't know if you felt it, I've been feeling watched for a while. I've looked around, but I see nothing. It's eerie. I cannot shake the feeling."

"Yes. I have sensed it myself. Almost as if it's from behind. Just watching. Until I found that saddlebag, I was thinking I imagined the feeling."

"We need to get some shut-eye, but not sure how good it will be. Carter was right about traveling at night."

"Yes, well, I suggest we keep watch on and off while we sleep. And… before I forget…" Jackson unrolled his bedroll and pulled out the gray braided uniform. "I don't know if I have the right of it, but Ella understands military rank. She knew the cords for a lieutenant colonel. I was impressed."

Thoughtfully, Nolan responded. "Yes, well, we've spent a little time talking about military rank, so that she would better understand my rank—your rank, too—so she could make sense of the cords and stars on the uniforms. Shortly after we brought her home from that awful situation with Jason…" He paused. "Anyway, we talked about it. She asked me what mine would look like. I thought nothing about it at the time…" He looked at Jackson with awareness. "You gave her the cords. Where did you find extra cords like this, during a war?"

Jackson waved his hand, cutting him off. "Never mind. Ella told me she needed the cords. I was promoted a while back and had some older ones. Now, we both need to get some rest and then we get out of here. I have plans when I get back."

"You continue to surprise me, Colonel. I hope I would be the same man you are if ever in a similar situation. This war has taken the ability to respect and trust each other away from us. Everything and everyone is suspect. It's nice to be wrong about a person, especially one that intends to become part of the family."

"I knew you were holding back but didn't push it because your presence complicated things enough. I hated not being honest with Marshall. I wanted to keep him out of this little episode in case I got caught. You should know, Marshall has a contingent of men out tracking these people. My hope is he finds them away from here, but indications are that they are closer to us than I would like."

Tired and hungry, the two men checked the loft. It appeared clear and clean, but they set up their bedding with the horses. The stall was oversized, and it was cooler on the lower level.

"Hungry?" Jackson reached into his saddlebag and pulled out a brown sack. Fishing into it, he extracted a handful of hardtack. "Here, have some. Maybe having some food in our stomach can help us relax."

Nolan nodded, accepting the snack. He fished into his satchel and pulled out a small packet wrapped in cloth. Sheepishly, he offered his to Jackson. "Carter slipped this in my saddlebag. I think it's... yes, it is." He unwrapped it. "Ol' Indie's cornbread. I swear there's none better. Have some. This will fill our bellies."

Sated, with their guns resting in their laps, they both leaned back, exhausted. Sleep, however tentative, came —

CHAPTER 27

And went! Gunfire and loud cursing from the wooded area behind the barn woke both men, bringing them to their feet, guns at the ready. The horses were quiet, almost as if they, too, knew this was the time for silence.

"I'm going up top to see what's going on." Nolan scrambled out of the stall and nearly flew up the ladder to the loft.

Straw trickled down through the upper floor, and he heard Nolan crack the window open. Noise from outside the barn suggested they had trouble.

"Two horses with riders just shot across the grounds followed by Union forces on horseback. There were at least ten Union soldiers. One shot just took out the front rider." Nolan's voice competed with the sound of horses.

"The other rider slowed, but then kicked his horse into a run towards the woods behind us. I recognize the man leading the soldiers," he uttered loud enough for Jackson to hear. "It's Marshall Jameson." Nolan turned around and threw his body against the wall. "This could be bad all the way around."

"What? Marshall's out there?" Jackson scuttled. He grabbed his gun and sprinted to where Nolan was watching the scene play out. A thousand questions flooded his mind at once. What if they stopped and came in the barn? How would he explain his and Nolan's presence here? How long had Marshall been watching the area? What time was it?

Jackson's left hand scrambled into his pocket, trying to find his watch. "Seven o'clock." They might have been in the clear if they had just gotten out of there a half-hour earlier. Now, they had to see what opportunities presented themselves. He would not show himself if he didn't have to.

Marshall and his men disappeared into the back wooded area. He fully expected them to reappear to check the dead man, who didn't seem too dead at all. The captive was crawling away. Jackson felt sure this was Sam Black or her husband. Poised to fire, he waited. Before the thought was cold, a shot came from the other side of the woods. Someone was firing at an injured man... no, it was a woman. Her hat fell off revealing her identity.

Confederate soldiers emerged from the woods. The damn Confederate pickets must have spotted Marshall in the area and gathered reinforcements.

Marshall's men rode back through the woods, their prisoner riding in tow. They did not understand they were riding into hell. They had captured the Blacks—both. One was dead, and the other was in ropes, bound to his horse.

Before Jackson could fire off a shot or do anything to warn his buddy that the Rebs had him surrounded, they attacked.

"Hell, and damnation! Marshall needs help. He won't escape this one, not unless those Rebel guns are filled with air."

"No, wait! He could still get out of this."

"I don't see how."

The fighting paused as the smoke cleared.

Five of Marshall's men were down, along with several Rebs, and the still bound prisoner, Black. There were at least three dead or wounded horses. Marshall's men, or what was left, turned and tried to escape into the wooded area with the larger Confederate force in pursuit.

Jackson didn't bother to count the Rebs on the ground. His heart stopped when he recognized that one of the wounded was Marshall. The movements Marshall made were small, but they told Jackson that his friend was still with him.

Marshall is still alive, but for how long?

"I've got to help him. You stay Nolan. Hide deep in the straw. When this skirmish clears, head back to your men." At odds with his words, he stopped and shook his head. "I cannot believe I said that. But I meant it, God help me."

"Wait, let me help you, Jackson. I will go to the Confederates. They may recognize me. You brought me this uniform." He scrambled into the uniform as he spoke.

"Get it on. Then get out of here, first chance you get. I don't want to tell your sister you died while I was trying to help you. Hide." He checked the scene out front once more. "I have to help Marshall." He climbed down the ladder, checked his horse, and then went to the front. "Lock this door if you see trouble," he called back as loudly as he dared.

Jackson peered out the front of the barn. It was clear. He wished it were darker. It would be soon, but he needed to move now. Marshall needed help before he was recognized as a Union officer and captured. He slipped out and moved towards the safety of a deeply shaded adjoining pen.

Think! There is a way out of this chaos. I need to think of it and quickly.

The wounded were all spread out, covering at least an acre. Marshall had stopped moving. The Rebs had pursued Marshall's men, into the forested area to the back. Shots were going off.

He tried to be hopeful.

Two soldiers had stayed behind, but they were busy stealing clothing and things from one of Marshall's badly injured men towards the back of the farm. From the looks, there was money, because they were whooping and pouncing all over the poor man. That couldn't last long.

Jackson needed to see how hurt he was before he could make any real escape. Blood was coming from his leg. That could be a blessing and a curse. Moving gingerly, he crouched down. Marshall wasn't too far from the barn.

Marshall was awake; his eyes bored into Jackson's own. While he asked nothing, his face demanded answers. Jackson just gave a slight nod his way and muttered, "Later." He hefted Marshall up and the two of them ambled away from the makeshift battlefield.

They almost made it, but the timing wasn't on their side. A gunshot cracked across the farm as the Confederates burst through the tree cover and surrounded them, guns drawn.

~

Nolan watched from the safety of the loft, chewing a piece of straw. He was deciding. The easy thing would be to do as Jackson ordered, but he couldn't. There was only one of him, and those were his men. He was almost sure. Jackson, the man who had saved his life and risked his own, was now being led away, likely to end up in the Salisbury Prison Camp, a place known to be worse than Hell.

Nolan looked at the sun. It was almost down. He needed more time. He locked the door to the barn and went back up the loft, waiting and watching.

Nightfall came, and it was time to move. The horses were still silent in the stall. They had gotten a sufficient fill of the hay and water. Good horses were scarce.

He needed to protect both Mason and his horse, but they had to be with him to make his escape successful. The smile was hard to hold back as he looked over Mason. He rode him, knowing how close the horse was to Jackson. If a mount were lost, it most likely would be the one in tow.

He got on Mason, and his own mare followed behind, perhaps relieved it didn't carry a man. The barn was dark; it was time.

Once outside he urged the steed forward. They quietly followed the voices off in the distance. He noticed how stealthily Jackson's horse moved. Jackson worked with his horse. Trusted him. It was unusual that a Yankee could sit a horse as well as a Southerner. He respected that.

His men had taken Marshall, Jackson, Black, and the others a mile or so down the road. They set up camp in the nearby woods, taking advantage of a nearby stream. Surely the loud celebrating could be heard all the way to headquarters in Kinston. It was an unexpected victory trophy to have two enemy officers in tow.

He winced as he thought of Marshall walking all this way, wounded. The man had aggravated him and taunted him with his attraction to Sara, and the attention he showed her. As much as he'd like to pay him back, that wasn't what he would wish for him.

His men were loud and easily followed. Not the best course of action for them, but he had counted on their miscalculation. Hopefully, he would have time to deal with that later.

The camp was surrounded by trees and bordered a small creek. The darkness shrouded the outer edges as light danced off the campfire, lighting the center of the activity. He spotted where the prisoners were being held. They sat close together, bound and gagged in a tent in the back of their camp.

Good fortune might be with him. The captured horses were tied up nearby.

Nolan tied Mason and his horse up to a tree out of notice, away from the other horses. He furtively moved towards the back of the camp, keeping his celebrating men in sight. They were full of themselves, bragging and talking big about how they were all going to get promotions for capturing two Union officers. One was holding up items stolen from the dead.

He could hear their revelry and could catch details he needed. Capturing the Blacks was their target as well. Mr. Black was bound, gagged and secured to a tree under a special guard. The body of his wife was still strapped to the horse in the distance. Nolan hoped the two Union officers being bragged about were still okay.

He moved quietly, pulling back behind a large sycamore tree when he saw the sentry at his post in front of the tent. If he cut the back of the tent, he risked being heard, especially if the men inside said anything. Going to the front would afford him the least surprise to the men inside. It depended on how alert the sentry was.

It was decided. He checked his pistol.

~

*D*amn! For Jackson, things had gone from difficult to bad to worse, and he didn't know how to fix it. His best friend had been shot and probably would lose his leg if he didn't get attention. He was supposed to rescue him, not get caught. Through all of this, Marshall hadn't uttered a word to him, not even a small "Hi."

Jackson figured it could all break loose if they got out of this, but he'd risk it. Anything, if they could escape. He knew he'd have to explain his presence at the same farm that Marshall had tracked the Blacks to.

Did they get anything from Black, any confession? Did Marshall even know about the Summers?

He and Nolan had buried them. He doubted it. Marshall hadn't opened his eyes in a while. Jackson poked him.

His eyes shot open. He gave a small glare and he shut them again.

"Fine," he whispered. "Be that way. I am sorry for this mess, but I was trying to help. We will discuss this later, not now."

The other men looked at him, obviously wondering what was going on between these two.

Yes, I'll explain once I figure out what I will say. It needs to be plausible. Argh! I need a miracle to pull me out of this.

A vision of Ella backed up onto his desk came to mind. He groaned. That was not the miracle he wanted, at least not right now.

Marshall's glare shot daggers at him.

Jackson knew he was getting no place with Marshall right now. He'd worry about that later. He closed his eyes. His body stirred with the memory of lustrous red hair and thoroughly kissed lips.

Transported, he went back to the library. He heard her soft moans of feigned protest as she arched her body closer to his. His blood heated at the memory.

The state of his clothing brought him back to the tent, his vision of Ella gone in an instant. He wouldn't risk looking down but could tell that he was near to bursting his pants open.

Ignoring good sense, he looked around anyway. The only eyes on him were Marshall's. They weren't cold and dark. No, they were full of mirth, amused at the predicament Jackson created for himself. Well, that was at least a change of mood in the right direction, even if it was at his expense. He'd take it.

Noise at the front of the tent got their attention. It sounded like a sharp blow and a body falling. *What now?*

⁓

Opting to create a backdoor, Nolan cracked the butt of his gun on the unsuspecting sentry's head. He had been sleeping. There would be changes when he got back to camp. This lack of discipline would be their undoing.

Sneaking around to the back, he grabbed the knife he had borrowed from the sentry. He tapped his pocket, making sure the gun he borrowed was there, too. A slice through the center and he was sure to get attention. He held his finger over his mouth, surprising everyone inside.

Nolan was dressed in the Confederate officer's uniform. This would probably be a good story told for a while. He hoped to not be recognized by anyone other than Marshall and Jackson.

Luck was with him. "Quiet now. Colonel, hold up your bindings." He cut them and handed Jackson the knife. Jackson reached around and cut the rest of the bindings from the men.

"Quiet, men. Don't talk." His voice was an urgent whisper. "We don't want to disturb the party going on out front." Smiles went up as the men followed Nolan and Jackson out. Once Marshall moved to the opening in the tent, Jackson and Nolan, together, pulled him out of the tent. Jackson gripped his arm under Marshall's and helped him walk.

"The horses are over there, in the tall brush." The men worked their way towards the horses and quietly mounted them. His voice a low whisper, Jackson ordered them to stay silent, move out slowly, and meet them at the road.

Nolan and Jackson helped Marshall mount his horse and sent him out after the men. "Mason is back here, waiting." The two men, sure the others had gotten away, moved towards their own horses.

"Thank you, Nolan. I was sure you would follow orders and be gone from here, but I appreciate that you didn't. I should have listened to you and waited. Ha! That is one Confederate strategy I learned from this day."

"Well, I don't listen to enemy orders." He smiled at Jackson, his hand extended. "Brother."

Jackson smiled and shook Nolan's hand. "I've learned much from this time we've spent together, Nolan. You are an honorable man. I wish I could do more for you, but I promise I will take care of your family until you return. And you *will* return. A smart, savvy, man like yourself—I only wish you were on our side. I'm glad to call you my brother, and also my friend. Godspeed."

Nolan's throat tightened with emotion. "I gathered up a few arms for you and the men. You may need them." He handed Jackson the gun he had taken from the sentry as well as a small sack of guns he had found lying outside the tent. He snorted. "They were the confiscated weapons that were being taken to the commanding officer."

"You are a constant surprise to me, Whitford. Thank you for that."

"One more thing." Nolan needed to tell him this. He trusted him, and he wanted a way to communicate with his family. "Carter—we talked, and there's a place we know that I will leave him messages—only messages for my family. I will send word once I get back to camp. It may take a little while for messages to get to you." He waited for Jackson's reaction.

Jackson nodded. "That makes sense. I won't ask any details, and I will not question Carter. I appreciate your trust."

The two men urged their horses forward slowly. Soon, each peeled off in a different direction. Jackson turned towards the road and joined his men. Nolan took a shortcut he remembered. He still had a distance to go before getting to Kinston.

Nolan wanted to make sure they got away, but he couldn't risk being caught with them in case they ran into a picket or other trouble. He pulled off the side of the road about half a mile ahead of Jackson and waited under a bridge.

His patience was rewarded when the sound of horses was almost upon him a few minutes later. Staying as still as he could, he let them pass over the bridge he stood under. Coming out to make sure it was Jackson, he spotted Jackson and Marshall pulling up the rear.

"Ah! The twin colonels," he said, smiling to himself. He could head to his camp in Kinston knowing he had taken care of things back home.

He mounted his horse and headed back the way Jackson and his men had come. With any luck, he would reach his men in a matter of hours. A mile or so later, he turned at Wyse Fork and headed into Kinston, darkness enveloping him. He kept to the side of the road, mindful of Carter's warning and determined to stay alive.

CHAPTER 28

It had been three days since he and Marshall returned. Marshall was mending. The two men still had not discussed his presence at the farmhouse. In fact, no one missed the cool indifference between them.

It was time. Today would be the day he talked to Ella and Marshall —got his house in order, so to speak.

He left the library and went to the kitchen. Aiden and Bo were just finishing breakfast. "Have you seen your sister?"

"She said she was going into town to see Sara. I saw her head out to the barn to gather eggs. Said she would be back to check on me before she left. She had something to attend to first."

"To town?" She had not discussed that with him. He fought the urge to throttle her and kiss her at the same time. She wasn't leaving this plantation without him, and she didn't need to sell her eggs anymore. He had Cook bringing eggs into Sara's kitchen once a week. The agreement was that Sara would send back her delicious rolls. It was a handshake deal that Ella had approved of, so what the heck was she doing?

Without preamble, he left out the back door, hoping to spot the redhead that teased and tormented his heart.

He spotted her standing by the wagon. "There you are!"

At the sound of his voice, she turned and smiled. "I've been waiting for you."

"You have?"

"You didn't think I was leaving without my armed escort, did you?"

Caught. Jackson's face reddened when he realized Ella and Aiden had tricked him. "Well, no. Aiden said you were taking eggs to Sara." He tried his best to deflect.

"Confound it, Jackson. I got you, admit it!"

She had him; he knew it. "Okay. I admit it. You've got me." He walked up to her and pulled her close.

She felt so good in his arms. He had given their relationship tremendous thought, and it was now or *later*.

So now.

He dropped to one knee and held her hand in his.

"Ella Grace Whitford, will you do me the honor of being my wife?" His eyes studied hers. *Say yes.*

Ella framed his face in her hands. "Colonel Jackson Ross," she began, taking a nervous breath. "Yes." Her voice trembled with emotion. "Yes, I will be your wife."

Jackson placed a small gold ring on her finger. Its oval solitaire caught the sun and sparkled.

"This ring is lovely. Where…how did you get this?"

"It was my great-grandmother's ring. It's been in my family for generations. My mother sent it with me when I left for good luck. It's curious that I never thought about it before, but…" He laughed, nervously. "It was a strange good luck piece. Perhaps she was hoping I'd find you."

She looked at the ring, her eyes filling with tears. "It's prettier than anything I've ever seen. But how will it work?" Her question was a whisper.

"Well, if you need instruction…" He smiled, wickedly.

She cuffed him. "You know what I mean."

"Yes, I do." He stood up and held her to him, whispering in her ear. "Believe it or not, I have already gotten Nolan's permission. And it will work because we want it to. This war cannot last forever. I don't know how long it will last, but I vow to be faithful to you, protect you, and try my best to survive to live out my life with the best thing that has ever happened."

Jackson looked around and noticed that everyone had stopped what they were doing. They were watching them. He'd make this worth their while. He claimed her mouth, his arms holding her as Ella twined her hands in his hair.

The entire yard erupted into clapping and cheers. He momentarily forgot their audience. So, what? He loved this woman.

"When?"

"When?"

"When can we get married, silly?"

"What about Sunday? That will give Cook and the mess sergeant five days to get the food put together. Is that enough time?"

"Five days?" She was still smiling up at him, her lips swollen from that kiss. "Sounds good. I'll get Lizzy to help me with the dress. Now I do need to go to town and talk to Sara. Her daddy can marry us, and she has to stand up with me."

"Well let's go. I need to talk to Marshall when I get back."

"You also need to work things out with him. You kept him in the dark and made him feel like a fool."

"Has he told you that?"

"No, but I know how I'd feel in his place."

Jackson was amazed at her ability to read Marshall's mood. She was no shrinking violet. Living with her would make life interesting in this camp—for everyone. "You are right. It's time we talked. He was next on my list."

"Go. I'll wait. He is standing at the window up there." She pointed to the bedroom Marshall had been staying in while his leg healed.

He gave her a quick hug and scurried inside, taking the stairs slowly. Jackson rapped on the door to the bedroom Marshall was using. His mind was still grappling with how he could fix this rift with Marshall. He had hated lying to him.

"Come in." Marshall was brusque. He stood at the window with his back to the Jackson.

Jackson started to make a joke but thought better. "I didn't expect you to make this easy." He took a deep, steadying breath. "I apologize. I was wrong on a couple of levels. But I'm especially wrong for leaving you—"

"And helping to aid the enemy?" Marshall confronted Jackson. "You told me to release him in that cabin with Jason. Did you think I didn't recognize him? He was a prisoner. A prisoner!" He thundered.

Jackson's face burned, and angry tension corded his neck. "Yes. I did. I mean no, I didn't. Hell! I *hoped* you didn't because I knew what I wanted to do, and I didn't want to involve you in case I didn't succeed."

"I'm not stupid. I won't ask why you did it," he spat. He looked at Jackson's face and rolled his eyes.

"Yes, there was that." He crossed his arms over this chest. Marshall was treating him like he was a friend *and* a traitor. He swallowed.

"All you will say is yes? There must be a better reason other than you lost your damn head." Marshall blustered, holding onto his crutches and kicking the wall with his good leg. "Damn it! Your career would have been ruined." He faced Jackson. "I never thought I'd say it, but you are a traitor," he said, drawing up, his chest heaving.

"I guess…" He started to reason with Marshall but stopped. "Yes. I am a traitor, but I think my reasons are worth knowing."

"More? There are *more reasons?*" He snorted.

"Marshall, I admit to very strong feelings…"

"Loving." Marshall cut him off.

"Yes, loving Ella. There, I said it. I love her. It happened. I can't imagine anyone else for me. But it wasn't all about Ella." He hoped Marshall would listen with an open mind.

"Get on with it." His tone was gruff, but not as venomous as before. If the tone was any sign, Marshall's voice gave Jackson hope his friend wanted to understand.

"I should have brought this to you and talked more. But I knew your compliance could have cost you your life. That was something I would not risk. But I love her. And it's more than the needs of the flesh. She challenges me, but in the best sense. Ella makes me feel alive. I see a future and am excited about it. And I spent a lot of time with her brother, trying to decide if he was even worth what I wanted to do, what I was risking."

Marshall stayed silent.

"Whitford is very much worth saving. War rarely gives you a chance to know the men you want to kill. But if that could happen…" he blew out a long whistle of air. "I think the state of affairs would be a lot different."

His friend gave the smallest of nods, but Jackson caught it. He persisted. "The knowledge of what was happening with the Rebs that came home early, wounded, haunted me. People involved in those murders could be here on Silver Moon. We had no solid leads. Nolan might never have made it to trial."

"Hadn't thought of that." Marshall chewed on the inside of his mouth, a habit Jackson had associated with Marshall rethinking something. He hoped that was the case.

"I'm not proud of what I did, Marshall. But I *believe* in what I did. I think it was the right thing for this situation." He spoke, his voice sounded sober.

"Yes. I can see that." Marshall uttered, subdued. He extended his hand. "White, I mean Whitford, saved his sister's and your life. Hell, even mine. He came back for both of us. He could have run."

Jackson clasped his friend's offered hand. "Thank you, Marshall. Your friendship means a lot to me."

"I still need more time to square this. I'm angry because you left me out of this—" He waved his hands directionless about him. "—this plan of yours. And now I feel like I owe my life to a Reb."

"Not a Reb. An honorable man."

Marshall cleared this throat. "Your heart may have led the way, but I admit, your head was in the fight." He shifted and reached into his pocket. "Anyway, picked these up for you."

"Cherry blend." He placed it in his mouth. "I like some of the amenities here." Jackson grinned, rolling the cigar around on his lips. "Here's a match." He pulled it from his pocket and lit both cigars.

Both men stepped back and puffed for a moment, content to let the issue lay where it was. Marshall broke the reverie. "I think there is more brandy in the library. He hopped around with his crutches and held open the door. "After you."

~

Less than a half-hour later, Marshall and Jackson walked out of the library, laughing and chatting like they always had done. Ella stood at the door.

"I've waited to tell Aiden. I thought you would tell him with me." She smiled.

"Go!" Marshall hobbled out from behind him. "Tell him, Jackson. We can finish talking later. I need to put my foot up. The stairs wore me out. Here behind your desk works great." He grinned, taunting him. "Go on. The boy will be excited. He's out back with Carter, I think."

"Thanks, Marshall. Hey, don't scuff up my desk. It would be hard to explain the marks."

Jackson felt great. Marshall had forgiven him, and he had told him the truth. His friend understood. He shouldn't be so surprised; he should have trusted him. They had always appreciated each other's points of view.

"Marshall, there's one more thing, I want to ask you."

"Which is?"

"Will you stand with me?"

"Of course! I'm still not *completely* over this other business—mostly because I felt left out if I am to be honest. But yes. I wouldn't have it any other way." Marshall hobbled over and extended his hand, signaling all had been forgiven.

They found Aiden just where Marshall said he was. Aiden and Bo were working quite a system. Aiden held the cow's teat, aiming the milk for the can but spilling half. Bo caught the milk that escaped the pail, lapping it up as fast as it squirted in his direction. Carter was laughing and trying to guide him at the same time.

It struck Jackson that this was where he would want to bring up his own children, giving them this experience. He hoped the war would leave this home intact. He had been hoping for a lot lately.

Clearing her throat, Ella addressed her brother. "Aiden, we have something to ask you."

He turned so fast that he shot poor Bo in the eye. "Like what?" Aiden let the teat go and stood up. Carter took his place.

"Well, it's actually both of us that want to ask." He picked him up so that Aiden could be eye level with him. "What would you say if I married your sister and we became a family?"

"Bo! I'm getting a colonel!" He screamed it in Jackson's ear. "Sorry, but yes!" Aiden looked up, all smiles. "You would be my other brudder, right?"

"That's right. A week from now, we will be family. We will live here with Carter and Lizzy and Ol' Indie, whenever she visits. And we will be here when this war ends, and your brother comes home."

He put down Aiden and pulled Ella into an embrace. "That is if that meets your needs." He whispered to her, so no one else could hear. "I plan to meet more than those needs."

"Well, one need I have is for a kiss." As he pulled her close, she murmured for his ears only, "I cannot wait to have you meet my needs. I will be meeting yours, as well." She leaned in and kissed him.

Jackson was a happy man. He would be married in five days.

Noise from the open kitchen door stole the attention of Bo and Aiden. "Cookies! Let's go and get our cookies!" Aiden took off in a tear with Bo fast on his heels.

"Jackson, the wagon is still out front. I need to run to town and see Sara. Are you coming?"

Grinning, he picked her up and swung her around, kissing her on the cheek. "You bet I'm ready. Let's hurry and we can get back before dark."

*H*ours later they returned to find everyone absorbed in activity. No one seemed to notice they were back. Not a soul was in the front of the house. Alone. Without overthinking the opportunity, Jackson pulled Ella back to him and whispered in her ear. "I don't know if I want to wait..." He nodded towards her bedroom upstairs.

Her grin and the quick kiss on his nose gave him his answer before she said a word. "Meet me in ten minutes. I'll be waiting."

"Suh, before you go back in there, I have something for you."

Startled, Jackson almost cursed. He hadn't heard Carter enter the hall and hoped the man had not heard his suggestive whisperings to Ella. "I guess I got carried away with my happiness and didn't hear you walk in here. I apologize."

"Suh, you got nothing to 'apologize 'bout." He looked around. "I got something for you." He handed Jackson a folded piece of paper. "Massa Nole sent dis."

"I appreciate this. And I won't ask questions. I'm just glad to finally hear from him. Thank you, Carter." He opened the paper and glanced at it, noting the length. There was more than he had expected. *I'll read it later when I have more time. Let me just make sure he got back.* He scanned it and smiled.

Jackson went to his office and locked up the note. His thoughts drifted to Ella. She had been so thoughtful, waiting to tell her little brother with him there. It moved him nearly to tears. He was a lucky man.

When he thought sufficient time had passed, he wasted no time heading upstairs. Moving discretely, he found Ella's bedroom door unlocked and opened it. She turned around, a smile warming her whole face. She was waiting for him, and it nearly took his breath away. Quietly, he closed the door and turned the key.

∽

*E*lla stood behind her closed bedroom door and looked around, her arms holding her stomach. He was coming up to her room. *Her room.* Butterflies swarmed in the pit of her stomach and heat pooled between her legs at the thought of seeing him in here.

She felt unprepared for these feelings, but she sensed something else would guide her. Instinct. She was too nervous to recall more than a couple of details from the candid and descriptive conversations about *the act* she and Lizzy had had over the last few years.

Lizzy had always been there when couples married and committed their hearts to each other; she was there as their friend, and for many, a confidante. She had listened as they often related some of the more intimate details of their lives. She sometimes shared these matters with Ella. It was her way, she once told Ella, of sharing the knowledge her mamma would have given her if she had been there.

She knew she only had a few more minutes. *First things first!* Swiftly, she moved to the washbowl and grabbed her tooth powder. While still brushing her teeth, she checked her reflection in the mirror and pinched her cheeks. Swiftly, she finished her teeth and pulled her brush through her hair, letting her locks flow around her shoulders.

Her door opened, and she turned, giving a brilliant smile to her visitor. "Ella." Jackson's voice caught. "Beautiful. You are so beautiful." His hands reached into her hair, and he combed his fingers through it. She loved the luxurious feel.

Pulling her face to his, he lightly kissed her before adding more pressure to her lips, then totally covering them. His teeth nipped at her bottom lip, coaxing her, teasing her, until their tongues danced together, tip to tip.

Moving her backward slowly, he lowered her onto her bed. Without breaking the kiss, he worked the buttons on her shirt and the ties on her chemise, freeing two pert breasts. He moved from her lips and took one of her breasts into his mouth. His other hand worked its way under her skirts until his finger found her warm, wet core. He moved his finger in a steady pulse, stretching her. She arched, pushing herself closer to him, to the promise of *what*, she wasn't sure. She knew she wanted this, wanted him. *But she needed to see him.*

She pulled herself up, propping up on one arm. "Take it off." She nodded to his shirt and looked down at his pants. "First, the boots."

He stood up and pulled off his shirt. "I love this side of you." Then, he sat down to pull off his boots.

"Allow me." She reached down and tugged, pulling one boot off and then the other. "Now your pants." She gazed at him, waiting.

Jackson divested himself of his trousers. His smalls followed. Unabashed, he stood in front of her.

"*You* are beautiful. I fantasized about what you might look like without your clothes..." Ella swallowed, nervously. "I've wanted to see you without your clothes since that day in the library." Hesitating, she looked up at Jackson. "Can I touch you?"

He nodded. "Please but be gentle or this can end before it starts."

Not sure of what that meant, she reached over and touched him. "It is the softest skin, almost velvet."

At her bold assertion, Jackson reddened.

Reacting to his blush, Ella pulled her hand away, but her gaze never left his face. Unconsciously, she licked her lips, the feelings in her body suddenly unbearable.

Jackson moved towards her, pushing her back on her mattress. He tugged on her skirt, pulling it off and tossing it to the vanity chair. "I want you." Smiling at her, he leaned in and claimed her mouth. His hand slowly stroked and kneaded her center. The steady pulse of first one, then two fingers slowly stretched her. Carefully, he moved his body over hers, adjusting himself between her legs.

"This will hurt a little, sweetheart, so I will make it as quick as I can. Then it will be much better for you."

Biting her lower lip, she nodded, not altogether sure of what he referred.

Jackson moved between her legs and positioned himself. Leaning down, he covered her lips with his. He moved slowly at first, pausing after each short push.

Her eyes widened in surprise when he thrust into her. He covered her mouth with his own, suppressing her cry with a kiss.

"That's all the pain, sweetheart. It will feel better now. I promise." He began again to move in a rhythm that, within a few slow strides, pulled her into tempo with him.

They climbed higher together, their soft pants and kisses the only audible measure of the pleasure of their lovemaking. At the pinnacle of their ecstasy, she arched into him and shuddered, smothering a cry of joy. Jackson's own body juddered after a final push. A moment later, he rolled over to her side.

Ella stared up at the ceiling, trying to contain the erratic heartbeat that lovemaking had created. The area between her legs was wet and pulsed. It was a new sensation for her. *This is what it feels like to make love and become a woman.* She hugged herself and looked over at Jackson resting. "That was more than I ever knew it could be."

"And there will be much more, *so much* more for us." Jackson leaned in and kissed her, again. "I should leave before we are discovered here and have to explain. I would rather not place you in that position. But I could not let this opportunity pass. Ella…"

"I loved every moment, Jackson." She interrupted and pulled him towards her, covering his chin with kisses and nibbling on his bottom lip. Her body was still thrumming with need for him. "Maybe we could have another… opportunity." She wanted more and shifted her body until she was close enough to feel his body responding to her invitation.

"Minx!" Jackson pulled her tightly to him and drove deeply into her. Their pace moved together slowly, gradually becoming more frenzied.

Ella's mind swirled with feelings of joy and a feeling she couldn't name. Completeness? She closed her eyes and tried to focus on the pleasure of his touch.

Jackson sought her lips and kissed her deeply as she began to arch into him. His body spasmed, and his kiss muffled their exclaims of pleasure. A minute later, he laid his head on her chest.

"Can you hear my heart beating for you?" Ella gently moved her fingers through his hair and down his neck.

"My sweet Ella." Jackson leaned up on one elbow and gazed at her. "I think I've always been looking for you, and now I've…" A noise downstairs stole his attention and he bolted up, pulling her with him. "Perhaps we should get dressed *now* before Aiden searches for us."

"Mmm. You're right." She sighed. "I'm glad I won't have to wait much longer to try that again."

"There is one more thing I want to tell you, Please, don't ask me how I know this, because I cannot share. But Nolan made it back to his men just fine."

"Thank you." She smiled up at him, her eyes watering. "I appreciate you telling me. I was worried about him."

"I love you, Ella. One day he will come home. Have faith."

She nodded.

Quietly, they dressed and left the room, one at a time.

∼

Ella woke up on Sunday morning, her stomach in knots. This was the day. She would be Mrs. Jackson Ross by the end of the day. She wished her papa and brother could be here, but Jackson had assured her that Nolan would be home when the war was over. Nolan had said as much in his letter to her. She knew neither one could promise such a thing, but Jackson's faith in her brother comforted her beyond measure.

She hadn't known what she would wear, but Lizzy surprised her, having located her mother's wedding dress in the attic. It needed cleaning but little alteration. It was comforting to know she could wear it. A part of her parents would be shared with her own wedding.

The dress was beautiful. It was candlelight satin with a sheer overlay of the most delicate cotton muslin she had ever seen. A darker ecru satin accented the edges and formed a V at both the bodice and the back in an accordion fashion. The sleeves were fitted satin on the top of her arms, blossoming out in a sheer puff of the cotton muslin that covered the elbow and flared just above the wrist. Seed pearls were placed sparingly within the muslin overlay to form an almost ethereal creation. Some of the fabric for the hoop skirt of her mother's time was removed so that the skirt had more of the flounce look that had become popular before the war. The extra materials went into her trousseau.

She looked over at the delicate wreath of orange blossoms and satin she planned to wear. Sara's dress of white muslin hung next to her own. Its bodice was styled to mimic her own.

Two hours to go. Aiden had popped in no fewer than four times already. His pants and jacket were pulled together from some of Nolan's old clothes. He looked very handsome. He was proud of his new clothes. Even Bo had a necktie.

Jackson had insisted that when the war ended, and Nolan came home, they would have a reception to celebrate his homecoming and their marriage. He was a thoughtful man, even if he was bossy and a Yankee.

She had only good feelings about marrying him. It was like he expected any qualm she could have and addressed it before she could. He told her he wanted her the way she was and wouldn't change so much as a hair on her head.

She wouldn't change him, either. Aiden loved him to death. The two of them and Bo had gone fishing by the creek three times this week. Aiden showed him what Nolan had taught him and called him his other 'brudder.'

The door opened, and Bo burst in followed by Ol' Indie and another dog she didn't recognize at first. "Rinny! Oh Rinny, you have a necktie, too!"

"Yes, chile. Your Ol' Indie isn't gonna allow her best baby girl get married without a proper dressed wedding party and send-off, now is she?"

Smiling, Ella jumped up to hug the old woman's neck. "You did it! Rinny is okay. Jackson told me about how he and Nolan saved him and..." Tears flowed from both women.

"I fixed him the best I know how. He seems good, but he was missing his people a powerful lot."

"That is so sad for him, but we will shower him with love. Sara plans to keep him with her some until Nolan gets back."

"He will like Miss Sara." The old woman declared, smiling, and scratched the dog behind his ear. "Now step back and let me check you out." She nodded in appreciation and smiled broadly.

"Lizzy, you missed dis little piece." She pulled on Ella's hand, opening it and placed a small cameo in her palm. "Besides dis dress being old and new, I thought a little more 'sump'um old' might be helpful. It's important to know where you been. Dis pin was your mamma's. Before she left us, she gave me this and asked me to make sure you wore it on your wedding day. I promised her, and Ol' Indie keeps her promises." She dabbed the corner of her eye with a lace handkerchief.

"I remember that pin. I thought we had lost it when Mamma died. Papa had looked for it. Momma wore it all the time. She told me it had been her mamma's." She squeezed her hand around the cameo and then pinned it on her dress.

Ol' Indie's gift turned on the tears.

"Lord, chile, this a happy day." She took her handkerchief and dabbed Ella's tears away. "Your mamma is smiling today. She knows dis be de right man for you."

"Thank you Ol' Indie." She squeezed the old woman and kissed her cheek. "You have given me the most perfect gift."

~

Jackson waited downstairs in the parlor. It was his wedding day. He didn't think he would ever marry, and then he met Ella. The woman had turned his life upside down. Her smile ignited warmth and joy and radiated a peacefulness he had never known. She owned his heart.

Lizzy sat down by the pianoforte and began.

It was time.

He looked towards the door and knew without a doubt he was marrying the most beautiful woman in the world—the only woman in the world for him.

Ella heard the music starting up. Checking herself in the mirror, she pushed back a stray tear. This was it. She was actually getting married. How would it have been to have her mamma and papa here?

Closing her eyes, she imagined she and Mamma together before Mamma had taken ill. She missed her so much, and never more than at this moment. Mamma would hug her close and tell her how much she loved her. She'd whisper how much she liked Jackson, and then smile at her. Mamma always smiled. Jackson would have loved Mamma, too.

Ella checked her reflection in the mirror once more and pinched her cheeks for color. She felt beautiful. The dress was once her mamma's. It felt soft and lovely on her skin. *She is here.*

Clutching a spray of orange-blossoms and rosebuds close to her heart, she stood in the doorway. Ella was anxious to start. Pastor Larson, Sara's father, traveled two days to get here. It wouldn't have been the same without him. He liked Jackson, according to Sara, and minced no words in telling him so, as well as what he would do if he ever hurt her. She smiled at that thought. Jackson would never hurt her, but Pastor Larson's concern touched her.

Jackson and Marshall stood ready at the front of the church. She took a deep, slow breath to ready herself, and caught Jackson's smiling face. He was so handsome in his uniform, even if it was the wrong color.

Aiden insisted on giving her away once he understood he wasn't really *giving* her away. Sara came behind her, and Bo and Rinny followed in tow.

Ella put her hand in Jackson's and the only sound she could hear in the room was the beating of her heart until Pastor Larson nudged her for her pledge. "I do." She smiled.

"*I now pronounce you husband and wife.*" The rest of his words faded to background. She was married. She was Jackson's *wife.*

The reception passed too slowly. Jackson was anxious to hold his wife in a way a man could only do in the privacy of his bedroom. He had had all the small talk he could handle. He looked at Ella. "Wife, are we ready to wave goodbye to our guests?" He leaned down and nuzzled her neck, and whispered, "So that we can discover other pleasures?"

"Yes, husband, I am ready." His breath tickled her neck, setting off the familiar warmth spreading throughout her lower limbs. "Let me say something to Aiden just so he won't worry about me."

She reached Aiden and leaned down, telling him it was time for her and Jackson to leave the party. She would join them tomorrow. To her surprise, Aiden grinned.

"Jackson told me about this. He said you have wedding games you have to play. And he wants to win," he whispered.

Shocked, Ella looked around and caught the smile on Jackson and Marshall's faces. Determined not to let him have the upper hand, she leaned down and kissed Aiden. "I plan to win at least once, Aiden." They both grinned.

"Come, wife. Let's bid these guests merry and leave."

Jackson reached down and picked her up. He carried her upstairs while she buried her head in his shoulder. The guests waved and then returned to celebrating the nuptials.

She was now Mrs. Jackson Ross. Conflict was all around her, but on this day, the only thing she surrounded herself with was love and Jackson. As they entered her room, she kicked the door closed behind them. Theirs would be a private celebration, one she had anticipated all week.

EPILOGUE

*New Bern, North Carolina
December 12, 1862*

Jackson and Aiden pulled the twelve-foot Loblolly pine through the front door, a cold breeze rushing in behind them. "Aiden, guide the rear towards the middle, son, so it won't hit the walls and get damaged coming through the doorway.

"Yes, suh!" The little boy clapped his hands, wearing his biggest smile. "This is so exciting. It's almost Christmas! We've never stuck a tree in the house before! I bet Ella will be surprised when she sees this beaut-i-ful tree. She always wanted a tree.

Bo followed behind them, alternating between tugging and barking at the rope tied to a secured bundle of pine boughs that Jackson and Aiden left on the porch. The pup had dragged them in until they became stuck in the doorway, lodged awkwardly. Bo gave a final tug and the boughs catapulted through the door, causing him to fall backward, sprawling into a landing on his bottom.

Aiden erupted into peals of laughter. "Bo! You are a funny dog. We were gonna get those!

Jackson bent down and loosened the package of boughs. "I'm amazed he got these into the house still in a bundle. I thought we would have to toss the ruined ones and cut more." He laughed. "Your sister will be surprised—that is, if she didn't hear us coming with all of our commotions." He smiled at his little helpers and gently chucked Aiden under the chin, gaining another big smile from the little boy and a bark from Bo.

"Let's see if Carter can help us get this into the parlor and stand it up. I think a third hand could help us keep it from dragging so we can keep some of those beautiful pine needles on the tree." He pointed behind him at the trail of pine. "What do you think, little buddy?"

"What's all the barking about?" A smiling Carter entered the hallway from the back of the house, carrying the newly built tree stand. "Suh, I think dis will work. Here is the twine you asked 'bout to tie it up into place."

Carter set the tree stand in front of the parlor windows. "Miss Ella always talked 'bout her wanting a Christmas tree right here." He gazed up and down the tree. "Oh boy! She gonna love des big tree."

Jackson and Carter finished arranging the tree in the stand with Aiden supervising. Stepping back, they admired their handiwork. "You recommended a fine Christmas tree, Carter. And you did a great job with that tree stand. It should hold it straight." He pulled the loose twine from his pants pocket. "Can you help me secure it to the window? Let's try to tie it from the top." He reached up towards one of the top limbs. "It won't show if we anchor it from behind. I want to trust it won't fall."

As they finished their handiwork, Ella walked into the room. "Oh! Don't want to think of that gorgeous tree falling!" She went to sit down on the couch but was almost mowed over by her young brother and his faithful companion. "There you are. I was worried about my little man. It's cold out there." She hugged him and kissed Bo on the nose.

"Looky, sista! Jackson and me, we found our tree for Santa Claus! Don't you think it's beaut-i-ful?" Aiden jumped up and down.

"Oh, it is, Aiden. Truly."

"Hurry! Let's decorate it!"

"Yes, let's start with this." She handed Jackson and Aiden some strings. "I'll keep stringing."

She took her seat on the couch and grabbed up a bowl of popped corn and her needle and thread, continuing to string popped corn. "I read about this in *Godey's*." Ella picked up a pile of strung popped corn and showed where she was still working on it. "I can tie this off and start a new string. That might be better. The drawing they had made the tree look pretty. I thought it'd look nice on our tree.

"It will be fine looking," Jackson agreed. He moved over to the fireplace mantle and withdrew a book-sized box. "It's a star. I carved it." He handed it to Ella. "Aiden, do you think you would do the honors and place this on top of the tree when we get all of the decorating done?"

"A new tradition. I love that. The star is perfect!" Ella got up, holding yards of popcorn on the string. We will need something to stand on to hang this." She pointed to a small ladder in the corner of the room, behind the door.

She stepped back, satisfied with her work. "Now this is done, we just have to finish the cotton angels. Aiden, you can help with these, if you'd like. I'm using this flour paste to glue these little cotton balls into small angel forms. Then I thread a string through the top and tie them off and we hang them.

The three of them worked together putting the strings of popcorn around it, watching a very festive tree take shape.

"Gee! This tree looks better than any Christmas tree I've ever had!" Aiden beamed.

Jackson chortled as he watched Ella and Aiden place the finished angels amid the strings of popcorn.

Ella tied off the last the few angels and handed them to Aiden to hang.

"Can we put it up there, suh?" Aiden held the angel up, pointing to the top part of the tree.

"Sure, I will be your ladder." He jovially lifted the little boy on his shoulders and walked around the tree, standing as Aiden hung the remaining angel.

∽

"It's beautiful. I don't think I will ever forget this day." Ella loved watching her little brother's enthusiasm as he hung the ornaments.

She reminisced as she watched them work, thinking back to the last Christmas her family was together.

Nolan had been home from school. Aiden had been only two. They hadn't had a tree that year. Instead, she had made stockings. She wondered where the stockings had been stored. Her thoughts turned to Nolan and she pondered what he might be doing and if he was okay.

A couple of hours later, the decorating had been finished except for the lights. Lizzy brought small candles in little wooden holders fastened to clothespins to secure on the limbs.

The help had thinned out. Aiden and Bo had both fallen to sleep in front of the fire. Jackson and Ella admired the tree from their place on the couch, warmed by a crackling fire in the fireplace. The star lay on top of the pianoforte in the far corner of the room, opposite the window.

"We'll wait to hang the star when they wake up." Ella laughed. She stared into the fire, mesmerized.

"A penny for the thoughts that have taken you away from this warm fire, darling?" Jackson stood and circled around the tree to her side. "You know, if someone had told me I would find happiness while fighting this war, I'd have never believed it." He rubbed her shoulders affectionately. "Yet, so much has happened in such a short time. I don't think I'll take even a minute of life for granted again."

"I never expected all of this. It seems like it was meant to be. But I don't know if it's fair that so much of our world is embroiled with grief, yet my life—our lives—have gotten better." She shuddered as she recalled thoughts of her brother and father. The silence was deafening. "I hope they are okay."

"Who?"

"Nolan and Pa. I wonder if...I think about whether they are safe if they are okay, and..." She couldn't finish her thought.

"I have heard nothing about Nolan, love, so my thinking is no news is good news. As for your father, I think Nolan mentioned he planned to ask and start searching."

"I hope he will find him, and that he is all right." She missed Nolan and her father, but today, her heart was full. She still had her family—Jackson, Aiden, and Bo. Her hand touched her stomach and rubbed it gently. In that moment, she decided.

"Jackson, I think I have the perfect Christmas present for you, but I don't want to wait."

"Then don't!" He laughed. "Surprise is overrated."

She leaned into him and ran her hand along the underside of his chin. Her hands moved up and curled in his hair. "Well...first, I should mention we will need to renovate the room next to Aiden." She bit her lip and waited.

"Why would that be?"

"Well," she started slowly, "That would be where our son or daughter will sleep." Ella slowly took Jackson's right hand and placed it on her stomach, holding her hand over it. She watched his expression change from pensiveness to confusion to wonderment. Waiting, she sucked in her breath, hoping.

A broad smile lit up his face.

"A baby?" He encircled her waist, pulled her closer.

She nodded, smiling.

"When?" He nuzzled her ear, kissing it and moved down her neck.

"Perhaps July, if I have my calculations right."

A small whimper of contentment escaped him, and he moved to her chest, covering the exposed skin with soft kisses.

Tingling, she felt a familiar heat ignite her middle. "I missed my monthly and didn't think about it until a couple of weeks later. I'm two months along, I think. I wanted to keep it until Christmas, but I couldn't wait another three weeks to tell you." She rested her head against his chest, breathing in the sandalwood essence of him.

"We will have another addition to our family." Jackson jumped up and slapped his knee. With giddy excitement, he picked her up, spinning her around. "I hope she looks just like you. Your eyes mesmerized me from the first day I met you. And your spicy, uncompromising spirit is perfectly matched by your beautiful red hair."

She smiled. "So, you won't be disappointed if this is a little girl? I was so worried you might be." A boy or girl would be fine, but she had only had boys in the house. She wanted this child to be a little girl.

"Absolutely not!"

Ella reached up and slanted her lips over his. Her tongue met his in a slow, familiar dance. Jackson moved his arms behind her, pulling up her dress inches at a time and moving her down on the couch. In minutes, low pants were coming from both.

Bo barked, and their kiss met an untimely end.

Ella and Jackson sat up, wordlessly adjusting themselves on the couch.

A muffled grunt sounded from under Bo, who was lying over his young master's face as if to cover his eyes. Aiden heaved his puppy aside and sat up, wiping the sleep away.

"Bo, you were smuddering my nose!"

Laughing, Jackson reached down and picked up his little buddy. "Aiden, what would you think if we told you we will have a baby?"

It seemed to take a moment for the question to register with Aiden, but the heart-stopping smile on his face gave his answer. "Really?" He squirmed to get down and ran over to hug his sister, touching her stomach.

"Yes, Aiden. Maybe a little niece or nephew," she whispered, kissing his head. "I will count on your help." Ella hugged her little brother and kissed Jackson.

This was the start of their Christmas traditions and their family.

She had the family she doubted she would ever have. Ella never believed she could have the love she had known her parents to have, but somehow it had found her. It was hard to forget that the war was here, but Jackson was determined to keep as much normalcy as he could at Silver Moon. Fear was still commonplace, but she held on to her faith.

Life had changed so much. Love and contentment had soothed the anger and hatred she once held towards the Yankees, and she looked forward to this new life. It held so much promise with Jackson, Aiden, and this child. She cherished her life.

Hope was what she felt now. Hers was no longer a life touched by embers of anger.

AFTERWORD

When New Bern, NC fell to the Union forces in March 1862, slaves flocked to the area looking to taste freedom, and soon James City (located a half mile south of New Bern) was born. Even though the Emancipation Proclamation was a year off, the slaves that made it to New Bern were free—they were protected by the union army. In many cases the slaves that had escaped the plantations sought work for the occupying Union soldiers, and were better off than their former masters because of the jobs and other help provided by the Federal Government.

ACKNOWLEDGMENTS

This book would not have been possible without the help of so many.

My husband, who actually reads my books—cover to cover—and continually encourages me. And my sister, Susan, whose enthusiasm about my stories is contagious!

Heather, Tina, Erin, Judy and Pat read my book and provided tremendous helpful feedback. Heather and Tina went beyond that- reading the book multiple times, and with their incredible patience and abilities they spotted things I might surely have missed. Together, all of these ladies gave so much inspiration and kept the fun going in this process.

Steve Shaffer, a highly-regarded New Bern historian, toured the New Bern (NC) battlefield with me on a very hot July day—both of us dodging snakes and mosquitoes, and enthusiastically educated me about the layout of the battlefield, the battle itself, and gave me tremendous insight on what went right and wrong that fateful day in 1862.

Jessica, my editor, made me realize this book was actually going to happen! Her support was unwavering and amazing.

Lastly...but never least...is Elizabeth, a truly wonderful friend whose expectations and subtle 'deadlines' pushed me to not only finish this book but has helped me in many immeasurable ways.

I've carried Ella and Jackson's story around in my head for years...and thanks to the help of so many amazing friends and family members, I finally finished this book.

Thank you...each of you.

ABOUT THE AUTHOR

Anna St. Claire is an avid reader, and now author, of both American and British historical romance. She and her husband live in Charlotte, North Carolina, where their once empty nest has filled with her cat, two dogs, and her two granddaughters.

Anna relocated from New York to the Carolinas as a child. Her mother, a retired English and History teacher, always encouraged Anna's interest in writing, after discovering short stories she would write in her spare time.

Her fascination with history and reading led her to her first historical romance—Margaret Mitchell's *Gone With The Wind*. The day she discovered Kathleen Woodiwiss,' books, *Shanna* and *Ashes In The Wind*, Anna was hooked. She read every historical romance that came her way. Today, her focus is primarily the Civil War and Regency eras, although Anna enjoys almost any period in American and British history.

She would love to connect with any of her readers at annastclaireauthor@gmail.com.

Made in the USA
Columbia, SC
19 January 2019